Twisted Tracks

The Clearwater Mysteries

Book two

Proofread by Ann Attwood
Cover Design by Andjela K

Printed by CreateSpace, an Amazon.com company.

ISBN- 9781096730446

Available from Amazon.com, CreateSpace.com, and other retail outlets.
Available on Kindle and other devices.

Also by Jackson Marsh

Other People's Dreams
In School and Out
The Blake Inheritance
The Stoker Connection
Curious Moonlight

The Mentor of Wildhill Farm
The Mentor of Barrenmoor Ridge
The Mentor of Lonemarsh House
The Mentor of Lostwood Hall

The Clearwater Mysteries
Deviant Desire
Twisted Tracks

www.jacksonmarsh.com

www.facebook.com/jacksonmarshauthor

Twisted
Tracks

Jackson Marsh

One

J ames Joseph Wright was born on January 10th, 1863 at the precise moment the world's first underground train delivered its passengers to Farringdon station. As the locomotive puffed and fumed from the tunnel, James' mother, some four miles distant, puffed and fumed through her own first delivery.

The boy arrived healthy and noisy, pink and robust, and survived childhood thanks to the care of a mother who doted, and a father who worked hard and provided well. James was planned and wanted, unlike too many other children in the city, and benefited from a poverty-free upbringing.

Where the underground was the first such railway in the world, so James Wright, inaugurated on the same day, was the first and only of his kind, or so he thought.

Although he didn't lack affection at home, he craved it from his school companions, but only from the other boys. When he reached double figures, and his friends talked about marriage and the playground-taboo subject of sex, they spoke about girls. James was uninterested and thought only about men until he realised he was the only lad who did so. He kept the secret to himself and lived a confused and quiet life in the semi-respectable neighbourhood of South Riverside imagining that one day he would wake up to an interest in the opposite sex. It wasn't until he became a telegraph boy at fourteen that he realised he didn't have to. There were others of his kind in the world; men who were solely attracted to men.

Work as a messenger brought with it all manner of opportunities, both for income and for companionship. The young men were drilled each morning by a senior hired for his military bearing. They were crammed into tight uniforms which soon loosened as they spent hours cycling and walking the streets. There were the social times when the lads would joke and mess together, telling stories of their conquests and their day's earnings, who they saw inside the hall at Lord X's house, and who had been seen at the upstairs window in Lady Y's when her husband was away. Life was a mixture of routine, running and raunchy behaviour towards girls, something his mates saw as a game of conquests, and something that bored James to tears of frustration.

Until he met Thomas. Since then he hadn't been able to get the man out of his mind.

He had been on his feet all day, running messages and waiting to take replies. It had been as mundane as usual until he was sent on an urgent errand to Clearwater House. There was nothing uncommon in the delivery except that he had never delivered to Lord Clearwater. It was usually someone else's patch, but that man was ill, and James was chosen because he was presentable and polite. It wasn't the address that brightened his day, nor the neighbourhood half a mile from his home but a whole world away. It was the man who answered the door that sent him reeling from the steps, trembling.

The chance meeting began with a standard, brief announcement, 'Telegram for Lord Clearwater,' but after that, nothing about the exchange was ordinary. Not the way the footman looked at him, nor the way James was suddenly lighter than air, and not the way the two swapped names as if they knew they would meet again. James had been met at front doors by many handsome servants, but the Clearwater footman was the first to stir more than just a casual interest. He caused James' blood to race, and as he left, he glanced back. Thomas was doing the same, and James sensed he had found a kindred spirit.

Admittedly, it was only a few hours ago, but all the same, he was determined to speak to his employer and see what he had to do to change his patch and deliver to Bucks Avenue and Clearwater House.

The Crown and Anchor was fogged with pipe smoke, clammy and noisy, but the seats were padded, and James' legs ached. He sat with a newspaper on the table reading the latest horrors committed in the East End. The Ripper had killed twice in one night, and there was no foreseeable end to his reign of terror. The police were useless, locals were rioting, and the city was gripped by panic.

'Huh,' he mumbled. 'Not in South Riverside.'

Luckily, the murders were taking place far from his home borough in the west where James sat sipping a pint of cloudy ale. He often needed a drink after the day's work, but today, he needed one more than ever. He was on his second pint and still his heart was racing, his mind tumbling over itself and his blood coursing with anxiety. Not even the grisly reports from Greychurch could distract him. Every sentence contained a reminder of his encounter with Thomas.

He read, "The neighbourhood of Greychurch was horrified to a degree of panic…" and remembered how he'd panicked when he first saw Thomas. Reading, "The circumstances of the murder are of such a revolting character…", his heart jolted in shock because people would think him revolting if they knew he'd instantly been attracted to another man.

"There are still no clues, and no-one as yet knows who the murderer is…" James had no clue how he could get to know Thomas, he only knew that he wanted to. More than that. He needed to.

'Damnit!' he growled, and turned the page hoping for more cheerful distractions.

He studied the House of Lords listing, reasoning that if he learnt more about Lord Clearwater, he might stand a better chance of being given the patch and thus more opportunity to meet the footman.

He'd begun work for the post office as soon as he was able. Having been taught well, he read fluently, and his handwriting was legible. He was chosen, however, for his stamina. He was not a sporty youth, but he was quick on his feet and was often complimented on his speed despite his stocky build. The hustle and bustle of the dispatch office was enjoyable although, at first, it was all he saw. He was promoted later in his teens and sent onto the streets of the capital with mundane deliveries, later still, he was entrusted with the urgent ones and given his own patch in the west of the borough. In winter, the days were dark and cold, in summer, hot and uncomfortable and he sweated in his uniform. He enjoyed every day of work, apart from those when the peasouper was so thick he could hardly breathe and had to feel his way to his destinations. Although the air wasn't always clean, James enjoyed the freedom to run and walk through the streets more than he would have done his father's irregular glimpses of the outside world and decided his career lay in delivering messages.

On bad-weather days, he envied his father working aboard ships that sailed to foreign waters. He sat with his younger sister at the parlour table reading her the names of the vessels that used the country's ports and describing their exotic destinations from books.

When his father was home, only for a week at a time and not very often, he would tell James of his adventures. First, when James was sitting on his knee asking more questions than his dad could possibly answer, and later, opposite each other at the table discussing the perils of ocean travel as men. Even now in his mid-twenties, James loved to hear his father's stories, the escapades, the storms, the heat of the sun on the equator and the frozen rigging when he sailed north.

He had wanted to join him in work and had asked it many times, but it wasn't until he was older that he realised why his father was reticent. He may have had adventures, seen the midnight sun and flightless birds who lived on icebergs, but only on rare occasions. Most of his time was spent in the steam and heat of an engine room, the pumps deafening him, and the fumes choking him worse than any city fog.

There was another side to being a messenger, and one which would have neatly rounded the edges of James' desires, which were to earn money to support his family and to find affection from another man. Another James Wright, but with a different name, someone with whom he could discuss why he wasn't attracted to the opposite sex. He had never known such a friend. Although he met many young men, none hinted at being open to a conversation should James ever dare to start one.

That was, until aged seventeen he was approached by an older messenger with the unlikely name of Lovemount.

James was relieving himself in the depot washroom when the handsome if lanky youth joined him at the trough. He flashed his cock blatantly and asked James if he was interested in making some money. As a way to extend the time he had to gawp at Lovemount's prick — one of the few he had seen — he asked for more details.

The senior messenger explained how his colleagues earnt extra shillings by doing favours for "discreet gentry, at home", the meaning of which was evident from his state of arousal.

James had been too shocked to reply. He knew that such things happened, but the knowledge that Lovemount was so open about it gave him hope. Finally, he was not the only James Wright in the world. He told Lovemount that he would think about it, but although the idea aroused him, he never mentioned the subject again.

If he was to be with another man, it had to be for more than the base acts his colleagues spoke of. Security and love were to come first, of that, James was sure. He reached that conclusion as he left Lovemount semi-erect in the washroom, and vowed that, when his first time came, it would be with a man he loved. The problem, of course, was finding such a man.

'Unlikely to be Thomas,' he muttered as he turned a page to read the shipping columns, hoping to find news of his father's current voyage. Even that didn't distract him from thoughts of the good-looking redhead.

How was he to know if the look that passed between him and Thomas meant anything? Maybe it was surprise on the footman's face, the same thrilling rush as James experienced. On the other hand, it might have just been the shock of not seeing their usual delivery boy.

In fact, it probably meant nothing and, as he finished his drink, he decided it was a pointless fantasy. Even if the footman was like him, there wasn't much about James to like, not physically. Five-foot-nine, 'big boned' as his mother said when really she meant bulky, he wasn't fat, but he was not slender and graceful like Thomas. His hair was military-short and blond which to some represented softness, and he had nowhere near as much in his trousers as Lovemount. Thomas was taller, his hair the colour of a new penny and he looked stunning in his uniform, whereas James looked like any other blue-and-belted courier.

As for what Thomas might have in his trousers, that wasn't James' first thought, not even his first desire. It was something else, something intangible he couldn't see, a thing he could only imagine; the touch of Thomas' lips.

He put his glass on the table, folded the newspaper and, as alone as when he entered it, left the pub.

The following day fate once again delivered him the man he had spent the night fantasising about. Not, this time on the steps of Clearwater, but at an agent's business in Riverside High Street. James, again asked to cover the patch for his sick colleague, entered the premises to find Thomas seated by a desk. At first, he was struck dumb at the chance meeting, and then it was panic which robbed him of his words. He stumbled over his delivery. Waiting for the agent to compose a reply gave him time to talk to the Clearwater footman, but not enough time to plan what to say.

He was relieved when Thomas seemed pleased to see him and engaged him in conversation. Thomas was waiting to buy a railway ticket with the last of his savings, he said. Having lost his job, he was travelling home to his parents' farm the next day.

'Is that what you want to do?' James asked, fearful that he wouldn't see the man again.

'No,' Thomas admitted. 'I want to be in service, but I've just been fired. No respectable house will employ me now.'

James was devastated to think he would lose Thomas as soon as he had met him, but kept his wits about him and thought quickly. Always one to find an opportunity in a crisis, he offered Thomas the use of his room should he want to stay in the city a few days while he thought things over.

Thomas was caught off guard and took a moment to think. He endearingly bit his bottom lip as his emerald eyes flicked from side to side. He raised them to James and smiled.

'Can I?' he asked, the realisation of the offer dawning on him.

'Why not?' James shrugged, although he wanted to scream with joy. 'My sister can go in with my mum, and we'll have my room.' The thought thrilled him with possibilities.

'It would be useful,' Thomas said.

James hoped it would be more than that. 'We'd have to share a bed,' he ventured.

He expected the man, essentially a stranger, to change his mind, but he didn't. He was no keener either, but he was still happy to accept the offer.

'I have some things to do first,' he said. 'I have to see someone in the hospital, but we could meet later?'

They did, and Thomas brought his bags to James' house that afternoon. They parted on the street, Thomas to visit the hospital and James to wander the pavements counting the hours until they met again. He was thanking gods he didn't believe in when he was suddenly overtaken by nervousness. Thomas was probably not interested in him that way. Even if he was, how was James to find out?

He didn't know it at the time, but once again, fate was waiting to dispatch an opportunity.

Two

Thomas Payne was deep in conversation with a post office messenger he had met only the day before when a man half a mile away changed the course of his life.

He wouldn't know the details of what Viscount Clearwater had in store for him, but even if he had been privy to his Lordship's plan, he wouldn't have believed it, particularly as he had been dismissed from his service only forty-eight hours previously. He hadn't been able to tell the viscount that he no longer worked for him, and Tripp had forbidden him to come to the house. That was painful enough, but he now had nowhere to live. Luckily, he had met by chance the cheerful blond man now sitting with him at the corner table.

The Crown and Anchor, as usual, was cloudy with smoke infused with the smell of ale and the tang of workman's sweat. A crackling fire heated the public house which, that night, was busy, and the sound of men's chatter, laughter and falling dominoes provided enough background noise to cover the discussion being had by the new friends.

'Like I said earlier, Tom,' James rested his elbows on the table, 'you can stay with us for as long as you need. Don't worry about it.'

'That's very good of you,' Thomas replied. 'I'm still shocked, I suppose, and haven't been able to work out yet what I am going to do.'

It was the content of a telegram James delivered that sparked the events leading to his dismissal. Thomas had read the message and, defying Tripp, the butler, acted on it out of loyalty to his master and with no thought for himself. He was still loyal to him and would always be, because his affection for Lord Clearwater ran deep. Until he met James, and before that his Lordship's new secretary, Silas, he had very few friends.

'Me mum don't mind,' James said and took a sip of his beer. 'If you don't mind the bunking up.'

James' interest in his plight was heartening. Although they barely knew each other, the man was affable, keen to know more about Thomas, and had offered to help in any way he could. Thomas knew that, in part, this was down to an instant physical attraction that had sparked between them on their first meeting. At least, that was what he hoped at the time. Such a notion, however, was not something he was able to discuss as openly as his current lack of employment, and although part of him hoped James' interest was more than platonic, Thomas had to tread carefully. So far, they had conversed merely as acquaintances, but James had taken him in. That, surely, suggested he had more than philanthropic motives.

'When I get some money,' Thomas said, 'I can give your mum something towards...'

'Leave it out,' James protested, laughing. 'I said, no need. Not unless you end up staying a couple of weeks, then she'd start grumbling, but she don't mind me having a mate stay over, especially not one what's fallen on hard times.'

James' kindness, and that of his mother, reminded Thomas of the generosity shown to him by Lord Clearwater and brought a stab of regret. He had lived to serve His Lordship since they were boys and, because they had known each other for so long, had reached a point where he considered the viscount a friend. It had been that friendship which overflowed into what the butler called an 'unspeakable attraction', one of the reasons he gave for dismissing Thomas with no wage.

'I'll pay you back,' Thomas promised. 'As soon as I find another position.'

'Will you though?' James asked. 'I mean, did you get a reference?'

'Not yet, but I'll write to His Lordship explaining my sudden departure and asking him if he can see his way. He wasn't the one who dismissed me, but he'll probably be amenable.'

'Sounds like a decent bloke.'

'He is, James, very. I often wonder if his decency might one day be his downfall.'

'Why do you say that?'

Thomas was not prepared to go into details. Instead, he searched for a way to bring up his own delicate subject; his attraction to the messenger. He sensed there was an unspoken reason for James' friendliness, but was unsure what. He might simply be an affable man, or like the viscount, he might also have an interest in the same sex.

It was not a question easily raised, but James was waiting for an answer.

'I don't mean anything by it,' Thomas said. 'He's generous, clever, looks after his staff and likes to help people less fortunate.'

'But he still fired you for… What was it? Helping him out?' His hazel eyes questioned beneath brown brows.

'It was his butler who fired me,' Thomas corrected. Again, he was not prepared to state exactly why. He had told James it was because he'd opened the private telegram, and the messenger, not understanding how things worked in a noble house, had accepted that as truth.

'Was the butler a tall stick of a man with a beak like an eagle?' James asked.

Thomas laughed briefly. 'Aye,' he said. 'Sounds like Tripp. Why?'

'He's coming this way.'

Thomas turned in his chair to see Tripp advancing on them, a head's height above the other customers. He wove through the tables sneering at a small glass of beer, and Thomas hoped he was not going to ask to join them.

'Damn,' he muttered. 'Quick, speak about anything.'

James, a young man of quick wits, found a subject instantly. 'There's always running work at the post office,' he said. 'Quite a few of us messengers and postmen are around our age, Tom. They calls us boys and some are, but you can earn a fair amount…'

He broke off as a shadow fell across the table causing Thomas to break into a nervous sweat.

'Would you excuse me?' Tripp's familiar voice droned in grating, affected tones. 'I would like to speak with Mr Payne in private.'

'Happen we're in conversation ourselves, Mister,' James replied with courage that Thomas found charming. 'What's your business?'

'None of yours,' Tripp answered in his usual patronising fashion.

Thomas' guts turned over. 'Yes, Mr Tripp?' he enquired without looking. 'What is it?'

'A word, please, Thomas.' Unnervingly, the butler sounded affable. 'To your advantage.'

James raised an eyebrow and tipped his head silently asking if he wanted to talk to the man. Thomas nodded once and rolled his eyes.

'He'll be with you in a minute,' James said. 'Me and Tom's just finishing a chat.'

Being told to wait by a messenger was not something he was used to and Tripp gasped. It was gratifying to hear.

'I will wait over there,' he said. 'But please inform Mr Payne that Viscount Clearwater is waiting for him at his earliest convenience.'

The smell of brass polish and pressed clothing drifted away, and Thomas relaxed.

'Don't know how you put up with sods like that,' James whispered. 'You want me to get rid of him?'

'No,' Thomas smiled. 'Thanks, but I'll have to face His Lordship sometime. Perhaps he has good news for me.'

'Why are you grinning?'

The answer was because Thomas was certain the viscount's loyalty to him was as intense as his to the viscount. He assumed Lord Clearwater had questions regarding his sudden dismissal, but would understand and take Thomas' side.

'I reckon he might let me have some wages,' he said. 'He's like that. I'll have to go. Sorry.'

'No, mate. You go.' James sat back cradling his glass. 'I'll be here an hour or so until closing. If you're not back, I'll be at home. Mum won't mind you letting yourself in.'

'Are you sure?'

'I keep telling you, Tom. You're me mate. Of course she won't.'

Thomas tried to read his expression, hoping to find a suggestion of something more intimate than a passing acquaintance, but there was none.

'You're a good man, James.'

They had known each other two days and spent one night sharing a bed, but James had indicated at nothing other than wanting to help a man he liked, purely as a friend.

'So are you, Tom. Trusted you from the start, I did.'

The speed at which he had latched on to Thomas might be

considered a sign of a more than platonic interest, but it was not something they could discuss. Thomas didn't know how to start such a conversation, an overt attraction between two men brought with it a lengthy prison sentence, not to mention the employment and social implications attached to being queer.

'I had better go,' Thomas said. He drained the last of his beer. 'I'll see you later.'

'No problem, mate. Key's in the place I showed you. Try not to wake me up.'

'Hopefully, I'll be back soon with some cash.' Thomas stood. 'I must repay you for your kindness.'

James waved it away. 'We'll think of something.'

His cheery smile caused Thomas' heart to flutter, but then James always had a smile, it was as if his face had been built only to be jolly. His last statement, however, could be taken a couple of ways and Thomas was unsure how to respond.

'Thanks again,' he said, standing. 'You're a lifesaver.'

'Ah, get out of here.'

Thomas left him and, tearing his imagination away from James, focused on Tripp, now waiting impatiently near the door with an empty glass. This was not going to be pleasant, but Thomas reminded himself that he no longer needed to be civil. He would be, however, for the viscount's sake.

'Yes, Mr Tripp,' he said, looking the man in the eye and holding his head high.

'You are to come with me.'

The butler wore his livery beneath a long overcoat, suggesting he was still on duty.

'To where?'

'Where do you think, boy?' Tripp growled. 'This is not the time for playing games.'

'I was with His Lordship only recently,' Thomas said. 'I can't imagine what he could want with me if I no longer work at the house.'

Tripp scowled and handed his glass to a passing customer who looked at it and told him to fuck off. That amused Thomas, but caused the butler to blanch. He put it on a table.

'Just follow me, and keep your mouth shut.'

Tripp left the pub, and Thomas gave a last wave to James, who grinned, held up a thumb and mouthed, 'Later.'

The walk to Clearwater House was conducted in silence. Thomas had no wish to engage Mr Tripp in conversation. He was still furious at the man for throwing him out of the house he had worked in for the last nineteen years. He wouldn't have given him the time of day had he not been on Archer's business, and he knew better than to ask questions. He also knew better than to think of His Lordship by his Christian name, despite the fact Archer had insisted on it. Archer wanted Thomas to consider him a friend, but only when appropriate. When he had been serving the man, that was any time they were alone. Now that he was free, he could do what he wanted, but the divide between them was still great. Archer was a Lord, and Thomas, the son of a dairy farmer. The only way they could acceptably mix was as master and servant. There was a far more personal bond, and many shared secrets, but again, nothing that he could speak of and definitely not with Tripp.

His nervousness increased as they neared the back of Clearwater House. He hoped that he was to be reinstated, but knew that if he was, Tripp would make his life a living hell. It could only be at a lesser post, and that would be worse than no job at all. Thomas' ambitions were simple, and he only had two. The first was to work his way up to the position of butler, but he had been robbed of the opportunity by the lanky man walking two paces ahead. The second was to experience the same personal happiness His Lordship had recently found with Silas. He wanted the same unconditional love and friendship, and James presented an opportunity for both. As soon as the viscount was done with him, he would return to James and further test the waters.

Tripp led him to the servants' hall where the other staff were seated at the table. They rose as Tripp entered, and Lucy flashed a huge smile at Thomas.

'Has His Lordship's dined, Mrs Baker?' Tripp asked.

'He has, Mr Tripp. His Lordship and his guests are in the drawing room. We are instructed to go up as soon as you return.'

'Then I will see if he is ready for us. Wait here, Payne.'

Tripp removed his coat and passed through to the stairs followed

19

by four pairs of eyes. Once his footsteps had faded, and the baize door closed with a dull thud, the gossip started.

'I hope it's quick.' Lucy yawned. 'What's going on, Thomas?'

'I don't know. Has Mr Tripp said anything, Mrs Baker?'

'Not a clue, Thomas,' she admitted. She sat, and the maids followed suit.

Thomas had a soft spot for the housekeeper and she for him. It was a mutual mother and son pretence that had started when Thomas first arrived at the house as a hall boy. Aged eight, alone and from the country, he had been homesick for a week. Mrs Baker, whose role in life had always been to keep house not a husband, took pity and offered a sheltering wing. If she knew anything about this business, she would tell him.

'He's not even said anything about you leaving,' the second maid, Sally said.

'But he has been in a foul temper since before dinner,' Mrs Baker added. 'And none of us can think why.'

'It's because Mr Tripp doesn't approve of Mr Hawkins in the green suite, or the Russian in the coach house,' was Lucy's view.

'And you will keep your eyes off both gentlemen, Lucy.' The housekeeper warned her with a glare.

'Mr Tripp doesn't approve of all the queer behaviour,' Sally decreed.

'Queer?' The word hit Thomas in the stomach. 'What do you mean?'

'All the goings-on.' The maid lowered her voice. 'Those meetings you had in the study. His Lordship and Mr Hawkins' injuries. Dressing up. Them two coming here from the East End, you know. Queer stuff. Odd like.'

Thomas relaxed. 'All to do with His Lordship's charitable project, as you know.'

'And also none of our business,' Mrs Baker had heard enough conjecture. 'We may well find out presently, until then… Where are you staying, Thomas? Do you have savings?'

Tripp's precise footsteps on the stairs brought the others to their feet and gave Thomas no chance to reply.

'To the drawing room,' the butler ordered. 'And in silence.'

Thomas' apprehension increased. The last to leave the hall, it occurred to him that he had climbed these steps thousands of times in his life. The first, as a second footman in the late viscount's time, he had nearly been sick with worry. Tonight might well be the last, and the same gut-churning state returned. Whatever the viscount had in store, Thomas had the possibilities that James offered. A new way of life, a friendship, possibly more, and that thought was enough to settle his mind and his stomach.

This, of course, was before he learned what Lord Clearwater had decided.

Three

Lord Clearwater stood with his back to the fire, one elbow casually resting on the mantlepiece. He was talking with Silas and Fecker when Tripp knocked unnecessarily on the open door. They were called into the drawing room in a line, with Thomas last. He stood by the door in what had been his customary position, but tonight he was out of place. Wearing his Sunday suit, he was neither guest nor footman.

He watched Archer closely. The viscount appeared remarkably well considering he had spent two days in an East End hospital after falling forty feet from a crane to the river, nearly drowning and barely escaping the Ripper's knife.

'Thank you, Mr Tripp,' Archer said, when everyone had filed in. 'I would like you to be comfortable. Take a seat.'

No-one moved. It was a running joke among the servants that although they cared for the lavish furniture in the house, they were never allowed to sit on it. The late viscount wouldn't have heard of it, but the new Lord Clearwater was what the papers were calling a 'new man', one who had respect for the lower classes and treated them humanely, unlike his predecessor.

'Please,' he prompted. 'Silas, would you bring a chair for Mrs Baker?'

Silas did as instructed assisted by Fecker the Ukrainian, and they set seven chairs in a line facing the fire. It took another prompt from His Lordship before the others sat, but he said nothing when Thomas remained standing. He didn't even look at him, a sign, surely, that this was not to be a pleasant conversation.

'I won't keep you long,' Archer said. 'It's late, and I am sure you have better things to do than listen to me, but there is some news which I want you all to know.'

He looked at Tripp, and an exchange took place. Both men kept straight faces, but Tripp inclined his head to the side. It was his way of saying that everything was in order and the viscount could proceed, but was more usually applied to the going-in for dinner, or when the maids had finished a room. This exchange had behind it a meaning that Thomas couldn't read.

'Now then.' Archer cut a handsome figure in his dinner clothes, his dark hair brushed back from his high forehead and his face recently shaved. The only visible blemish was a patch of dark bruising around his temple. 'What I have to say will come as a surprise to you all, as it was to me. Sadly, Mr Tripp is leaving us.'

Thomas' heart paused its hurried rhythm when the words sank in, but Archer gave him no time to speculate on the announcement.

'Yes, it's all rather sudden,' he continued, and we shall, of course, be very sad to see him go.'

Tripp stared intently at the viscount. His bloodhound face, limp in silent interest, gave nothing away.

'Apparently, there has been something of a family crisis, and Mr Tripp must put family first, a very noble act, and I quite understand that time is of the essence. Therefore, dear old Tripp will be leaving us in the morning.' There were more gasps which Archer ignored. 'We have already spoken on the matter,' he said, 'so I won't embarrass you further, Tripp. Is there anything you would like to say?'

Thomas' heart was beating again, but his mind was as skittish as the flames in the grate.

Tripp stood and cleared his throat. 'Thank you, My Lord,' he said. 'Only to say what an honour it has been, and to apologise for the suddenness of my departure.'

The two men regarded each other coolly, and Thomas was convinced there was another reason for Tripp's leaving which Archer didn't want to share.

'Not at all, Tripp,' Archer said. 'Needs must and all that.' He turned to the housekeeper. 'We should have discussed this with you, of course, Mrs Baker, and I would have done so were it not for the urgency of the situation and the fact we only learned of it this evening.'

Mrs Baker appeared not to mind. Thomas suspected that she, like everyone else in the room, was silently relieved.

'And there we are, Mr Tripp,' Archer said. 'I thank you for your service, as does my family. Please keep in touch, and we wish you every success in your retirement or your new enterprise or… whatever you decide to do.' He took two confident paces, shook Tripp's hand and returned to the fireplace. He had still not acknowledged Thomas. 'And that, I think, ends the matter,' he said. 'You may now stand down.'

'If Your Lordship has no objection,' Tripp said, 'I will spend an hour of the morning bringing my books up to date, and then stand down.'

'Of course. You're catching the early train I believe?'

Apparently, this was news to Tripp. He was momentarily shocked, but his dour demeanour soon returned.

'Quite,' he said.

'Then goodnight and godspeed, Charles.'

Tripp was a civilian from that moment, and the use of his first name caused Lucy to giggle. A glower from Mrs Baker soon put a stop to that.

'Goodnight, Sir,' Tripp said with a bow. 'And thank you for your generosity.'

He clearly didn't mean it.

Tripp turned to the doors, his eyes straight ahead, ignoring Thomas.

'Oh,' Archer stopped him. 'One moment.' He turned to the housekeeper. 'I have gifted the Battle of Agincourt centrepiece to Mr Tripp for his long service. My father was as fond of it as he was of Tripp. I will sign it off the inventory, Mrs Baker if you could make a note.'

The housekeeper nodded, and Tripp sailed from the room a free man and probably rather wealthy. The centrepiece was solid silver and, as far as Thomas knew, the only one of its kind. Whatever had happened, the viscount had set the man up for life.

'If everyone else could stay behind a short while longer,' Archer said watching as Tripp closed the doors behind him. 'I have a few apologies to make.'

To hear the master of the house apologise was not something the maids were used to, and it distracted Lucy from her yawning.

'First, however,' Archer went on, 'I need to clear up a few things. The past week has been an unsettling time as you are aware, and there have been some changes at Clearwater. There will be more. I am not my father, and the house will, from now on, be run according to my rules as much as good housekeeping and etiquette will allow.' He bowed gracefully to Mrs Baker, who repressed a smile and nodded approvingly.

Archer addressed Fecker who sat nonchalantly picking his nails, his forearms on his knees studying the pattern on the Turkish rug. 'Mr Feck...' He stopped himself from using Fecker's nickname, fully aware that everyone in the room would understand its inappropriateness. Instead, he used the man's Christian name. 'Mr Andrej is to be our new coachman. We have been without someone to care for Emma and Shanks in the stables, and much as I enjoy being with the horses, it will be good to have a driver again. Mr Andrej will also assist below stairs as Mrs Baker sees fit.'

The housekeeper considered this and approved, as did Lucy who stole a quick look at the giant Ukrainian.

'Da.' Andrej was a man of few words.

'Mr Hawkins you also know,' Archer continued, turning to Silas. 'He will be living with us in the green suite as my private secretary and advisor. As you might be aware, I am involved in the setting up of a charity to assist the less unfortunate men of the East End, and Mr Hawkins has been instrumental in my research, as has Mr Andrej. He is not staff, as such, and so will be treated as a guest.'

This came as less of a surprise to everyone, particularly Thomas who knew the depths and intimacy of the relationship. Silas' suite was directly opposite the viscount's, only a few paces from bed to bed. Thomas let a pang of jealousy subside as he reminded himself that the house and what took place there was no longer his concern. Archer was working along the line of chairs, and Thomas wondered what he had in store for him when his turn came.

'My first apology,' the viscount said, 'is to Mrs Baker.'

'Oh?' She was surprised.

'I should have come to you with all of this first,' Archer explained. 'I have rather dumped it on you. Andrej will need a livery, suitable clothing and something to wear when not on duty, and I will give an allowance for that. Perhaps you would help him in the morning?'

The housekeeper looked Fecker up and down. At six-foot-four, he was almost as broad as he was tall, and she would have no idea

25

what a nineteen-year-old Russian would wear in his spare time.

'We will do our best, My Lord,' she said.

'Thank you. And please inform Mrs Flintwich of these changes would you?'

'Of course.'

'And my second apology is to Thomas.' He finally looked at him, his face displaying regret. 'I was unaware that Mr Tripp had dismissed you,' he said. 'And it's a matter we can discuss in the morning if you wish.' He addressed the other servants again. 'You won't be aware, but Mr Hawkins and I had a bit of a scrape in Limedock two nights ago, and things would have been much worse had Thomas not come to our aid, you could even say rescue. He not only braved the East End alone at night, but he also pulled me from the river, was of great assistance to Mr Hawkins, saw to our treatment at Saint Mary's and paid for it from his own pocket. I have only just discovered he did all that after Mr Tripp terminated his employment.'

His annoyance was easily detectable.

Among the questioning looks and glances from the staff, Archer walked over to Thomas and offered his hand; an unusual approach between a viscount and someone of a lower class. Thomas' back stiffened. Perhaps he too was to be sent on his way with a silver centrepiece and a cover story. If he was, he would act with decorum. He owed his previous employer that much.

'Beyond the call of duty, Thomas,' the viscount said as Thomas shook his hand. The grip was firm, the skin smooth and the appreciation in Archer's eyes palpable. 'Thank you.'

'Not at all, Sir,' Thomas said. His throat was so dry his voice cracked.

Archer returned to the fireplace. 'It will be hard,' he said. 'Adjusting to calling you Mr Payne. That is…' He repressed a smile. If you are willing to stay with me as my butler?'

Where there had been carpet beneath Thomas' feet, there was suddenly air. Where it had been cold beneath his shirt, his skin now glowed, and where his thoughts had been centred on how he would survive, they were now scattered in disbelief.

'I am lost for words, Sir,' he admitted.

'Well, don't be. Tripp has trained you well. Mrs Baker will see to your uniforms. Oh, and there will be an increase in salary, Mrs Baker. Thomas knows the role, house, cellar and everything as much as any butler, so pay him whatever Tripp was on.' He returned his attention to Thomas, who was stunned. 'And in the morning, you can begin the process of finding me a footman to replace you. He can be your first appointment, if you would.'

All eyes were on Thomas. Of course he would. Apart from the job, the security and the accommodation, he would be back under Archer's roof, and his first ambition would be fulfilled.

'I know it's unusual for a man of twenty-seven to be a butler,' Archer said, reading Thomas' surprise as uncertainty. 'But I can think of no-one better. Don't you agree, Mrs Baker?'

'I do indeed, Sir.' She was happy for Thomas as, he suspected, were the others.

'So, it's down to you, Tom.' Archer was waiting.

'I would be more than honoured, My Lord,' he said. 'Thank you.'

'Then that's that.' Archer clapped his hands. 'One more apology and you can all go to bed, and it's you again, Thomas. I mean, Payne. I'm sorry, but can I delay you from your free time one minute more? Everyone else, thank you for your indulgence. Clearwater House will be staffed again when Payne finds us a new footman. Unless you still need a hall boy, Mrs Baker, in which case come and see me. As I said, there will be changes, but in time they will become normality, and everything will find an even keel, so...' He'd run out of words. 'Goodnight.'

The servants rose, Fecker and Silas returned the chairs, and Mrs Baker led the maids from the room.

'You need me?' Fecker asked.

'No, thank you, Andrej. You get to your quarters. See Mrs Baker in the morning, and afterwards, Thomas can talk you through your duties. I hope you'll be happy here.'

'I don't need to sell my cock?' Fecker asked, unused to what was an acceptable conversation in a stately drawing room.

'No, mate, no more talk like that,' Silas punched him on the arm.

There was no need for either of them to be back on the streets selling themselves to survive, and now, after a few days of uncertainty, there was no reason for Thomas to worry about his future. He would miss the excuse to stay with James. His promotion would prevent him from forging a closer friendship, let alone anything else, but what was that compared to the stability of a good job in a house like Clearwater?

Fecker left, and Thomas closed the doors behind him. As soon as he turned to face the room, Archer was on him, pulling him close and embracing him hard. Surprised, Thomas gently returned the hug.

'You're not my butler until Tripp leaves the house,' Archer said. 'And the same rules apply from now onwards as did before. You'll always be Tom to me, my friend, but we will have to continue the pretence of master-servant when in public.'

'I understand.'

Archer released him and stood back. 'By God, you're a good man to have around. I am so sorry Tripp took it on himself to dismiss you. Bloody nuisance. The man didn't know what you had done for us, and I had no idea you did it in your own time, off your own back and with your own money. I will settle up with you immediately. Now, either stay here or wherever you have been, but be here at midday tomorrow, Tripp will be well out of our way by then. Can you do that?'

'As you wish, Sir.'

'Come now, Tom,' Archer chided playfully. 'The doors are shut, it's just Silas and us.'

Thomas relaxed. He wanted to burst into tears. His life had been a series of ups and downs, confusion and clarity these past few days, but now, there was an end to it. The Ripper had fallen to his death, Archer had nearly done the same, and Silas had almost been murdered. On top of that, Archer had declared his platonic love for Thomas and shown him that to love another man was not the sin he had been taught. He had been able to accept himself.

Silas was with them now, also shaking Thomas' hand. 'Good one, Tommy,' he said, grinning that overly cute, cheeky grin of his. 'What do I have to call you now?'

'Mr Payne in public, whatever you want in private,' Thomas said.

'Come, Tom.' Archer led him to one of the settees. 'Sit down while you can legitimately use the furniture.'

'If it's alright by you, Sir,' Thomas said. 'I have a friend waiting for me at the Crown.'

'Oh.' Archer said, taken aback. 'Of course. I was only going to talk about what happened, but we can do that tomorrow.'

'But I will happily stay if you want me to. You must be exhausted.'

'I am a bit.' Archer flopped onto a settee, Silas beside him. 'Everything aches and my head is full of questions. Have you heard any more news of the Ripper?'

'No, Sir. The newspapers continue to speculate, but there have been no developments that I have heard of.'

'I'm guessing the man's at the bottom of the river,' Silas said. 'And good fecking riddance to him.'

'I am sure Mr Hawkins is correct,' Thomas said.

'Oh, Tom,' Archer sighed. 'Will you promise me one thing? Please? For my sanity's sake?'

'Of course.'

'Don't start sounding like Tripp. Yes, play your part when you must, but don't let yourself become supercilious and grand like him. I tell you what…' Archer rose and entered his study. 'Why don't you go and find your friend, finish your beer and do whatever you want,' he called from the depths of the next room. 'You can stay here tonight, but I imagine you might feel uncomfortable until Tripp has gone.' He reappeared with a five-pound note. 'Here, have a drink, enjoy your night of freedom and either way, we'll see you tomorrow.' He handed Thomas the note.

'I can't take that.'

'For the hospital and everything else.'

'But…'

'Birthday present,' Archer said, opening Thomas' fingers and slapping the money into his palm.

'That's not until…'

'I know. Shut up and get drunk.'

'I'd rather not.'

'Then buy yourself something. I don't know, Tom, I'm only trying to say thank you and it's the only way I know how.'

'I think reinstating me, promoting me and treating me as a friend is payment enough, Sir.'

'Archer.'

Thomas gave in to the warmth of friendship that flowed between them. 'Thank you, Archer,' he said and put the note in his pocket.

'Right, well, I don't know about you two,' Silas said, getting to his feet. 'But I've got pains in places I didn't know I had, and I need to sleep for a week. I'm going to bed. Goodnight, Archie.'

'Sleep well,' Archer said and kissed him.

'You can keep me awake if you want,' Silas smirked.

'If you're still awake when I come up, I will.' Archer threatened playfully.

That was something else Thomas would have to adjust to; their openness. He glanced at the mantle clock to avert his eyes and wondered what it would feel like to kiss James.

'As for you, Tommy.' Silas patted him on the cheek. 'Thanks for saving my life and all that stuff.'

Silas was blushing, and Thomas found it hard to suppress a smile. The youth was bold to the point of insolence at times, as open as a book and as rough as gravel, but it was impossible not to like him. Thomas had tried and failed.

'Anytime, nipper,' was all he said before Silas left and he was alone with Archer.

'Happy, Tom?' The viscount asked once he had heard the door click shut.

Thomas nodded, allowing his smile to roam free. 'Are you?'

Archer dropped into an armchair. 'I am, Tom,' he sighed. 'But I fear shock is now presenting itself and I am about to blub.'

'Go ahead, Archer. It's what I've been doing this past couple of days.'

'Have you? Why?'

'Forget I said that. Not your concern.'

'What possessed the man?' Archer, his mind elsewhere, was referring to Tripp. 'How dare he? And Quill!' He glared at Thomas as if he was responsible for the Ripper's killing spree. 'How can I know a man so well and yet not know him at all?'

Thomas had no answers and let the viscount ramble on. If he missed James at the pub, he would find him later at his house. Archer needed someone to listen, and Thomas would stay with him for as long as it took.

The viscount spoke about his friendship with the doctor, the years they served together and the things they'd seen. He spoke of the time when his own brother tortured him and his lover, Lieutenant

Harrington. He wept for the dead renters, the poor youths who had lost their lives at the hands of Doctor Quill in his mad attempt to corner Archer and exact revenge.

Thomas reassured him that there would be no more killing and, slowly, Archer calmed himself. Sniffing back tears, he let out a mighty sigh. When he finally admitted his exhaustion, his eyes were droopy, and his mouth more downturned than usual. Thanking Thomas all the way to the front door, Archer saw him out in a manner that, from the next day, Thomas would adopt with him. For now, the role-reversal was entertaining and showed that despite everything, the viscount had not lost his humour.

Thomas walked to the Crown and Anchor through an unusually warm October night. A church clock struck midnight, and he knew James would have left for home. He turned that way and whistled, secure in the knowledge that he was protected and valued.

What he didn't know was that during Thomas' absence, James had taken a drink with someone else. A while after Thomas left, Mr Tripp returned to the pub. James' anger rose when he saw him approaching, and he wished he hadn't just ordered another pint.

'Thomas ain't here,' he said.

'You should be careful of his kind.' The butler helped himself to a chair. 'I've come to see you. I know you messengers have low morals. How do you want to earn some good money?' He took James' drink from his hand.

Before James could object, Tripp engaged him in a conversation that was as interesting as it was exciting. The old man with the eyebrows that crested like foaming waves and grey jowls that hung like rotting curtains offered more than intrigue. A large sum of money was available for a covert job discreetly but well done.

James' Christmases came at once and with several measures of decent whisky paid for by Tripp. He left the pub with the chance to be wealthy enough to pay for his sister's schooling and the rent on the family house for years to come. His mother could ease off on work and let her hands recover, and he could take time to find a better job.

At twenty-five, he was old enough to be a postman, and too old to be a messenger, but until something came up he was forced to stay where he was and be the laughing stock of his colleagues. Now, Tripp had made him an offer impossible to refuse. James' family needed the money, and all he had to do for it was discover information by seducing someone he already desired.

Unfortunately, that man was Thomas, and James was tempted.

Four

James lived in a cramped two-up two-down cottage a mile from Clearwater House towards the river, where Thomas arrived a little after midnight to find no lamps burning. In the yard, he located the hidden backdoor key and let himself silently into the scullery where he groped the windowsill for a candle. With that lit, he removed his shoes and, doing his best to make no noise, crept up the narrow stairs to the bedrooms. Mrs Wright and her daughter shared the front room while her husband was away at sea or when they had guests, and James currently had the back room to himself.

He had left a candle burning on the dresser, so Thomas extinguished his and put it outside the door in case anyone else needed it during the night. He was undressing when he realised James was awake and watching him.

'Where have you been?' he asked.

'Did I wake you?'

'No, I was waiting for you.'

Thomas hung his jacket on a hook and removed his trousers. He kept his underwear on because his long johns were tight fitting. The soft cotton helped confine the erection he had suffered last night when lying beside the messenger.

'What did that man want?' James asked as Thomas climbed over him. James liked to sleep at the edge of the bed and Thomas had to squeeze in beside the wall.

'Long story,' he said. 'But I have a job again.'

'Yeah? That's great, mate, well done.'

'I had no say in it,' Thomas admitted. 'But like I said, Lord Clearwater is a good man. He's promoted me.'

'Get out! Why?'

'Because I'm good at what I do. And Tripp had to retire suddenly.'

'That's the man who came to the pub?'

'Aye.'

Thomas wriggled under the covers. They were damp and musty. He would never allow that in Clearwater House. Thinking the name brought on a wave of panic.

'I hope I'm up to it,' he said, lying on his back and watching the candle flame flicker on the low ceiling.

'You got enough room?' James asked. Their thighs were touching in the narrow bed, causing Thomas all manner of inappropriate thoughts.

'Aye,' he replied. 'I'm fine. You?'

'Can't really move much more, or I'd fall out.'

'I'll be gone tomorrow. The viscount gave me some money, so I can leave that for your mum.'

'She'll appreciate that.'

James shifted to find a more comfortable place. He was also on his back, his hands behind his head where his elbows jabbed Thomas in the shoulder. When Thomas turned to look at him in the semi-light, their faces were only inches apart. James smelt of beer and pipe smoke mixed with a manly smell of a day's sweat. As he moved, his leg pressed against Thomas who couldn't help but wonder if that was a sign. Their brief acquaintanceship hinted at nothing other than friendship, despite James' eagerness to offer him his bed. Thomas didn't dare read too much into his kindness for fear of giving himself away.

'So, you'll have your own room again?' James asked. Although speaking quietly, his voice cut through the stillness of the night and when he stopped, the silence was more intense.

'I'll have several,' Thomas answered, crossing his arms on his chest and trying not to elbow the other man. 'A suite on the top floor and a pantry below stairs.'

'Nice. How big is Clearwater House?'

'Oh, it's grand, James,' Thomas enthused. He took him on an imagined tour of the downstairs listing the various rooms and his duties before mounting the stairs and guiding his friend through the viscount's floor. 'It's divided in half upstairs,' he said. 'The Dowager has two suites on one side of the stairs when she's in town, and the viscount has two on the other. Us servants are also segregated on the top floor, men one side and the maids the other. Mrs Baker has her rooms in the basement...' He was no longer tired, he was too excited about his prospects, and James had to tell him to slow down.

'I can see you like it,' he said. 'But who's going to replace you?'

'That's another thing...' Thomas leant up on one elbow, facing James who turned his head to watch. 'I'll have to place an advertisement and interview for a footman. We have more at Larkspur, the country house, and I could bring one down, but I think the viscount wants to refresh the staff and put in his own.'

'Well, Tom,' James said. 'I'm happy for you, but it's getting late.'

'Sorry. My head's in a spin.'

James laughed. 'So I see.'

He ruffled Thomas' hair, sending warm shivers through his body and causing his cock to tingle.

'I really appreciate your kindness,' Thomas said. It was the first time James had done anything like that, and it was hard not to read too much into the contact.

'I'm a nice bloke,' James said.

'I agree.' Thomas was unable to think about sleep. Recent events, his dismissal and promotion, the challenge of the job ahead, being given what he always wanted and now lying in a bed with another man and James' close physical contact crowded his mind with uncertainty. He harboured a driving desire to let his hand flop from his chest and land on James' hip. It was as if Thomas' cock had a mind of its own; he could feel its heat and wondered if James' was in the same solid state. He needed to know if what he felt was reciprocated, but to ask would be a huge risk.

'How come you don't have a girl?' He hoped the question wasn't too obvious. 'Thought they'd be all over someone as good-looking as you.'

'Ha!' James snorted. 'I ain't good-looking.'

'Yes you are.' Thomas pressed the point further. 'At least, I think so.'

'Nah, too chubby.'

'You're stocky. Nothing wrong with that.'

'Some people don't like it.'

'Girls, you mean?'

'Ain't got time for them, Tom.' It was a cryptic reply and begged the question, why?

'No, me neither.' Thomas' breathing was shallow, his pulse quickening and he fought against the itching in his fingers which wanted to travel the short distance from his chest to James'.

'Girls are complicated,' James said, and yawned.

'I know.'

'Never met one I fancied.'

'Really?'

Anticipation hung heavily in the air, thickening the silence. Thomas had opened a gate and hoped against hope that James would accept the invitation to follow.

'Have you?' James asked, breathless. 'Fancied a girl I mean.'

This was surely some kind of code. 'No,' Thomas admitted. 'Don't get much time in my job.'

'Does the viscount have a wife?'

There was no way Thomas was prepared to talk about Archer, not even if James rolled onto him, declared undying love and begged. The viscount's private life was no-one's business.

'He has plenty of friends,' he replied, keeping it vague.

'Ah, I see,' James said. 'And you don't?'

'No.' It was a sad fact but true. 'Again, not much time. I know some of the staff next door, but don't often get to socialise.' The conversation was drifting from suggestiveness to things more prosaic, and Thomas didn't want to lose the moment. 'But now I've met you,' he said, 'I can say I have at least one good mate.'

James laughed again, once and briefly. 'You hardly know me,' he said.

'But I'd like to know you more.'

Another long pause, another insinuation.

'Yeah? How's that?'

Was James fishing for the truth, or just making conversation? It was late, he had to be up early for work, and he'd said he was tired, yet he seemed as unwilling as Thomas to let the conversation end.

'You know,' Thomas said, stumbling for words. 'More about you, what you like. What you do.'

'Deliver telegrams.'

'When you're not at work.'

'Drink at the pub.'

'And after that?'

'Come home and sleep.'

'Alone?'

'Some men don't have a choice.'

Did that mean what Thomas hoped it meant?

'But do you…?' Thomas' pulse drummed in his ears. 'That is… Do you ever wish you had someone to be with? At night.'

'Like this you mean?'

Was James flirting? The candle was dying, and Thomas could no longer see his face.

'Aye, like this.'

Longing filled the pause between their words and offered all manner of fantasies while he waited for James to make the next move.

'Sometimes,' James admitted. 'But you can imagine what my mum would say if I brought a girl to stay the night.'

Sickness knotted Thomas' stomach. 'Aye, girls are difficult,' he said. His throat was constricted as if the muscles there didn't want him to voice what was in his mind. He swallowed and heard every sound inside his head amplified. It was underscored by the rush of adrenaline through his veins. 'But your mum doesn't mind you sleeping with another man?'

'As long as we're only sleeping, Tom,' James said, and Thomas' hopes died.

James sighed and shifted, uncomfortable. That might have been because of the cramped space, or it might have been because he knew what Thomas was hinting.

'I heard some men do more than that.' Thomas screwed up his eyes, expecting a barrage of insults and outrage.

James said nothing.

'What do you think about that?' It would have been an innocent enough question were it not for the situation.

James' head moved, and his pillow rustled. He looked at Thomas, who kept his own eyes on the ceiling. The yellow dance of the dying flame faded before his eyes, and the room slipped into darkness.

'What do they do, these men?' James whispered.

'I don't know.' Thomas trembled. 'I heard they touch each other.'

It was a ridiculous thing to say as it meant nothing.

'Like they'd do with a woman?'

'I suppose.'

'They wank each other?'

Thomas froze. 'Must do.'

The chasm of silence returned. His cock was painful now, and he had a choice to make. He could reach over and touch James' to see what state he was in, but that would be uninvited, and if Thomas had misread the situation, he would give himself away. Or he could stay lying on his back, screaming from the inside out, do nothing and never know if James felt the same way.

Thomas was not a man to live on regrets.

'Do you fancy it?' he said and every muscle in his body tensed.

'With you?'

It was a case of now or never. 'Aye.'

Thomas expected rejection or worse.

'It's illegal, Tom,' James said. 'Could lead to all kinds of trouble.'

That wasn't a no, and it wasn't a yes. It was as if James was testing him.

'I'm used to a bit of trouble.' Thomas' heart felt like it would shut down at any moment. Too much hope prevented him from thinking straight, and he was sick with anticipation.

'Is that what you want for me, Tom? Trouble?'

How was he to answer that? Archer always said to be honest, no matter what.

'No,' he said. 'I don't want trouble for you. I was just interested.'

'Why?'

'Because I like you.'

'You fancy me, you mean?'

'I like you, James.' Thomas' head was hurting. 'I'd like to say thank you for helping me. Happy to do what you want.'

He jolted when James took hold of his hand and lifted it. Saying nothing, he moved it over his body and pressed it to his crotch. He was hard beneath his underwear, and Thomas felt the heat and pulse through the material. He curled his fingers around the solid rod of his erection, his own stiffness pressing urgently against James' thigh.

James lifted his hand away and put it back on Thomas' leg.

'Sorry, Tom,' he said, rolling onto his side. 'I need to think about this.'

Again, not a no and not a yes, but the touch had stoked a fire. It was as if Thomas had built up a boiler of steam which had no outlet, and if the safety valve didn't blow soon, he would explode.

He was still resting on his elbow, now facing James' back and his arm hurt.

'Sorry,' he said. 'Didn't mean anything.'

'Go to sleep, Tom.' Sighing, James pulled the covers up to his chin. 'It's late.'

'Aye. Sorry.'

Thomas admitted defeat, and knowing he wouldn't be able to sleep so close the man, rolled onto his back, an arm across his face to shield his pain from the darkness.

'Stop saying sorry, mate,' James sighed. 'I ain't saying no, just saying… Maybe.'

'I won't mention it again.'

'You can,' James said. 'But give us a bit of time, yeah? I've got to be able to trust you.'

'You can.'

'Prove it.'

Was that another offer? 'How?'

James reached behind and found Thomas' arm. He dragged it around his chest, forcing Thomas to spoon into him. He was unable to hide his aroused state, and his cock pressed into the soft mounds of James' buttocks.

'Just go to sleep,' James said. 'Like this is good. We all need to be warm.' He bumped his arse against Thomas' length and wiggled it, sniggering. 'Just keep that monster to yourself.'

If he carried on doing what he was doing, Thomas would blow his load.

Luckily, James stopped. He continued to hold Thomas' hand, though, and that had to be a sign that more might be possible. Thomas controlled his breathing. He was desperate to kiss the back of James' neck and do more, but his friend's message was clear. If he could be trusted to leave him alone, James would be more inclined to take things further in his own time.

It would have to do for now.

Accepting that this was all the affection he was to receive that night, Thomas lay awake until his breathing slowed, his grip loosened, and he fell asleep.

It took James a lot longer, though he pretended to be sleeping as soon as Thomas' arm was around him. This was exactly what he had hoped would happen when his invitation to stay had been accepted. Thomas wanted what he did, they were both being cautious, but James could turn to him, kiss him and that would be that; the start of a path he was desperate to travel.

But then there was Tripp. 'Play it calmly,' he had advised. 'He will rise to the bait more keenly and give more away.'

Tripp was not queer. He hated them and had said so, and had not quizzed James on the subject, merely assumed that because of their city-wide reputation, all messengers were open to bribery and keen to make money from whatever source. James had remained silent, taking the man's advice as heaven sent guidance as to how he could approach Thomas and win him.

'Win him first, delve later. I shall tell you everything you need to know.'

Tripp's voice was in his head. It had made a home there, and as much as James wanted rid of it, the dull, monotonous drone continued, reminding him what was expected, and what he had to do to earn his money.

Five

The following Saturday morning, Archer was woken by a gentle knocking on his bedroom door. Whereas Tripp had knocked four times and each one sounded like the toll of a death bell, Thomas rapped the door as if he was playing a minuet. Light and cheery, it made for a much more pleasant start to the day.

'Come!' Archer called, sitting up and stretching as the butler entered.

'Good morning, My Lord,' Thomas greeted him. He placed a tray of coffee in Archer's lap before attending to the curtains.

'Morning, Tom.'

'Fair weather but chilly today, Sir,' Thomas announced.

'I'm not going anywhere.'

'Lady Marshall is due at one, Sir, and Cook wondered about salmon.'

'Mrs Flintwich is always wondering about salmon but rarely decides on it,' Archer smirked. 'Lady Marshall has an aversion only to bad fashion and trout. Tell Cook that I have relieved her of her stress and *asked* for her salmon.'

He had been adding sugar to the tarry liquid in his cup and looked up as he replaced the teaspoon.

'Good Lord, Tom,' he exclaimed. 'Her Ladyship was dead right about your colours.'

In need of new uniforms, Archer had asked his godmother to advise on what was modern and daring. He was keen to rid his house of any vestige of his father, and Tripp's black, grey and white liveries — made, as his godmother said, by Messrs Dour and Duller — had never been to Archer's taste. They were far too 'last decade' Lady Marshall decreed, falling on the task like a rabid hound. It had taken all of Archer's tact to keep her focused on what was suitable in the city rather than the latest flounce and feather from France, and Mrs Baker, whose job it was to keep within a budget, put up an equally rigorous fight on the financial front. The compromise was seen in the new uniforms for the Clearwater butler and footman. Black tailcoats again, but a modern cut and trimmed not with black velvet, but emerald green, dark and rich. The traditional white shirts were still to be worn, but the choice of attachable collars increased. The waistcoats proved more controversial, but to Archer's mind, were a vast improvement. For Thomas, Her Ladyship had suggested russets, and she had been right. The dark, autumn red was a perfect match for his hair, and his green eyes were reflected in the edging. His clothes had been cut to accentuate his slender figure, a design which worked perfectly, and the overall effect was to emphasise the uniqueness of the man who wore the uniform with pride.

Thomas was a handsome sight, but Archer's greatest joy came from seeing the pleasure the livery brought his friend.

Archer had been staring as well as reminiscing. 'Sorry, didn't mean to gawp,' he said. 'What time is it now?'

'A little after eight,' Thomas said. 'Mr Hawkins has been up for some while.' He disappeared into the dressing room. 'Will you bathe this morning, Sir?'

'No thanks, Tom.' Archer sipped his coffee. 'Tonight perhaps. Something casual for the morning?'

Thomas' face popped around the door. 'The Ashton tweed?'

'Hell no. It smells of straw, and I feel like a bushel.'

'The Derby linen?'

Archer shook his head. 'It's only my godmother,' he said. 'Yesterday's trousers, any shirt, no collar, and one of my smoking jackets.'

'Very good, Sir.' Thomas nodded his approval. 'The question, of course, is which? Will it be the Oriental dragons in a choice of gold or jade? Perhaps the bamboo, the lion or the embroidered lily?'

Thomas was half-smiling, and Archer liked his playfulness. Tripp wouldn't have given him any choice. Knowing exactly what outfit Archer's father would have worn, he would have laid out the same for him the night before. He was much happier with Thomas' lighter approach.

'Whatever you think best, Tom,' he said, returning the grin.

Thomas retreated to the dressing room where, after a quick wash, Archer joined him.

'Do you object to playing valet?' he asked, tucking in his shirt as Thomas helped him dress.

'Not at all,' Thomas replied.

'You won't have to do it when we're up at the Hall.'

Archer's country house, Larkspur Hall, was miles west of the city and another world entirely. His widowed mother entertained in the Hall when Archer was away but lived in the dower house in the grounds. Whereas the city home required only a small staff, Larkspur had an army of them, most of them unnecessary, he thought.

'When we're next there...' Archer said, '...and I hope we will be for Christmas if not before, you will have a heap of staff to see to. I doubt we'll get much time alone.'

'It will be a challenge,' Thomas said, handing him the black smoking jacket with the jade dragons and silver flames. 'The late viscount's valet needs replacing. Robert is keen on the job, but I'm more than happy to be doing this.'

'We'll see,' Archer said, putting on the jacket. 'I've written to Larkspur, so everyone knows the situation with Tripp, but...' He turned to Thomas tying the belt. 'Is everything alright, Tom?'

'Why do you ask?'

'There's something changed about you and not just the butler role. I sense you've something on your mind. Am I right?'

Thomas blinked his long, blond lashes and the half-smile returned. 'You can tell?'

'I can, and so can you. By which I mean, you can tell me what the problem is if you want to. You know you can, don't you?'

'I do, Archer.' Thomas used his first name to show he was sincere. 'And I will, if I need to, but please, don't worry.'

'I must if it is to do with the house. Are you managing? When do you interview?'

Thomas attended to the jacket with a soft brush. 'It's not exactly to do with the house, and I am managing, yes. You'll let me know if I'm not,' he said. 'I am expecting replies to the advertisement today.'

'As you wish,' Archer said. 'You know where I am.'

'Thank you, Sir.' Thomas nodded formally, ending the intimacy.

'Will there be anything else?'

'No, thank you, Payne.' It was odd to call Thomas by his surname, but Archer did as he must. 'Let me know when you have the applications, I should be interested to look through them. Oh!' A thought struck him. 'I don't mean to imply that I don't trust you...'

Thomas held up a hand. 'I would be delighted.'

With that arranged, Thomas left to see to his business leaving Archer free to visit Silas.

'Who is it?' Silas called when Archer knocked.

'Archer.'

'Oh, come in.'

When he stepped into the room, Archer understood why Silas had questioned. He stood surrounded by piles of clothes wearing only his underwear; not a state in which to be discovered by a maid. The sight reminded Archer that he had yet to settle the clothing bill, and not only for what her Ladyship had arranged for Silas, but also the new uniforms, and clothes Mrs Baker had acquired for Fecker.

'Your godmother's order arrived,' Silas said. 'I hope there ain't no more. I don't know where to start.' He held up a shirt.

Archer closed the door and walked over to him, took the shirt from his hand and flung it onto the bed. 'You can start here,' he said, wrapping Silas in his arms.

They kissed passionately, and the feel of Silas' slim body nearly naked and pressed to his own, soon had Archer's cock raging. His hands slipped to Silas' buttocks. He loved the feel of one in each hand, and in return, Silas' hand dived straight to his erection.

Archer groaned with pleasure when Silas sank to his knees, undid his trousers and took his cock between his lips. He had just drunk coffee, and his mouth was hot, intensifying the pleasure.

'My God,' Archer whispered. 'You're beautiful.'

Silas, holding Archer's dripping length in one hand, looked up, his impish smile growing. 'Fuck my mouth,' he leered, panting.

Archer took his head in his hands. He adored the man's ears and the feel of his dense hair, but more, he worshipped the touch of his tongue.

He began slowly, almost gracefully, watching his sturdy cock vanish between Silas' lips, but soon — too soon — he was driving harder, his legs buckling, and he came deep in his lover's throat.

Silas gagged and swallowed, refusing to let Archer go until he had licked every sensitive part, and Archer was begging him to stop.

As soon as he was allowed, Archer lay Silas down among his new clothes. There, he returned the pleasure, bringing Silas to distraction gradually in a series of gasps and jerks until he thrashed at the clothes, bucked and fired a series of hot bursts into Archer's mouth.

Archer let Silas' cock slip from his lips and marvelled at its dark skin, stretched to its full six-inch capacity, the stocky balls tight and darker beneath. He kissed them before working his way back up Silas' body where they shared the taste of each other in a long, lingering exchange.

They caught these moments of intimacy whenever they could, but restricted them to their rooms and at times when they would not be disturbed. Sometimes snatched in fleeting moments of opportunity, sometimes a whole night, every time was an exploration of new pleasures as they learnt from each other and grew together. The only people in the house they had to hide from were the housekeeper and the maids, but it was good practice to behave with decorum in case their passion should boil over at an inopportune moment. At Clearwater House, there was an above stairs, and a below stairs divide, a private and a public way of life, and, despite Archer's unconventionality, both had to be seen to be separate.

'Hey, Boss,' Silas said, as Archer cradled him in his arms. 'I think I should finish getting dressed.'

Conventionality returned to Archer's life with the arrival of Lady Marshall dead on one o'clock.

He was in the drawing room scanning the newspapers for any mention of the Ripper or the finding of Quill's body when Thomas crossed the hall. A few seconds later, the front door opened and closed, and he appeared in the room standing to attention.

'The Lady Marshall,' he announced and stepped aside.

Archer's godmother wafted in on waves of chiffon and silk, cut too provocatively for a lady of her age, and announced, 'Archer! Behold the descending angel.' With that, she turned, took Thomas by the elbow and led him back into the hall.

45

Archer followed, wondering what she was up to, and found her arranging the butler on the turn in the stairs. She came down, leaving him there, and stood back.

'Isn't that just fabulous,' she said, admiring the uniform as much as the man. 'I knew greens and reds were the way to go. Do you like it, Payne? Honestly.'

'Very much, Your Ladyship. Thank you.'

'Don't thank me,' she replied. 'He's paying for it.'

'Dolly, don't be vulgar,' Archer admonished her. 'Thank you, Payne,' he said, and behind Lady Marshall's back, gave his butler a wink.

Back in the drawing room, Her Ladyship made herself at home in her usual place on the grandest settee, and as soon as Archer entered, began questioning him about the house. They had met only briefly since Archer had fired Tripp, and he had not provided her with all the digestible details. He told her only what he wanted her to know, staying with the fiction of Tripp's family crisis, and was eventually able to turn the conversation to the purpose of their meeting; their charity.

'Mr Hawkins is in the East End today,' Archer informed her. 'He and Mr Andrej have begun investigating suitable properties. There is an agent who has provided a list.'

'Makes perfect sense,' Lady Marshall said. 'As they know the area. Have you been back since the night of the riot?'

There had been much unrest in Greychurch because of the Ripper murders, and Archer had told her he had been caught up in one such disturbance while on one of his research visits. He hadn't, of course, he had been dispatching the Ripper to a watery grave, but no-one, not even Lady Marshall could know that, or his connection to the murderer.

'No,' he replied, honestly. 'I have seen enough for now, but you and I will have to visit when Silas finds an appropriate building.'

'I'm looking forward to the opening,' she said. 'My niece has discovered an outlet for *Français pauvre*, as she's calling it. The starved look, I say. Very rustic. I will fit right in.'

Archer thought it best not to remind her that they were building a hostel for rent boys and not a fashion house.

'The rents are very cheap,' he said, immediately regretting using the word. 'I've instructed Marks to draw up the principles for negotiation, and everything else should be signed off at the next meeting of trustees.'

'How jolly.'

The conversation continued in a similar vein until Thomas reappeared to announce lunch. He seemed flustered.

'Thank you, Payne,' Archer said.' Did the applications arrive?'

'They did, Sir,' Thomas replied.

'Is everything alright?'

'Er... Yes. I have just finished reading them.'

'You can always borrow one of mine until you find someone suitable, Payne,' Lady Marshall offered.

'I am honoured, Your Ladyship.' Thomas bowed his head. 'I think I have seen one who is more than suitable, Sir. Shall I put the letters on your desk?'

'If you would. We can look through them later.'

They crossed the hall in silence and observed their version of the luncheon formalities. At Clearwater, now that Archer was viscount, this meant he and his godmother could sit opposite each other at the side of the table, not at the ends where they would have to raise their voices across the distance. They were served by Thomas and Lucy, discussed their charity and the deplorable state of the poor in general, and when the meal was over, retired to the drawing room to take a whisky-coffee, a decadence of which they were both fond.

It was while they were discussing how the servants at Larkspur would take the news of Tripp's departure, that Thomas passed the doors once more. Archer was expecting no other visitors, and his mind was only half on Lady Marshall as he speculated on who it could be.

He received his answer a minute later when Thomas appeared with a silver salver.

'My apologies, My Lord,' he said, when Archer acknowledged him.

'Who is it?'

Thomas advanced and offered the tray. 'Inspector Adelaide.'

Their eyes met, and Archer instantly knew what his butler was thinking. Adelaide was the man investigating the Ripper murders. Someone had made a connection between the killer and Archer.

Quill's body had been found with some incriminating evidence. Thomas' face was strained, but Archer knew to keep a cool head. He took the inspector's calling card.

'Thank you, Payne,' he said. 'Show him in.' He nodded reassuringly, and Thomas backed away.

'What could he want?' Lady Marshall enquired rhetorically.

Archer had little time to gather his thoughts and calm his nerves before Thomas was back to formally announce the visitor.

He stepped aside to reveal a tall, wide-set man with a barrel chest barely contained by a tight-fitting suit. The hair that was missing from the centre of his head appeared to have been rehoused beneath his nose in the form of a moustache with which Lucy could have swept the kitchen floor. His face sagged as if he had known too many tragedies, and his eyes were ringed with dark shadows.

'Inspector.' Archer rose and waited for the man to approach. 'What an unexpected pleasure.'

Thomas left, and the policeman advanced.

'My apologies, My Lord,' he said, his voice gruff and accented. 'Rude of me to arrive without an appointment.'

'That's alright, Inspector.' Archer shook his hand. 'You've become something of a celebrity of late. Oh, The Lady Marshall.'

Adelaide bowed to her before addressing the viscount.

'And some have fame forced upon them,' the Inspector misquoted. 'If it's inconvenient, Sir, I could return later.'

At least the man was not here to arrest him.

'I can't imagine what your business might be,' he said. 'But if it is of an indelicate nature, I am sure Her Ladyship would excuse us. We could talk in the library.'

'It might be considered a little indelicate, Sir,' Adelaide said.

'In which case, sit down and give me all the details,' Lady Marshall enthused. 'Unless Clearwater is against the idea.'

'Actually, Ma'am…' Adelaide turned to her. 'Your presence could be useful if you don't mind.'

'I shan't know if I mind until you tell me what you are about,' Her Ladyship challenged playfully.

'Please, Inspector, sit.' Archer offered a chair and resumed his own place before his legs buckled.

'I'll stand, Sir,' Adelaide said. 'If it's all the same. I'll not keep you.'

'As you wish. Coffee?'

'No thank you.' Adelaide took a notebook from his pocket and flicked to a page.

'This looks official.' Archer tried to make light, but it came out as a concern.

'In a way, Sir, but I hope not. It concerns a missing person known to be of your acquaintance.'

'Oh?' That could be anyone, but if Adelaide was on the case, it could only be Ripper related. 'Who?'

'A Doctor Benjamin Quill.'

A shattered image of Quill falling beneath him into the death-black waters of the river passed across Archer's mind, and he shuddered inwardly.

'Benji?' he asked, with as much surprise as he could fake. 'Missing?'

'Apparently so, Sir. He hasn't been seen for several days.'

'Men go missing all the time, Inspector,' Lady Marshall said. 'They always reappear in some frightful state, reeking of alcohol and French tarts. Usually in the House of Commons.'

Had they been alone, Archer would have laughed, but with the policeman bearing down on him, he thought it best to let the comment pass, as did Adelaide.

'He was last seen by his wife on Sunday,' he said, referring to his book. 'When she woke on Monday he was no longer at home. Assuming he had left early for his practice, she thought nothing of it. When he had still not appeared by Wednesday morning, she became alarmed and contacted his secretary. It turned out that he hadn't seen him since the previous Friday when he left for home. Assuming he was unwell or called away, he said nothing, but after two days of absence, contacted Mrs Quill. Their messages crossed, but the disappearance was reported to us on Wednesday morning.'

This made no sense to Archer. The inspector must have the days wrong, but to question him would arouse suspicion.

'And how can we help?' he asked, reaching for his cup as calmly as possible. It rattled in the saucer when he lifted it, and he put it down.

'I hear that he is connected with you through some charitable endeavour.' There was a blank in the man's book, because he turned several pages as if he had the answer there somewhere.

'He is on our board of trustees,' Lady Marshall confirmed. She had noticed Archer's shaking hand, but said nothing.

'When did you last see him, Ma'am?'

Her Ladyship's eyes stayed on Archer as she thought. 'For my part, at least two weeks ago,' she said. 'When we met with Marks, the trust's solicitor.'

Adelaide made a note before raising his eyebrows to Archer who immediately felt on trial.

'We had lunch last week,' he said. 'I can show you my diary, but it was Thursday. That's a week last Thursday, not the one just gone.'

Another note in the book and Adelaide asked, 'Where was this?'

'The Grape Vine at Five Dials. I have the receipt somewhere if you need it.'

'Your word is more than acceptable,' the inspector said. 'But you have not seen him since?'

It was against Archer's nature to lie, but there was no other choice. 'No,' he said. 'We are due to lunch again in a fortnight and, unless I have some illness for him to attend, I don't expect to see him until then.'

'I see.'

What did he see?

'Is that it, inspector?' he asked. 'Because I have something to ask you.'

Adelaide stared at his pages before flipping the book shut. 'Yes, Sir?'

'Our charity will be centred in Greychurch,' Archer said, and Adelaide's ears pricked up. 'And I know you are very active in the area at the moment.'

'We are doing what we can, Sir.' The inspector glanced cautiously at Lady Marshall.

'Have you caught the madman yet?' she asked. 'I've not read of any more ripping or arrests.'

'The case is on-going, Ma'am,' he replied. 'But there have been no more murders since the double event, as the papers are calling it.'

'Well, let's hope that's an end to it,' she said.

The double event had been two days before Archer confronted Quill at Limehouse, but that was not what was troubling his mind.

50

'Let us hope so indeed,' he said. 'But, Inspector, perhaps when you are not so busy, I might speak with you about the policing of the area and how we may work together. You see, the men we are hoping to assist are the very same as the Ripper has been attacking.'

It was a bold confession in more ways than one, but if Archer was to stand up for what he knew to be right, he had to be prepared for the knocks that would follow.

Contrary to his expectations, Adelaide didn't look surprised.

'That sounds mightily noble,' he said, a west country accent trickling through. 'Those poor bug... young men need assistance as well as taking in hand. The Commissioner has tasked me with clearing the streets and anything that will help... Well, it will help. Please feel free, Sir,' he added, 'to contact me when I can be of service.'

'Thank you, Inspector.' Archer needed clarification on another point. 'May I just ask you to repeat... When was Benji, sorry, Doctor Quill, last seen? On Sunday night?'

'That's right, Sir. Mrs Quill says he had been away on the Saturday evening and returned in the early hours. Again, not unusual for him. As you probably know, he likes to dine and stay at various clubs. So, Sunday evening he went to bed, Monday he was gone.'

'That's very disturbing,' Archer said.

Quill had plunged into the river on Saturday night. Far from perishing, as Archer had thought, he had survived.

'But that wasn't the last time he was seen,' Adelaide added. 'The last reliable sighting puts him at North Cross railway station on Wednesday night. He spoke with a patient of his, a man of good standing. He caught the night express to Averness and here is where things become even more strange. That sleeper service only stops at one place, a siding on the North York moors where there's only the water and coal depot and nothing for miles.'

'How is that strange?' Lady Marshall asked.

'Because, when the steward went to wake the doctor at Averness, he was nowhere to be found.'

'Oh, I read one of those mysteries,' her Ladyship enthused. 'Probably suicide.'

'Apparently not.' If the inspector was annoyed at her flippancy, he didn't show it. 'His luggage was also missing, suggesting that rather

51

than fling himself from the carriage, he had disembarked in the ordinary manner. However, his wake-up call was an hour before arrival, and the train was searched before it reached Averness. Therefore, he must have alighted on the moors.'

'How very odd.'

'Indeed, Ma'am. And that's our concern.' He addressed Archer. 'We will find your friend, Sir,' he said. 'The local constabulary is making enquiries, and I am sure there is a simple explanation. These things usually work out, and we're not overly worried.'

'I am surprised you are dealing with this,' Archer said. 'It is, I hope, unrelated to your Ripper investigation.'

'Oh yes, Sir. The Commissioner is also a patient and friend of Doctor Quill, hence my involvement.'

'Well, he's put his best man on the job,' Archer flattered. 'I am sorry I can't be of more help, but if I hear anything, I shall dispatch a telegram.'

'Very kind, Sir. To be frank, as there appears to be no foul play, there isn't a great deal we can do.'

'Well, thank you for taking the trouble to tell me personally.' Archer stood, bringing the matter to a close. He was alive with concern and needed to be alone. 'I appreciate you coming rather than sending one of your men.'

'Oh, yes,' Lady Marshall agreed. 'A policeman knocks at a door in this street and society is alive with ridiculous gossip for a whole season.'

Archer rang the bell for Thomas. 'Is there anything else, Inspector?' he asked as he would have done any other caller.

'No, Sir, that's it.'

'Well, keep up your good work, and I will be in touch about the charity if I may.'

Adelaide bowed, and Thomas appeared at the door. He must have been waiting outside. Butlers always did that, Archer knew, always listening, but in this case, he was glad.

'The inspector is leaving, Payne,' he said.

'Your Ladyship. My Lord.' Adelaide made his formal farewells and left.

Back at the settee, Archer waited for the sound of the front door before collapsing in a heap.

'You are as white as a sheet,' his godmother said. 'And have been for some time. You think very fondly of Benji Quill, don't you?'

Nothing could have been further from the truth.

Six

Thomas came to the viscount's study in the late afternoon. Lady Marshall had left, and the house was quiet. The female staff were taking an hour off for tea in the servants' hall, but Archer was behind his desk, visible from the drawing room as Thomas crossed it, checking that everything was in its place. He knocked, and Archer looked up.

'Ah, Tom,' he said, closing a book and pushing aside papers. 'Everything under control?'

'Yes, My Lord. May I?'

'Come in, take a seat, stand, as you wish.'

Thomas stood on the other side of the desk, noting that Archer had been reading the footmen's applications. 'Is now a convenient time?'

'In a moment,' Archer said. 'You heard my conversation with Inspector Adelaide?'

Thomas hesitated.

'It's fine, Tom,' Archer smiled. 'I expect my main man to look out for me.'

'In that case, yes, I did. What should we do?'

'You don't have to do anything. I'm thinking it over.'

'Tell me if I can help.'

'I will. When I have fully considered the situation, we will talk. Now...' Archer gathered the letters. 'I have had a look through these. Only five?'

'More may arrive, but I think, within these five, there is one who stands out. At least...' He hesitated, anticipating a clash. Not between himself and Archer, he couldn't imagine any situation where they might fall out, but a clash between what was customary and what was not.

'At least?' Archer queried, glancing at each letter.

The best way to deal with the viscount was to tell the truth and, much as it sometimes embarrassed Thomas to be so open with him, it was the only way.

'I think one of these men will be suitable,' he said. 'That is, if you don't mind taking a risk.'

'A risk?'

'Perhaps I should sit after all.'

'I wish you would, Tom. Close the doors.'

Thomas did as instructed, and pulled up a chair opposite his master.

'One of these poor chaps can hardly write,' Archer said, dropping one letter to the side. 'This one is in his sixties, which beggars the question why is he still a footman and not a butler, retired or dead?' He scanned another page. 'This one has a neat hand but no experience, the fourth is barely in long trousers...'

'Before you go on,' Thomas interrupted. 'It is the one with no experience that interests me.'

'Oh?' Archer sat back, throwing the last papers down and holding the arms of his chair. 'Why?'

Thomas calmed his nerves. 'I know him,' he said.

Archer's neatly groomed eyebrows rose, and he leant forward to collect the appropriate application.

'This one? James Wright?'

'Yes, Sir.'

Archer read the man's details aloud. 'Twenty-five, lives locally, no experience of service whatsoever and has been in the employ of the post office since he was fourteen.' He looked up at Thomas sharply. 'Is this the man who took you in?'

'Yes, Sir, but that's not the only reason I have an interest.'

'Go on.'

'Mr Wright was very helpful towards me,' he said. 'He allowed me to stay at his parents' house when I returned from Limedock that night, rather, early morning, and his mother was kind enough to house me there for a couple of days. I had a little time to get to know the family and they are good people.'

'Yes, all very well, Tom,' Archer said. 'But he knows nothing of service. I think this chap might be worth speaking to.' He pulled out a different letter and read parts. 'He's working for Lord Ashwort as an under-footman at Herring House...' A surprised expression crossed his face. 'Herring House?'

'My point,' Thomas said. 'He has experience, but can't write. It's Lord Ash*worth* at *Derring* House.'

'Bit fishy, eh?' Archer joked.

'A bit slovenly,' Thomas replied. 'If a man can't compose a letter or have someone do it for him, then...?'

'Very well, Tom,' Archer said. He considered another application. 'And Mr Sykes?'

'To be direct, Sir, I am not sure having a man of fifty years' experience working under me would be comfortable — for him, I mean. Reading between the lines, I smell another Tripp.'

That was a tricky thing to say, because it crossed acceptable boundaries of respect for one's elders. Even if one had no respect for them, the game must be seen to be played.

Archer was not concerned. 'So, out of these first few, you would like to consider a younger man with no experience who has been tramping the streets with messages and who offered you a bed for a night or two.'

'Yes, Sir,' Thomas said. His chest fluttered and his face flushed, but he added, 'His bed.'

'That was very kind,' Archer said, not picking up on Thomas' meaning. 'But it's not really a criterion for...' The penny dropped. 'His?'

Trembling, Thomas nodded.

It was hard to read Archer's face. He was a man who knew how to disguise his feelings behind quizzical looks and noncommittal expressions. He appeared to be thinking, but Thomas sensed he was troubled by something deeper. Archer was an intelligent and thoughtful man who put other people's needs before his own. In this case, Thomas hoped he would understand why he wanted James at the house and accept his recommendation without asking too many questions.

He was to be disappointed.

'Do you have feelings for him?' Archer asked, nearly knocking Thomas from his chair with his directness.

The only way to reply was in the same manner. 'To be honest, Sir, I believe I do, but they would not interfere.'

56

Archer paled.

'How can you be sure?' he asked.

'I would insist on it,' Thomas said. 'The affection I feel for James... For Mr Wright, is... It's hard to explain, Sir, but I want to help the man in the way that you have helped Silas.'

'A messenger is hardly a street-rat renter,' Archer huffed. 'Though I hear some are one and the same.'

Thomas knew what he was alluding to. 'I am aware of the reputation of a few,' he said. Telegraph boys were well known in certain circles as boys willing to earn an extra shilling from an extra service. 'But this man is different.'

'It's still tricky, Payne.' The use of his surname suggested that the viscount was not interested in Thomas' personal attachment, and he was thinking purely of the man's suitability for the job. 'To employ a man with no experience who has possibly another less reputable string to his bow and a history that might arouse suspicion... Can you trust him?'

'I believe so.'

Thomas wanted to trust James as much as he wanted him living upstairs. If the viscount could have happiness, why couldn't Thomas?

Archer put down the letter. 'He writes neatly,' he said. 'He might know who is who in society, I suppose, and he sounds keen.'

'His letter also suggests some knowledge.' Thomas was quick to point out other positives. 'It would appear he has had some schooling from someone who knows the running of a house. He may not have worked up from hall boy, but he has held his job for several years. A reference from the post office would, I am sure, be favourable.'

'I'd hope so. He's old to be a messenger, I thought they stopped at twenty-one.'

'He said it was a stable job and he was expecting a promotion to postman soon.'

Archer glanced at him, still considering, and stood.

'Has anything happened between the two of you?' he asked.

The intimacy of the question caught Thomas unaware, but he shouldn't have been surprised.

'Not exactly,' he admitted.

'Not exactly?' Archer had his back to him, examining a shelf of books.

'Is it relevant?'

'Yes, Tom, it is.' The viscount turned to face him, vexed and possibly even angry. 'You have to consider that this man may have seduced you because he wants a job.'

'I have, and I don't believe that's the case.' Thomas also stood, and, being eye to eye with the viscount was more secure.

'But you have been "not exactly" intimate with him. I assume you want to be "exactly" intimate, but that's not yet happened?'

Thomas remained silent. His heart was pounding, and anger was growing in his chest.

'Consider this,' Archer said, returning to his books. 'I employ him, you chase him, and he turns you down. Or, you get what you want, and he uses that in some blackmail scam.'

'I don't think that's likely, Sir.'

'You're blinded by love, Payne.'

'I don't think that is the case either.'

Archer rounded on him, his face burning and his eyes narrow. They had none of their usual compassion or softness, but were hard, and his lips taut.

'Then what is the bloody case, Tom?' he roared. 'Will you please tell me the truth!'

Thomas was so stunned he ran a check-list in his head, placing the maids and other staff in their current locations. He was relieved to find they were either out or below stairs. The outburst would not have been overheard.

'Well?' Archer was waiting for an answer.

'The truth, Sir?' Thomas squared his shoulders, prepared for any backlash. 'Is that I feel affection for this man in the way that you do for Silas, and if you can have that, then I don't see why I can't.'

'Because you're a bloody butler, Payne, and butlers don't have private lives. They don't marry and they certainly don't appoint strays because of their unnatural tendencies.'

'You do.'

Thomas had reacted instinctively and in the stunned silence that followed, his mind returned to practical matters. He wondered how long it would take him to pack. That was surely what the viscount was going to order him to do next. He should have apologised immediately and offered to resign because of his insolence, but Archer's hypocrisy hurt.

'I am inspired by your example, Archer,' he said, not caring if he should be formal or friendly. 'I always have been. I kept thought and feeling inside for all of my twenty-seven years until you showed me what's really important. I think I've found that, and I, like you, want to help someone with whom I can be myself. I understand what the world out there thinks, and I know what's legal and what isn't. But there's nowhere else in this stinking city that I can feel safe apart from here, and I can't think of nowhere else where a man in your position would understand. If two men can't be safe at Clearwater, then there's no hope for any of us.'

It poured from him like an avalanche, fast and shocking, and it wasn't until he gasped for breath that the full horror of what he had said sank in. Suffering a bout of nausea, he prepared for dismissal.

The viscount, still with his back to him, lifted his hand to a book. He pulled it gently from the shelf and judged the weight of the leather binding and its pages before slapping it into the other palm. He tossed it on the desk where it skidded, scattering papers. He tapped his forehead against the shelves twice and sighed.

'Anywhere,' He said at length. 'I can't think of *anywhere* else. Double negative. Thomas, come here.'

'I think I should...'

'Come here!'

There was no arguing. Thomas came to stand behind the viscount.

Archer turned almost imperceptibly, his head hanging. He lifted it to face Thomas, his eyes ringed with red.

'Why can't a man have it all?' he asked, his voice wavering.

Thomas didn't understand.

'Why, Tom, can a man not have it all?' He lifted his coffee-brown gaze. 'I have. I have the title, the money, the houses, friends and a man I am in love with and, because of understanding friends like you, I have the security to be who I am. But I want more.' He raised his hand and placed it against Thomas' hot cheek. 'Do you remember, when we were eleven and thirteen, at Larkspur, in summer?' A smile began to grow. 'We escaped to the upper woods and fell down the bank, ended up in a heap, you on top of me.' He was losing himself in a memory. 'By the frog pond. You didn't get off me. You, the hall boy, lying directly over the Honourable Archer Riddington and holding him down.' His other hand came to Thomas' face. 'Your manhood was digging into me and you moved it from side to side. Then the gamekeeper came over the hill and the moment was over. You remember?'

Thomas had often relived that time. He nodded.

'That was the nearest we ever came, wasn't it, Tom? I've often wondered how it would be to have such a moment again.' He pulled Thomas an inch closer. 'But without the gamekeeper's interruption.'

Their lips were close enough for Thomas to feel the viscount's breath in his mouth.

'Hell, Tom. This is so difficult.' Archer whispered. His lips parted.

Whatever it was that had aroused the viscount, it had the same effect on Thomas. He closed his eyes, ready for the kiss he had long imagined and wanted.

'But we can't.'

Archer let him go.

'There must be limits,' he said. 'Particularly for us. Fecker and Lucy can flirt and misbehave, but his Lordship with his butler? Sadly, you are the one thing I can never have. It would cause too many complications. However, I want you to be aware of my feelings for you, which are and always have been, extreme friendship to the point of love. I hope you will forgive me.'

'There is nothing to forgive, Archer,' Thomas whispered. 'If I was as good with words as you are, I'd say the same thing. I can't be with you in the way we've always wanted, so, like you, I must direct the physical love I have elsewhere. I'm the one who is sorry.'

'Damnit, Tom!' Archer spun away and crashed into his chair. 'Why wasn't I born below stairs? It's where I feel most at home and the only part of my house I spend no time in. Why can't a man have everything?' He leapt up again. 'Tom, come here.'

Archer hugged him and for one blissful moment, their groins rubbed together as if for old time's sake. They broke apart, but Archer gripped Thomas' arms.

'You were right to say those things,' he said. 'I was jealous. It was the first time I realised that just because I can't be with you, doesn't give me the right to stop you finding someone else. I will have to get used to that. So yes, invite Mister Wrong, or whatever he was called.'

'Wright.'

'Right. Of course. You deserve to be happy too, but for god's sake, be careful.' He released Tom and pointed to a chair.

They sat facing each other across the desk.

'If we were to be found out,' Archer continued. 'Or if some scandal occurred, I am in a better place to deny and cover than you are. I would stand up for you without question, but it would bring you immeasurable pain. If you love this man, hell, even if you're only infatuated, I will take the risk and help you, because I love you. If I can't have you, at least I can see you happy. But, please, again, be careful.'

'I will.'

'I mean, sound him out before you offer him the job. Be prepared for him to spurn you directly after.'

Thomas was shocked. James wasn't the kind of man to do that.

'It happens,' Archer said. 'And you're to say nothing about Silas and me, not until I feel I can trust him. If he is... one of us.'

'Understood.'

'And no canoodling on the back stairs.'

'Certainly not.'

'No fucking in the kitchen.'

'Not even in the scullery, My Lord?' Thomas couldn't help but smile.

Archer was doing the same. 'Not unless I can join in,' he said.

'I hadn't thought of that, Sir.'

'Liar.'

The smiles were now leery grins.

'Any more of this and I shan't be able to answer the bell for an hour.' Thomas looked at his lap.

'You need a footman to assist you,' Archer said. 'In more ways than one.'

He slapped the table and stood, unbothered about the swelling in his breeches, in fact, he seemed proud of it, and rightly so. Thomas couldn't keep his eyes away.

'Right!' Archer said. 'Tom, we are friends again, yes?'

'Always were, Sir,' Thomas said, also standing. If Archer could to display his untouchable manhood so blatantly, so could Thomas and he was well-equipped to match it.

'Good, because I've made up my mind on the Quill disappearance and I need your advice. What time is Silas due back?'

The sudden change in conversation and atmosphere caused Thomas to finally wrench his eyes away from Archer's trousers.

'Around six,' he said and inspected his pocket watch.

'Then we'll wait. While we do, why don't you fire off a letter to Mr Incorrect. You can do it at the writing table.'

'Mr Wright,' Thomas laughed. 'James Wright.'

'Well, write to Wright and give him some right good news,' Archer joked, rearranging the weight in the front of his breeches. 'Tell him I want to see him. As soon as you like.'

Thomas took him up on the offer and sat at the writing desk. It was in his mind to pour out his feelings towards James which he was sure ran deeper than lust, but that was not how things worked. Instead, he constructed a formal letter while imagining how perfect his life was going to be.

Seven

Archer paced the study, a copy of Bradshaw's Railway Guide open in his hands, but his eyes on the wall. He had removed an oil painting and hidden it behind the couch. The painting depicting a fox being torn apart by hounds and had given him nightmares when he was a boy, probably because that was all he had to look at when his father thrashed him, something he did on several occasions. He'd been meaning to be rid of it for weeks, but hadn't found anything to replace it with until now. He'd fixed a large map of the country to the wall using tacks Thomas had found in the stable. When Archer dispatched him there for more just after six o'clock, the butler returned with Silas.

'Shall I ring for tea, Sir?' Thomas asked, having shown Silas into the room.

'Not for me,' Silas said. He kicked off his shoes and made himself at home on the couch where he tucked up his feet.

The sight warmed Archer's heart, because it told him Silas was happy. Archer had never been totally at home in the city house, not until Silas came into it. Admittedly, the last ten days had also brought confusion, drama and more than a fair amount of soul-searching, but they had also brought something previously lacking; joy.

Thomas was hovering in the doorway.

'Come in and close the doors, Tom,' Archer said. He put down the travel guide and kissed Silas before taking a seat in one of the armchairs. 'Dinner's at eight,' he said. 'A glass of something?'

'I'll get it.'

Silas was rising when Thomas told him to sit. He closed the doors and the curtains before pouring them drinks while Archer enquired about Silas' day.

'We looked at five places,' Silas said. 'Some of them no good, one that's possible and the other would be best, but there's more to see.'

'I didn't think there were that many empty places in the East End.'

Archer's mind was elsewhere, and he was only half-listening. He had a more important matter to discuss, but it would be impolite not to talk about Silas' work first.

'Yeah, more than you think,' Silas continued. 'A few abandoned church missions, a factory that's relocated but that's the building that's not right.' He gave Archer a few more details but must have seen the viscount wasn't paying attention, because he said, 'Then Fecker fucked an old trick, and we made us ten shillings.'

Archer looked up sharply from the carpet. 'What?'

'Thought you wasn't there,' Silas said, accepting his drink from Thomas. 'What's up, Archie?'

'I don't know. At least, I am not sure. Tom, have a seat, have a whisky.'

Thomas did as he was told, but declined the drink.

They sat opposite him, Silas curled on the couch, Thomas more upright in an armchair, both attentive and concerned. Silas' smooth cheeks glowed from his recent journey, his hair was windswept and his clothes dusty, but no matter how he looked, or what he wore, he always made Archer's heart miss a beat.

'We'll talk about the charity tomorrow,' Archer said. 'I have some other news which I can only share with you two.' He looked at Thomas, grave-faced. 'The discussion after lunch. Did you hear it clearly?'

'Some,' Thomas admitted.

'I'd have called you in to hear all of it,' Archer said. 'But that would have seemed suspicious.'

'What discussion?' Silas asked.

'I had a visit from Inspector Adelaide.'

'Oh feck.'

'Yes, indeed.'

Archer sipped his drink. The tang of the Scotch burned his lips, but as he rolled the liquid around his mouth, he imagined it cleansing him of the sickening fear that had been with him since Adelaide's visit. 'He wasn't here to discuss the Ripper,' he said. 'Or he didn't realise he was. Quill is still alive.'

He expected Silas to be stunned, but instead, he shrugged and said, 'That's a kick in the money bags.'

'Er... What?'

'What's happened?'

Archer repeated the story, emphasising the days on which Quill had been seen following the fall into the river.

'So, it's definitely him?' Silas had finished his drink and was eyeing the sideboard.

'Yes,' Archer said. He downed the rest of his in one, suddenly feeling the need for more.

Thomas collected the glasses. 'Can you run it by me again?' he asked as he unstopped the decanter.

'We last saw him on Saturday night, Sunday morning,' Archer said. 'His wife, on Sunday night. No-one on Monday or Tuesday, but on the Wednesday, a witness has him at the station. He gets on a train going to the north of Scotland, a train that only makes one stop, and when it reaches its final destination, he doesn't. That's it.'

Silas scratched his head as he thought and ran his fingers through his hair, teasing out knots.

'First thing that comes to my mind,' he said, his gaze on the fireplace. 'Is that he's done a runner.'

'Makes sense,' Thomas agreed. 'He knows you can identify him, but he doesn't know if you have gone to the police. He's fled in case you do.'

'He knows I can't,' Archer said. 'Or that I won't.'

'Then think it through logically.' Thomas handed around the drinks and remained standing. 'Imagine it from his point of view. His entrapment scheme didn't work, or he is now too crazed to see it through, whatever happened up there, you and he fell. You both survived. Maybe he was washed further downstream, who knows? Doesn't matter. He makes it home on Sunday. Now...' He leant on the mantelpiece. 'By the sound of it, there was nothing suspicious about his state of dress. There can't have been, or his wife would have said something, and Adelaide said there was no suggestion of foul play. Correct?'

Archer nodded.

'Which tells me,' Thomas continued to think aloud, 'that he didn't go straight home. He would have been covered with mud and treddles like you were. So…'

'One moment,' Archer interrupted. 'Covered with what?'

'Sorry,' Thomas grinned. 'Covered in… muck. My point being that he must have changed clothes somewhere other than home. Or washed and dried them at least. Either way, he went elsewhere first.'

'And why's that important?' Silas asked.

'It's not really,' Thomas shrugged. 'I'm just going through it in my mind.'

'Go on, Tom,' Archer encouraged. 'You're doing well.'

Thomas blushed. 'His wife sees him on Sunday, they go to bed and…' He circled a long-fingered hand in the air, imagining the scene. 'He can't sleep. At the back of his mind there's this thing… How do you describe it, Archer? A fluttering bird in a cage that bangs the bars and can't get out? It keeps him awake while he worries over it, finally realising what it is. It's the knowledge that he can't lie there doing nothing. You might go to the police at any moment, and even if he thinks you're dead, other witnesses could identify him. Us two. He knows three people know his secret.'

Thomas paced the room, his attention on a fixed point on the wall.

'He gets up, quietly so as not to disturb the missus, and packs his bags. The mention of him having luggage on the train suggests he is travelling rather than running in panic. And that suggests it's premeditated. Like his murders, he has a plan. Prepared, he creeps out of the house and lays low.' He turned to Silas. 'Where is he?' And to Archer. 'Who is he with? Where or what is his shelter?'

'Inspector Adelaide could do with you on his team.' Archer beamed, loving the way Thomas threw himself into the mystery.

'In fact…' Thomas paced to the map. 'He's not missing for two days, but three. The night train from North Cross leaves at eleven, that's nearly a whole third day he was, presumably, in the city. Doing what?'

'You've got loads of questions, mate,' Silas said. 'But not many answers.'

'I know.' Thomas turned, and the enthusiasm dropped from his face. 'But there's a point to me blabbing all this.'

'Which is?'

'What strikes me as strange, gentlemen,' he said, sinking to sit on the arm of the couch. 'Is the witness at the railway station.'

'A patient of his,' Archer said. 'Reputable man apparently.'

'I'm sure of it,' Thomas agreed. 'And of the noblest birth no doubt, with a reputation clad in armour.'

'I sense cynicism.'

'I smell a rat,' Silas said, catching on to Thomas' meaning.

Archer, however, was still to understand. 'What are you saying?' He sat forward.

'Well,' Thomas looked at Silas for permission to be the one to explain, and Silas bowed his head gracefully. They both looked at Archer as if he was stupid.

'What?' he said, laughing nervously.

'How,' Thomas began, 'can anyone, let alone an eminent physician, be so clever as to vanish in this city for three days, make sure he wasn't noticed, and yet allow himself to be seen boarding a train...'

'... that only goes to one destination?' Silas finished.

Archer had still not grasped their point. He shook his head, his mouth open expectantly.

'He *wanted* someone to see him,' Thomas said, kicking himself to his feet and again approaching the map. 'He wanted someone to know that he was heading north.' He pointed to Averness at the top of the country.

'And to know he stopped off somewhere on the way,' Silas added.

'Here.' Thomas pointed to the North Yorkshire Moors, halfway up the map.

'Why did he want to be seen?' Archer asked.

'We need to be in his mind.' Thomas stood beneath the gas lamp, and it threw his face into weird shadows. 'Can't sleep on Sunday, but no-one's come for him yet. The city isn't the place to hide, but he needs to make arrangements. He's watching the newspapers, but sees no mention of himself, other than the Ripper murders. Whether the police are after him, or you are, he needs to get away and plan what to do. But, to hide all that time and then get off in the middle of nowhere? Reeks of a plan.'

'Then,' Silas said, 'there's the witness. He wanted to be seen. He might even have paid the man...'

'... Or he could be an accomplice...'

'Either way, he was there for a reason, Archie.'

'And that is?'

'So word would get back to you that he's alive, you fecking eejit.' Silas laughed.

'Quite.' Thomas was more reserved.

'And he wants me to know... Stop laughing, Silas,' Archer added with a grin. 'He wants me to know he's still alive... Why?'

Silas came to him and kissed him hard on the lips.

'You're gorgeous,' he said, before returning to the couch and lying down.

'I can only think it's a message,' Thomas said, moving away from Silas' feet. 'I mean, it is, clearly, a message.'

'Or an error on his part.'

'That is possible, Archer, yes,' Thomas conceded, studying the map. 'And as to why... Does he want you to live in fear? Will this be a repeat of the torture your brother inflicted on you? You said yourself that he was present at the time and saw what it did to you, so is he playing with you?' He ran off the list as if he had studied for years under Sherlock Holmes, and Archer was impressed. 'Or is it because he wants you to chase him?' Thomas continued. 'Is he in some mental state of mind where he believes the only thing that will stop him killing is for him to be killed? If so, who better than his friend since school? His lunch partner, his equal in cunning and intellect? The perfect adversary.'

'For heaven's sake, Tom, now you're sounding like The Penny Illustrated,' Archer laughed. 'So, he wants me to find him and kill him. After what he's done, I'd do it happily, and Inspector Adelaide will give me a medal.' He stood, and the blood rushed to his head. When the room stopped swaying, he approached the map. 'But do I just wait?' He followed the route of the train from the city to the northern moors. 'If Adelaide is right,' he said, his voice quietening. 'Then he got off somewhere around here in the early morning. He could have gone anywhere. What does he expect me to do?'

'You could just wait and see,' Thomas suggested. 'It's highly unlikely he would come after you, so I am sure you would be safe.'

'I'm not worried about that.'

'Or,' Silas said. 'You could investigate.'

'Investigate what?'

'Where he might have been for those missing days,' Thomas suggested. 'Who was the witness?'

'What's on the moors?' Silas put in. 'If you start looking at it, you might find answers that put you one step ahead of whatever game he's playing.'

It was a fair point. What did Archer have to lose?

'And where do we start investigating?' he asked, returning to his chair. 'Tom? You're the logical man. Where would you start?'

'Personally, I'd begin with the idea that he has an accomplice,' Thomas said. 'If there are any records of his communications earlier this week, they would give us an idea of who. And if that "who" is the witness, or happens to be in the North York area, then...' He waved his hand in the air. 'Then you have some clues, and you do whatever you must do.'

Archer had known Thomas for so long he could read him like a gentlemen's periodical.

'And how do we access a man's private communications?' he smirked. 'Tens of thousands of telegrams fly around this city every day.'

'Through the telegraph office and their records,' Silas suggested, the last to understand where the conversation was going. 'Mind you, you'd have to know someone on the inside. I can break in, but we'd need to know what we were looking for.'

'Do we know anyone who works for the post office, Thomas?' Archer raised his brows knowingly.

Thomas grinned. 'I could deliver my letter by hand to the Crown and Anchor this evening,' he said and bowed. 'With your permission, My Lord.'

'Good idea, Payne,' Archer smiled. 'We might even join you for a drink.'

Eight

Thomas decided it would be better for him to see James on his own, and Archer agreed. It would be too unorthodox for a viscount to call at a high street pub, find a messenger and invite him to discuss employment as a footman, not to mention the delicate matter of asking him to do something illegal without telling him why. Thomas was unsure if he could achieve what was needed, but any excuse to find James and be alone with him was welcome. He had little free time in his new position, but the viscount let him go after dinner when he and Silas were entertaining themselves in Archer's private sitting room.

The walk through the leafy borough of Riverside was not unpleasant. The October nights were growing colder, but a constant stiff breeze from the south drove the nightly fog higher where it hung over the city like a veil. Beneath it, daily life continued as the well-to-do returned from their clubs and restaurants, and coach wheels and horses' hooves clattered through the hushed streets. Messengers busied themselves with their deliveries, running up steps to wide front doors, touching their peaked caps and distributing dispatches. Newspaper sellers headed home, the evening editions all sold, and Thomas walked among them proudly wearing the two-tiered winter cloak Lady Marshall had recommended.

He had changed from his butler's livery into a dark suit, and with his Yeoman's bowled hat, in the latest 'fall' style crowning his auburn locks, he held his head high. To anyone passing, he was a middle-class gent on his way to an evening of cards, or perhaps a late supper with a mistress.

For Thomas, his clothing and the responsibility Archer had given him represented a new start. As Archer had been elevated unexpectedly from second son to viscount, so Thomas had been elevated to the most important member of his household, and, after their sudden but intense discussion earlier, almost to the level of Archer's equal.

Riverside High Street was alive with pedestrians and carriages even at ten at night. The lights of the Crown and Anchor burned brightly through leaded windows, its sign creaking gently in the breeze. No-one loitered outside, no hurdy-gurdy played, and there were no prostitutes eyeing him up and calling obscenities. It was a far cry from a few days ago when he had visited the East End, and he marvelled at how far his life had come in such a short time.

Full of confidence, he entered the pub to be greeted by a clammy atmosphere and the smell of wood smoke hanging over the aroma of hops and sawdust. The public bar was packed. He politely pushed his way through, expecting rough tongues and insults, but nobody paid him attention. He was similarly dressed to the other men who stood or sat in small groups debating the latest news, business and their wives. He was almost as middle-class as they were.

He found James at his usual corner table, except now he wasn't alone. He sat with two other young men, deep in conversation over their pints of beer. James didn't even notice him as he approached, and Thomas' confidence ebbed. He feared James had changed his mind, but whatever happened between them, he vowed not to forget that his loyalty lay with the viscount. He coughed to draw attention.

When James noticed him, his face exploded into a smile, and Thomas' fears vanished. The messenger was sincerely happy to see him, and surely that was because of their mutual attraction.

'Tommy!' he exclaimed, putting down his glass. He offered his hand. 'What you doing here?'

'Good evening,' Thomas said, removing his hat before accepting the handshake. 'Sorry to disturb you, gentlemen, but may I have a word with Mr Wright?'

'Course you can, Tommy.' James stood and wiped his mouth on the back of his hand. 'Be back shortly, lads.'

Knowing the pub better than Thomas, James led him through to the saloon bar where there were fewer people, and they could talk privately. The room was less stuffy, and Thomas was able to hang his cloak and hat on a stand knowing they would be safe.

'So, Tommy,' James said as he slid into a seat. 'What's up?'

'Good to see you, James,' Thomas said, making sure he faced the room. He wanted to be sure no-one passed by and heard their conversation.

'You too, mate,' James said. 'Want a drink?'

'If you're having one. There are a couple of things I want to talk to you about.'

'All ears, Tom.'

James was intrigued. He leant on the table, his fingers laced, and his brow furrowed.

'I have two delicate matters of business to discuss,' Thomas said. He had another, but the third was personal and would have to wait. He had planned the conversation during his walk, and he hoped that he could stick to the script.

'Did you get my letter?' James leapt in.

'I did. Very unexpected.'

'Hope you don't mind me not warning you. I didn't want you to think I was using our friendship in my favour.'

Friendship. That was a good start.

'Not at all, though it does raise some questions,' Thomas said. 'Your applying and our…' He wanted to say relationship, but that was too intimate a word. 'Our new friendship.'

'Ask away. Anything you want.'

Thomas pulled down the cuffs of his jacket and rested his forearms on the table. 'Thank you,' he said. 'I am here on official, semi-official, and personal business.'

'Sounds like a lot. Better get that drink in.'

James waved at the barmaid who came out from behind the tankards and bottle-cluttered bar bringing a friendly smile.

'Yes, gents?'

'Two beers.' James sifted the change he drew from his pocket and put down the right amount of money. It left him with very little.

'Let me.' Thomas paid.

'Very kind of you, Tom,' James said. 'It this your way of easing the blow?'

'No.' Thomas shook his head. 'But your generosity might be seen as a bribe.'

'I get you.'

'Right.' Thomas was aware that it was exactly how Archer changed a conversation. 'First of all, I am here on His Lordship's business. He wants to see you about your application.'

'Oh?' James seemed genuinely delighted.

'I can't promise it will lead to a job. He, like me, is concerned at your lack of experience.'

'I'm a fast learner.'

'I don't doubt it. The viscount can, of course, appoint who he wants, but I asked him specifically to consider you over others who are already in service. You, I think, have had none.'

'That's right. Been a telegraph boy since I was fourteen. I like the job but it's going nowhere, you get me?'

'I can imagine. So, that's the first thing. He is willing to interview you with me, and together we will decide if you are suitable. Now, it sounded from your letter that you have been asking about the job and what it entails?'

'Right again.' James folded his arms and sat back. 'I know a man who worked in service all the way up from hall boy to footman to butler. He's given me some background.'

'That shows initiative,' Thomas complimented. 'But Clearwater House runs on slightly different lines to the average city house, and, if you are successful, you will also have to work at Larkspur, the viscount's country home.'

'Sixteen bedrooms, first, second and two ordinary footmen, seven upper housemaids, seven all-work maids, lady's maid, viscount's valet and the stables,' James said. 'I've done my asking.'

'Very commendable,' Thomas grinned. James obviously wanted the job. 'The position at Clearwater is for second footman, and it brings a salary of twenty-five-pounds per year.'

James' eyes widened.

'Plus tips that guests or the viscount may award, accommodation, meals and uniform. And,' he added with a grin, 'there's not as much of the drilling and army-style training your lot give you at the CPO. Quite the opposite in fact.'

'That's eased off,' James said. 'They have matrons looking after the boys now, to keep them safe from the older ones, but it's still fairly strict regards uniform and turnout. Anyway, I thought the viscount was a military man.'

Thomas was impressed that he had done his research. 'Navy, but he left that two years ago. My point, James, is that you would be well-rewarded, but only if you worked hard.'

'Same as any job.'

'Not at all.'

'How so?'

Thomas did his best to explain how Archer worked without giving too much away. 'His Lordship is unconventional,' he began. 'If he likes you, he helps you, but his generosity is not to be misconstrued or taken advantage of. He can dismiss you as easily as he drops a collar stud, but, by the same token, he can elevate you just as quickly. Look at me.'

'I am, Tom,' James replied. 'And I like what I see.'

Thomas' cheeks flushed with hope more than embarrassment, but he kept his thoughts in order.

'But,' he said, holding up a finger. 'The thing you have to...'

The barmaid reappeared with their beer and put down two foaming glasses before flouncing away.

'What you have to remember,' Thomas continued, 'is that I would be responsible for you and anything you may do wrong.'

'So, you'd be taking a big risk. I get it, Tom. Or should I call you Mr Payne?'

'Tom is fine for now. But if you come to be interviewed and certainly if you are given the job, then Mr Payne.'

'Understood.' James reached out and put his hand over Thomas'. He squeezed it once and let it go. 'I'm very keen, Tom,' he said.

It was a comment that could be taken in various ways, but Thomas told himself James was only talking about the position and all that would come with it.

'You're not there yet,' he said, withdrawing his hand and taking a more professional approach. 'The second thing is a completely different matter with which His Lordship might want your assistance.'

'Oh?' James' round face twitched with interest.

'It's to do with where you currently are.' This wasn't going to be easy. Tact was the way forward, but Thomas thought it wise to impose a boundary. 'Let's see this as a test of discretion,' he said. 'A vital requirement for any servant.' He waited for James to nod agreement before continuing. 'If, for example, I asked you to undertake a matter out of your general sphere of postal duties, how would you react?'

James thought as he took a sip of beer. 'Depends,' he said. 'If I was asked to do something dodgy, then I might not be so happy. What did you have in mind?'

'I am speaking hypothetically. You know, as in…'

'I know what that means, mate.' James winked. 'I can read. Have to, as a telegraph boy.'

'Of course. But say, in your position as a messenger, you were asked to trace messages. Can you do that?'

'How d'you mean?'

'Look back through records of a certain time and find copies, assuming they are kept. Is that possible?'

James sat back, cradling his beer and eyeing Thomas suspiciously. 'This got anything to do with what goes on over at Cleaver Street?' he asked.

'Cleaver Street? No.' Thomas didn't understand.

'Not to worry then,' James said. 'There's a bit of a scam going on over there, and some of the messengers are involved. Not to worry. Answering your question, yes, it's possible. I know where the records are kept for this borough and those nearby. It depends where you wanted to look, and why. It's not exactly legal.'

'Ah,' Thomas said. 'If you were asked to do such a thing by your potential employer, would you?'

James glanced over his shoulder and leant in. 'Tom,' he whispered. 'If I got the chance to work in a grand house like Clearwater, live under the same roof as my new mate, and earn a decent wage, I'd do whatever my butler or master asked, no questions.'

Again, an answer which could hold two meanings, but it was precisely the kind of response that Archer would want.

'You would be allowed to ask questions,' Thomas explained. 'In fact, His Lordship values staff who question him. With the appropriate respect of course. But only if their questioning is pertinent. You never ask the viscount why, but if you have doubts, you voice them.'

'Fair enough.' James took another swallow of beer. 'All sounds very matey, but where's this leading?'

It was Thomas' turn to take a pause, drink some beer and gather his thoughts. He replaced his glass, and said, 'His Lordship has a favour to ask, but it has nothing to do with the possibility of an interview.'

'And what's the favour?'

It was too early for details.

'I can't go into that yet,' he said. 'But I need to know, on principle, if you were willing. It's hard to explain and here is not the right place.'

'So, you want me to take something on trust.' James clarified. 'You want me to say I'd do just about anything as long as I got the job?'

'No, that's not it.' Thomas thought he had been clear. 'What I am trying to find out is if we can trust you. Without knowing you for a long time and without seeing your work, the only thing we have to go on is a reference from the post office. That's fine for the formal part of this business, but the rest is… Let's just say that things can sometimes be very informal at Clearwater. Unorthodox, to say the least.'

'I'm more intrigued by the minute,' James grinned. 'But, how can I prove you can trust me?'

He moved his leg beneath the table, and their feet touched. It could have been unintentional, but when James brushed Thomas' ankle, he knew it was a message. They held each other's stare. Thomas maintained a passive expression, but his mind was alive with possibilities. James beamed enthusiastically and, with a hint of impishness reminiscent of Silas, rubbed Thomas' leg.

'What's that for?' Thomas asked, his throat suddenly constricted and his heart beating faster.

'Think you know, Tom,' James replied. 'I reckon you and I already trust each other and for the same reason. Right?'

Thomas checked the bar; no-one was listening.

'Didn't exactly go very far,' he whispered. 'More like we were just keeping warm.'

'Believe it or not,' James said, 'that was new to me. Very new, but very right. You understanding me?' He rubbed Thomas' leg. 'I'm doing it because I want to.'

Thomas nodded. 'Because of me?'

'I wouldn't be doing it to no-one else I know. Never have.'

'Then we both feel the same way.'

Nothing had been explicitly said, but this was the crux of Thomas' third matter.

'I know how you feel,' James said. 'I felt it the other night.' He took another drink, but his stare remained with Thomas who was again blushing. 'You look even sweeter when you do that.'

Thomas moved one of his feet to reciprocate what James was doing, and the smile on the messenger's lips grew to encompass his whole face.

A moment passed during which Thomas was convinced that James was sincere. Not only that, but he would fit right in at Clearwater. He was just the kind of man Archer liked to have around. Not the most handsome in the world, and therefore no distraction, but apparently keen, loyal and not adverse to unconventionality. Having satisfied himself that he had found the right man for Archer's business, a potential footman and as willing to engage with him as he wanted to engage with James, Thomas left his beer and moved his foot.

'Then I think we understand each other,' he said. 'And I have found the man I want. However...' He raised his finger before James could jump in with some scandalous double-meaning. 'This doesn't guarantee you the position. That will be decided by His Lordship, and anything else that he might ask of you will have nothing to do with it.'

'And what about anything you ask me to do?'

The question was loaded with a salaciousness that thrilled Thomas. 'I will only order you to carry out your duties,' he said, trying to keep the excitement from his voice. 'Anything else asked of you will be personal and would only happen in private time. You do understand?'

James nodded.

'And would never be discussed.' Thomas added for emphasis.

'My lips will be sealed, Tom,' James said. 'Except for when I need them open.'

There were times when Thomas wished he could control himself, and this was one of them. His cock was growing at the suggestiveness, and he imagined how it would behave should he find himself sharing the top floor with this man. They would spend most of their personal time there together with a locked door between them and the female staff, and no-one prying.

'Good,' he said and cracked his knuckles as if to draw a line beneath that more interesting side of the discussion. 'So, I have written to you formally...' He produced the letter. 'It invites you to interview. Uncertain of your working hours at present, I have asked you to suggest a time over the next few days.'

'Anytime, Tom,' James said, opening the envelope. 'I can pretend to be sick and bunk off.'

'Excuse me?' He had only been in the role a few days, but the butler took over. 'Bunk off?'

James looked up from where he had been reading and the joy on his face morphed immediately into horror.

'I won't ever do that with you, Mr Payne,' he said. 'I meant it as an expression. My boss will let me have an hour or two for an interview, Mr Hicks is a decent chap.'

'If,' Thomas said, 'you find yourself indisposed for a legitimate reason, then you tell me immediately. If you need time away for something personal, you do the same. If you are genuinely ill, the viscount will probably pay for the best treatment, but only if you are devoted to him. Try anything else, and you'll be out on your backside.' He hated himself for sounding like Tripp but understood how effective it was to be grand and supercilious. James blanched.

'I'm really sorry, mate... Mr Payne,' he said, flustered. 'I am faithful when I find the right man... You know, employer. You can ask at the post office. I've been promoted twice in eleven years.'

'Yes, very well, James.' Thomas believed him, and not just because he found the man compelling and craved his friendship.

'I'll have to be called James, will I?'

'Not necessarily. His Lordship used to call me Thomas and Tom, Tommy occasionally, and when we were young, a few other things which have no bearing on this discussion. He may choose to call you Jim, Jimmy, James or "You blithering idiot" depending on his mood. The thing you have to remember is that if you get the job and if you take it, your life will be completely different. In fact, your life, like mine, will belong to Viscount Clearwater for as long as we are lucky enough to be in his employ. Are you prepared for that?'

78

'Hell yes,' James said. 'If I get this job, I'll do anything for him, and you. I'd be so grateful.'

Thomas did wonder why, but only for a second. The meeting had gone better than he had hoped, but it was getting late and he had to report back.

'Can you come tomorrow?' he asked before finishing his beer.

'I can come whenever you want, Sir,' James said. 'Do I call you Sir?'

'Not usually. I can teach you all that and the other etiquette if you are successful. I need to go now,' Thomas said, rising. 'Come to Clearwater House at eleven tomorrow morning. Is that possible?'

James nodded enthusiastically, his broad smile had still not faded, and it was contagious. 'As you wish, Mr Payne.' He said, standing. He thought quickly and fetched Thomas' hat and coat, offering them haphazardly with one hand.

'And I will show you how to present a gentleman with his belongings,' Thomas said, with comedic outrage. 'And it's not like that! You should only be an hour at the house, but if his Lordship requires you for longer, you will, I trust, be able to stay.'

'You trust right, Mr Payne,' James said. 'Like I said, I'm happy to do whatever he or you wants of me.'

Thomas left the Crown and Anchor satisfied that he had achieved what he set out to do. James had given all the right answers, and Archer would be pleased. Thomas, of course, would be even happier if James moved into his life on a more permanent basis. He popped his hat onto his head and let his cloak flap open as he strode homewards, certain that Archer's troubles would soon be at an end.

He might not have been so confident had he seen James return to the public bar where, ignoring his colleagues, he passed through to the yard.

Outside, he peeked around the gates and found Tripp waiting in the shadows just beyond the spill of lamplight. He was there most nights, waiting in case James discovered anything about Clearwater and his private life.

'Well?' he said, impatient and gruff. 'Have you still not learnt anything yet?'

'Hold on, mate,' James replied, turning up his collar. 'This was only the first time I've seen anyone, but I learned plenty, Mr Tripp. I've got things set up now and so well, my price just increased.'

Nine

The following morning, James turned into Bucks Avenue, a long thoroughfare lined by trees as tall as the mansions and took a moment to remind himself of the importance of what he was about to do. His mother's fingers had become so bad she was unable to work, his father's payments came irregularly, and his sister's extra lessons had to be paid for. His post office job, although a good one, didn't bring in enough income, and now he was twenty-five, he was expected to provide in his father's absence. A position in service would not only provide sufficient income, but it would also mean less expense. His wage wouldn't have to cover his food or uniforms, leaving him more to give to the family. It would still mean a lifetime of hard work. At least, it would have done were it not for Mr Tripp's offer of fast cash for firm information. Information he would be able to gather easily if he could get himself appointed to the position he was about to be interviewed for.

The problem was Thomas.

Was he a man James wanted to be closer with? Definitely. Was he the man who could get him into the house so that James could earn Tripp's money? For sure. Was it right for him to mix the two ambitions? No, but for the next two hours, he had to concentrate on securing his place in the house. That would knock down three skittles with the same ball; stability, Tripp's payment, and Thomas.

First, though, he needed to impress the viscount. Without Tripp's advice and inside knowledge, he wouldn't have stood a chance, but the old butler had told him what to expect, what to say and what to ask. He had explained what Lord Clearwater liked in a servant and thus, forearmed, James had no cause for nervousness.

He crossed the road confidently and took the side alley to the mews, arriving at the tradesman's entrance with a calm air and a friendly expression. After ringing the bell, he turned to admire the yard. A coach house stood to the side where two horses watched him with disinterest. They were not the only animals stabled there, however. As he admired them, a man appeared from an outhouse carrying a saddle. He was tall and solidly built, and his long hair was tied back in a tail to match those of the horses he cared for. He wore an open waistcoat over a dark shirt, and riding breeches far too tight for any man let alone one so well endowed. James' eyes were drawn directly to the groom's groin, a habit he was unable to control, and he gulped at the sight, wondering if this was the viscount.

'No staring at cock,' the man said in a heavily accented complaint.

James tore his eyes away and to the man's face. He appeared more confused than angry, but nodded his head politely enough before taking the saddle into the stable.

The back door opened, and James turned to find a maid.

'Yes?' She said, taking in all of him with a quick up and down.

'James Wright to see Mr Payne,' he said, removing his hat.

'Mr Payne's expecting you.' The maid stood aside to let him in.

He followed her through to a kitchen and then a large room beyond. Tripp had told him this was the servants' hall and the butler's pantry where he would be interviewed was along the passage. He sailed past other staff at work in the kitchen, aware of their looks, but ignoring them, and followed the girl into the gloomier recesses below stairs, finally arriving at an oak door set into a dull, plastered wall.

The maid knocked twice and waited to be called before showing James into the room.

Thomas sat behind a small desk, a ledger open beneath a lamp. A basement window allowed very little light, but the lamps caused silver and glass to glint inside their cabinets. A fire burned in a small grate and the room smelt of woodsmoke and polish.

'Mr Wright to see you, Mr Payne,' the maid announced.

Thomas thanked her and stood, putting on his tailcoat which had been hanging on a hook beside him.

'Mr Wright,' he said, setting the formal tone. 'Sit, please.'

James did as he was asked, his confidence waning at the thought that the handsome man was no longer his acquaintance, but his potential superior. Thomas was a different person; no smile, no nod, no sense of friendship or attraction. He adjusted his lapels, flicked his tails and sat. The lamp bathed his face in a warm shade of orange, and as the light flickered, it washed waves through his copper hair.

Adrenaline pumped, fuelled by physical attraction and anxiety.

'His Lordship will see you presently,' Thomas said, completing an entry in his ledger. 'But first, I have a few things to explain and ask.'

Thomas finally looked up, the professional butler, not a friend. James sat straight and did what his mother had always told him to do; he kept his big ears open and his bigger mouth shut. He listened intently as Thomas told him every aspect of the job, most of which he had already learnt from Mr Tripp. He asked about James' experience, read the reference he had brought, and asked him to explain why he wanted to come into service.

Again, Tripp had given James fair warning, told him what to say, and prepared him well.

The fact that Thomas knew most of James' story already didn't affect the butler. He remained upright and attentive, interested and slightly sceptical all the way through James' replies.

'Thank you,' he said, when he had heard enough. 'Do you have anything to ask me before we go up?'

James was startled to learn he would be taken upstairs. 'I'm not really dressed to meet nobility,' he said.

'And usually, you wouldn't, not yet. But His Lordship is his own man, and how can we expect you to dress like a gentleman unless we employ you as one?'

James appreciated the reassuring words.

'Can I make sure I'm right?' he asked, before Thomas could open the door. 'I greet him as His Lordship first and then call him Sir?'

'Correct, Mr Wright. You wait at the door until called over. You do not offer your hand, but if he offers his, you take it. One quick squeeze is how a gentleman does it these days. You may nod your head if you have any military background.'

James didn't. 'Is that it?'

Thomas opened the door. 'That's not even the start of it,' he said. 'But His Lordship understands your inexperience.'

They climbed the stairs to the next floor where he was made to wait at a green door as the butler entered the main house. He was away for less than a minute, but it gave James time to glance up the stairs, back down and around, trying to find his bearings and taking in the layout. Everything had been brown and white, plain and faded so far, and he wondered what he would see on the other side of the door.

Whatever he was expecting, it wasn't what he found. Thomas returned and told him to follow. The door swung open, and James had to squint against the light.

The cold autumn sun glared through the multi-coloured glass surrounding the front door. Above, a crystal chandelier as round as his front parlour was long caught the rays and held them in rainbow colours, while beneath, a highly polished table reflected its splendour. There was little time to take in the paintings and the rugs, the figures on pillars and the mirrors before he was following Thomas through a room, the likes of which he'd never seen. Sofas, plush chairs, fancy tables painted gold and blue, more paintings and a fireplace the width of a workman's cottage. That was without fully appreciating the glass doorknobs, the panelling, the bookshelves, decanters, flower arrangements and trinkets.

His apprehension increased when Thomas stopped at another pair of doors. He turned to James and inspected him, flicking dust from his collar and straightening his lapels.

'Remember to be yourself,' Thomas said. 'Don't be intimidated and expect the unexpected.'

James nodded, his palms sweaty. He gave them one last wipe on his jacket while Thomas opened the doors, stepped in and announced him.

The messenger entered a new world; there were no other words for what he saw.

The room was designed for work.

Every wall was a bookcase. A leather-topped desk and two tables were strewn with books and maps, portfolios, pens, inkwells and reading lamps. A globe stood tilted on its own stand. Crossed swords and a collection of firearms adorned the walls above the bookcases along with a collection of framed knots and a barometer in the shape of a ship's wheel. Everything was dark and lush, the colour of oak, or deep red and vibrant green.

'It's a bit much, isn't it?' A man's voice, deep and lilting, rang through the room, and at first, James couldn't see where it had come from until a smiling, smooth face appeared around the corner of a wing-backed chair. 'Come and sit down, Mr Wright.'

It was not until Thomas had shown him to the chair opposite that he took his first proper look at the viscount. He had a long face, with a cleft chin and a high forehead. Between, a dimple in his lips creased in perfect symmetry with his regal nose and ears that protruded behind black sideburns. James had been told Viscount Clearwater was nearly thirty, but he didn't look a day over twenty-one.

'I'd sit if I were you,' the viscount said. 'It could be the last chance you get.'

James had been paying too much attention to the man's face and corrected himself.

'Thank you, My... Your Lordship.'

His legs were suddenly weak. Not because of the man's looks, he was handsome, but nothing compared to Thomas, now pulling up a third chair. It was because the viscount appeared so open, so interested and eager to entertain. James felt as if he had known him for years and it was not what he expected.

'Did Payne offer you a lemonade?' the viscount asked.

'No, Sir,' James said, perched on the edge of his seat.

'Good, then we'll have a Scotch. Just a small one, Payne.'

Thomas glided to a sideboard where glasses tapped and chinked as he poured a measure for the viscount and what could only be described as a spit for James.

'Right!' the viscount said, when he had been served, and James thought he was calling his name. 'Mr Wright, is it James or Jimmy?'

'Whatever pleases Your Lordship,' James said. 'My friends call me both, but maybe James is more formal.'

'Quite right,' the viscount agreed. 'So, James, I know you've not worked in service, but Thomas tells me you are a man of character.'

'That's very kind of him, Sir.' Tripp had told him to be polite, but not obsequious. He had looked up the word first thing that morning and was determined not to be it.

'And what is your character?'

'Sir?'

'You, James, who are you? What's your background?'

'I'm afraid you would find it dull, Sir.'

'I hope not,' the viscount said, taken aback. 'No-one's youth should be dull. You're twenty-five, I understand. What has happened in those years?'

James was off to a good start when he told of his birth coinciding with the arrival of the first underground train. His Lordship found that amusing, and he encouraged James to tell more stories of his childhood. The family was not poor, but they were not rich. His grandfather had been a merchant seaman as was his father, his grandmother and mother had made straw hats, but now his mother's fingers were bad, she was unable to work, and James was the breadwinner.

He had been raised by a religious mother, he said, and she read from the Bible every Sunday. Unlike other people he knew, she was not banging the book on his head and cramming righteous words down his throat. His mother's approach to the Good Book had been to highlight the passages about love and kindness, charity and chastity, with perhaps more emphasis on the parts about chastity than should be demanded of a teenage boy. Her readings hadn't enamoured him towards a particularly Christian way of life, he never attended church, but they had left him with an ingrained sense of what was right.

His Lordship seemed impressed with that.

James mentioned his sister in passing — she was several years younger than him and more trouble than she was worth — and he said how much he enjoyed working for the post office.

By the time he had brought the viscount up to date and stated his reasons for applying for the job, he was sure he had bored the man to tears.

'My God,' the viscount said. 'You sound like a decent fellow.'

James was embarrassed. 'Just doing what needs doing for the family,' he said. His mother had also instilled humility, and although he didn't always show it, it was a good act to have ready.

'Admirable, bravo,' His Lordship mumbled as he read James' reference. He put it down, still grinning about something, and looked at Thomas. 'Do you have any qualms, Payne?' he asked.

'Only those we have discussed,' Thomas answered, making James wonder what had been said.

The viscount nodded in thought before returning his gaze to James. 'May I ask you an impertinent question?'

'You can ask me what you want,' James replied without thinking. 'I mean, of course, Sir.'

His Lordship huffed a laugh, apparently amused at James' error, but his expression changed in an instant.

'Have you ever been in trouble with the law?' he asked. 'And the truth cannot harm you here.'

James wasn't sure what that meant, but he answered honestly. 'No, Sir. I can say with my hand on the Bible that I have not.'

'The Bible, eh?' The viscount glanced at Thomas.

'Like I said, I was brought up on it, Sir,' James said. 'But not within it.'

That was a line directly from Tripp's advice, and it had the desired effect. Lord Clearwater also had little time for religion.

'On it but not within it. The same as the law?'

James was stumped. 'I was brought up... Sorry, Sir, I don't understand.'

'My fault,' His Lordship said. 'What I was trying, unsuccessfully, to allude to was a very specific question. The Bible tells us to do all manner of things both good and bad. Love thy neighbour, but stone him if he has a different belief. How does one square that circle? We can't, and so people live outside of some of the book's teaching, but within the parts that suit them. I respect people's right to find faith in the pages of a book but have no need of it myself, and I have no time for hypocrisy. The law, however different in concept, is the same thing. We must live with laws, but, as with the Bible, some men prefer to pick and choose which commands they obey. The questions is, are you prepared to act outside the law?'

Thomas had warned him that the man could be unconventional, and James was not concerned by his question. He knew the viscount had a favour to ask.

'It would depend.'

'But you're not averse to the idea?'

Everyone had to earn a living, and most would do anything to feed their family, but in this case, James knew the right answer.

'Whether you employ me or not, Sir,' he said. 'I'm happy to check out some old postal records if it puts me in Your Lordship's favour.'

He raised his glass, a little cheeky perhaps, but the viscount raised his own.

'However,' His Lordship said. 'If I were to ask such a thing of a stranger, how would I be assured of his discretion?'

'May I speak honestly, Sir?' James knew what he wanted to say, but couldn't put the words into a polite order.

'Mr Wright.' The viscount was grave. 'If I employ you, you won't be permitted to speak in any other manner. Go on.'

'Thank you, Sir. Well, the only way to be certain of my discretion is to employ me. It's simple. I'll do this other job for you, because I want to help Thomas, and he wants to help you. Yeah, you're taking a risk as you don't know me, but then so am I. Let's face it, if I get caught, no-one's going to believe you paid me to do it. I'm the one that's got most to risk, see? But, I trust you, you've got that thing in your look that tells me I can, and, being frank, I need money for my sister's schooling. 'Course, if you hire me permanent and all, that's even better.' He ran out of words. 'Sorry.'

'Not at all, James.'

Lord Clearwater lifted his eyes to Thomas, and James did the same. Thomas was the one to make the decision, it seemed, and he studied James while he decided.

'I think,' he said, rising. 'Mr Wright would be a positive addition to the staff, Sir. He has that "thing" in his look.'

'I agree, Payne.' The viscount winked at Thomas before addressing James. 'You will have much to learn, and if, after a reasonable period, we discover that the position is not for you, I will have to find someone else.'

'That's fair enough, Sir.'

'Then that's settled.' The viscount clapped his hands once. 'How long until you can start?'

James was so flushed with excitement he didn't know how to answer. 'I will have to tell them at the post office,' he stammered. 'But... tomorrow?'

'Will that give Mrs Baker enough time to arrange the new livery, Payne?'

'Yes, Sir.'

That quick? James had been joking. He was supposed to give notice, after eleven years it was only fair. He would have to invent a story, or just walk out. They wouldn't pay him, but last night he had screwed another five pounds out of Tripp as an advance. It would pay for his sister's teaching until his first wage from Lord Clearwater, and the sooner he was in the house, the sooner he would be closer to Thomas. Nothing else mattered.

'I shall write to your employer, Mr Wright,' the viscount said. 'I will explain my predicament and offer to recompense him for any inconvenience. Collect the letter before you leave. I will put it in the hall, Payne. That should clear up that matter.'

'If you can stay a while, James,' Thomas said. 'I will show you the servants' quarters and tell you what to bring.'

James nodded, still in shock. He was to have his own room. Hell, his own bed.

'But before that...'

His Lordship's voice brought him back to his senses. From now on, he was more or less owned by this man. It was a sobering thought.

'Before you go, James, will you permit me to explain this other matter. The interest I have in the telegraph records?'

'Of course,' James said, adding, 'Sir,' a moment later.

Thomas refreshed their glasses, and James prepared to listen.

'It's quite simple,' the viscount said. 'I am trying to track down an old friend.' He and Thomas exchanged an uneasy glance. 'A rather sick old friend who appears to have gone missing and who we think might be a danger.'

'In danger, Sir?'

'No, James. A danger. To myself and many others.'

Ten

Archer took an instant liking to the man and had no qualms about taking him on. The expression on Thomas' face was a good enough reason to go out on a limb. He displayed a constant glow of wonder as James spoke, but became the butler when necessary. There wouldn't be any problems there. As for the man's fidelity, he had been correct. The only way to test it was to trust him, and Archer would rather trust a man on Thomas' recommendation than hire a private detective to do his dirty work.

However, James must not know the truth. The circle must be kept small and tight if his reputation was to be maintained. For this reason, he chose his words carefully as he explained what he wanted from the messenger and asked how much he would charge for the service.

'Can I make sure I've got this right?' James questioned when the viscount had finished. 'You want to track down any messages that might have been sent by this Doctor Quill?'

'Correct.'

'But you don't know where they might have been sent from? If they've been sent at all?'

'Sadly not.'

'And you are aware how many messages are actually dispatched each day?'

'Sadly, yes.'

James' eyes widened, and Archer was able to appreciate their colour. Flecks of green floated among brown reminding him of the bark of a mossy tree. There was something earthy about the man, his round cheeks were ruddy, his eyebrows the colour of soil and his hair the colour of corn. He was not what Archer would call handsome, but he could see what Thomas found attractive. He wasn't as bullish as Silas, but he had confidence, and although he was stocky, he wasn't fat, suggesting he was not lazy. He wouldn't look out of place on a university rugger pitch.

He may have been staring for too long because Thomas gave a cough.

'May I suggest, My Lord...?' he prompted.

'Yes, Payne?'

'Can you think of any likely locations from where Doctor Quill might have sent a telegram? I believe he was at his home on the Sunday. Perhaps the office at Five Dials might be a starting point?'

'Good idea,' Archer agreed. Quill could have been anywhere during the days before travelling north, but close to home seemed a sensible place to begin a search.

'Can you access the offices at Five Dials, James?' Thomas asked.

'I can, Mr Payne,' he replied. 'In fact, I reckon I can do better than that.'

'How so?'

'Well, Your Lordship...' James sat straight. 'I have a friend who works there. He's an older man who used to sail with my father. We called him Uncle John when we were little, so a family friend. I'm sure I could ask him to let me see the records, and I might be able to ask him to check other offices too. He is one of the men who gathers and stores the receipts, you see. As I'm sure you know, most customers bring what they want sending already written out. If not, the office writes it down before passing it to the wireless operator who then taps it through. The original is kept with the payment slip and stored for six months. John does all of that.'

'But I don't want to cause alarm,' Archer said, concerned about bringing in yet another man. 'My friend's disappearance is probably quite innocent.'

'John won't ask questions,' James said. 'I can say I'm on official business. Wearing my uniform, he won't be surprised.'

Thomas, having considered this idea, nodded.

'Then let's start there,' Archer decided. 'The most likely day is Sunday, but there are three other days, and as he wasn't at home, he could have been anywhere.'

'I see,' James nodded. 'And the problem there is, the originals are kept at each local office until a Thursday. That's the day the week's worth is collected and taken to central storage at Mount Pleasant.'

'Oh,' Thomas exclaimed. He stepped closer. 'Then that's perfect. All communications for the period we are interested in will be at the central office by now.'

'Are they stored in any particular order?' Archer asked.

James grinned, and Archer noticed that his two of his top teeth slightly overlapped in the centre.

'Now there's a job no-one wants,' James laughed. 'Did it once, didn't like it. There's a huge room where they're all sorted by name of sender so that when someone complains that their urgent invitation never arrived, someone at Mount Pleasant can look for it and confirm it was sent. The office at the other end, also noted, gets the blame.'

'Therefore...' It was Archer's turn to clarify. 'You can go to this storage place tomorrow and legitimately browse any correspondence from Doctor Quill made on those dates?'

'Yes, Sir.'

'It's not very private, is it?'

'We all have too much to do to go snooping.' James glanced at the mantle clock and smiled. 'But I can go any time,' he said. 'John will let me stay. The office runs all night.'

'You shall be well rewarded for your time, James,' Archer said. 'And more so if you alarm no-one and don't state who has sent you.'

'It'll all be legitimate and anonymous, Sir. I'll have left the post office by the time my boss finds out. Can't see a problem.'

'That's good news,' Archer said. 'And it only leaves two things. One, to say thank you, James, and the sooner you can do it and start working with Mr Payne here the better. And two, you've not said how much you want for this unusual service.'

The man's face fell. Archer expected it to light up as he announced some ridiculous sum, which he would have paid, but instead, James looked at Thomas who nodded encouragingly. James wasn't after encouragement, though, and Thomas' reaction made no difference. It was as if he was struggling with the decision to agree, rather than how much to charge. He swallowed as he returned his gaze to Archer.

'I'll happily do it for nothing, Sir,' he said. 'As a way to show I can be trusted.'

Archer appreciated his attitude. 'I will find some way to repay you,' he said. 'And that, gentlemen, completes our business. Unless you have any other questions, Mr Wright?'

Thomas gently kicked the back of James' chair, telling him it was time to leave.

'I'm sure I have many, Sir,' he said, rising. 'But if Thomas is showing me around, I can ask him.'

'Then that's that.' Archer stood and offered his hand. 'Welcome to Clearwater, James,' he said as they shook. 'Payne will show you the house and your quarters. Have Mrs Baker measure him would you, Payne?'

The boyish excitement on Thomas' face was entertaining as he showed James to the door.

'Oh, Payne? Where has Mr Hawkins gone today?'

'Mr Andrej is instructing him on how to ride without falling, I believe, Sir,' Thomas replied. 'He mentioned St Mathew's Park and said he would be home for lunch.'

'If Andrej is back in time, have him drive James wherever he needs to go. If not, get him a cab. I look forward to seeing you tomorrow, Mr Wright,' Archer said. 'And remember discretion.'

James touched his forelock, but Thomas knocked his hand away. 'You're not a tradesman,' he tutted and hurried the man from the room.

James didn't know what he was. He had entered the house as Tripp's spy and was to leave it as the viscount's footman. He had met Thomas on the front step not one week ago, fallen for his chiselled looks and green eyes, and now here he was about to visit what would be their shared apartment. His life had been rocketed in a completely unexpected direction as opportunity fell into his lap from two sides, and he didn't know which way to turn. What Tripp wanted of him was easy to deliver, and he was in the perfect place to do it, but it meant turning against the men helping him. He would have to betray not only Thomas but also the viscount, a man the likes of whom he had never encountered.

Messenger, spy, footman, friend or lover, he could not be all things, and he had much thinking to do.

Clarity returned as they passed through the drawing room and Thomas led him towards the back of the house. Whichever way he decided to go, whichever side he took, both depended on his working at Clearwater, but as they entered another room, he wondered if he had made a mistake.

'What's this?' he asked standing in awe.

'The library,' Thomas explained. 'His Lordship uses it only occasionally for entertaining and sometimes to play the piano or billiards.'

The piano stood at the far end, the billiard table in the centre, every wall was lined with old, thick books, and two windows looked out over a small garden and the park beyond. It reminded James of illustrations of a gentlemen's club.

'His Lordship likes reading,' he observed, stunned.

'Actually, this is his father's collection,' Thomas explained. 'His Lordship's are now in his study which, by the way, is a room you do not enter alone.'

'Oh?'

'One of his rules. Lucy is allowed to clean the grate and make the fire, and I may enter to leave post on his desk, but otherwise, no-one goes in the study unless the viscount is there or instructs you to enter in his absence.'

'Understood,' James said. 'I assume that's because he has private papers or something?'

'Ours is not to reason why.' Thomas ushered him into the hall and closed the door before leading him to the stairs. 'Through there is the dining room, you will spend a lot of time in there, and behind it, the breakfast room. Follow me.'

They ascended the stairs. Wide and carpeted they turned beneath dark portraits and landscapes lit by individual sconces. The largest painting showed a man not dissimilar in looks to the viscount but wearing a medal-adorned military uniform. His hair was peppered with silver, his expression stern and behind him, a rambling country house was depicted with a hunt meeting in front of it.

'The late viscount.' Thomas pointed as they turned to the second flight. 'He passed away only a few months back. A fall from a horse at Larkspur, ironically enough during one of the hunts he was so fond of. He was fifty-two.'

James didn't know what to say, which was probably a blessing.

94

Ears open, mouth shut, he followed Thomas to the first floor.

There, Thomas pointed out the east side of the house which contained the dowager's suite and her guest rooms, and the west side which was the viscount's.

'His Lordship's private drawing room,' he said putting his hand on a door. 'His bedroom here, Mr Hawkins has the green suite here...'

There were more rooms that James could comprehend, and he wondered if the job came with a map. Before he had a chance to ask, they were exiting the corridor to the back staircase.

'These lead up and down at either end of the building,' Thomas said, climbing. 'And the central backstairs run behind the main staircase...'

James was used to walking the streets, running sometimes, but most of the time he was on the flat. It kept him fit, but climbing so many stairs was new to him, and by the time they reached the top floor, he was gasping for breath.

'You'll get used to it,' Thomas said. 'The trick is, when summoned, not to arrive panting or sweating. Take a moment before entering the house from below stairs, compose yourself and take a breath. Do the same before entering a room. Here...'

They entered the servants' quarters on the men's side and a long passage that mirrored the one below, but with a lower ceiling. It was nowhere near as grand, but there were paintings on the walls and carpet on the floorboards.

'We have several spare rooms for visiting staff,' Thomas said. 'Also for if the other footmen are down from Larkspur. The women live on the far side of that door which is only opened by Mrs Baker. There's no need for the maids and us to mix up here, we're quite private. And this is where you will stay.'

They entered a bedroom with a sloping ceiling and a large garret window. Beneath it stood a single bed and a nightstand. A mirrored wardrobe stood against one wall and a chest of drawers on the other beside a small fireplace with a modern gas heater. A desk and armchair were the only other furniture, and the walls were bare apart from the lamps.

'This was my room.' Thomas said. 'It's warm, you can open the window in summer, and the only downside is the rattling roof tiles

95

when it's windy. The bathroom is next door, and it is shared by all the male servants.'

'It's inside?'

Thomas stared at him in surprise and then a wry smile grew on his soft lips. 'Yes, James, it's inside, and there's running water, hot and cold. That was only put in last year. Before then we had to bring up hot water in buckets. Now then…' He led James back into the corridor. 'You need to bring your own clothes for when you are not on duty, but dress appropriately as it will become known you are His Lordship's footman. Can't have you going about publicly in tat, but from what I've seen, you like to dress well.'

'I dress as well as I can afford, Sir, yes.'

'Not Sir, James. Mr Payne. Unlike in other houses where you must provide your own, you will be supplied the appropriate uniforms, outdoor and carriage coat, cloak, hat, gloves and so on, and shirts, collars and studs. You will not abuse His Lordship's generosity. It's up to you to keep them clean, and us men are responsible for keeping our quarters tidy and swept. I shall keep a close eye as will Mrs Baker, the housekeeper.'

He rattled off several more details that James knew he wouldn't remember, and finally, showed James his own bedroom.

Except it wasn't just a bedroom. Thomas also had a sitting room and a lot more furniture, bookshelves, two armchairs and his fireplace was bigger. This room, smelling of fresh paint, was at the front of the house facing south towards the river. Its garret window overlooked the rooftops and chimneys of Riverside. The top floor of Clearwater was twice the size of James' whole house, and he couldn't wait to see his mother's face when he told her the news.

'Now then…'

He returned his attention to Thomas standing beside the double bed.

'We need to speak as James and Tom,' the butler said. 'Come here.'

He patted the bed and sat, sending James' stomach turning over as he approached.

'I don't want this to be awkward,' Thomas said, as James sat beside him, 'but I would like to speak about that night when I stayed with you.'

'Fair enough.' James had thoughts on the subject too, but kept them to himself.

'This is all very new to me and rather strange,' Thomas began. 'But, I think our brief conversation and what happened after it was enough for us both to realise that there was something… going on. At least, that is, if I have read the situation correctly. If not, tell me, and we'll say no more.'

It occurred to James that he was sitting shoulder to shoulder with a man for whom he had what others called unnatural feelings, and they were alone in his bedroom. The feelings were not unnatural to him, and apparently not to Thomas either, and yes, he had read the situation correctly. The attraction was stronger now Thomas had gone out of his way to help him, and the pull was irresistible. What compounded his affection was the way Thomas' actions were not a bribe in the same way that his new job was not dependent on him searching the postal records. Everything was unconditional, and that was not something James was used to.

'You got to understand,' he said, his eyes falling on the unlit gas heater. 'This is new. I don't just mean the job, or even sitting here with you, Tom, but the whole thing.'

'I'm not sure I do understand,' Thomas said. 'What do you mean?'

'Well…' James took a moment to think how best to explain himself. 'Alright, yes, you did read things right. I want to tell you stuff, but it's not stuff we're meant to talk about. Unnatural things, and I ain't never said them to no-one before.' He glanced at Thomas who was also studying the grate. 'You know what I mean?'

'Affection towards another man?'

'Yeah, that's it.'

'Aye,' Thomas nodded, and James heard a hint of a country accent. 'I thought the same way,' he said. 'Least I did until recently. Now, here, under this roof, I am safe enough to think about them. And, after the other night, I think I am safe to talk about them with you.' They faced each other. 'I am safe, aren't I?'

'Yeah.' James' mouth was dry, and his pulse had quickened. 'You and I are the same, Tom,' he said. 'The other night… I was nervous. Not had another man in my bed like that, not one I… you know…'

'Fancied?'

James nodded.

'Same for me,' Thomas said. 'And it's now become so much more complicated.'

He had no idea how complicated this was for James. He had Tripp on one shoulder like a tempting devil offering instant wealth for information, and on the other, the kind hearts of the viscount and Thomas offering stability in return for loyalty.

'Complicated, because what we want to do shouldn't go on anywhere?' James queried. 'Not out there, not here in private?'

'And certainly not between butler and footman.'

'I bet it happens all the time.'

'You may be right.'

'So, others must find a way around it.' James wanted reassurance, but it involved asking a personal question about his employer. Just the kind of question Tripp sought an answer to for his own unexplained reasons. The problem was, it didn't feel loyal to ask it.

'What are you thinking?' Thomas slouched, so their shoulders touched.

The only way for James to move forward was to ask the damn question. 'I was wondering about Mr Hawkins and the viscount,' he admitted feeling rotten.

Thomas moved away. 'That's one of the things you and I will not discuss,' he said.

James was relieved. Thomas' refusal gave him the excuse to ignore Tripp's directive. He was, however, worried because the viscount's private life was what Tripp was paying him to evidence.

'What it comes down to is this,' Thomas said. He walked to the window and stood looking out. 'How do you feel about me? Not as your butler, but as a friend. Could you work with me, be told off by me when necessary, be taught your job by me and behave as a footman without that getting in the way of friendship? If you were not here in the viscount's employ and remained as a messenger, would we still meet in the pub? Could I still stay at your house some nights, and would we... be ourselves?'

James joined him. The view was spectacular, particularly as the high-up breeze had cleared the smog, and the sun, though faint, lit damp rooves through a layer of silver cloud.

'I would have liked that,' he said. 'I ain't talked like this before, but I reckon we're whistling the same tune.'

Thomas nodded. 'Once again, I agree.'

'Then, we'll work it out. If that's what you want.'

'Is it what you want, James? Can you tell me that you want the same thing as I do?'

James wasn't sure that he could voice the words. Instead, he took the bold step of putting his arm around Thomas' waist, expecting him to move away. He didn't. Silently, he returned the gesture, and they stood holding each other gazing over the city.

'We should have a rule,' Thomas said at length. 'That we only do this up here and when off duty. Outside our rooms, I am Mr Payne, and you are James, the footman, and we must behave as such. But in our privacy, it's Jimmy and Tom, and neither of us speak a word about anything beyond our doors. Agreed?'

'Definitely.' James leant his head on Thomas' shoulder, and the man's grip tightened.

He wanted Thomas so much it was painful. His guts were churning with anticipation, his heart fluttering and God knows what was going on at crotch level, but up top, his mind was a jumble. A battle was taking place between what he wanted and what he had agreed to do. If only this had happened without Tripp's involvement, he would be home and dry with a good job, a man he could share his desires with and security on all fronts.

'You can trust me, Tom,' he said. 'But you've got to understand I don't know what to do next.'

Thomas let go and faced him. 'I'm going to say this while I can.' His jade eyes glittered in the sunlight. 'I've fallen for you, James, and I want to fall further, but it's going to take me a while to trust you. Not because I am uncertain of you, but... well... in these times, a man such as me — men such as *us* — must be protective of our secret. We need to keep our friends close, but in matters such as this, you can never be sure who your enemies are. Your discretion means everything... and not just to me, to His Lordship as well. Don't be offended if I need time to get to know you.'

James swallowed at the sight of Thomas' kind face. 'I ain't offended,' he said, raising a trembling hand to touch the man's cheek. 'I wanted you as soon as I saw you. It was physical, yeah, but then when we got talking... It's more than just that, you know?'

As an answer, Thomas took his hand and pressed it to his lips.

'Like the backstairs,' he said. 'One step at a time.'

Thomas' fingers were long and his skin soft, but his grip was powerful. James grinned and returned the gentle kiss.

'And I for one can't wait for the next one,' he said. 'Can I kiss you?'

'I wish you would,' Thomas smiled. 'But, I'm worried that if you do, I won't be able to let you go, and we'll be in trouble for not getting on with our work. Maybe, tomorrow, when you've moved in...'

James couldn't wait that long. He pulled Thomas to him and locked their lips together. Thomas gasped, but the sound soon became a murmur as they held each other, kissing deeply but inexpertly, until the rage in James' groin forced him to break apart.

'Sorry,' he said, panting. 'Couldn't help myself, but any more of that and... well...'

'I know.' Thomas coughed to clear his throat. 'Tomorrow, Jimmy, I promise. But for now, duty first.'

This was how it was going to be, and it would continue in this double-life way until James either sided with Tripp, discovered the information he wanted by deceit, or gave into his true feelings for Thomas and told Tripp to go boil his head.

'Yeah, we should get on,' he said, unable to keep the grin from his lips.

'We should,' Thomas agreed. 'In a moment.' He rearranged the front of his trousers, and James did the same.

They left the room suppressing laughter and bumping each other like schoolboys plotting mischief, trying to catch the other's hand until they reached the backstairs.

'Follow me, Mr Wright,' Thomas said, straightening his uniform and his behaviour. 'And I shall introduce you to the other servants. Mrs Baker will arrange your livery and your room ahead of tomorrow.'

They took the stairs as butler and footman, and James had the uneasy feeling that whichever way he decided to go, Tripp or Clearwater, he was coming down from the clouds and about to hit the ground with a thump.

Eleven

Maps, timetables, plans, questions, notes… Archer stood bent over the reading table between the windows staring at sheets of paper, newspaper cuttings and headlines. He was getting nowhere. Quill was out there somewhere, and, contrary to what Silas might think, he was not 'doing a runner'. If he wanted to flee to the continent, he wouldn't have gone to the northern moors. He could have stowed away on a boat at Limedock, gone to the eastern ports or to Westerpool and taken a ship to Ireland. The north made no sense, as did allowing himself to be seen boarding a train. The only explanation he could come up with was what Thomas had suggested; he wanted Archer to know he was still in the country.

Why?

Archer, Silas and Thomas were probably the only men who knew Quill was the Ripper. Why send such a message? What did he want?

'Horses are like a whore with the clap,' Silas proclaimed as he entered the study. 'Looks like a good ride but you don't want to get in the saddle.'

He walked stiffly with his legs apart, possibly because his breeches were tight, but more likely because he was in pain. His face was red and his hair in disarray. He checked there was no-one behind him before kissing Archer, resting his head on his chest and groaning.

'You actually like doing all that, do you?' he said. 'Fecking torture.'

'Did you fall off?'

'Ha!' Silas, grinning, kissed him again before crossing to an armchair. 'More like, did I get to sit on the bloody thing for longer than ten seconds? I thought Fecks was a mate. He's trying to kill me.'

He lowered himself gingerly into the chair keeping his weight on his arms and emitting grunts of various degrees of discomfort until a final, 'Ahh,' accompanied a look of relief. 'I know where I am with a chair.'

'Did Andrej take James in the trap?'

'Is that his name?' Silas asked as he wrestled with a boot. 'Yeah. Who's he?'

'Thomas' replacement footman,' Archer said. 'He's gone to see if he can track down any communication from Quill during the time he was allegedly missing.'

He left the table and sat at his desk, rocking back in his captain's chair and cracking his knuckles.

'Just his replacement?' Silas asked.

'Why do you say that?'

Silas winked and touched the side of his nose. 'Takes one to known one,' he said. 'The man's as queer as I am.'

'How can you tell? He doesn't act it.'

'You saying I do?' Silas laughed. 'Yeah, you're right. He looks as straight as anyone, but the look on his face when he said goodbye to Tommy, you'd a thought he was off to war leaving his sweetheart weeping like a widow.'

'Maybe he is as we are,' Archer mused.

'He's one of us to be sure,' Silas said. He freed one foot from a boot and sighed with joy before starting on the other. 'Which is why you've trusted him to get involved in this, I take it.'

'But, that's not our business.' Archer smiled. Silas was always right. 'Our business,' he said, glancing at the writing table, 'is spread out over there and up on the wall.' He pointed to the map. 'What the hell is Quill playing at?'

'I'd like to say I was thinking about that while Fecks led me around the park like a dog on a lead,' Silas moaned. 'But all I could think about was how my bollocks were being crushed.'

'You're doing it wrong.'

'Never done anything wrong with my balls, mate,' Silas said with a leer. 'Want to nip upstairs and rub them better?'

Archer laughed. 'Every minute of the day,' he said. 'But we can't just now. I've got Quill on my mind.'

'There's a nasty thought.'

'Indeed.' He screwed up a piece of paper and threw it at the map. 'Why has he gone to the north?'

'You know him better than anyone,' Silas said, grappling with his other boot. 'Any more news?'

'None.'

'Well...' His foot came free. 'Thank fuck for that. Last time I get on a horse, I swear. Well...' he continued once he'd wiggled his toes. 'I reckon there's nothing to be done until we get some message from him, or until the new boy turns up something.'

'And I think you're wrong.'

Silas was surprised. 'How?'

'There is much we can do,' Archer said. 'For a start, I've been looking at the route he took. It's five hours to the depot on the moors, so he would have arrived there around three in the morning.'

'I think we knew that.'

'Correct, but I also looked at where the train goes first. Agreed, it doesn't stop as it does on other nights, but does it slow down enough to allow him to alight anywhere else?'

'And?'

Archer shrugged. 'I'm not a railways expert,' he said. 'But we should be able to find someone at the station who is. Bradshaw's...' he indicated one of his guide books, 'doesn't mention the depot. There's no reason; it's not a local attraction. It does, however, mention towns along the route of the Highland Express, none of which the Wednesday train stops at. However, it might slow down enough to allow someone to alight safely, and if we can confirm that it doesn't, we can concentrate on the depot.'

'And if we discover it does?'

'Then it's all about needles in haystacks, and as you say, there's nothing we can do until he makes another move. But, in the meantime. How do you fancy a trip to North Cross railway terminus?'

'As long as I don't have to sit in a fecking saddle.'

Archer walked to the bell-pull and tugged. 'Hungry?'

'I could eat a horse,' Silas said. 'Preferably the bastard one that's squashed my nuts.'

The afternoon was cool, November was approaching, and with it the breeze which wafted the city fumes away to the south, but brought temperatures from the north. Archer and Silas sat in the relative warmth of a hansom, the viscount in his travel-cloak and Silas beside him wearing a coat over a new brown suit. He also wore a bowler hat which Archer said made him look like a businessman.

Holding Silas' hand on the seat between them beneath the cover of his coat gave Archer more than its usual thrill. He was infatuated with the man, and could never imagine himself being anything else, but to touch him intimately and semi-publicly added to the frisson. The warmth of his skin, the way he moved a finger, absentmindedly rubbing Archer's palm as a coded message that he was still there, and the way his grip tightened when he saw a new and, to him, thrilling sight intensified the delight.

The cut on Silas' chin had healed, and the stitches would come out soon.

The thought reminded Archer to contact Doctor Markland. He had agreed to oversee the East End mission when it opened, and Archer had promised to invite him for dinner. If he managed that in the next few days, the doctor could also see to the stitches. Perhaps, he thought, he would also agree to be his personal physician. Archer liked the man for his plain speaking and professional attitude towards the sick no matter what class they were from, but he had yet to sound him out on his thoughts on sexuality; he already trusted him enough to broach the subject. It didn't have anything to do with his work, of course, but Archer was keen to support any man who was 'on the same crew.'

He shelved the thought as they left the leafy borough of Riverside, the driver taking them around the top of the busy West End to avoid traffic.

'Even smells different,' Silas said, gazing out at the women in long, black dresses, the men ducking beneath their wide-brimmed hats as they passed, doffing their own bowlers and caps.

'You can thank Bazalgette for that,' Archer said.

'Where's that?'

'Not where,' Archer smirked. 'Who. Sir Joseph. A friend of my mother, some say an old affair, but I prefer not to think about such things where Her Ladyship is concerned. He designed the new sewer system.'

'Nice.' Silas grimaced.

'There are miles of tunnels beneath us,' Archer said. 'Some

large enough for a steam engine and bigger than the new circular underground railway. Fascinating what we can do these days.'

'Yeah, well, your man needs to pop down to Greychurch and start digging.'

'The East End also benefits.'

Silas laughed. 'Sorry, Archie,' he said. 'But it doesn't. Not much. Why d'you think Markland told you to watch out for cholera after you fell in the river?'

'Good point.'

Archer squeezed his hand and resisted the temptation to kiss him. The drive could only have been improved had they been allowed to lean against each other, or if he could tuck Silas beneath his arm. He brushed his leg against his lover instead.

The hansom trundled unhindered along the Great East Road until it delivered them to North Cross station where Silas paid the cabbie as Archer considered the best way forward.

'I think,' he said as they stood facing the grand frontage of the city's busiest terminus, 'that you seek out the station master and tell him I would like an audience. I'll play the nobility card, but it's best you deal the hand.'

'As you say, Boss.' Silas tipped his hat with a wink. 'What shall I say is your business?'

'A general enquiry to start with, but also a personally urgent matter.'

They entered the concourse and threaded through passengers to the over-grand Café De Paris, an ornately fronted building set within the high arches facing the tracks. Above, the glass and iron roof echoed with the sounds of whistles, voices and rumbling luggage as porters dragged carts, people called farewells, and pigeons flapped, their wings clattering as they escaped the unwanted advances of small children. All life was here, it seemed, from the staff to the nobility, and from country folk in for the afternoon to suited men going about their business.

'Railway stations are worlds within worlds,' Archer mused as they parted company. 'I shall wait inside this one.'

Silas followed a sign directing him to station's offices while Archer entered the humid warmth of the café. It too was busy with middle-class passengers queuing for tea at a counter, segregated by a velvet rope from those travelling first-class. He found a table close to the window from where he watched the outside-inside world go by until Silas returned ten minutes later.

'So,' he said, as he slipped into the opposite chair. 'The man's name is Burrows, and he's more than happy to see you. I told him that I didn't know your exact business, but that you were very keen to have him help with a matter of great personal interest. I hope that was alright?'

'Perfect,' Archer said, collecting his top hat. 'Lead on, Mr Hawkins.'

He followed Silas at two paces, close enough to show the gap in status. It was a gap he hated, but there was no way he could be seen to treat his secretary as an equal, not in public. In reality, he and Silas were equal in many ways although Silas knew more about sex than Archer. At the bottom line, they were both criminals, and everything they did together in private was punishable. That was enough to draw the viscount emotionally closer to the man he could no longer bear to be apart from, and it was the nobility of love that helped him keep his head high as he walked.

His impassive stare drew attention, but he ignored those around him unless he gave a polite nod of the head in deference to a person of equal standing. Their route led them past the outer track and an impressive locomotive waiting for departure, its funnel pumping smoke into the industrial atmosphere. The smell of oil and steam pervaded the air as they approached a door marked 'Station Head Office.' He had formulated his plan and was not at all nervous, certain that his visit would not arouse suspicion.

Silas confidently entered the offices as if he worked there and held the door for his master. Archer was met by a startlingly attractive man in a blue uniform who he at first mistook for a doorman.

'Lord Clearwater?' the man said, bowing politely. 'I am Stamp, clerk to Mr Burrows who is expecting you. If you would care to follow me.'

The greeting was conducted according to convention, despite the noise and mess around them. Men worked at desks in lines facing away from the office's glass frontage as if they were not allowed to look on the marvels their employment sustained, and each one was busy at a desk writing in ledgers beneath oil lamps. Their sleeves rolled up, they wore visors to shield their eyes and concentrated on their work.

'What office is this?' Archer enquired of the clerk.

'Accountancy, Sir,' he replied. 'And through there we have scheduling, and beyond, maintenance offices and secretarial.'

'I never knew so much went on.'

'We are a hive of activity,' Stamp said, raising his voice above the sound of pistons, whistles and trundling trucks that echoed beneath the vaulted, glass ceiling. 'There are a few stairs I'm afraid.'

He led them to a spiral staircase at the back of the building. The fancy metalwork was ornate for an office but in keeping with the rest of the wrought iron that held the station together. At the first landing, Stamp opened a door to allow the guests to pass through and, as soon as he closed it, the outside hubbub was silenced. Archer's ears rang with the sudden drop in volume, and he was still adjusting a moment later when Stamp knocked on a second door. He didn't wait for a response before entering the station master's office and announcing, 'The Viscount Clearwater', in a tone that would not have been out of place in any stately home.

A burly man rose from behind a partner's desk, framed by the glass frontage of his domain. Behind and below, station life busied itself in silence while nothing in the office moved apart from Burrows buttoning his jacket and coming around his desk to welcome the unexpected visitors.

'An honour, My Lord,' he said, observing etiquette and waiting for Archer to approach, should he want to shake hands.

Archer did. Many men in his position wouldn't have bothered, but he wanted this meeting to be friendly. He intended to extract as much information from this man as he could.

'I must offer my apologies, Station Master,' he said, gushing somewhat. 'Not to have telegraphed ahead was amiss of me. I hope I am not an inconvenience.'

'Not at all, Sir.' The man seemed genuinely happy to be interrupted. 'May I offer you refreshment?'

'No, thank you,' Archer smiled back. 'We shan't keep you any longer than we must.'

'Thank you, Stamp.' Burrows nodded, and the clerk left the room. 'Will you sit, My Lord?'

'I will.'

Archer took the seat he was offered, and when Burrows suggested Silas might prefer to wait outside, he dismissed the idea, saying, 'I need my man with me.' It gave him a secret thrill to utter the words. Silas was his secretary, but he was also his man in every other sense. 'Mr Hawkins will make notes if he may?'

'Of course.'

Silas sat behind Archer and produced a notebook and pencil. Archer knew his handwriting was not the best and had told him to pretend to use a form of shorthand to cover the fact. It was an act; Archer would remember anything important that might be said.

Once they had observed the formalities, Burrows asked how he could help.

Archer opened his mouth to speak, but was interrupted by the loud clanging of the station clock which vibrated rather than sounded through the office.

'One becomes accustomed,' Burrows said, passing it off.

'I hear from your accent that you are from the northern counties,' Archer observed.

'I am, Sir. Lancashire by birth.'

'One of our great industrial areas?'

'Carnforth, actually, rural but not far from the cities and, of course, now joined to this great metropolis by the wonder of the railways.'

'Indeed.' Archer thought it time he got to the point. 'But it is with the eastern line that I have an interest,' he said. 'And I wonder if you might give me some information about the Highland Express. Sleeper service.'

'Certainly.' Burrows beamed, apparently ready to impart all and any knowledge. 'We are very proud of that service.'

'And rightly so, I am sure.' Archer's compliment was well received, and the man was warming to him. He wanted to make sure he warmed further and said, 'I would have sought the advice of a driver or engineer, but I always think it's best to speak with an expert, and I am sure there is no-one better than yourself.'

'I am honoured you think so.'

'Quite right.' Archer was somewhat patronising, but he suspected Burrows was used to that. 'Also, this is rather a delicate matter, and

Mr Hawkins...' he indicated Silas, 'has heard of your reputation as a man of discretion.' He didn't explain how, because he couldn't, he'd just made it up, but Burrows shined more brightly.

The flattery now seen to, Archer turned to the meat of the meeting.

'I have two requests, Mr Burrows,' he said. 'Firstly, are you able to furnish me with details of the route taken regularly by the Highland Express?'

'I can provide you with a route map if that would suffice.'

'It won't, I'm afraid.'

'Oh?'

Archer smiled inwardly when Burrows become intrigued.

'That is, Sir, it will partly fulfil my needs. What I would be most interested in is the more technical details of the route.'

'Technical?'

'Yes, as in, the speed of the locomotive as it passes stations, crosses bridges, viaducts and so forth. I, and my colleagues in the House are fascinated by your new technology.'

'As we all should be, Sir.' Burrows agreed. 'It is the way forward.'

'Quite. Tell me, are such things recorded and available to the public?'

'Yes and no, to be honest with you, Sir. Yes, I can have Stamp find the reports, but no, we would not usually allow the public to see them.'

Silas coughed pointedly, and Burrows caught his meaning.

'As you are not the general public but a member of the House of Lords, I see no harm in providing you with such information. In fact, I should say that the Great Northern and Eastern Railway Company would be honoured to encourage whatever interest your Lordship has in us.'

'Oh, it is purely personal,' Archer clarified. 'But also invaluable. I shall, of course, recompense you for any trouble or additional work my request involves.'

'It's a simple, matter of sending Stamp to the basement.' Burrows rang a handbell that tinkled so quietly Archer could barely hear it.

Stamp, on the other hand, must have been tuned to it as he appeared at the door a second later as keen as a hunting dog. He was instructed to fetch the speed trial and running records of the express train's journey and vanished in a swish of eager subservience.

'I am indebted, Mr Burrows,' Archer continued. 'And now, the second matter. Are you able to furnish me with passenger information? Now, before you throw up your hands in horror at betraying the confidence of your customers, a reaction I would fully understand, allow me to be more specific.'

'That would be appreciated, My Lord.'

This was the part where fact and fiction would have to mingle, and Archer chose his words carefully.

'A very dear friend of mine took the Highland Express on Wednesday last,' he said. 'And he has caused me some confusion. I thought, as I was indulging myself with this visit about the engineering specifications, I might ask you to clarify this matter and put my mind at rest.'

'With pleasure, Sir, if I can.'

'You see, my friend promised to send me one of those picture postcards from his destination which was Invermoor.'

'The train terminates at Averness, Sir,' Burrows corrected as Archer knew he would. 'It is the only stop.'

'The only stop?'

'Apart from the Barrenmoor depot where it halts to re-water and fuel, and where the post is exchanged.'

'Then I stand pleasantly corrected,' Archer said. 'You see, I thought my Doctor friend told me he would contact me from Invermoor, and I received a card from Averness, unsigned, so that clears my confusion, and all is well. It must be from someone else.'

'Would this be Doctor Quill?'

Archer tried not to show his surprise. 'Why do you ask?'

Burrows twiddled his fingers nervously as if he was about to ask something extremely delicate. 'No reason,' he said, but clearly there was. 'I know he has many society patients, and he came to see me before boarding the train. I've suffered from a bad chest, you see, and he wanted to enquire after my health even though he was in a hurry. I thought it very good of him and not out of the ordinary until...' He searched the room for a suitable cover story, and Archer was prepared to wait until he found one. 'Another gentleman enquired after him regards the same journey. It makes

110

no matter, but I am glad to hear he arrived safely.'

'You saw Doctor Quill board the night train?' Archer asked it as innocently as he could. 'I didn't know he was taking the trip.'

'Oh. Then the man of interest to you is not Doctor Quill?'

'No, Mr Burrows, another man entirely. But who was asking after Doctor Quill? Perhaps I could assist.'

'I am sure it's nothing to worry yourself over, Sir.'

If he guarded his trains as effectively as he guarded his secrets, then his passengers would be treated with the utmost discretion.

'And I am sure you are correct, Mr Burrows.'

It was obvious that he was trying to avoid mentioning Inspector Adelaide, and Archer was not going to press the point. The man's bluster was proof enough that he was the witness the inspector spoke of and, by the sound of it, not one paid by Quill to provide an alibi.

'I have used up enough of your valuable time,' Archer said. 'I should leave you to your good works.'

He stood, and Burrows' chair scraped as he did the same.

'The pleasure and honour have been mine,' the man said. 'Ah, here is Stamp.'

His clerk sailed into the room slightly out of breath. 'As you requested, Your Lordship,' he said, offering an envelope. 'It is a copy, so there is no need to return it. If you would like me to explain any of the more technical aspects...'

'Thank you, Stamp,' Burrows interrupted. 'That will be all.'

Stamp left, and Burrows made the same offer. Archer assured him that he would be in touch if any explanation was needed, and passed the papers to Silas.

'Mr Burrows,' the viscount said as Silas handed him his hat from the stand. 'Once again, thank you for your time. My apologies for the inconvenience, and may I say congratulations on your station. It is something of a marvel.'

'A new age is upon us, My Lord,' Burrows said. 'We must embrace it.'

'Quite, quite. Hawkins?'

Silas left the office ahead of him, and Archer thanked the station master once more and with a deference which the man soaked up like a dry sponge.

Downstairs, they left the industrious hum of the accounting office and entered the melee of the concourse, soon to be lost among the luggage and travellers, the steam and smell of hot metal.

'What a charming man,' Archer said as they sought a hansom cab on the street.

'Bit of a creep if you ask me,' Silas mumbled. 'Stamp was cute enough. Nice arse.'

Archer repressed a smile. 'Apparently, it's a new age,' he said. 'But, I don't think the likes of Mr Stamp are quite ready for that kind of observation. I, on the other hand, am.'

'Eh?'

He nudged Silas and winked. 'I have a friend who is suffering a riding injury that needs my attention,' he said as if discussing the weather. 'I've heard a massage, gently but deeply penetrating, is the best cure when saddle-sore. Ah, a cab.'

Twelve

The evening saw Archer and Silas take a quiet dinner served by Lucy and Thomas during which nothing was said of their business. Instead, they discussed Silas' riding lesson and the founding of Archer's East End charity, the details of which they didn't go into when the maid was present. Afterwards, they retired to the study and Archer asked Thomas to send the housekeeper.

'Mrs Baker,' Archer greeted her cheerfully and beckoned her closer when she bustled into the room. He collected a letter from his desk as he sat. 'I know the city is not your favourite place in the world and you much prefer Larkspur, and this past couple of weeks have seen an upheaval in the usual routine of the house. You must all be quite exhausted.'

'Not really, My Lord,' she said. Her beady eyes flashed to Silas reading at the table and then back to Archer.

'That's good to hear,' he said and waved the letter. 'Particularly as Lady Clearwater needs you.'

'Oh?' Mrs Baker was as flattered as she was interested.

'She has written asking if I can spare you. Apparently, my mother, ending her period of mourning unfashionably early, has announced a ball, and that can only mean one thing. She needs your guiding hand.'

A brief smile twitched at the corners of the housekeeper's thin mouth, but was quickly disguised.

'This came by the afternoon post,' he continued. 'She asks if I can spare you. The ball is next weekend, and apparently...' He studied the writing as if he had forgotten when all he was doing was thickening her intrigue. 'Ah, apparently, Mary is unwell. You know how Her Ladyship is when her lady's maid is unavailable. Mary has also been keeping house. She stresses, rather vehemently, that Larkspur is in danger of decline without you.' He put down the letter and fixed her with an intent stare. 'Your place really is with the mistress of the house and as there isn't one at Clearwater, would you be happy returning there to save the day?'

'If it is your wish, Sir,' she said. 'Although…' She hesitated.

'Yes? Please, whatever your concerns, I will know them.'

'With no disrespect, My Lord,' she said. 'Mr Payne is new in his post. If Mr Tripp were here, I would have no qualms, but the accounts, the ordering, and now a new footman…?'

Archer put on his most charming, lost-boy expression. 'You are, of course, correct, Mrs Baker,' he said. 'It will be a struggle, but I am loath to leave my mother at the mercy of the staff. Robert is a fine first footman and is managing the male servants, she says, but without overall leadership… You can imagine. And this ball is important to her. Would you return to Larkspur and put my house in order for me? At least until I can get there.'

Mrs Baker tipped her head, and when she lifted it, she seemed more relaxed. 'Of course.'

'Thank you. Have you seen to James' livery?' Archer asked.

'I have, Sir, as best I can. I insisted one uniform at least be delivered tomorrow morning, but told the tailor the rest could come in a day or so, to minimise the cost.'

'Good thinking as always. Mrs Flintwich and Payne can see to the ordering, Lucy to the rooms. I think we will manage. I can't imagine you have anything of major significance outstanding around this house.'

'Certainly not, Sir.'

'I thought so. I'll have Mr Andrej drive you to the station in the morning if that's not too soon. Take Sally with you for the company.'

As suspected, Mrs Baker was more than happy to leave the city she hated, and her face lit up. Her place was with his mother, the mistress until Archer married.

'As long as Mr Payne can manage,' she said. 'And you are sure, Sir, I will speak with Sally. She will be grateful for the change of air.'

'And a chance to flirt with Robert, no doubt.' Archer lifted his eyebrows suggestively, which surprised her, but the slit of her lips twitched again.

'I don't know what you mean, Sir.' She did, and it was plain to see.

'Us boys will manage down here,' he said. 'But if I have any problems, you shall be the first to know.'

'I'll need to put a few things straight.' The housekeeper began organising immediately. 'Mr Payne will have to see to the accounts, but if you're happy with that, I can go first thing.'

'Perfect, and you have a good time, Mrs Baker. It won't be a holiday of course, but the air is cleaner, and you've been in the city since before father died. It's about time the men managed alone. I am sure Mrs Flintwich will keep us well fed and under control. Take what you need for the fares from housekeeping, and thank you.'

Mrs Baker left the study with a spring in her step, a very unusual sight but a pleasing one.

'What was that all about?' Silas asked, turning in his chair.

'It was actually all true,' Archer said. 'She's bored here and uncomfortable. I don't need a housekeeper when it's just the two of us.'

'And Tommy, this new man and Fecker. You turning this into a molly house?'

'Now there's a thought,' Archer laughed. 'And not one to be aired in public. Good Lord, can you imagine the fuss? No, Silas. Mother needs her housekeeper, and we don't. Right!' he slapped the desk and stood. 'Brandy?'

'Yuk, no thanks. Gives me indigestion.'

Archer rang for Thomas and, when he appeared, instructed him to close the doors. By then, he had served himself a large Cognac and was back at his desk.

'Take a seat, Tom,' he said. 'Kick off your shoes, throw off your tails and lend me your mind.'

Thomas kept his shoes tightly laced but took off his coat and rolled up his sleeves. Silas drew him a chair to the reading table, and Archer joined them, bringing several papers.

'Tom,' he said. 'I've sent Mrs Baker and Sally away to Larkspur. There will just be the four of us and Lucy in the house from tomorrow. I thought it best to have fewer servants around while you train James and we deal with this Quill matter. I hope you agree.'

'I do, Sir,' Thomas said. 'Particularly as you have guests for dinner tomorrow night.'

'I do?'

Thomas reminded him that he had invited Lady Marshall and Doctor Markland, the physician who attended him at St Mary's.

'As long as you can manage with just Lucy,' Archer said. 'Or we could borrow someone from Lady Marshall when needed and ask Andrej to help with service.'

Silas laughed, but cut it short when he saw Archer was serious.

'Sorry, Archie,' he said. 'But that'd be like asking a docker to dance in a ballet.'

'I rather agree with Silas,' Thomas said. 'I will take James in hand and...'

'Oh yeah?' Silas leered.

'Don't be vulgar.' Thomas tapped him playfully. 'And I am sure lady Marshall will be sympathetic. Doctor Markland, if I have read him right, will be as out of place as James, so he won't notice if the new footman does anything wrong.'

'As you say, Tom,' Archer conceded. 'No news from James, I take it?'

'No,' Thomas replied. 'Fecker came back in the late afternoon. James had told him not to wait any longer. There was a lot to look through, but he said he would bring any news as soon as he had it, as long as it was not too late.' He glanced at the clock. 'It doesn't look like he's coming tonight.'

'That's a shame,' Archer said. 'But we can't pressure him. He doesn't yet know our purpose.'

'Which is what, exactly?' Thomas asked, taking the papers from Archer. 'What's this?'

Archer told him about their afternoon visit to the railway station and explained the sheets of information. Thomas read as he listened and looked at the bookshelves while Archer finished his story.

'Can you excuse me a minute?' he said, rising.

'Of course.'

Archer watched as he left the room. He was exchanging a mystified glace with Silas when Thomas hurried back, put on his tailcoat and left again.

'Did you learn anything from that stuff?' Silas asked, indicating the railway information.

'I hardly understood a word of it,' Archer said. 'All volumes and distances, weights and pressures. I was hoping for something less complicated.'

'What's your plan? You have got one, haven't you?'

'Not really.' Archer sipped his drink. 'But I do have a feeling.'

'Which is…?' Silas left it hanging.

'That we have not heard the last of Quill.'

'Because…?'

'Because I have a suspicion.'

'You know,' Silas said putting on his cheeky grin. 'That's another bloody thing that's so likeable about you.'

'What?'

'You can act so helpless with Mrs Baker you've got her around your little finger, but you know what you're doing, don't you?'

Archer winked. 'And that's what's so lovable about you,' he said. 'You read me like a book.'

'Ah, but only sometimes. What are you up to? Why do we need the house to ourselves?'

'We don't, particularly,' Archer admitted. 'But I think that having as few staff here as possible is a sensible thing. I have this feeling…'

'You and your bloody feelings.'

'I have this notion then, that we are in for a disturbing time and the fewer people who know about it the better.'

'Have another brandy, mate,' Silas laughed. 'Maybe that'll make you talk straight.'

Thomas arrived bearing the weight of several large books and staggered to the table where he dumped them unceremoniously in the centre.

'What's this?' Silas sat back to give him room. 'The butler's guide to etiquette?'

'I couldn't carry that on my own,' Thomas joked, removing his jacket. 'Some of the late viscount's reference books,' he explained. 'From the bottom shelves.'

Only the heaviest tomes were kept on such shelves, otherwise their weight would bow the wood. The late viscount had a penchant for books and had collected several hundred. He had always intended to read them in old age, but his love of hunting and alcohol had put an end to that.

Sitting, Thomas spread out the books.

'You are fuelled by intuition, Archer,' he said. 'I was brought up to think intuitively too, but about cows and calving. However, my dad did encourage in me a sense of logic.' He laid the station master's specifications before them. 'Here is the route of the train,' he said. 'And here are the relative speeds at which it is legally allowed to travel over certain terrains…'

Impressed, Archer listened as Thomas read out the names of stations and the speed the train would travel through them. Silas wrote them down, and Archer watched the pair over the rim of his brandy glass, glowing with pride. Once that information was collated, Thomas dragged the largest book towards himself and opened it. It was an atlas of the country with one county per page, several topographical maps of the land and others detailing specific areas. The centre pages showed a spread of the whole island with major towns and cities clearly marked.

'The slowest points are here,' Thomas said, turning to a map of the capital and pointing. 'Obviously there's the part of the journey before the train picks up speed and we can't discount the possibility that Quill jumped before he left the depot. Having said that, I think it unlikely, else why bother to make the point of being seen boarding a train to get your attention and not just be seen in the street? The next possible opportunity he would have to get off safely wouldn't be until this tunnel where the train enters at… five miles per hour.' He pointed to a town a little way to the north. 'But…' Turning to another page, he showed Archer the place. 'As you can see from the Ordnance Survey, the tunnel is long, and the train picks up speed before leaving it. Even if he risked getting off inside, in the dark, the chances are he would be injured. And again, it's so close to the city, why bother?' He followed the route with one of his slender fingers, and Archer noticed how well he kept his nails. 'The bridges…' He conferred with the railway notes. 'Are all straight, and according to this, there is no need to slow the engine, not on the night train when there is little traffic on the tracks. It reaches full speed here, so that's out of the question…'

He mumbled away to himself as Silas and Archer shared a look. Both sat back and folded their arms, happy to let him do the work.

'No,' Thomas finally said. 'There is no suitable place other than the depot, as we thought, but at least that is now proved.'

'So, we reckon he definitely got off at Barrenmoor?' Silas sought clarification, and Thomas nodded.

'Unless he committed suicide with his luggage, I agree,' he said. He closed the atlas and reached for another hefty book. '"Porter's Guide to the Northern Moors",' he explained, reading the index before finding the page he wanted.

'And what's at Barrenmoor?' Archer leant in to read.

'Not a great deal, it seems.'

Silas reached for the atlas and found the map of the area. He studied it while Thomas and Archer read.

Archer could see nothing which sparked a memory or an idea, and yet he was convinced Quill had gone there for a reason. He shifted his chair to sit closer to Silas and pressed his shoulder against him to see more clearly. Silas held his leg beneath the table, and a tremor ran through the viscount. It was ridiculous to think that he might, out of curiosity, go chasing after a man who had nearly killed his lover, let alone himself, but it was equally ridiculous that he should let the Ripper get away if he had a chance to capture him.

'If only we had something else to go on,' he said. 'I feel like we are looking for clues where there are none.'

'Does the name Barrenmoor mean anything to you?' Thomas asked. 'The locations of his East End murders triggered your suspicions.'

'Barrenmoor?' Archer considered it. 'I can't think of anything. What else is nearby? Arriving at that time of the morning, he either had someone to meet him or somewhere to walk to.'

'Inglestone?' Silas asked, reading out the names of the nearest villages. 'Muchmoor, Wiltington, Saddle... What's that?'

'Saddlebroughton,' Archer read. 'No, nothing occurs to me.'

'Good, I want nothing more to do with saddles. Fecking nightmare.'

'You'll get used to it.'

'Tell you what, Archie,' Silas said. 'As you know, my arse can take some fair hammering but that bloody...'

'Yes, alright,' Thomas interrupted, blushing. 'Shall we stay on the point?'

'Sorry, Tommy.' Silas coughed, and squeezed Archer's leg harder.

They had returned from the railway station and headed straight for a bath and bed, in this case, Archer's, and they had shared both. Silas was as hungry for Archer's body as he was for his lover's, and it had only been Thomas' discreet knocking that had woken them from their post-sex slumber, curled naked together in blissful afterglow.

'And there is nowhere beyond the depot that would allow him to step from the train?' Archer queried.

'In the dark, travelling at speed anywhere is dangerous,' Thomas said. 'But the only place these specifications might allow is the new Invermoor viaduct, and that is even more remote, not to say extremely high. Unlikely.'

'This is hopeless,' Silas sighed. 'We're fishing in the dark and stabbing at ghosts.'

'And several other mixed metaphors,' Archer mumbled under his breath. Louder, he added, 'Let's get away from the table and take a drink. Perhaps that will clear our minds.'

They moved to the armchairs and sat facing the fire. Silas took a whisky and Thomas a glass of soda.

'All we can do for now,' Archer said. 'Is hope that Thomas' new friend comes up with something.'

'Sir,' Thomas said, forgoing Archer's first name to indicate he was talking shop. 'James is our new footman and a stranger to us all. It would be wrong to call him a friend.'

Thomas was right as usual. 'Correct, Tom,' he said. 'And again, we must not let him know what we are about. However, I did notice the way you were with him and if you want to consider him your friend when you are upstairs…' he pointed to the ceiling, 'that's up to you. I trust you to do the right thing.'

'Thank you.'

'And when I say right thing, I also mean what is right for you personally.' He reached over and took Thomas' hand. 'Just because I have Silas,' he said, 'doesn't mean I care about you any less.'

Thinking that could be misconstrued, he did the same to Silas. 'And just because I care about Thomas as my friend', he said, 'doesn't lessen my love for you.'

'Oh, Christ,' Silas said rolling his eyes. 'You read too many bloody books, Archie.'

'You're a cheeky little guttersnipe,' Archer teased.

'Yeah, but you love me.'

A knock on the door made Thomas leap to his feet and scramble for his tailcoat while Archer and Silas moved apart.

'Hold!' Archer shouted, calling, 'Come!' when they were ready.

Mrs Baker stepped into the room to discover Archer and Silas reading, and Thomas in the process of serving brandy.

'Sorry to disturb you, My Lord,' she said. 'A special post has arrived.' She shot Thomas a glare as if it was his fault that she had been called to the front door.

'That *is* late,' Archer said, accepting an envelope from the salver she offered. He dismissed her with thanks and opened it, discovering a picture postcard inside. When the housekeeper was beyond the drawing room, he passed the delivery to Thomas. 'What do you make of that?' he asked.

Thomas read the back of the card but was as dumbfounded as Archer, as was Silas when he took his turn to read the writing.

'It makes no bloody sense,' he said. 'So I'd say it's what we've been waiting for.'

'It's very unorthodox,' Archer agreed, taking it and rereading the message.

'Of course,' said Thomas. 'Murderers tend to be unconventional.'

Thirteen

His head ached, his fingers were sore, and he was tired, but James still had enough energy to tell his mother his news when he returned home just after ten that night. She was at first surprised, and then delighted to hear about his new position. His sister, on the other hand, was less than pleased that he would now be able to pay for furthering her education, but he made her understand how beneficial that would be and told her she would no longer have to share a bedroom, at which point she relented.

He lay in bed that night unable to sleep. Despite his exhaustion, his mind would not allow him to rest, and it tumbled from one concern to the next. How the post office would take his sudden departure, the little he knew of household service, and what to make of Viscount Clearwater were the most pressing matters. The viscount's letter, which he would take to work in the morning, would see to the first, his brief introduction from Tripp reassured him about the second, but the third took more time to restlessly contemplate. The viscount seemed a generous man but one who acted on impulse. Surely there were better trained and more suitable applicants for the post, so why had he chosen James, a man with no experience?

As he thought about that, Tripp's words came back to him. 'Things happened at Clearwater House which would shock the most hardened, righteous man.' He was alluding to Archer's sexuality in coded words so obvious he may as well have written them in a telegram. James needed Tripp's money and was, at first, happy to act as his spy. Now, having met the viscount and experienced his generosity, he was loath to act against him. On top of that was the knowledge that Thomas was keen to return James' affection; unnatural affection which was what Tripp, for his own unexplained reasons, wanted to prove was rife at Clearwater House.

He was in a no-win situation and had to make a choice. Either spy for Tripp and make a lot of quick money, or lose the opportunity by believing in Thomas and giving his loyalty to the viscount. He could think of no safe way to do both and knew he wouldn't sleep until he had decided.

The decision, when it came, was easier than he expected, and once James' mind was made up, there was no shifting it. The candle died at two in the morning. The light was extinguished on his old life, and his future began in darkness.

His mother woke him at his usual time to give him breakfast and insisted he wore his best clothes. She had been awake since before dawn and had packed a suitcase with all the things Thomas had said to bring. There was no tearful goodbye, he would be living less than a mile away and promised to visit during his time off, but still, it was a wrench to leave the only home he had known. As a way of reassuring his mother that he was doing the right thing, he gave her what money he had, saying that he would no longer want for anything.

He realised that he wanted for a lot when he arrived at Clearwater later that morning and looked up at the massive building. In the yard, he counted the attic windows in from the right until he saw the room that would be his, but even the thought of his own bed did little to steady a sudden attack of nerves. The maid led him through to the servants' hall where he was acutely aware of unfamiliar sounds and smells. Pans clattered, and the echo of footsteps that belonged to people he didn't know greeted him as he entered the kitchen. A scrawny woman was bent over a sink, and it took him a moment to realise this was the cook and that she would be preparing his meals from now on.

A severe woman met him in the servants' hall. Her grey hair was tied back as though shocked from her face by his appearance, revealing a fixed scowl and an air of distrust. She told him to stay where he was, and her authority reminded him of his first day at the post office. He had been scared out of his wits and nearly burst into tears when asked his name. Today, he had more confidence, mainly brought about by Tripp's forewarning and the knowledge that somewhere in the house was Thomas.

'Under normal circumstances,' the woman said, 'I would have a say in your appointment.' She looked him up and down. 'But, these are not normal circumstances. I am away at any moment and must leave you in the hands of Mr Payne.'

'I understand, madam,' he said.

'No.' She shook her head. 'It's Mrs Baker. You call no-one madam. Wait there.'

She turned and swept from the room leaving him alone among the lingering smell of toast. He waited as patiently as he could, wondering if he was allowed to sit, and was about to take off his coat to alleviate his nervous sweating when the chestnut-haired maid reappeared. She gave him a brief, sympathetic smile as she passed through the room carrying bed sheets, but was gone in a second.

He waited a minute more, listening to laughter in the kitchen, and let his eyes wander over the dressers. This room was not so much different from his parlour at home, except it was larger and lavishly equipped. And this was only for the servants.

'Who are you?'

He turned at the sound of a thickly accented, deep voice to find the huge, blond groom from the stables filling the doorway, and stepped back more in awe than shock.

The man wore a long, dark grey coat, double-breasted and buttoned, a straight high collar showing beneath, and below, he wore tight trousers tucked into high black boots. He carried a top hat in one huge hand, and James realised he was the coachman, not a lowly groom.

'James Wright,' he said, and stood to attention.

The coachman laughed for no reason and put his hat on the table.

'Where you from?' the man asked.

'South Riverside.'

'What you do?'

'I'm the new footman.'

The man nodded, studied James for a moment and took a step towards him. He was several inches taller and intimidating. The riding crop he carried had something to do with that, but he placed it on the table before offering a hand.

'Andrej Borysko Yakiv Kolisnychenko,' he said, taking James' hand and nearly crushing it as the words rolled exotically from his tongue. 'Fecker. Ukraine.'

Before James had a chance to ask him to explain, Mrs Baker was back carrying a parcel wrapped in brown paper.

'I will be five minutes, Mr Andrej,' she said. 'Sally is on her way. My bags are outside my rooms.'

The coachman said nothing as he headed deeper into the house leaving James alone with the woman in black.

She gave him the parcel and said, 'Come,' before turning on her heels.

He followed, passing another maid coming down the backstairs. Although busy with a suitcase she eyed him with interest.

'Can I help you with those, Miss?' he asked, thinking it a good way to break the ice.

'No,' the housekeeper ordered, and the maid, smiling apologetically, struggled past.

He was led to the same room where Thomas had interviewed him, and Mrs Baker knocked before entering.

'Change in here,' she said. 'Mr Payne will be with you shortly. Touch nothing. Goodbye.'

With that, he was left alone.

Yesterday, he had been too intent on Thomas to notice the room in detail, and his nervousness increased as he took in the sight of silver and pewter, the arrays of glasses and a pile of ledgers on the desk. A stone sink was set in a wooden counter beneath a barred window which looked onto a brick wall, and two clocks ticked on the mantlepiece, both reading the same time to the second. The room was a mix of practicality and studiousness, with cleaning materials on one shelf and a dictionary and reading books on another.

He unwrapped the parcel carefully but quickly — as everything so far had suggested things happened swiftly but efficiently below stairs — and took out what could only be his uniform. It consisted of a double-breasted tailcoat, a waistcoat of dark green shot through and shimmering with crimson, black trousers and a small bow tie. At least, he assumed that was what it was; it was little more than a length of silk, also dark green and an odd shape. Hoping that no-one came in, he stripped to his underclothes and was wondering what to do about a shirt when the door flew open, and Thomas appeared.

'Good Lord!' he exclaimed when he saw James topless and wearing only long johns and socks.

'Good morning, Sir,' James said, standing to attention and saluting as was the way at the post office.

Thomas' dazzling eyes widened, and he kicked the door shut with a foot.

'No,' he said. 'Mr Payne.'

'Sorry.'

'My apologies.'

'What for?'

'You should say, My apologies, not Sorry. And don't salute. His Lordship hates it, and you don't do it unless you are a military man, which I know you are not.'

'Right-oh.'

'Heavens no,' Thomas said, horrified. 'We are not Americans. As you wish, Very well, Of course. Anything but right-oh.'

'Very good, Mr Payne.'

'Better.'

Thomas' face, until then wrinkled in thought, relaxed and his eyes, which had been hovering at James' groin as if unable to look anywhere else, found his face. Thrilling though it was to be semi-naked in front of the man he desired, James was embarrassed that Thomas had stared. He wished he had more for the man to admire.

'Try on your uniform,' Thomas said.

'Do I wear my own shirt, Mr Payne?'

'Damn, did they not send them? Do you have a white one?'

'Yes.'

'Then wear that for now if it can take a collar. Yours will arrive in due course.'

Thomas busied himself at a cupboard while James put on the trousers and found his best shirt from his suitcase. He was about to ask about a collar when Thomas handed him one and two mother of pearl studs.

'Blimey!' James exclaimed. He had never been given jewellery before. 'My shoes?' he asked, but Thomas held a pair in his hands.

'Mrs Baker said these should fit you,' he said. 'If not, bear with me, and I will send for some to arrive with your other livery.'

'There's more?'

Thomas smiled and perched himself on the table, his arms folded, admiring James as he dressed.

'You have much to learn, James,' he said. 'And I shall enjoy teaching you. It will take time, but for now, the important thing to remember is that you only do what I tell you. If in doubt, ask me, but not in front of His Lordship or his guests. Understood?'

'Yes, Mr Payne.'

'You will have this livery for the mornings, another for lunch and afternoons and a more formal one for evening dinners and other occasions. Lady Marshall has yet to design a royal livery for times when you might be required to travel with His Lordship to state occasions, but he has no plans in that respect, and it will come in time. All of them will be kept immaculate every minute of the day. By you, that is. Aprons and overalls are provided for when you are washing the plates, sweeping the hall and cleaning the silver, and there are gloves for the glass work and serving. You'll get the rhythm of it.'

'I hope so.'

'Nervous?'

'Like the first day at school.'

'Here.'

James was struggling with the bow tie until Thomas, having pushed himself from the table, came to him and took it. He turned James to face a mirror and showed him how to tie the material, standing behind with his arms over James' shoulders. The intimacy of the position was thrilling and, James hoped not lost on Thomas. Remembering their conversation and the dual role they had agreed to play, the new footman behaved and said nothing of what was in his heart. He wanted to thank the man as much as he wanted to take his hands and hold him, but he couldn't, not here. Where he had to learn his duties and appropriate behaviour, he also had to learn to control his feelings. It wouldn't be easy, and when Thomas turned him again, it was all he could do not to kiss the man.

With the waistcoat and jacket, both of which fitted perfectly, and the polished shoes, which did not, he was complete.

'Now,' Thomas said, returning to his desk and sitting. 'His

Lordship won't expect you to be perfect in your duties, not today, but come tomorrow or the day after, you are expected to be adept, so watch and learn. Ask privately when necessary and try not to be nervous. I am here for you, James, as you know, and I mean that on… on both floors, shall we say.'

His words were reassuring.

'The house runs slightly differently to Larkspur where there is a larger staff. I'm expected to valet His Lordship, as you may be. The late viscount's man retired after the master died, and a new one has not yet been appointed as there's no need. So, we have dual roles, but there's no cause for panic. For now, I have seen to breakfast. 'We have a small dinner party this evening, and you'll be expected to serve. Meanwhile, His Lordship is at work in his study and will ring when he needs us. I'll tell him you are here as he is anxious to ask how you got on yesterday. As am I.'

'Oh, well, I…'

'Not yet.' Thomas interrupted. 'One thing at a time. For now, I will answer the bells, and you will follow me everywhere, understood?'

James nodded.

'Good. First, however, you should take your things to your room. I've made up the bed and aired it. From now on, you will see to that yourself and to your own laundry changes, though Lucy will do your washing. Any questions?'

'Hundreds.'

'Of course, and they will be answered.' Thomas rubbed his hands together while examining James' livery and, it seemed, liking what he saw. 'For now, I have one to ask of you.'

Thomas locked the door, an action which increased James' heart rate, and returned to stand facing him.

'This is the last time such a thing will happen down here,' the butler said. 'Tell me, James, our discussion yesterday, upstairs, do you still feel the same?'

James knew what he meant. 'If it's possible,' he said, unable to keep the grin from his lips. 'More so today than I did then.'

'In which case…' Thomas took a step closer. 'This is definitely the last time this will happen here, and if you tell anyone, you will be fired.'

He took James' head in one hand and drew him to his lips. James lost himself in the kiss, wishing it didn't have to end, and by the time they did break apart, breathless and happy, his nervousness had drained away.

'Thank you,' he whispered.

'What for?' Thomas was still holding him, and if he didn't let go soon, James wouldn't be able to hide his swelling enthusiasm.

'Everything,' he said, shrugging. 'Just everything.'

'I know you won't let me down.' Thomas released him. 'But, more importantly, I know you won't betray the trust His Lordship has placed in you. Come along.'

They left the butler's pantry and made for the backstairs with the word 'trust' ringing loudly in James' ears and guilt gnawing at his heart.

The next two hours passed in a blur as Thomas showed him how to lay the dining room table and set the sideboard for lunch.

'Don't be surprised if His Lordship changes his mind about eating,' Thomas said, measuring the distance of the wine glasses from the table edge. 'And don't take it to heart if you spend an hour preparing the dining table only to be asked to deliver a tray to his rooms.'

Satisfied with the table, he led James into the hall to show him the correct way to answer the door, explaining how the bell system worked and how they would alternate the door answering. James had noticed the bells earlier and seen that each one had beneath it the title of the room to which it corresponded.

'Arrive at the door,' Thomas said, taking him to the drawing room. 'Check your livery and your composure before entering. It's only necessary to knock if the doors are closed, in which case you wait to be called. If they are open, like now...' He walked into the room. 'Stand here and wait to be addressed. You can knock if the matter is urgent. Got that?'

'I hope so.'

At that moment, the double doors to the viscount's study opened, and a man appeared. When James had seen him yesterday, the man, younger than him, smartly dressed and boyishly handsome, had been swaying in the saddle of a horse led by the blond coachman. He had appeared unconfident, but today, he strode with authority.

Thomas straightened his back and James copied.

'This must be Jimmy, right?' the man said, his familiarity taking James by surprise. He had an Irish accent and, as he drew near, James was able to see his eyes were a deep blue. The eyebrows were jet black and slanted towards his temples giving him a look of severe concentration.

'James,' Thomas corrected.

The youth appraised James with his hands on his hips and his head to one side. The inspection over, he nodded.

'Very smart,' he said. He slapped James gently on his shoulder as he passed by. 'I'll be back in a minute, Payne. His Lordship wants you.' He continued into the hall where James heard his shoes squeak on the tiles.

'Mr Hawkins,' Thomas whispered. 'His Lordship's secretary. You call him Mr Hawkins first time and Sir thereafter. We'll go into the study now. Remember, Your Lordship, and then Sir. Come.'

Thomas walked ahead, and James tried to copy the way he glided across the carpet, but was unable. He'd spent most of his working life tramping pavements and dodging traffic, and here he was treading on rugs in the most extravagant room he could imagine. Keeping his hands by his sides and his head erect took all his concentration, and he wondered if he would ever be as calmly skilled and confident as Thomas. He admired his wide shoulders and broad back, his sculptured features and perfect hair, but mostly, he marvelled at his calm assurance.

There was no time to think on the matter. Arriving at the study, Thomas entered completely at ease while James waited nervously on the threshold.

The viscount stood at a large table between the two tall windows, his head down over an atlas. He was in his shirtsleeves, and his waistcoat hung open.

'You wanted to see me, My Lord?' Thomas asked, coming to a stop in the centre of the room.

James watched the butler, but from the corner of his eye, saw the viscount glance over his shoulder.

'Yes, Payne,' he said, returning immediately to his book. 'Did Mrs Baker get off alright?'

'She is leaving shortly, Sir. Her and Sally both.'

'Good, good.' The viscount was preoccupied. 'And James?'

Thomas gave a polite cough with enough meaning to draw the man from his work, and, behind his back, signalled James to approach. He took a few paces into the room and waited.

The viscount turned, a pen in one hand and a sheet of paper in the other. He seemed surprised to see James, but his expression soon changed.

'Well, I say.' A charming smile lit his face. 'You cut a fine figure. Don't you think so, Payne?'

'I do.'

'Come, stand nearer the window,' the viscount said. It wasn't an order and yet there was no way to refuse.

Thomas nodded permission, and James approached the table. Unsure where he should look, he kept his eyes on the atlas.

'Lady Marshall certainly has a flair for colour.' The viscount appraised James in much the same way as Mr Hawkins had done.

'The other uniforms will be here by tomorrow,' Thomas said. 'But we had to improvise with the shirt.'

'How are you, James?' The viscount offered his hand. 'Welcome to Clearwater. I hope you will be happy here.'

James didn't move.

'If His Lordship offers his hand,' Thomas said. 'You may take it.'

James did, and the handshake was firm but brief. It gave him an excuse to look the man in the eye, and he was calmed by the expression returned.

'How did you get on?' the viscount asked. 'Did you have any luck?'

Hesitating in his reply, James again looked at Thomas for permission to speak. Lord Clearwater caught the moment, and the next thing James knew, had slapped a hand on his shoulder and was leading him towards the fireplace at the far end of the room.

'No need to be nervous, James,' he said as if they were friends. 'I know this is not what you are used to, so don't worry about getting anything wrong. Thomas... Mr Payne, speaks highly of you after only knowing you a few days, and I intend to learn why.' He stopped and again stood back to look James over. 'Apologies for inspecting you as though you were a lot at auction,' he said, grinning. 'Old habit from navy days. I want you to feel relaxed in your duties and around me. Thomas has explained my most important house rule, I hope?'

Thomas coughed, this time with mild annoyance.

'Sorry. Mr Payne.' The viscount emphasised the name. 'Actually, would you do me a favour, Payne, and fetch my diary? I left it in my sitting room.'

Thomas nodded once and left.

'Maybe you will feel more talkative if we have a moment alone,' the viscount smiled knowingly.

James was too nervous to talk. The idea of becoming a footman in a grand house had excited him up until the moment he walked into this room. Now it was frighteningly real. Yesterday, he was Jimmy Wright the messenger. Today he was James the footman, a completely different person in an unfamiliar role.

'I'm... That is...' The words didn't come, and he faltered.

Far from being angry as James expected anyone to be with his ineptitude, the viscount fell into an armchair, saying, 'I hate this as much as you do.'

'I'm sorry?' He regretted it immediately, he should have said something else but couldn't for the life of him remember what.

'This standing on ceremony business,' the viscount explained. 'But it must be done. James, please, remember the golden rule of Clearwater House, and you shall be fine.'

James had to say something and opened his mouth in the hope that the right words came out, but a voice at the door interrupted him.

'Ah, leave him be, Archie.' Mr Hawkins was back and lounging against the doorjamb. 'I can see he's trustworthy.' He pushed himself upright and sauntered to the couch. 'The first rule in this man's life, Jimmy, is honesty.' He winked.

'Quite right. So, James. Tell me, honestly, how did you get on yesterday?'

He was back on familiar ground talking about his job — his previous job, he reminded himself — and this time, the words flowed.

'I ran into some problems,' he said, forgetting to call the man Sir or My Lord or whatever. 'The messages had been delivered to Mount Pleasant in the usual Thursday roundup but had not been collated. I had to go through each office's batches day by day, but at least they were in alphabetical order. It took me a few hours.'

'Did you get in trouble from the post office?' the viscount asked, concerned. 'Anyone ask questions?'

'No, Sir.' He was pleased with the way he had managed the task. 'I explained my absence to Mr Hicks, my old boss, this morning, and your letter really helped. Thank you for that.'

The viscount waved it away.

'And no questions were asked at the records office,' James continued. 'I came away with one message. I have it in my suitcase if you want to see it. It's a copy, of course, I was unable to take the original, but it was the only one sent by Doctor Quill.'

The viscount sat with his elbows on his knees and his hands on his cheeks, staring intently at James.

'He sent just one?' he queried, his voice faint. He glanced at Mr Hawkins before giving James his attention. 'Do you remember what it says? When was it sent and to whom?'

'If I may, Your... Sir. I would rather fetch it, so you can read it word for word.'

'Fly like the wind,' Mr Hawkins laughed.

'Yes, alright, Silas.' The viscount nodded enthusiastically to James. 'Would you, please?'

James remembered enough to bow before leaving. He crossed the drawing room to the hall and started on the stairs two at a time only to meet Thomas coming down.

'What the hell...? No, James, up the backstairs. What are you doing?'

'His mastership wants to see the message I found,' James explained, breathless.

Luckily, Thomas burst out laughing. 'Just this once then,' he said. 'Be quick and come back down the backstairs. You only use these if attending the first floor and only then if you must. And for God's sake, get the word mastership out of your head, whatever it is. Hurry.'

James ran to the next floor and only then realised that the main stairs went no higher. He opened a door on the landing thinking it led to the backstairs but instead found a cupboard full of hat boxes. A second door led to a large green-papered bedroom where clothes were heaped on every chair in disorder, and another to a neatly ordered sitting room. He remembered the door at the end of the passage and took the stairs two at a time. Beneath the eaves, he found his room, unearthed the message from his case and ran back the way he had come. This time, he passed the first floor looking for a way into the hall only to find himself outside the butler's pantry in the basement. He stumbled from there, his heart racing and, in a panic, walked into a boot room where the blond coachman appeared to be wrestling with something in the corner. The sight drew James up short.

'Sorry,' he flustered.

Mr Andrej leapt away from whatever he was doing as if caught in the act of robbery and James realised that he had been canoodling with the maid. She, flaming red in the face and adjusting her hair, scarpered, leaving the massive blond as surprised as the footman.

'I'm sorry, Sir,' James said, not knowing which way to turn. 'I was on an errand.'

'Hey!' The man took two strides and was in James' face before he could flee. 'You say nothing, or I kill you.'

If the size of the man wasn't threat enough, the tone was unmistakable, and the weight of the hand that crushed James' arm left no room for doubt. James was by no means weedy, but Andrej could have broken his neck with a twitch of his fingers.

'No,' he stammered. 'I won't tell anyone. Honest.'

'Mr Andrej?' The woman in black was calling his from the corridor, but the coachman took no notice.

James was drilled by a pair of fierce blue eyes and frozen under the man's glare until the face suddenly cracked into a laugh. The force of it was enough to move James' hair from his brow.

'You good man,' the coachman announced and tapped James' cheek. It was more like a slap, but with the laugh and the change of expression, it was not meant as one. 'You shut mouth, we be friends. Where you go?'

'Er, the study?'

Before he knew what was happening, the coachman was carting him by the elbow to the stairs. 'Up, green door,' he said. 'You James? Da?'

'James, da… What?'

'Fecker. Silence or death.'

With that cryptic remark, James was set free.

Back in the hall, he recalled Thomas' advice and paused to catch his breath, straightening his uniform before composing himself and continuing as sedately as his weak legs would allow. The study doors were open, and there were voices within. Was he meant to wait, knock, or do both?

He decided to do both, but as he raised his hand, Thomas waved him in. The viscount and Mr Hawkins stood at the table backed by daylight, and Thomas, on the other side of the desk, held a large diary open in his hands like a minister reading from a psalter.

'There you are,' the viscount said, all hint of good humour gone from his voice. 'James, please, tell me this message was addressed to someone in Yorkshire.'

James was confused. 'No, Sir,' he said, unfolding and offering the paper. 'Sorry. It was sent express delivery at the highest charge, so utmost urgency.'

'That's a blessing. Read it. Quickly, man!'

Thomas nodded permission, and trembling, James read the message.

'Birthday gift planned. Stop. Be assured. Stop. Matter in hand. Stop. Restoration awaits. Stop. BQ.'

In the silence that followed, three men stared at James is if he was mad.

'The receipt confirmed that BQ stood for Benjamin Quill,' he said, hoping it meant something to someone. 'Oh, and it was sent on Monday morning from the Greychurch office.'

'Makes sense,' the Irishman said. 'Does that mean anything to you, Archie?'

The viscount's stare remained on James, and he swallowed. Unless James was mistaken, the viscount was suddenly as nervous as his new footman.

'And the delivery address?' he asked, his voice wavering.

James read the unfamiliar words to himself twice before speaking them aloud.

'The Rotterdam Institute, Dordrecht, Sir,' he said. 'And it was addressed recipient only, a Mr Crispin Riddington.'

Fourteen

The viscount was the first to break the silence, but it wasn't with his voice. It was with the sound of his fists slamming onto the table top accompanied by an angry growl. The force of his reaction shocked James, but Thomas discreetly held up his hand for calm, instructing James to remain where he was.

Lord Clearwater took a long, deep breath and straightened his waistcoat. Turning to James, he said, 'My apologies, James. Gentlemen.'

'If I may, My Lord.' Unfazed, Thomas came around the desk. 'Lunch will be served presently. Perhaps James and I should attend to it.'

The viscount nodded. Thomas took the message from James and handed it to Mr Hawkins before leaving.

Back in the drawing room, he closed the study doors, and James followed him to the hall. He knew better than to ask what the outburst was about and remained silent until Thomas spoke.

'Take no notice,' he said. 'Some bad news is all. Now then. Your first lunch.'

It was an easy introduction to his serving duties, there being only the viscount and his secretary at the table. Neither said very much, but when they did speak, it was about general matters concerning the viscount's charitable work and fascinating though it sounded, James tried not to listen. Instead, he concentrated on Thomas, watching his every move and copying him. Thomas served His Lordship, and James served Mr Hawkins "from the left and with the left" in silence. The atmosphere was strained to say the least, and James gained the impression that the stilted conversation about buildings and facilities, running water and staffing was more for his benefit, as if the pair had something else they wanted to discuss, but couldn't. The telegram was no doubt to blame and had a deeper meaning beneath its garbled words. James had been the one to discover it. He had unearthed the mystery they wanted to discuss, and yet he was excluded.

During the afternoon, Thomas formally introduced him to the cook and Lucy the maid before showing him his post-lunch duties which were mainly washing the plates and putting them away. James listened intently to a lesson in cleaning silver and glassware and, by the time the simple two-person lunch was finally dealt with, his feet were aching, and his eyes were sore.

'We can now sit down and have a cup of tea,' Thomas announced, and James was surprised to see him make it himself.

'You want me to do that?' he offered, but Thomas declined.

'When we go to Larkspur,' he said, 'we have hall boys and all-maids to do his kind of thing, but here with a small staff, we're expected to pitch in.'

'As long as you don't ask me to cook,' James joked, but Thomas, like his master, was not in the mood for pleasantries. 'Is everything alright?' he asked. He wasn't sure how informal he could be. They weren't above stairs, but they weren't in their own apartment either.

'Aye, James,' Thomas said. 'Nothing for you to worry about.'

'I did search every single record,' James said. 'I was there until gone nine, but that really was all I found.'

'I'm sure it was.'

Thomas sat at the head of the table and, at four o'clock after they had eaten, the coachman joined them. He gave Thomas a simple nod as he entered, but lingered longer over James, staring at him until James felt uncomfortable.

'Did you meet Mr Andrej?' Thomas asked, passing the man a cup and saucer as he sat. 'Andrej is from the Ukraine,' Thomas explained.

James wasn't sure where that was and said so.

Thomas' reply, 'Russia,' brought a scoff of derision from Mr Andrej. Apparently he wasn't keen on being called Russian, and James slipped that nugget of information onto the long list of other things to remember.

'Natural born horseman,' Thomas said. 'Do you ride, James?'

'I can,' James admitted. 'But I am out of practice. I haven't had much time.'

'You come riding with me,' Andrej said as if James had no say in the matter. 'Banyak is shit.'

James looked at Thomas for a translation.

'Banyak is Fecker's nickname for Mr Hawkins,' he said.

It didn't help. 'And Fecker is...?'

'Sorry.' Thomas tutted. 'My mind is elsewhere. Fecker is Andrej's nickname.'

'And what's yours?'

'Bolshoydick,' Andrej said, causing Thomas to splutter on his tea.

'Do you mind!'

James wasn't sure whether to laugh as Fecker was doing, or pretend he hadn't heard.

'Big penis,' the Ukrainian said.

Thomas leant to James. 'He's a fine one to talk,' he said, raising an eyebrow and a smile. 'But this conversation never happened.'

He collected a newspaper from the sideboard.

'No more dead?' Fecker asked.

Thomas shook his head. 'Thank God.'

'Ripper murders?' James assumed.

'Ghastly business.' Thomas glanced at Fecker who agreed with him, but said nothing. 'Hopefully now at an end.' He changed the subject. 'Oh! I see someone has found a way to make pictures move.' He showed the article to James. 'A man in Leeds has discovered a way to put images together like a zoetrope, but project them, so they appear to have motion. Whatever next?'

The conversation continued away from nicknames and murders until Thomas announced that it was time to prepare for the evening.

'I did warn you that the hours were long,' he said. 'How are you doing?'

'I'm fine, Mr Payne. Didn't sleep much last night, and my head's not big enough to hold all the information, but I think I am doing okay alright.'

'You are doing splendidly,' Thomas said. 'You're what me old fader would call a spry lierner and not unhandy.'

'Is that a good thing?'

'Aye, you be a good'un.' Thomas grinned. 'I'm from Kent, but I don't get to use my dialect much. Being in service is all about playing a role,' he explained. 'You speak well for a city boy.'

'I been playing a role since I joined the post office,' James said. 'We all got a-keep ourselves as what folks expect to see.'

'Then I am even more impressed. Have another progger afore we set about our doings.'

'Another cup of tea before we get to work?'

'Aye, nipper, that be it.'

James couldn't help smiling. Every time Thomas switched his voice, he became more intriguing, and his friendliness set James' heart turning. Whatever it was that attracted him to the man, it was more than his looks, and if Fecker was to be believed and from what he remembered, what he had in his trousers.

The rest of the afternoon was spent preparing for dinner. The viscount was expecting two guests at seven-thirty for eight. James would not be free of his duties until much later, but the cook prepared an early supper for him and Thomas which helped to refuel his energy. His other uniforms arrived earlier than expected, and, up in his room, he was able to change his clothes including his shirt and shoes. Everything fitted perfectly, and he presented himself to Thomas in the servants' hall, having found it without getting lost, where he was paid one compliment after another until his head was swelling.

'Now then,' Thomas said, after he had inspected James' tails and brushed a blond hair from his lapel. 'Come with me to the dining room, and I'll run through the order with you.'

James hadn't seen the viscount all afternoon, and the study doors had remained closed. They still were when Thomas took him into the drawing room and showed him how to make up and light the fire, trim the lamps and brush the furniture.

'His Lordship works hard,' James said, as he helped Thomas lay the dining table. 'His secretary must be invaluable.'

'Mr Hawkins is as new in his post as I am in mine,' Thomas admitted. 'But what goes on in the study, as elsewhere, is no concern of ours.'

'Like that business with the telegram?'

'Exactly.'

'But it's been on your mind, hasn't it?'

Thomas looked up from the cutlery he was polishing for the

second time. 'Why do you say that?'

'Because you're not as relaxed as you were when we met in the pub.'

'You can hardly compare the two locations.' He swept his hand from the chandelier to the oil paintings.

'Yeah, I get that,' James said. 'But I can't help noticing these things, and if you want me to obey the first rule of Clearwater, I've got to say I'm concerned about you.'

Thomas looked from the doors to the drawing room. There was no-one in sight. 'James,' he said. 'I know this is new to you and I know our... relationship is unusual in all respects, but I must insist you keep personal talk to our rooms.'

'Sorry,' James said, frowning. They weren't being overheard, but he lowered his voice just in case. 'You know what the hardest part of today has been? Being so close to you and not being able to touch you.'

Thomas stiffened. 'Not down here, James, please.'

'Just being honest, Mr Payne.'

'And thank you for that. If it helps focus your attention, I feel the same way, but as I said earlier, we have our above-stairs roles.'

'I just want to tell someone my news, how I feel, how excited I...'

'You can't,' Thomas emphasised. 'None of us can. Tonight, we must be butler and footman.'

'All night?' James asked, insinuating.

'Maybe not all night,' Thomas replied with the faintest hint of a smile. 'We shall see. But definitely not while on duty.'

'Just after reassurance,' James said.

'And you have it. Later. But now...' Thomas checked his pocket watch. 'Now I must attend to the wine. You should wait downstairs for the bell and if I am in the cellar, answer the door.'

'On my own?'

'I can ask Lucy if you're nervous.'

'No, I'll be fine.'

'We're expecting the Viscountess Delamere,' Thomas said as they left the dining room. 'You open the door, bow your head, take her coat, stole, wrap or whatever she offers you, and hang or place them on the stand. With Lady Marshall, it's best to be prepared for anything, as it often is with His Lordship. She is his godmother, by

140

the way. We are also expecting a doctor who works in the East End, Doctor Markland. He and Mr Hawkins will be your responsibility at dinner. I will serve His Lordship and Lady Marshall. I suggest you watch and copy me, but only after I have served. It's a question of status.'

'I see. And what do I do with them when they get here?'

'Well, you don't leave them standing in the hall, that's for sure.' Thomas walked him through the procedure of announcing callers before they headed downstairs to continue the preparations.

As seven-thirty approached, James stood watching the bells, part of him hoping Thomas would reappear and half of him hoping he didn't. He was keen to show his ability and, nervous though he was, he was sure he could manage. The front-door bell tinkled at exactly half-past and, alone, he left to answer it.

The hall echoed with the sound of the clock which had just announced the time. It would chime many more times before his duties ended.

Praying he could stay awake and alert, he checked his uniform and opened the front door.

He knew of, but had never met the Viscountess Delamere. She was one of the few women who had been given a title in her own right, and the person he found on the step was not what he was expecting. She wore a fashionable, hooded coat that fitted tightly at the waist but flared to the hem in the Gothic fashion, its buttons a darker red than the velvet material. The hood was up, and at first, James thought it was jewelled, but then he realised it was sparkling with droplets of rain.

'Good lord,' Her Ladyship said, sweeping the hood from her head to reveal real jewels in a narrow headpiece. 'You're a handsome one. What's your name?'

'James,' he said, quickly adding, 'Your Ladyship.' He stood back to allow her to enter.

'Where's Tripp?' She was in the hall and had taken off her cloak before James had a chance to assist.

'Mr Tripp has been replaced by Thomas, er, Mr Payne Your...' Was it Ma'am or Your Ladyship?

'Ma'am,' she said as if reading his mind. 'New?'

'Yes, Ma'am. Shall I take your coat, stole, wrap or whatever?'

She looked at him in amused shock, before saying, 'It's a whatever. I'll do it.' She marched to the stand to hang it, leaving James redundant. 'What happened to the tortoise?'

Was it, I beg your pardon, or I'm sorry? 'I haven't yet seen one,' he said.

The woman laughed and spun to face him. Her dress was startling. Also crimson, it reached the floor, pinched above her narrow hips and blossomed at her shoulders in silk ruffles. It was cut low enough to show off several rows of diamonds at her neck, but not so low as to reveal cleavage, and was trimmed in a material that caught the chandelier's light, making every thread sparkle.

'I meant Tripp, James,' she said.

The use of his Christian name by a titled lady came as a pleasant shock, but the talk of Tripp reminded him of his dishonesty. 'I'm not sure, Ma'am,' he said, swallowing.

'Ah, Dolly!' The viscount appeared in the drawing-room doorway. 'Put James down and come in. Payne is bringing absinthe.'

'Oh no,' Her Ladyship complained, sweeping across the hall like an elegant statue on unseen, well-oiled wheels. 'I've done with that filth. Tripp is no more, I understand?'

'Still living, but not with us,' the viscount said. 'I shall explain all. How are you? Thank you, James.'

They disappeared into the drawing room leaving James wondering what he should do next. He didn't have long to decide as he heard a carriage pulling away and footsteps approaching the front door. He opened it to a dark-haired man in a three-quarter length coat and a top hat. The guest was watching the street as he reached for the bell-pull, but turned to reveal a serious face, the centrepiece of which was a bushy moustache in the fashion of the young well-to-do. James put him in his thirties.

'Doctor Markland,' the man said, lowering his hand. 'I am expected.'

'Good evening, Sir,' James bowed his head, something which he'd forgotten to do to Lady Marshall.

He stood back, and this time was allowed to take the offered hat and coat which he hung before inviting the man to follow him to the drawing room. There, he knocked once and announced, 'Doctor Markland.'

'Thank you, James,' the viscount beamed, as he approached. 'Ask Payne to join us would you?'

There was no sign of the viscount's earlier black mood, and his cheerfulness was reassuring.

'Of course, My Lord,' James said, congratulating himself on his correctness as he left.

'And there's no need to knock if the doors are open,' the viscount called after him, slightly deflating his ego.

He found Thomas on the backstairs carrying several bottles of wine. 'How did you get on?' he asked.

'I think I did alright. They're in the drawing room, and His Lordship wants you.'

'Thanks, and well done. Go and wait downstairs.'

James waited nervously in the kitchen with the cook. She, like Fecker, was someone who said little, but she did explain each dish and told him how to serve it. Accepting he was new to service, she asked no questions and spoke clearly though rather sharply. She was protective of her creations and, he sensed, protective of him. That might have been because she wanted him to do justice to her cooking, but it left him with the sense that he had another ally.

At five to eight, Lucy left to ring the first dinner gong, and Mrs Flintwich said, 'That's your time to go up. Good luck.'

As it turned out, James didn't need luck. He followed Thomas' every instruction and movement, remembering to clear plates with both hands and from the left. He didn't drop anything and when not attending to the table, kept his eyes on the wall or, more enjoyably, on the butler.

'Your new man seems to know what he's doing,' Lady Marshall said, as she examined the soup Thomas had carefully ladled into her bowl. 'Both of them.'

'Thank you,' the viscount said. 'This is James' first day, so we must be gentle with him.'

'May I ask, James, how you came to be in service?'

The question came from the doctor. James hadn't realised he was allowed to speak to the guests, but a quick nod from Thomas told him he could reply.

'By the good grace of His Lordship,' he said. He wasn't sure if that was correct, but it sounded like the right thing to say.

'On Payne's recommendation,' the viscount clarified. 'And you know how much I value his opinion.'

'But I believe you were a messenger?' This came from Lady Marshall.

'That is correct, Ma'am. Until only yesterday.'

'They have something of a reputation,' the doctor said. 'I mean no disrespect to the footman, but we hear stories.'

James said nothing.

'I have always found them flighty,' her ladyship commented. 'And I have never met one as handsome as James.'

'Behave, Dolly,' the viscount chided. 'Thank you, James.'

That was James' cue to return to his place, the soup having been served, and he stood with his hands behind his back, his chin raised.

The conversation turned to the meal, but after the first course, shifted to a discussion of Lord Clearwater's charity. James couldn't help but listen and made sure he didn't react when they spoke about renters and men who prostituted themselves to other men for money. He knew the score. Several of his ex-colleagues made money from doing just that, but privately in gentlemen's homes. He was glad he had refused Lovemount's offer to become involved. The subject didn't upset Lady Marshall. In fact, she approached it with gusto, apparently as keen as the others to do something for those in the East End who had no other option but prostitution. Thomas didn't react to the discussion either, keeping his gaze on the wall and occasionally checking the table, ready to attend when His Lordship called him.

'And what's your take on it, Mr Hawkins?' the doctor asked. 'I believe you have a working knowledge of the matter.'

'Perhaps that's a discussion for later,' the viscount suggested, tipping his head to indicate James.

'My apologies.'

'I don't mind, Doctor,' Mr Hawkins put in. 'A man can't help his past, and I reckon we can trust James.'

'Can we trust you?' Her ladyship looked up from her fish, her grey eyes narrowing.

With what? Was what James wanted to ask, but instead, he said,

'Certainly, Ma'am,' and received a nod of approval from Thomas.

'Yes,' Mr Hawkins continued. 'I used to do that, Doctor, up until a while ago. But His Lordship rescued me.'

'Oh, please, Silas,' the viscount laughed. 'You flatter me.'

'Much as your butler rescued you from the clutches of Saint Mary's,' the doctor said.

'Yes. How did you end up in that place?' That was Lady Marshall. 'You never did give me the details.'

'And it's best that I don't,' His Lordship replied. 'But you are correct, Markland. Thomas, and Silas both had my back when the crunch came, as did you. On which note, remind me after dinner to discuss the hospital's needs. I know you're moving over to the Cheap Street hostel — we must find a better name — but I promised to write to Lady Clearwater with my first-hand experiences of St Mary's, and I fear I've quite forgotten.'

'One should never forget one's mother,' Her Ladyship said. 'The poor creatures are the ones who bore us into this life and continue to do so until we bear them to their graves.'

'I shall, Your Lordship,' the doctor said, having smiled thinly but politely at Her Ladyship's observation. 'And please, call me Philip, if you will.'

'I would be honoured,' the viscount said.

'The honour is all mine.'

'Now you are flattering me, Philip.'

'It is no less than your philanthropy demands.'

'Oh, for heaven's sake!' Lady Marshall threw back her head and laughed so loudly, James thought he saw the drops of the chandelier tremble. 'You boys,' she said, recovering. 'It's like some kind of cockfight preening ritual. Can we just accept that you two should clearly be friends, that we all have the good of the renters in common, and that James has undoubtedly heard worse than four people talking about what men are forced to do with their penises.'

The viscount choked on a potato, and James fought to suppress a nervous laugh. It didn't help that Mr Hawkins winked at him.

'Dolly!'

'Oh, come on, Archie. We're all men here,' she continued. 'Not physiologically perhaps, Markland, but underneath I have equal mettle. Silas, what exactly did you have to do to earn your shillings?'

145

'Really, Dolly. Must you?' The viscount's eyes were wide.

'Yes. How else will the doctor know what we may confront in our mission?'

'I have been researching, and am happy to tell your ladyship without the need to embarrass Mr Hawkins,' the doctor said.

'You can't embarrass him,' Lady Marshall scoffed. 'Tell me I am wrong, Silas.'

'No, Your Ladyship,' Silas smiled. 'You're right there.'

'Except she isn't.' The viscount addressed his godmother. 'Dolly, I am metaphorically kicking you under the table.'

'Ineffectually.' She poked out her tongue at him.

'I must attend to those stitches, Mr Hawkins,' the doctor said, in an attempt to change the subject. 'It looks like you have healed quickly.'

'All coming along nicely, Doctor,' Silas said. 'Thank you.'

'Maybe we could find somewhere private after dinner,' Markland said to him, with a brief nod towards the viscountess. 'It's a simple procedure, but not to everyone's taste.'

'I have seen far worse.' Her Ladyship said. 'But tell me, Markland, are you of an *achillean* persuasion?'

The question, which came out of the blue, shocked the doctor, caused the viscount to draw in a sharp breath, and turned James' blood cold with fear.

'I beg your pardon?' the doctor spluttered.

'Well, everyone else around this table prefers men, with the exception, perhaps, of the footman.'

Lady Marshall raised her eyes to him. James could feel them, but his own fixed on Thomas who remained static.

All other eyes were on the doctor. He flushed a shade of red to match the wine, knowing the conversation was not going to continue until he answered.

'You may speak freely and safely in Clearwater,' the viscount assured him. 'But there is no need to answer such an impertinent question.'

The doctor put down his knife and fork and cleared his throat. 'Your Lordship,' he said. 'We are aware of the consequences that may befall a man making such an admission, hence my reticence. I have treated you professionally and been invited to dine as an acquaintance. I mean no disrespect when I say that I am not yet honoured enough to be considered a friend of such an intimate nature that, despite your generous outlook...'

'Here we go again,' Lady Marshall tutted. 'If it helps you break through the barrier of conventionality, Doctor, you are in one of the few houses in this metropolis where walls have no ears. Silas has decreed that we can trust the new footman, and I know we can trust Payne. Out with it.'

'I would rather not, Your Ladyship, for fear of shocking you.'

'Unlikely,' she said. 'But maybe the lower orders can guide you.' Turning to James, she asked, 'What are your thoughts on the subject young man?'

Thomas paled but gave him no guidance.

James thought quickly. If he understood the situation correctly, the viscount and his secretary were a couple, just as Tripp suspected. He knew Thomas shared the same inclinations, and he knew that Tripp was after as much incriminating evidence on the subject as he could supply. If he admitted that he, too, liked men, he might learn more — from Hawkins perhaps, if not from Lord Clearwater himself. On the other hand, the titled guests might be trying to trap him, or it could be a test of his honesty set up by Lord Clearwater, a man whose trust he needed.

The dinner party was waiting.

He took a deep breath to steady himself. Strangely, his uniform gave him the confidence to find words he imagined Thomas might use. 'I would like to say, Ma'am, that although I have been in the house only a few hours, I have already found it the most welcoming place to work. It is because His Lordship has placed his trust in me, an unqualified amateur, and it is because of the leadership shown to me by Mr Payne that I am compelled to answer with all honesty.'

'Yes, yes, dear,' her ladyship hurried him along. 'Very noble and well said, but the answer is?'

'You won't lose your job.' The viscount was watching him with interest. 'And you are perfectly safe here. Either way.'

'Thank you, My Lord. Then the answer, Ma'am, Sirs, is yes. I am, but I would never admit nor discuss the matter beyond these four walls.'

He'd done it. Gone, from ashamed messenger to self-confessed lover of men in less than twenty-four hours. He had no compunction at admitting the fact. It was as if the building as much as its occupants allowed it. He had found a haven where danger only came to those who lied.

'Bravo!'

Lady Marshall approved, Silas winked again, and the viscount looked at Thomas, who still gave no reaction.

'Well,' His Lordship said. 'This is all most illuminating.' He addressed the doctor in a softer voice. 'Philip, please consider all of us your friends if that's possible.'

'Thank you, Sir. As it happens…'

'Archer,' the viscount corrected, and the doctor nodded.

'Archer, Lady Marshall. Before we return to the discussion of the charity which I feel we should, may I be permitted to say that, like James there, I too have never encountered such free-thinking and welcoming company. It is something of a shock, and believe me, I have seen some shocking things in Greychurch. Like James, I too have no intention of discussing the subject beyond these safe walls and thus, to repay the trust you have shown me, and inspired by your footman's sincerity, I would like to answer Her Ladyship's initial question.'

'So that's a yes then, is it?' Mr Hawkins said, smirking.

'Not exactly,' Markland replied. 'I am of a rare species that finds itself attracted to either sex or, I should say, both.'

'Lots of men like that,' Silas said, as if the confession was nothing. 'I used to come across them regular. Or they'd come across me.'

Thomas coughed pointedly, and the viscount looked like he might pass out.

'Really, Doctor?' Lady Marshall drew back her head in amazement. 'I should find it rather confusing.'

'Not at all, Your Ladyship.'

'But surely you have too many options? Where, for example, does a man decide to insert his… '

'Payne?' The viscount interrupted, throwing a helpless look at the butler.

'Shall we clear, Sir?' Thomas stepped forward, stately and unaffected. 'Mrs Flintwich has constructed your favourite dessert.'

Fifteen

The conversation about sexuality ended with the delivery of a work of art otherwise known as a blancmange. James was terrified to touch it, but luckily Thomas served, leaving him free to remove plates to the kitchen. With dinner over, he and Thomas tidied the drawing room before the guests gathered there, and left them to their discussion of the charity.

'Is that what the viscount does?' James asked, as they descended to the servants' hall. 'Raise money to help poor people?'

'Not exactly,' Thomas answered. 'For a start, he doesn't need to raise money, his land and investments do that. 'But he does have an interest in helping those less fortunate than himself, particularly renters, as you heard.'

'I heard a lot of things. Did I answer right?'

'You answered correctly, yes. Actually...' Thomas stopped him on the turn of the stairs. 'I was rather proud of you.'

'Proud? I only spoke the truth as you told me to, and I meant it. I wouldn't speak about that kind of stuff out there and, before today, wouldn't have spoken of it anywhere.'

'It's the house,' Thomas said, looking to the ceiling as if he could picture the whole property through it. 'There's no point hiding secrets at Clearwater. His Lordship sees through them eventually.'

James' heart received a stab of guilt, but he calmed it with a deep breath. 'So, what do we do now?'

'Unless we are dismissed for the evening,' Thomas explained, 'we wait until the guests depart, and then I will close the house. I suggest you get yourself something to eat if you're hungry, have a cup of tea and put your feet up.'

They continued to the servants' hall where James made tea. Thomas sent Lucy to bed, and once her light footsteps had died on the stairs, said, 'You might as well go up as well. You look done in.'

'I'll be alright,' James replied. 'I'm enjoying being alone with you.'

'As you wish, but it could be a long wait.'

'Give us time to talk.'

'About what? The best way to clean silver?'

'Never put them in the knife cleaner unless they are already clean and free of grease,' James said, and earned himself a look of approval. 'No, about what they were saying. Does His Lordship really not mind people knowing he's... you know?'

'I don't think it's a question of minding,' Thomas said. 'He has, as far as I know, only shared the secret with a few people and only when he knows he can trust them implicitly. He would mind, however, if the news was out there on the streets. He manages, somehow, to cover it up. He doesn't dress flamboyantly apart from his smoking jackets, and he doesn't behave in that hideously affected, feminine way that I have seen some men do. I've even read about them dressing as women, itself a cause for arrest unless it's on the music hall stage.'

'So, he must trust me then.'

'If Mr Hawkins thinks you are trustworthy that is good enough for Lord Clearwater.'

'And you think I am?'

'Obviously.'

Another stab of guilt caused James to growl inwardly. 'What's Mr Hawkins' story?' he asked. 'I mean, he's only been his secretary for a short while, but he was a renter before. Is that right?'

Thomas nodded.

'Is it love?'

'It's not for us to speculate,' Thomas said. 'But we don't need to. Yes.'

Thomas was tired, James could see it in his eyes which, until then had been alive and dazzling like the emeralds of Lady Marshall's rings. Now, they were glassy and drooping.

'Have you ever been in love, Tom?' he asked. 'Or is that subject out of bounds?'

'We're alone, James,' Thomas replied. 'But it's wrong to discuss such things here. Do you mind?'

'Of course not. Sorry.'

'Having said that...' Thomas got to his feet with a groan and stood behind the footman. He put his hands on his shoulders and leant so they were cheek to cheek. 'The answer is yes, but it was not to be.'

'How does it feel?'

'A little like this.'

Thomas kissed the top of his head before he moved away.

'You mean it?'

Thomas dragged his fingers through his hair like a row of ploughs turning furrows at sunset, his smooth features set in a semi-smile. His arms extended behind his back as he stretched and yawned, his mouth opening wide to reveal the damp, dark pinkness inside. His tailcoat parted, and James wallowed in the sight of his slim waist and slender legs.

'As me fader would say...' The country accent was back. 'Bain't no other reason fur me a-feel like I been swept away be-a bessom.' He relaxed and shook his shoulders. 'You look worried, James.'

'Yeah, well, it's been a long day, and everything's happened so fast. Sorry, I'm not worried, but maybe a bit apprehensive.'

'About what?'

James was dog-tired, it had been an exhausting day, and his feet had not touched the ground. Moving from one job to the next, the experience of dinner, the knowledge that here at Clearwater he could be himself, and now hearing that Thomas had fallen for him in the way he had fallen for Thomas... It was too much to soak up, and with Tripp's mission floating around like scum on an otherwise pure pond, he was drowning in uncertainty.

'Can I really be myself here?' he asked, as Thomas returned to his chair. 'I mean, I can talk about this stuff with you, my boss, and no-one's going to know?'

'You could talk about it with His Lordship if you wanted,' Thomas said. 'But I wouldn't, not just yet. He has other things on his mind. You could chat with Mr Hawkins, he'd be open to that, but I'd give yourself some time to get to know him first.'

'Which leaves you.'

'Oh, you can talk to me as much as you want.'

'That's another thing,' James said. He may as well admit it. 'You and me, if we get to... that, you know.'

'If? Ask me, it's a question of when. At least for my part.'

That was good to hear, but the knowledge that something was going to happen between them was as worrying as it was thrilling. James reminded himself of the first rule of Clearwater.

'I ain't done it before,' he said. 'Have you?'

Thomas didn't answer directly. Instead, he said, 'If it's right, it'll take care of itself.'

The drawing room bell rang.

'Oh good, they're leaving early,' Thomas said, rising and straightening his uniform.

'Shall I come?'

'May as well. There's not much to do, but you can watch.'

Upstairs, Thomas collected Lady Marshall's coat and stood with it ready to place around her shoulders, and James did the same for the doctor. They came from the drawing-room laughing together and with Her Ladyship hanging from the man's arm. Lady Marshall was swaying slightly.

'Look at the two of them,' she exclaimed, releasing Markland and making a beeline for Thomas. 'Handsome boys in earthy russet and green. Servant colour is quite the fashion in the best houses.'

'Her Ladyship designed your livery,' the viscount explained. Like Thomas, his eyes were ringed with red. He had stubble on his chin which James noticed bore a scar. He might have seen it before, he was too tired to remember.

'You have many talents, Lady Marshall,' the doctor said. 'May I drop you home?'

'Philip, I live not sixty yards away, but perhaps I might impose on Archer to lend me James to guide me. He is something of an expert at deliveries, I believe.'

'Of course,' His Lordship said. 'Would you, James? It's stopped raining.'

'It would be an honour, Your Ladyship,' he said. 'If Mr Payne has no objections.'

'He's not allowed them,' Lady Marshall decreed, taking James' arm. 'It's not far, you won't catch cold.'

He waited awkwardly, held firmly by the old woman's hand and yet reassured by it. Everyone said their farewells, promised to meet again to discuss matters further, and along with other pleasantries, thanked the viscount for his hospitality. Thomas held the door and raised one dark-blond eyebrow secretly to James when he led Lady Marshal from the house.

The air chilled away his drowsiness the moment he stepped into the porch.

'We should walk slowly,' Her Ladyship said, once they were on the pavement. She waved farewell to the men, and James noticed Fecker had brought the trap around and was assisting the doctor into it. He wondered how and when that had been arranged, and marvelled at how things just seemed to happen in the house. Everyone knew what they were supposed to do and when, and he resolved to pay more attention in the future, so Thomas would see he was quick to learn.

'How did you enjoy your first day?' Her Ladyship asked, her arm tucked through his.

'Very much, Ma'am,' he said.

'You think this work is for you?'

'I hope so.'

'And so do I, James. You do my designs justice.'

'Thank you.'

'Ah,' she said, drawing him to a halt and looking behind. 'We are safe.' She gave a gentle tug and moved him closer. 'I hope I didn't embarrass you at dinner.'

'Not at all, Ma'am.'

'I have an eye for these things,' she confessed. 'And I care immeasurably about my godson's happiness. As you may have gathered, I am not what society calls conventional, and I love it that way. What do you say?'

He wondered if this was a test of some sort and reasoned that if it was, the only way he would pass it was to tell the truth.

'I haven't met any titled ladies,' he said. 'Only their servants at doors, so I don't have anyone to compare you to.'

'Sensible answer,' she said. 'Trot on.'

They continued, passing the point where Clearwater House abutted hers.

'Now listen, James,' she said, again drawing him to a halt. 'None of what happens inside Clearwater must be discussed outside. Am I clear on this?'

'I understand, Ma'am. In the postal service, we respect privacy, and I was trained from an early age to keep my mouth shut.'

'That is good to hear,' she said. 'But I do need to give you a word of warning.'

'Oh?' He couldn't imagine what she was going to say next.

'There's something not right with Archer. Lord Clearwater. He is changed of late, and I am concerned for him, you understand?'

'Not entirely, Ma'am.'

'I want to ask you a favour,' she said, continuing the walk. 'I can't discuss it with Mr Payne, and Archer would never tell me, but I do feel that I can put my faith in you. Maybe it's because I don't know you, but I rather think it is because of your wonderfully blatant honesty at dinner, for which, I might add, you should receive an accolade. You are going to fit right into my godson's way of life and his household. But all that aside, if you notice him suffering, will you tell me? I mean if he falls into any trouble, you come and find me even if there is but a suspicion. Yes?'

'Would I be betraying his confidence if I did so, Your Ladyship?'

'I don't think so.' She thought for a second. 'No, but if you did and he made a fuss, I'd sort him out, and you wouldn't be punished. I'm not asking for gossip, I don't want to know what he and Mr Hawkins get up to for example, but of late, he has not been himself.'

'I am unable to judge as I have only known him a few days.'

'I know, it's a difficult task, but you will know if there is something amiss, and I will know how to deal with it.'

They reached her steps, and she put more weight on his arm as they ascended.

'That's all I wanted to say, James,' she said. 'That and thank you for humouring an old lady.'

'Hardly old, Ma'am.'

'Oh, I love you more by the second. I must get one just like you. Where did Payne find you?'

'On the steps of the house when I delivered a telegram,' he replied.

'Well, that makes sense. And he's another lovely young man,' she added, aiming a jewelled hand at the bell-pull and missing.

James rang it for her.

'I've always admired Payne's loyalty,' she said. 'He put up with so much under the tortoise. I am quite glad Tripp has gone. Look after Thomas too, if you can. That man carries more affection than is good for him, and he needs an outlet. I study people, James… May I call you James? Of course I can, I'm a bloody viscountess, I can do what I want.' She laughed loudly once, and the sound echoed along the avenue. 'But sincerely, James. Keep your eye on Archer for me and be a good friend to Thomas. You will do well to do so.'

An immaculately dressed butler opened the door.

'Ah, Saunders,' she said. 'I shall be one moment.'

The butler bowed his head, gave James a quizzical look and stepped back inside leaving the door open.

'One last thing,' her ladyship whispered. 'My ear is always open to you on any matter.'

'Thank you, Ma'am.' Her conversation had been both flattering and confusing, but he put that down to the way the woman had taken to him so quickly. It was unnerving to be so trusted on first sight. 'I'll say goodnight, Ma'am, but can I ask you one thing?'

'Anything, dear boy.'

'When I return to the house, should I enter through the front door, or the back?'

'If I were you,' she said, putting her lips to his ear. 'I'd enter from behind. I hear that's how men like it.' She nudged him, sniggered and in a completely different tone, called, 'Yes, Saunders, alright. I am coming. I can hear your disapproval from here.'

James returned as quickly as his sore feet would allow, passing Clearwater House and taking the alley to the yard. He was about to ring the back doorbell when he stopped. There was no need. This was his home.

He found Thomas in the servants' hall, and having locked up, they headed for their rooms high above. There, James realised he'd not had time to light his fire.

'Light the gas while you wash,' Thomas suggested. 'It soon warms up. You can take a bath if you want, but join me for a drink before you turn in?'

'You can drink in your room?'

'We can do what we want, but you need to be on duty by seven in the morning. I'll wake you, I'm in the habit of rising in plenty of time.'

James, also tired, decided to bathe in the morning, but he

stripped to his underclothes and washed, shivering despite the gas fire which hissed and glowed in the grate. He had no dressing gown, and he knocked on Thomas' door wearing his shirt.

'What are you doing?' Thomas was amused when he saw him. He found a dressing gown that was far too big for James and poured them each a small glass of wine. They stood at the window looking out across the city. Streets were picked out as rows of dotted lights, coming together in the distance to form one dull, yellow glow, while above, scattered clouds gave way to stars and hung in uneven shapes.

'Well? Thomas said. 'Did Her Ladyship say anything of interest?'

'She was very flattering,' James replied. 'Told me her door was always open, which I thought was strange seeing as she doesn't know me.'

'We all get that talk at some point.' Thomas said. 'She's part of the family, or part of the furniture. It's good that she's taken to you.' He yawned.

'I should let you get to bed.' James downed his drink. His body ached, but his mind was picking over the events of the day, and he wanted to stay where he was.

'Aye, we should sleep. Tomorrow will be an even longer day, but His Lordship isn't receiving visitors, so I'll have more time to show you what else we do and at a slower pace.'

'That'd be good.'

He was waiting for Thomas to make a move and return to their conversation of earlier in the hall, but he doubted that even if he was invited to stay the night, he would be able to do anything. Apart from being exhausted, he was nervous. His apprehension increased when Thomas lay on his bed in his stockinged feet and invited James to join him, 'Just for a moment.'

James sat next to him, leaning against the headboard and wondering what he should do with his hands.

'Lie down,' Thomas said. 'We've shared a bed before.'

'Feels different now, though.'

'I know. Very strange,' Thomas admitted. 'I've never had a man in my room, let alone like this.'

He was making no move, and, in a way, James was grateful. He had been unsure about Thomas' previous advances and was hesitant, but aroused. Now, he was certain what he wanted, but didn't know where to start. It was as if the moment was too planned. Perhaps that's why Thomas was staring at the ceiling, waiting for James to make the first move.

He mustered his courage. 'Can I do this?' he asked and rested his head on Thomas' chest. It was awkward with his arms by his side pressed against the man's hips.

'Come here, you loon,' Thomas cajoled.

He put an arm around James' shoulders, and, the ice broken, they fumbled their way into a position where James was cradled against him, one leg over Thomas', an arm beneath him and their faces close.

'Feels nice,' James whispered.

They stroked each other's hair. Thomas' was thick and lightly oiled. He smelt of spices and soap, and his body was warm. James could hear his heartbeat, steady and slow.

'It's like all my birthdays at once,' he said. 'I could do this all night. And more.'

By way of a reply, Thomas squeezed him gently. 'One step at a time.'

James felt the touch of his lips on his hair and repaid the gesture with a murmur of pleasure, holding the man tighter and kissing his cheek.

He had never known such contentment, but it was still not complete. After all James had heard and learnt today, after the way he had been treated and valued, there was no way he could carry out Tripp's wishes, but the man was still at the back of his mind, eating away at his happiness and stirring up dissent.

It was something to be thought about in daylight. Tonight, with the gas low and Thomas breathing so close, he was safe. He remembered Thomas' words from earlier when James had asked what love felt like. 'A little like this,' he had said, and James now understood what he meant.

The mantle clock ticked, the church bell rang midnight, and the scattered clouds gradually merged into one black and brooding mass as the pair drifted into sleep innocently cradled in each other's arms.

Sixteen

Thomas woke alone. James had returned to his own room at some point during the night, but had left his impression. Not on the bed, but in Thomas' thoughts. He instantly remembered the feel of the man, the softness of his hair, the sound of his breathing and the heat of his solid body. They were enough for now, and as he swung himself from the bed, not even the sound of rain on the roof and the whistle of wind about the eaves dampened his enthusiasm for the day ahead. Archer's business was less of an attractive thought. There were many unanswered questions, and with everything else that happened yesterday, he hadn't had time to apply his mind to the mystery of the postcard, the telegram and the other matters yet unresolved.

He woke James with two loud raps on his door before taking a quick bath and dressing. They met in the passage just before seven, washed and presentable in their morning uniforms.

'You look very smart,' Thomas said, seeing that everything was in order.

'Thank you, Mr Payne.'

'Not yet,' Thomas grinned. He pulled James to him. The joy on the man's face was as obvious as his own. They kissed and when they finally broke apart, Thomas said, 'Strangely, that didn't feel as odd as I thought it would.'

'Odd?' James protested.

'As in, kissing a handsome man inside His Lordship's house. Actually, holding you like this and kissing you feels perfectly natural, but it will take me time to adjust.'

'I fell asleep,' James said. 'Sorry.'

'Nothing to be sorry for. It was perfect.' He kissed him again, lightly this time. 'But now, we must leave all this until later and turn our minds to work.'

'Fair enough.' James smiled, and when he did, his cheeks swelled, and his eyes lit with interest. 'What do I do now?'

Thomas cleared his throat, ridding his mind of affectionate thoughts and replacing them with the day's duties in a logical order.

'Did you sleep well, James?' he asked in his butler's voice.

'I did, thank you, Mr Payne,' the footman replied. 'And I am refreshed and ready for the day. My mind is uncluttered, but between you and me, my heart is a mess of excitement and happiness.'

'You sound like His Lordship,' Thomas joked. 'On which note. Breakfast.'

As they descended to the basement, he explained what James had to do. It was a long list. Cleaning boots, shoes and cutlery, trimming lamps, brushing the furniture, sweeping the hall, checking the flower arrangements, laying the breakfast room table, and then cleaning himself up before attending to Mr Hawkins.

'Mr Hawkins prefers to dress himself,' Thomas explained as he ironed the daily newspaper to fix the print. 'If he's not already awake, knock twice, wait and if called in, ask if he needs you.'

'I've still not got the measure of him,' James admitted. 'He keeps winking at me.'

'It's just his way. You'll get used to it,' Thomas said. 'Once he's done with you, come back down here and help Mrs Flintwich with breakfast. Will you be alright?'

'I hope so.'

'Don't panic,' Thomas reassured him. 'Mr Hawkins is as unused to living in a grand house as you are.'

'Do I say anything about last night's conversation?' James asked, worried. 'The dinner thing and being... you know.'

'Only if asked, in which case, the simplest thing is to adopt the first rule of the house.'

'Got it.'

Upstairs, outside the gentlemen's bedrooms, they shared one last friendly smile and then set about their responsibilities.

'Morning, Tom.' The viscount was up and washed when Thomas entered. He was at the window examining the grey scenery beyond.

'Good morning, My Lord,' Thomas replied. 'Did you sleep well?'

'Not at all, Tom.'

Thomas had all but given up reminding him that he should be called Payne.

'Sorry to hear that, Sir.'

'All I could think about was that bloody message and what it means. It even pervaded my dreams. It's raining.'

'So I understand.'

Archer turned to him, dressed in only his underclothes. A fine figure and an attractive one, he always caused Thomas' heart to skip, but today, for the first time, it only did it the once. Not because the viscount's attractiveness was waning, but because Thomas' hunger for love was now fed by someone else.

He focused on his work. 'Are you at home today, My Lord?'

'I am Thomas. And I'd like you and Silas with me in the study. We have a troubling puzzle to consider and much to do. Last night's dinner rather took the steam from the engine, as it were. I think we should sit down and work out what the hell Quill is doing.'

'As you wish.'

'How's James?'

Thomas received two heart-skips at the mention of the name.

'Ah, I see from your face that you are pleased with him,' Archer said.

'Am I that obvious?'

'I know you well, Tom,' the viscount said, as he entered his dressing room. 'I'm happy for you.'

Thomas followed.

'He did well, I thought.' Archer was examining a row of shirts. 'Seems to pick things up quickly. Was he offended at Lady Marshall's behaviour?'

'I don't think so, Sir. If he was, he didn't say anything to me. In fact…' He stopped himself. It wasn't his business to talk about another man's private life, but it was his duty to report back on his staff.

'Go on, Tom,' Archer encouraged, selecting a shirt.

'He told me that he found the discussion refreshing. I think he was surprised at first, embarrassed perhaps, but he won't admit that. Then, when he discovered that he was able to talk freely, he found it liberating. I think that was the word he used.'

'He's intelligent,' Archer said. 'I like that.'

'And I think we will find him loyal. He is attending to Mr Hawkins.'

'I hope they get on.' The viscount held the shirt against himself and stood before a full-length mirror.

'Cravat and smoking jacket?'

'The gold floral with the black lapels,' Archer said. 'Something to combat the dreary weather.'

'Brocade or plain? Or with the shawl collar and frog-feet closures?'

'Frogs,' Archer said as he put on his shirt. 'It's a wet day after all. I'll breakfast with the morning paper then perhaps you will join me in the study.'

'Of course.'

'Tell Mrs Flintwich two for lunch, and a cold supper will do today, it's her half-day isn't it?'

'It is.'

'How's Lucy?'

They chatted about the other servants as Archer dressed, and as was His Lordship's way, put all the plans for the day in order before they left the bedroom. Lucy was waiting outside with the ash bucket, and Archer greeted her warmly.

'I hope you are not too lonely without Sally,' he said. 'Would you rather be at Larkspur with the others?'

'I am quite happy here, My Lord,' Lucy said, with a small curtsy.

'That's good to hear, but tell Payne if you change your mind.'

As Thomas followed his master downstairs, he whispered, 'I think she would rather be wherever Fecker is.'

'Yes, I've noticed that too,' Archer said. 'Well, on their own time is fine, but in the absence of Mrs Baker, you'll have to have a word with her about pregnancy.'

Thomas nearly missed a step. 'I will see what I can do,' he stammered, dreading such a conversation.

'Ask Mrs Flintwich for advice,' Archer said. 'She's been married a hundred years and never calved down. There must be a trick to staying out of trouble.'

'I think her looks might play a part.'

'Tom, don't be rude,' the viscount sniggered. 'Right! Let's get shipshape.'

Silas was already in the breakfast room reading the newspaper, following the lines of tightly-fitting print with his finger. James, Thomas was pleased to see, was standing to attention by the sideboard, and seemingly quite at home.

Morning greetings done, the viscount and Silas read while they ate. Thomas and James attended them, and after the meal was over, stayed behind to tidy the room.

'His Lordship requires me in his study,' Thomas said as they carried the last of the plates to the kitchen. 'It often happens. Have something to eat, take a short break and then set about the dining room grate. Ask Lucy to show you. You'll find overalls in the cloakroom. Listen out for the bells, too.'

With James organised, Thomas was free to attend the viscount. He found him at the reading table opposite Silas. The table had been tidied, the books stacked to one end and the only other things on it were the postcard, the telegram and the atlas.

'Tom,' Archer said, as Thomas closed the doors. 'Time to get your sleeves rolled up. Have a seat.'

'How's your boy doing, Tommy?' Silas asked, swiping his fringe from his face. It fell back again immediately.

'Settling in.'

'Getting used to living in a house full of queers?'

'Silas,' Archer chided. 'We're here to work. Besides, I don't think Fecker, Mrs Flintwich or Lucy would take kindly to being called queer. I'm not sure I do.'

'Oops,' Silas giggled. 'Right then, let's go over this again starting with the obvious question. What the feck is Quill playing at?'

'We drew a list yesterday.' Archer extracted a paper from among the books and passed it to Thomas. 'We've been through everything and came up with many questions but few answers.'

'I think,' Thomas said as he sat, finding himself at the head of the table, 'that we should approach this as a mystery which is, after all, what it is.'

'Er, yeah,' Silas said. 'Bit obvious.'

'Have a look at that list,' Archer said. 'See what you can add.'

Thomas read while the other two waited.

'As you say,' he said, when he had finished. 'Many questions, but that's all. What we need are answers.'

162

'You should work for Inspector Adelaide.' Silas rolled his eyes.

Thomas ignored his sarcasm.

'To start with,' Thomas said, and made his own list as he spoke. 'The most pressing items are the postcard and the telegram. Taking those first, if this is the only communication he made between when we last saw him and when he boarded the train, we have to assume he had no help. The telegram was sent from Greychurch.'

'So he was hiding there?'

'Not necessarily, Silas,' Thomas said. 'He could have been anywhere and travelled into the East End to send the message. As we know, the place is crawling with people and he would be less likely to be recognised.'

'Fair point,' Archer agreed. 'As I see it, he was biding his time, waiting for the Wednesday night train. Otherwise, he could have left the city at any point. Why didn't he go on the Sunday, or any other day?'

'Because the night train only makes the one stop on a Wednesday night,' Thomas reasoned. 'It leaves late, passengers retire early, and he more or less has the train to himself. On other nights, it makes several stops, and there's much coming and going. It's in your Bradshaw's, Archer. I looked it up.'

'Good,' Archer said. 'We can be fairly certain he alighted at Barrenmoor. Then what?'

'When was the telegram sent?' Silas asked.

'Monday, it doesn't say an exact time.' Archer fetched his diary from the desk. 'I was thinking about that,' he said, sitting and finding the monthly planner. 'He dispatched it to the mental asylum by express. We know from experience that it takes that institution a fair time to respond, but we don't know how long it took to arrive. I've always assumed telegrams were immediate, but what do I know?'

'Why is that important?' Silas asked.

Thomas took a clean sheet of paper and began drawing a chart listing the days of the week on one side and known facts on the other.

'Birthday gift,' Archer read the message. 'And Crispin's birthday is coming up. October twenty-fifth, the anniversary of the Battle of Agincourt.'

Thomas noted it on his plan. 'Assuming the birthday in question is your brother's,' he said, thinking aloud. 'That doesn't give us long to figure this out.'

'But it gives Quill time enough to arrange whatever he is planning, assuming the message was delivered promptly,' Archer said. 'Listen…' He reread the telegram. 'Birthday gift planned. Stop. Be assured. Stop. Matter in hand. Stop. Restoration awaits.'

'Phrase by phrase,' Thomas said. 'The message was sent to your brother, and you are assuming it's his birthday that's being referred to.'

'Well, it's not Quill's.' Archer turned the pages of his diary. 'That was two months ago.' His head shot up. 'Oh hell.'

He left his chair and hurried to the desk where he wrote a quick message, put it in an envelope and, that done, pulled the bell-pull.

'Anything I can do?' Thomas asked, intrigued. He glanced at the mantle clock and noted the time.

'No, nothing related,' Archer mumbled as he returned to the reading table. 'Carry on, Tom.'

'Birthday gift,' Thomas said. 'Quill has a gift for your brother.'

'Assumption,' Silas said.

'As is everything else. "Restoration awaits." Does that mean anything to you, Archer?'

'Possibly.' Archer was concerned. His face was stony with concentration and his down-turned mouth more of a frown than usual. 'Restoring his title.'

'It's your title,' Silas said. 'Can he do that? He'd have to be proved sane, wouldn't he?'

'Well, Quill is a doctor,' Thomas reasoned. 'It might be possible for such a man to arrange the release of a patient, but your brother is in the Netherlands, and we know Quill didn't have enough time to visit, confer with the medical men there and get back to be seen boarding a train on the Wednesday evening.'

'Which suggests advanced planning.' Archer concluded. 'Which in turn suggests this was orchestrated before, or during, his killing spree in the East End.'

'A fall-back plan?'

'Exactly, Tom. If he didn't catch me there, he had something else in mind to lure, trap and kill me. The end is the same; to restore

Crispin to the title of Lord Clearwater.'

'Don't know why he didn't just murder you in your bed or poison you at one of your posh lunches,' Silas joked.

'Thank you for that, Mr Hawkins.' Archer kicked him playfully under the table before brushing his leg with his own. 'Either would have been too obvious. He doesn't want to get caught, and I think we can assume he likes to play games. A cat with its prey.'

'Shit-head games,' Silas complained. 'Can't find any place near Barrenmoor he might have gone. Got a map with more on it?'

'I can get one,' Archer said.

A knock on the door brought Thomas to his feet, and he buttoned his tails.

'Come!' Archer called.

James appeared, stepping in and standing attentively as he had been shown. Thomas checked the time again and was pleased to see James had responded promptly to the bell. He arrived unhurriedly and with nothing out of place. Thomas was warmed by pride.

'Ah, James.' Archer rose and took the footman into the drawing room leaving Thomas and Silas to exchange quizzical glances.

'He's a good-looking lad, Tommy.'

'And one who knows how to behave above stairs, Mr Hawkins,' Thomas said with a gracious, but pointed bow of the head.

'Point made, Payne.'

Archer returned a few minutes later and closed the doors.

'I've asked James to run an errand,' he explained. 'He shouldn't be long. He's gone for a map. That should help. I interrupted you, Tom. Where were we?'

'The telegram. Birthday refers to October twenty-fifth. The rest suggests Quill is working to have your brother released and reinstated. That's a guess, but it gives him a motive. We know he wants you dead, Archer, but it looks like he is planning to do it with your brother's knowledge. What about the postcard?'

'Oh, bugger!'

Archer was on his feet again. Agitated, he hurried to the bell-pull and tugged it twice.

'Now what?' Silas grinned. 'What's in that handsome head of yours?'

'A second opinion,' Archer said, leaving the mysterious comment in the ether as he came back to join them. 'So!' He clapped his hands. 'Moving on from the telegram for now, what's this all about?'

He picked up the envelope and removed the postcard.

'Postmark?' Thomas inquired.

'You're one step ahead as usual. There are three, and they make no sense.' Archer examined both sides of the envelope. 'I can't read one of them, it's smudged, but it looks like it was either sent from here in the city, or a place called Inglestone, or a third place I can't read. It's Quill's writing, so there's no mystery as to who sent it, and it's dated the day after he would have arrived at Barrenmoor.'

'Hang on.' Silas flipped pages in the Bradshaw's guide. 'Yeah, there it is. Inglestone is about five miles from Barrenmoor Ridge which, you will be fascinated to know, is one of the highest peaks in the country, according to geographers and, according to this chap, "Of outstanding natural beauty, but suffers from sever conditions in winter".'

'I think that's *severe,*' Thomas corrected.

'Yeah, alright, professor.'

Another knock, another 'Come!' and James reappeared just as unflustered as before.

'James,' Archer said, beckoning him closer. 'Before you go, could you answer me a question or two?'

'If I am able, Sir.'

Thomas glanced at Silas as he covered his papers, concerned that Archer might draw James into the mystery.

His concern increased when Archer handed the footman the envelope. 'What do you make of these postmarks?'

James read the stamps, inspected the back and opened the flap to peer inside. 'They look standard to me, Sir.'

'But what do they tell you?'

'That this letter was dispatched from an office in Inglestone on…' He raised his eyes, and his lips moved as he counted days. 'Last Thursday.' He examined the back. 'It passed through the Essex-Road sorting office on Saturday and… Oh!'

'What?' Archer's eyes were alive with excitement. 'What is it?'

'Just a coincidence,' James said. 'Sir, sorry. It passed through Mount Pleasant on Sunday morning. It might have been leaving the building as I arrived.'

166

'You can read that smudge?'

'You get used to it, Sir.'

'It arrived here on Sunday, late,' Archer said. 'Is that unusual?'

'Not particularly, Sir. Not with this amount of postage paid. From Yorkshire to the city should be no more than tuppence depending on the weight, but the sender has paid double, suggesting he considered the message urgent. It wouldn't have made a difference. The tuppenny post is handled quickly no matter the postage paid.'

'Do you know Yorkshire, James?' the viscount asked.

'No, Sir. But general geography was useful to know in my line of work.'

'I thought you just delivered messages,' Silas said.

'Always keen to better my prospects, Mr Hawkins. The more a post boy knows, the faster he will be promoted.'

'Well, I'm surprised you aren't the Postmaster General by now, James.' Archer was impressed. 'Can you tell me anything else?'

James lifted the envelope to his nose and sniffed the back. 'The envelope was made locally,' he said. 'As opposed to abroad.'

'How the fu… How can you tell that?' Silas' face was a picture of disbelief.

'Again, Sir, you become accustomed. It's the smell of the paper, see? It's a standard, cheap envelope, not of the quality someone such as Your Lordship might use, but it was wax sealed.'

'Incredible,' Archer beamed. 'Wax sealed? There was no seal.'

'It was stuck down before it was opened.' James was confident. He showed the men the envelope flap. 'Most of us would use glue if we didn't have sealing wax, a stamp or a signet ring,' he explained. 'It's the easiest way, but this was sealed with a thin veil of wax under the flap. It's more secure, but not everyone goes to the trouble.' He handed the envelope back.

'Unbelievable,' Archer said. 'That you can tell so much from one piece of paper.'

'One piece of *folded* paper, Sir. Made from pulped wood, cut in a short-arm cross, folded to be sturdier than the average, sealed with wax and available in any shop that sells them. A common thing that has travelled further in the past five days than I have in my life.'

'Bloody hell,' Silas said. 'You need to get out more.'

'I hope that was of use, Sir?'

'I think so,' Archer said, looking at Thomas. He asked a silent question with his eyebrows, and Thomas nodded. Archer's eyes flicked to the postcard on the table and then to Silas, who drew in a short breath, clicked his tongue as he thought, and nodded.

'James,' Archer said. 'Before you go, can you tell me what you make of this?'

He handed James the postcard, and the footman gave it his full attention, first examining the front and then flipping it over to look at the back.

'Not going to sniff it?' Silas joked.

'No need, Sir.' James was unmoved by his tone. 'Postal cards, as opposed to letters, have been in use for over forty years and have improved in quality. This one is not standard issue from the post office, though. There's an image, and it was not pre-stamped. The picture, as I am sure you have seen, is a tourist one, showing some kind of ruined building and yet with no title plate. There is no information as to what that building may be. There is a recent trend to mark the backs with such detail, you see. It was inside the envelope I take it?'

'Correct,' Archer nodded. 'There's no stamp on the card.'

'Quite, Sir. It's a simple thing. The sender bought the card but didn't trust the delivery service not to read it, so he enveloped it. It's a common practice. Nothing remarkable.'

'Have you seen the image before?'

'My job was more the delivery of telegrams,' James said. 'A different department, but I was sent to work in the general office from time to time. Even then, however, there is little time to admire the artwork of such things. I don't recognise it at all.'

'And what about the writing?' Thomas asked, and received a glare from Silas.

'Yes,' Archer agreed. 'James may as well give us his thoughts on that, Silas. He appears to be an expert on the mail. How are you on handwriting, James?'

'Anything but an expert, Sir,' James admitted. 'My own is school-taught enough and legible, but this, I would say, was written in a hurry. It's not easy to read.'

'But you can?'

James didn't answer as he read the back of the card. As he

concentrated, his brows came together and his mouth twisted at the corners in a way that Thomas found irresistibly attractive, but then, everything about the man was attractive. His pride burned brighter. He could tell Archer was rapt with admiration for the man too, but hopefully not for the same reason.

'Ah,' James said. 'May I?' He pointed to the window.

Archer waved his hand in the direction. 'Do whatever you need.'

The men watched in various states of wonder and confusion as James took the card closer to daylight and pulled back the net curtains. The glass was rain-splattered and the view beyond dim in the drizzle, but apparently that was enough for his purpose. He held the card to the light and again examined both sides.

'Don't tell me you're an ink expert as well,' Silas said.

'Sadly not, Sir,' James replied, letting the curtain drop. 'But this card was written with a narrow nib, you can tell from the letters of course, but also, it has pressed through to raise some letters on the front. It was resting on something soft when it was written as opposed to being on a desk or similar.' He handed the card back to Archer. 'As for the meaning of the message...'

'Yes?' Archer prompted when James didn't continue. 'What?'

James' eyes fell on the atlas and travelled via Thomas to come to rest on the viscount. He bit his bottom lip before he took an audible breath.

'Please excuse the impertinence, My Lord,' he said. 'But exactly what kind of trouble are you in?'

Seventeen

Archer's heart landed in his stomach. How on earth could the man tell there was trouble just from reading some random words on a postcard? He heard Silas gasp, but kept his eyes firmly on James. The footman hadn't been impertinent, he had been intuitive, and now he showed no expression other than patience as he waited for the viscount to speak.

'My Lord?' Thomas prompted, but Archer held up a finger for silence.

Thinking through his options, he found only two.

He could send the man about his duties and say no more about it, or he could use whatever resources he had to offer.

The problem was, he didn't know James. Last night he spoke flatteringly enough of Clearwater House and his treatment, his trust and himself, but any man finding himself in a new job would be keen to say what he thought wanted to be heard.

Messenger boys had a reputation for being slippery characters when it was to their own advantage and Archer erred on the side of caution.

'Before I answer you, James,' he said. 'I would like you to see to that other matter, but differently. I shall explain in a moment.' Turning to Silas and Thomas, he added, 'This won't take long. Could I ask you gentlemen to leave us for a minute?'

Confused, they agreed.

'Come here, James,' Archer said, calling him to the desk when they were alone. 'It's an odd request, but would you look out of the front window while I do something?'

James did so without question, something Archer appreciated.

He rewrote his instructions and slipped the note into an envelope. At the fireside bookcase, he pulled back a volume of poetry which opened a panel made of fake spines revealing a combination safe.

He withdrew twenty pounds, closed the safe and the panel, and returned to the desk.

'Thank you,' he said. 'Over here.'

James came and stood attentively on the other side.

'Take this.' Archer handed him the envelope. 'Mr Andrej doesn't know this part of town so well, therefore I suggest you ride up front with him to give directions.'

'Very good, Sir.'

'No need to look so worried. He's quite tame. Take that letter, you know its contents, but instead of asking them to deliver, I want you to bring it back. They won't keep you long.'

'Are you sure, Sir?'

'Perfectly sure. They have it ready.'

'I mean, are you sure you want me to do this?'

'Yes.'

'And they will let me walk out with it?'

'They will when you show them my revised instructions, and...' He handed James the twenty pounds. 'When you pay them.'

James gawped at the money.

'Take it.'

The footman did as he was told and put the money into the envelope.

'I'll expect you back within the hour,' Archer said, offering a supportive smile. 'You'd better take a cloak. Lucy will find you an umbrella.'

'Very good, Sir.'

'And before you go, James, not a word to the others.' He took a pound note from his pocket. 'Andrej will need to know what you're about, so give him this and tell him it's for him to spend for the same purpose if he wants. Off you go.'

James bowed and left the room. A moment later, Silas and Thomas were back, Thomas shutting the doors firmly.

'What are you up to now?' he said, rubbing his hands and grinning. 'And how did he know we're in trouble?'

'It's not how he knew,' Archer said. 'It's the fact that he used the word trouble. We don't know if we are. Quill's playing a mind game. For all we know, the message means nothing.'

'Yeah, well that's hardly likely is it?' said Silas.

'May we ask what that was about?'

'No, Thomas,' Archer replied. 'You don't need to. If my intuition is as sharp as I think it is, you will find out within the hour.'

'And if it isn't?'

'Then I am a little lighter in the pocket. But enough of that. I felt we were getting somewhere, and I think it's about time Thomas took a trip to the attic.'

'For what purpose?' Thomas asked as he stood.

'The chalkboard from my old nursery. That's stored up there isn't it?'

'As far as I know.'

When Thomas left, Silas sat back in his chair, eying Archer suspiciously.

'I know I've not known you long,' he said. 'But I've not seen you be so devious before. What's going on?'

'That, I can't tell you, Silas,' Archer said, reaching for his hand. 'Not for another sixty minutes. Will you forgive me?'

'Archie, you don't need to ask. I'm intrigued, that's all.'

'Well, turn your enquiring mind to the clues, if that's what they are.'

While Silas continued to search the map of the Yorkshire moors for a location that might relate to the image, Archer examined the words on the postcard. Only a few made sense.

They were still in silent contemplation when Thomas returned with a chalkboard. He propped it on the table beneath the map of the country.

'I brought chalk,' he said. 'And took the liberty of asking Lucy to bring coffee.'

'Good man,' Archer mumbled, his head down over another guide book, also looking for images.

'Have you found anything possibly relevant?' Thomas took the notes and transferred them to the board.

'Nothing,' Silas said. 'Except that it's five miles from the Barrenmoor depot to Inglestone, and the card was posted from there on Thursday morning. So, we know he was there then.'

'Meanwhile,' Archer added, 'he's gone to lengths to ensure I know, while possibly arranging for Crispin to be discharged into his care.'

172

The mantle clock ticking its steady rhythm was the only sound in the study, apart from the scratch of chalk and the occasional sigh of frustration. Lucy brought a tray, and Thomas served coffee.

They worked for nearly an hour until Silas said, 'Your man's got another five minutes.'

Archer wondered if he had made a mistake.

Apparently not. James returned, his hair wet and his face flushed. He waited at the open door.

'Here he is,' Archer said, relieved. 'Come in.'

James was holding a small box in one hand and a large bunch of roses in the other. Archer clocked Silas' intrigue as he threw aside the book and sat up straight.

He asked the others to move to the armchairs. Thomas dusted off his hands into the fireplace and wiped them on a handkerchief while Silas used the couch, sipping cold coffee in what he thought was a genteel manner.

'A gentleman holds the cup by the handle,' Thomas corrected him, tutting as he sat.

'How did you get on, James?'

'All done, My Lord.' The footman wiped his forehead. 'Apologies. I ran straight up, haven't had time to dry off.'

'Then go and do it,' Thomas barked.

'Easy, Tom. It's doesn't matter, James. I want us to take a pause,' Archer said, closing the doors as James' hands were full. He took the box from the footman. 'It's my brother's birthday on the twenty-fifth,' he said. 'But in all the recent bother, I forgot that it is Silas' today.'

'And you bought me flowers?' Silas was confused.

'No, actually,' Archer said equally confounded by the roses.

'From Mr Andrej,' James explained, and blushing somewhat, offered them. 'He said, Mr Hawkins, that he would also take you for a drink with the change if that was acceptable to His Lordship.'

'Of course.'

'He was keen that I also pass on a private message.' James bent to Silas and whispered in his ear.

Silas burst out laughing. 'Yeah, well, when you see him, you can tell him I don't need him for that anymore.' He flashed a mischievous smirk at Archer. 'Nice offer though, coming from him.'

'Was there anything else, James?' Archer held back a smile. He knew exactly what Fecker had offered and knew how much Silas would enjoy it, but he was equally as secure in the knowledge that the offer would not be accepted.

'I also picked up the map you wanted.' James handed it to him along with the box before delving in his pockets. 'And your change, Sir. Six pounds, four shillings and sixpence ha'penny.'

'You keep that.'

'You what? I mean, I'm sorry, but… I'm not allowed.'

Archer laughed. James would do perfectly at Clearwater. Thomas had chosen well, and he would reward the butler later. The delighted outrage on James' face showed the footman had been rewarded enough. The money represented three months' wages.

'You are permitted to keep tips,' Archer said. 'You're not a telegram boy now, you are a gentleman's footman. Put the change in your pocket, James, and thank you for running the errand. Gentlemen…' He placed the box on the desk and addressed the others. 'I need to apologise. The purpose of the errand was two-fold,' he said. 'Firstly, because I hadn't remembered to collect Silas' birthday gift. Sorry about that Silas, we'll get to it later. Secondly, because I wanted to see if I could trust you, James. I sent him to Hennell's,' he explained to Thomas who knew of the jeweller. 'As you can see, the man is completely trustworthy. Anyone else would have run off with the money. Wouldn't you agree?'

'I wouldn't have done,' Thomas said, with a slight edge of annoyance.

'Don't be upset, Tom,' Archer said. 'I know you wouldn't, but I don't need to test you. None of us know James, but I think he has proved he can be trusted, and, now that he can, I think we should offer him an explanation. What say you?'

'You're the boss,' said Silas.

'The East End matter?' Thomas was dubious.

Archer watched James for his reaction. He stood staring at the wall as he had been taught to do. He could be of great service to them, and had suggested he understood the cryptic postcard.

'The other matter.' Archer considered. Maybe his knowledge of the Ripper murders was too much information just now. He curbed his enthusiasm. 'James?'

'Yes, Sir?' James paid attention.

'Would you like to sit down? And there's no need to look at Thomas. My study is the only place in this world I can truly be myself, and etiquette beyond the door doesn't apply in here. Sit. Would you like coffee?'

'No thank you, Sir. Shall I pour you some?'

'Just sit, James,' Thomas sighed. 'Are you sure, Archer?'

'Yes, Tom.'

When James had perched himself uncertainly on the edge of a chair, Archer took up his favourite position at the fireplace.

'James,' he said. 'We have recently been involved in some dangerous business. You don't need the details at this moment. For now, all you need to know is that the old friend of mine I asked you to help find is unwell, as I said. His illness, however, is of the mind. He is a treacherous man and needs to be caught. That is what we are trying to do here.'

He allowed James a moment to look freely at the wall map, the chalkboard and other research before he continued.

'The card was sent to my brother, and I will leave it to Tom to explain about Crispin, who is, or at least was incarcerated in a mental institution in the Netherlands.'

James tried hard to keep a blank expression, but his brow furrowed. 'The Rotterdam Institute, Dordrecht?' he asked.

'Bravo. The man we seek is, or rather was an old friend of us both. We served together in the navy before circumstances forced me to retire.'

'His mental brother tried to kill him,' Silas said, cutting to the denouement. 'Sorry, Archie, but if you're going to tell a story, you might as well make it quick.'

'Thank you, Silas. Yes, James, Crispin tried to kill me, because of an affair I had with another man. He was also the object of Quill's desire, although I didn't know that at the time. My brother's mental condition has worsened over the years, but has never been satisfactorily explained, although my father spent a great deal of...'

'Jesus, Mary and Joseph,' Silas mumbled. 'Shall I do it, Archie?'

Silas had that look. That one where he mixed damn cheek with sympathy, as if Archer couldn't help being a verbose idiot, his lips curled at the edges, and, of course, it came with a wink. The impertinence didn't annoy him. A spirited jest was Silas' way of showing he was comfortable with Archer and those around him.

'Go on then.'

'Thing is, Jimmy,' he said. 'Archer... His Lordship fancied another man on his ship. His brother went mental and tortured the boyfriend 'till he topped himself. Or the brother had him killed. Either way, Archer had it out with his brother, who then tried to cut him in half. Now then, Quill also fancied the boyfriend — before he died, of course — got jealous of Archer, set a trap, nearly caught him, but Archer got away. Now we think he's having another go. So, we've got a doctor who should be in the bedlam and a brother who already is. The brother wants his title back, but can't get it until the doctor gets him out of the madhouse which he can't do while Archer's still alive. They're both nutters, and both want *my* boyfriend dead.' He grinned. 'Welcome to Clearwater, mate.'

'That was hardly succinct,' Thomas muttered.

'Do you want me to repeat any of that, Jimmy?'

James swallowed, took a breath, but was unable to speak.

'If you are uncomfortable, James,' Archer said. 'Then say so and go about your duties. You hardly know any of us, and we've already displayed rather eccentric behaviour, but...' He approached, and James made to stand. 'No, stay there.' Archer crouched to him. 'I know you're one of us, James. Thomas saw it straight away, I see it now, and of course, Lady Marshall sniffs us out at a hundred paces. The point is, if you want nothing to do with this, then say so. I trust you not to discuss anything with anyone, and you are under no obligation to help. Either way, you remain in my employ, and the status quo is maintained.'

James raised a smile, but it was replaced a second later by confusion. He held Archer's gaze and squared his shoulders, reaching a decision.

'Sir,' he said. 'I don't know what to say.'

'Say what's on your mind.'

'Very well.' He took a deep breath. 'Yes, I am happy to help if I can, and no, I won't discuss anything. I know I've only been here a day, but last night after I got back, I stood at the door and thought, this is where I live. I couldn't believe it. Then I thought, no. It's not just where I'm going to live; it feels like home — even more so now

176

you've taken me into your confidence.'

'That's splendid,' Archer said and stood, his legs aching. 'I can assure you, James, there are no other houses where this kind of discussion would take place, let alone permit the outrage at dinner last night.'

'I enjoyed that, Sir,' James admitted. 'As in, I enjoyed the freedom to speak and said things I'd never been able to before. That was once I remembered house rule number one.'

'Ah ha!' Archer grinned. 'Quite right. You should understand, James, in case you were wondering, that although Thomas is my butler he is also my best friend and has been since we were children.'

'I know he is very fond of you, Sir.'

'And me of him.'

'Ah, everyone loves Thomas,' Silas quipped.

'And I don't need to explain what my secretary is to me,' Archer said, throwing Silas a smirk. 'So, that said. What say you? Will you help us?'

James hesitated.

'It's up to you, James,' Thomas said. 'There's no wrong answer.'

'It's not that, Mr Payne. But... Well, the thing is...'

Archer watched, fascinated as James' eyes pinked. He screwed them up and swallowed. Fascination turned to horror when he started to cry.

'Good God, man.' Archer stood back. 'What on earth is it? Are you not used to kindness?'

'It's not that, Sir,' James snivelled, searching his pockets. Concerned, Thomas passed him his handkerchief. 'I have a confession to make concerning Mr Tripp.'

Archer's blood chilled. 'Tripp?' he exclaimed. 'What's he got to do with you?'

James wiped his nose and composed himself. When he had cleared his throat, apologised and sniffed back the last of his sudden tears, he embarked on a story so outrageous it was all Archer could do not to take his ceremonial sword from the wall, leave the house and search out his old butler.

'He paid you to spy on me?' he fumed, when James had finished. 'Is that why you applied for the job?'

James shook his head, tears welling again.

'Have you spoken to him since you have been here?'

Again, James protested the negative.

Archer believed him. It would have been easy for James to have made off with the twenty pounds, found Tripp, told him of the dinner conversation and vanished. He owed no loyalty to Archer, and yet he had been faithful despite the temptation. If there were sides to be taken, and there clearly were, he had sided with Archer. Not only that, he had spoken honestly at the risk of losing his job.

Thomas watched him closely, and even Silas fell serious, waiting to see what Archer would do next.

'You poor chap,' he said, returning to the footman. Kneeling, he took his hands. 'I am sorry Tripp did this to you, it's bloody unfair. But please assure me you will have nothing more to do with him, and you have not found your place in my household because you intend to continue his despicable work.'

'Honestly, Sir,' James said, wide-eyed and sincere. 'I didn't apply for this job because of that, although Tripp did prep me for the interview.'

'You genuinely wanted to come into service even though you could possibly make more money as a messenger?' Archer queried. 'What with commissions and so on?'

James nodded. 'I did, Sir. I was with them long after I should have been a postman, but even that's not the reason for coming here.' He looked at Thomas. 'Sorry, Tom,' he said. 'Tripp told me to seduce you so you'd want me here.'

'That's disgusting,' Archer seethed.

'But, Tom, honest, that's not why... I mean, I fancied you the first time I saw you. I mean that. I went for the job because I...' He looked at Archer, frustrated with himself and pleading.

'Just say it,' Archer whispered.

''Cos I fell for you, Tom,' James said. 'You know, love and that.'

'Well, you are here now,' Archer said, to draw attention away from Thomas' blanched face. 'I am sure Tom believes you. I do. Thank you for your honesty.'

'The first rule, eh?' James sniffed.

'Quite. If you ask me, Thomas is a lucky man.'

It was hard to tell if James' crimson cheeks were caused by embarrassment or crying.

The footman pulled himself together. 'My apologies, My Lord,' he said. 'If you still wish to employ me, you have my assistance in any form.'

The man was admirable. Archer rose and gripped his shoulder.

'I have no intention of sending you away, Jimmy,' he said kindly. 'Remember the second rule of Clearwater. In private, we are friends. In public, we have our stations. Rule one is to be honest, and rule two is, if you like, to be dishonest, but only to those who seek to harm us. I will ponder the Tripp situation, but for now, with only a few days until my brother's birthday, we have another matter far more interesting than a butler's duplicity. As Silas would put it, what the feck is Quill up to?'

'He'll be up to his neck in shit when I get hold of him,' Silas grumbled. 'Any more coffee?'

He served himself while Archer returned to the writing table.

'James? Will you join us and lend your expertise, or is this too ridiculous to contemplate?'

'You believe me, Mr Payne? I've not lied to you.' James was still fixated with Thomas' concern.

Thomas refused to return his gaze. He stood at the window and looked out saying, 'His Lordship is waiting for your reply.'

James' shoulders slumped, and Archer sympathised. 'In my Navy career,' he said, 'I faced many difficult times, but none as grim as when admitting my mistakes to my superior officer. You and Thomas must talk privately, but for now, Tom is correct. Time is of the essence, James, and I believe we could do with your help.'

'If Mr Payne has no objections,' James said.

'Do what you want.'

Archer was not prepared to chastise Tom for his truculence, it would only alienate him. He held James' arm to reassure him. 'Up to you,' he said.

'I will do whatever you ask,' James said, and in an attempt to brighten his mood, added, 'I'm fond of a puzzle.'

'Good man.' Archer released him. 'Gentlemen, now we have James on board, we should hold a council of war.'

'You haven't told me what's in the box yet,' Silas said, ogling it.

'That's for later.' Archer winked. 'If you can wait?'

'I had to wait twenty years to find you, didn't I? I can hold on.'

Archer pulled a fourth chair to the table. 'James,' he said. 'Please explain what you saw on that postcard that made you speak of trouble.'

James sat, and the others took up their places, one man on each side, the map and chalkboard opposite Archer. James twisted in his chair to read it. When he turned back, he picked up the postcard and, between quick, sad glances at Thomas, reread the words.

'Well, Sir,' he said. 'I've seen many telegrams in my day, and I'm used to truncation. There are parts of that message that suggest a shortening of meaning as some people do to save money. That was the first thing odd.'

'That would make sense on a telegram,' Archer said. 'But Quill is not short of money, and this is a postcard within an envelope.'

'Right. So why not send a letter? And another thing, I'd have thought a doctor would know how to spell. Apart from those things, it's the manner of the message.'

'The manner?'

'It's not exactly an invitation to a dance, is it, Sir?'

'No, you're right. And there's no need to keep inserting Sir, it gets on my nerves.'

'My Apologies, My Lord.'

Archer huffed a laugh and let it go. 'What do you mean about spelling?'

James pointed to words on the card. 'He's spelt "I read" as *I reded*. And "public" with an A on the end. *Publica*.'

'The Latin word for State,' Archer said.

'Oh, I see. And does that make sense?'

'None of it makes sense.'

'Except we know who it is from,' Thomas said. 'And, as you say, it's not meant to be pleasant. Maybe if you read it aloud, Archer?'

James was surprised at Thomas' use of the viscount's first name, and Archer imagined he was having trouble taking in their familiarity.

'Very well,' he said, taking the card. 'What we have here is a picture of a ruin. I first thought it might be related to Quill's telegram in some way. It looks like a ruined abbey or a monastery, and the word "Restoration" appeared to link the two messages. But then I realised that Quill didn't intend us to find the telegram,

180

so the card and the message are not meant to be taken together. Whatever Quill is planning, we have the advantage because he doesn't know we have intercepted his communication. Meanwhile, we should take this postcard as intended for us. The witness drew our attention to his boarding the train, and Thomas was correct; he wants us to know he is alive. He also wants us to know where he is and what he is doing, else why bother sending this?'

'Silas sighed. 'He could have just told us.'

'It's not how he works,' Thomas reasoned.

'Quite. So, we address the coded postcard.' Archer held it up. 'And here is what he has sent.

He made sure all eyes were on him and read it aloud.

'"Once more unto the breach. (IV. III) The way you twisted words to a scabby tale B ireded today or your truth embed publica."' He put the postcard on the table. 'See? No sense whatsoever apart from the quote.'

'Quote?' James queried.

'"Once more unto the breach",' Archer explained. 'From Shakespeare. A famous speech, and for me, a call to do battle again with the man who would take me down. However, that's only to draw my attention to the play. The numerals that follow point to a different speech in act four, the night before the battle of Agincourt which took place on St Crispin's Day.'

'And is the rest of the message from the same play?' James asked; a sensible question.

'Not at all,' Archer said. 'I spent yesterday reading and rereading the whole thing, and nothing came to mind. I think the reference is simply to set the date.'

'Perhaps,' Thomas said. 'His misspellings are intentional.'

'He's a madman,' Silas huffed. 'Sounds too logical.'

'Which is why we have to work harder,' Archer said. 'St Crispin's Day is three days off, and whether he again intends to lure me to my death, or whether he intends to set my brother free to wreak his revenge in his stead, he must be stopped. We need to think hard, think fast and, I fancy, be prepared to travel.'

'Where to?' Silas sat up.

'Quill likes to lure me by use of locations,' Archer reasoned. 'This time he has contacted me from the Yorkshire Moors. The ruined building is important, else, as James says, why not send a letter? I suggest we work out where this is,' he tapped the picture postcard, 'and pay it a visit.'

'Play right into his hands again?' Silas was sceptical. 'We could just ignore him and not give him the satisfaction.'

'We could,' Archer agreed. 'But I am prepared to take the fight to him. We know his motive, and we know the date, but we must know his battlefield. If there is to be trouble, I would rather it happened amid the anonymity of the North York moors than here on my own doorstep.'

'But why lure you to that specific ruin?'

'That, Thomas, is what I intend to discover.'

Eighteen

By the time the lamplighter had lit the world beyond the windows, Archer had formulated his plan. His men worked hard during the afternoon, each assigned a role which they accepted willingly. Silas was dispatched with Fecker to arrange train tickets while Thomas and James put their minds to the image on the postcard and its possible location. He wanted the two of them to work together in the hope that Thomas' stony looks and sharp words would soften. They didn't. Despite James' best efforts, Thomas remained uncommunicative apart from when discussing their task, or ordering him to attend to footmen's duties. The light in his eyes had been extinguished the moment James admitted his story about Tripp. It was sad to see, but not Archer's main concern.

Quill's message might be cryptic, but its meaning was clear. He was, through his twisted use of the postcard, inviting Archer to a confrontation, and on a particular evening; the night before his brother's birthday. Perhaps he intended to take the news of Archer's death as his gift.

'Oh hell,' he said as a thought occurred.

Thomas looked up from his book. 'What?'

'Just an idea.' Archer compared the telegram to the postcard. 'Not a pleasant one and no evidence, but I have a suspicion Quill might be planning… No, it's ridiculous.'

'Go on,' Thomas encouraged. His jacket was off, and his sleeves rolled in his customary fashion.

'I wonder if Quill is planning to leave the country after all. His birthday gift suggested in the telegram is the restoration of the title to my older brother. Quill would have to be with him to pronounce him sane. What better gift than to arrive at Crispin's side on his birthday with news that I no longer stand in his way?'

'Because he's killed you?'

'Which he will try to do on the eve of St Crispin's Day.'

Thomas pouted as he thought, his full bottom lip turned down giving him a comic appearance. 'We're stretching to reach other conclusions,' he said. 'Might as well stretch that one too, but how would it help?'

'Ships,' James suggested.

'Ships?' Archer looked at him. Like Thomas, he had removed his jacket and undone his waistcoat. With his closely trimmed short hair, rounded face and open neck shirt, he looked like a casual young clerk.

'I've been studying the map,' he said. 'Inglestone is not far from the coast. I mean, it's a few miles, but there's the port of Littleborough to the north.'

'Oh yes!' Archer exclaimed, rising from his chair to look over James' shoulder. 'That makes sense. Lure me to a place not far from where he plans his escape. Kill me and sail to Crispin's side.'

'Hm,' Thomas pondered. 'Two questions. One, why? And two, are there any boats due to sail to the Netherlands on that day from that port?'

'Thomas is always logical. That's why we like him.' Archer gripped James' robust shoulders. He gave them a squeeze of encouragement. 'That and the way he easily forgives,' he added, trying to convey to James that Thomas would come around, and to Thomas that he should. 'As for why... He wants his revenge. I don't know the workings of an insane mind, but I doubt reason has much to do with anything. And as for the possibility of a ship's sailing...'

'I'll look for timetables,' James offered.

He turned, and Archer wondered if it was because he was uncomfortable being touched. Other people would think it extremely forward, but not the viscount.

'I can look in the Times,' James said. He gazed eagerly into Archer's eyes, seemingly unbothered that his master was holding him. 'Or do you have a current Lloyds list?'

'No,' Archer said. 'But today's newspaper is in my room. Start there.'

'Shall I fetch it, Sir?'

'If you would, James. If it's no good, I'll go to Lloyds.' He tapped him on the shoulders and let him go. 'Good man.'

As soon as they were alone, Archer drew a chair close to Thomas.

'What's going on?' He kept his voice low.

'How do you mean?'

'I believe him, don't you?'

'Who?'

'Come on, Tom. James? I saw it in your eyes even before I met the man. Now I have, I can see he's perfect for you and you for him, he has the same hopeful look. Or had, until he made his confession. Now you have a face like a wet flannel, and he's as sad as a lost puppy.'

'Tripp told him to seduce me,' Thomas complained. 'I thought he was genuine. Now?'

'Now you have a chance to show him how you feel by believing him,' Archer said. 'I'm prepared to let him into our inner circle, and he's practically a stranger.'

'You work on intuition,' Thomas said. 'I prefer realism.'

'You saw how hard it was for him to admit. He did it because he cares about you. Yes, my intuition tells me he is sincere. I don't know what Tripp promised him nor what his motives were, but I am certain that man is falling in love with you. Don't throw away the chance. Take a risk.'

'We're not all as brave as you, Archer.' Thomas returned to the book he was studying.

'Oh, Tom, you're as stubborn as an ox and as blind as a mole.' Archer left him and poured himself a small whisky. 'Sort it out, would you?' he said. 'If we're going into battle against Quill, I need my first officer on point.'

'I will be.'

'I want you to be happy, Tom. I meant what I said. You are my best friend.'

'Thank you, Sir. It is an honour.'

Archer threw up his hands. 'Have it your way,' he said, slumping into his chair.

James returned with the newspaper a few minutes later, his face white. He stood at the door, and making sure Thomas didn't see, showed the viscount a page.

Archer understood his concern immediately and beckoned him closer. He had forgotten that he had ringed certain passages relating to the Ripper murders, a story which had not died despite the lack of new victims.

James raised his eyebrows questioningly, a shocked expression on his face. He pointed to the words, "The Ripper" and Archer nodded.

'The same,' he said. 'Are you happy to continue?'

He expected James to be horrified, but the opposite happened. He smiled as if he was impressed and said, 'Definitely.'

Archer nodded to Thomas' back. 'Some things are worth fighting for,' he said, and James understood.

'Rotterdam, wasn't it?' the footman asked before taking the newspaper to his place at the table and laying it open.

'That would be the nearest port to the asylum,' Archer said. 'Look for cargo ships as well as any passenger steamers.'

'Right you are, Sir.'

James set about his new task with diligence, only occasionally raising his eyes to look at Thomas. Each time, he found him comparing the postcard to the plates in the book, or turning a page, his gaze anywhere but on James.

'Nothing that looks remotely like any church, abbey or monastery near Inglestone,' Thomas announced, throwing the book to one side and reaching for another.

'Try widening the field,' Archer suggested. 'Look coastwards rather than inland. I think James has hit on a good idea.'

Thomas continued his research and silence descended on the room, broken only by the ticking clock and the turning of pages.

'Nothing sailing from Littleborough,' James said at length. 'Nor Haverpool which is also nearby.'

'I still think it's a correct assumption,' Archer encouraged. 'Broaden your search too.'

The work continued until Silas returned.

'Afternoon all,' he said, as he waltzed into the study brandishing an envelope. 'Tickets as requested, Archer. The night train leaves at ten.'

'Stopping at Barrenmoor?'

'That it does, and several other places. It's not the express, so we won't pass Barrenmoor until gone five, but I checked with the ticket man, and he confirmed it will stop there.'

'Did he ask questions?'

'Yeah, but I said we were a party of bird-watchers, 'cos apparently it's a pastime. I told him we were keen to get off there to see a rare breed that's only found nearby.'

'He believed you?'

'Not only that, he offered to inform the guard who would bring steps. I said there was no need. Apparently...' He affected the air and voice of an older man, mimicking the ticket seller's superciliousness. 'It is not uncommon for passengers to alight at halts if they are closer to their desired destinations than a station if they don't mind the inconvenience of the dismount — or something equally as naff. He still charged me full whack to the next stop.'

'And you bought five tickets?'

'All returns too,' Silas said. He glanced at the others before leaning over the desk and kissing Archer firmly on the mouth. 'I did think about only getting four returns, just in case, you don't make it, but...' He grinned impishly.

'Shut up.' Archer knew he was teasing, but it was a reminder to himself that his relaxed attitude to the mission needed to be tightened. He refused to allow nervousness, however, and was confident he would be coming back alive. 'This could be our last chance to catch Quill,' he said. 'One way or the other, he's not to get away from us.'

'You really are prepared to kill him?' Thomas asked, without looking up.

'If I must.'

Silas laughed. 'Kill Quill,' he chanted, heading to the door. 'I'm going to change.'

'Who will look after the house?' Thomas asked, closing another book. 'We can't leave Lucy on her own.'

'A good point, Tom.' Archer considered leaving Fecker to guard the house, not that he expected any trouble at Clearwater, but he wanted his strongest man beside him. 'Maybe you should stay.'

'Now that's not going to happen.' Thomas stood and stretched his back. 'James is too new. Silas?'

'Could you imagine the riot that would cause?' Archer laughed. 'No. Perhaps you would deliver a message to Lady Marshall. I'll ask her to put one of her stevedore-cum-footmen people in the house.

He can give the silver a good going over.'

'And what reason will you give for our absence?'

'I'll think of something.'

'If I might, Sir,' James piped up. 'Her Ladyship told me last night to come to her should I suspect you had any problems. I had the impression she was suspicious of something. You might not want to add fuel to her fire.'

'Don't speak to His Lordship that way,' Thomas chided. 'And don't presume to know Her Ladyship as he does.'

'Yes, thank you, Payne.' Archer was annoyed at Thomas' tone. 'James is right to warn me.'

Thomas dropped his next book onto the desk with a thud, saying nothing, itself an impertinence which Archer ignored.

He wrote a short note explaining he was taking his men with him on a trip to the country and left it vague.

'Will you deliver this?'

'Yes, Sir.' James replied.

'Not you. Thomas.'

Thomas glared.

'You know her better than James,' Archer reasoned. 'She may ask questions, and I can trust you to evade them. Not that I don't trust you, James, but you're new to her, and she will manipulate you. God knows she tries it on enough with me.'

Thomas took the note, gave it and Archer a cursory glance, collected his tailcoat and flounced from the room. Archer watched him go. Saddened at his behaviour, but understanding of it, he addressed James.

'I am right to trust you, aren't I, Jimmy?' he asked, inflecting mild cynicism.

'Yes, Sir,' James replied, looking up from the newspaper after placing a finger on it so as not to lose his place.

'I'm not sure Thomas does.'

James' face fell. 'Understandable,' he said. 'I haven't been honest with him.'

'How do you feel about him?'

James shifted uncomfortably in his chair.

'You're not used to being asked such a thing?'

'No, Sir, though I've asked it of myself a lot these past few days.

To be honest, this whole set-up is new to me, and I don't just mean the job. I'm more than honoured that you've taken to me so quick, and I meant my words last night when I said I felt welcomed here, but... Well, I don't know what to do about Thomas.'

'May I be embarrassingly frank?'

James nodded, swallowing.

'When you came for the interview, I immediately saw that you were in awe of Tom. He is, let's face it, a handsome man, but he has other qualities which you will discover in time. I wouldn't normally have appointed someone such as yourself — without experience, I mean. I'm not questioning your character. But I saw in Thomas the same look of awe and admiration towards you as you have for him. Now, don't tell him I said this, but what you feel may be new to you, but it is equally new to him. It has taken him a long time to reach this place, and he only recently found the confidence to accept himself. Give him time while you learn your job and allow him room.'

'I don't know what to say to him.' James shrugged helplessly. 'My head's in a whirl, and my feet aren't on the ground what with the position, Your Lordship's kindness, the way you are with us and now all this.'

'Something of a shock?'

'On many fronts, but I can cope, Sir. I'll take your advice, and I won't let our situation interfere with the task you have graciously allowed me to assist with.'

'Bloody hell, Jimmy,' Archer laughed. 'How much schooling did Tripp give you?'

'Only an hour or two.'

'Then you must be a natural at obsequiousness. Remember, out there you're a footman, in here you're a member of my crew, no need to grovel.'

'Sorry.'

'Think nothing of it, but be yourself, not Tripp. By the way, do you know what he intended to do?'

'Do?'

'With whatever information you were going to give him?'

'No, Sir. He told me that... How did he put it?' He withdrew his finger from the newspaper so he could fully face the viscount.

'Something about unnatural vices or unspeakable acts, but he was alluding to men sleeping together, which of course immediately made me want to work here. Not because I wanted to be a spy, but because I'm… well… the same. You know.'

'What was he offering in return?'

'A lot. I got some money off him in advance which I gave straight to my mum, and he said when I furnished him with information he could use, he'd give me another twenty. I mean, that was like a year's wages.'

'Probably sold the hideous centrepiece,' Archer said. 'Good riddance to both. Are you to see him again?'

'Not straight away. I told him it would take time.'

'Do you know where he is?'

'No, Sir. He said he would be at the Crown and Anchor regular and look for me.'

Archer shuddered. All he'd done was sack the man for acting above his station, and because he reminded him of his father. That was not a good enough reason to dismiss a servant so long in his post. Tripp knew that as well as he knew that Archer's behaviour was not gentlemanly.

'I am right to put my trust in a man I hardly know, aren't I, James?' he asked again. 'Reassure me one last time.'

James sucked in his cheeks as he thought, scanning the room to find the words. He nodded to himself and returned his puppy gaze to the viscount.

'Yes, is the simple answer,' he said. 'But like you said, you'll have to give me time to prove it. If it helps, it would make no sense for me to incriminate myself in a scandal or whatever Mr Tripp had planned, and now that I know you and your kindness, it makes even less sense. But what seals it for me, what made me change my mind and confess, if you like, is Thomas.'

'Because you have fallen in love with him?'

'Sir, it was bigger than that.' James' reticence to talk about himself left him in a blink of pale lashes. 'I was bringing a telegram, and Thomas answered the door. I mean, that was it. Never met him before, but soon as I saw him, it was like I'd known him all my life, like everything made sense, you know?'

'Just as I experienced when I first laid eyes on Silas.'

190

'Yeah, but you two behave as though you've been married for years like my mum and dad. A double act I suppose.'

Archer chuckled at the man's innocence. 'I don't know how your parents behave together,' he said, 'but I know what you mean. They are comfortable together. My parents were the opposite, and it was hard to see the woods of love for the trees of their behaviour. It was not a happy relationship. In fact, our adversary, Quill, used to refer to their marriage as "A grim era."'

'Oh dear,' James said, but Archer's words had raised the hint of a confused smile.

'*A grim era* being a cognate anagram for *marriage,*' Archer explained. 'Not one of his best. But the point I was attempting to reach, was that not every pair is well matched. As soon as we met, Silas and I knew we were meant to be together even in a world where we shouldn't be, or can't be. One instantly understood the other. We have what he calls an easy friendship. It is, of course, deeper than that, and behind closed doors, devilishly physical.'

'Oh,' James said, looking away and blushing.

'I take it you and Thomas haven't…?'

'No, Sir. Luckily.'

That was an odd thing to say. 'Do you not have feelings for him after all? Or has he put you off with his sulk?'

'I reckon I've put him off, but I say luckily, because, to be frank, I wouldn't have a clue where to start.'

The penny dropped. 'Ah, I see. Then I shall embarrass you no more, my apologies.'

'Not at all, Sir.'

'Once again, Jimmy, not a word until the time is right, but what is as yet unexplored for you is equally as unexplored for Tom. Also once again, you will hear this in no-one else's company but mine. I, for one, hope that you are both able to explore the delights ahead, together and soon. You'll find a way, trust me.'

'I do, Sir, and I will.'

'Any news on your shipping theory?'

Silas was approaching through the drawing room. Archer waved to him so that James realised why he had changed the subject so curtly.

'I'll get right back to it,' the footman said, already in tune with

Archer's way of working.

'Getting anywhere?' Silas asked, entering and making directly for the decanters.

'Not yet,' Archer admitted.

While James was busy scanning the newspapers, Archer took the opportunity to draw Silas to one side.

'I wanted to give this to you tonight.' He spoke quietly and handed Silas the box. 'I was planning a bath and some time alone in the private sitting room tonight, but instead, we shall be speeding into the unknown. So, would you mind if we celebrated at a later time?'

''Course not, you daft eejit,' Silas laughed. 'What is it?'

'Open it.'

Grinning, Silas undid the ribbon and lifted the lid.

'Fecking hell,' he gasped, his grin vanishing beneath a wave of disbelief. 'Archie!'

'I hope you like it.'

Silas lifted the gold and gemstone ring to the lamp where it glistened. 'It's got our initials in it,' he said.

'It's a green tourmaline,' Archer beamed. 'Green for your homeland.'

'Westerpool?'

'Well, I meant Ireland, so, green for your heritage.'

'S and A written in a jewel. Me mam wouldn't have believed it. For me?'

Silas' delight was reflected in the happiness his expression gave Archer.

'Sorry that wasn't a very romantic presentation.'

'Ah, get away with you.'

'It reminds me of another time,' Archer said. 'And, as Hennell has engraved the letters entwined, I hope it will remind you of how much I—'

He wasn't permitted to finish the sentence. Silas' lips were on his, and he embraced Archer tightly.

'Hold on.'

They broke apart at the sound of James' voice and turned to see him staring, open-mouthed. He'd caught them kissing, but a hint of red on his cheeks was the only giveaway.

'Sorry,' he said. 'But I've found one.'

'Show me?'

James folded the paper and drew a line in red ink. 'There,' he said as Archer came to look, leaving Silas dewy-eyed and examining his signet ring. 'The only one I can find. A ship called De Raaf, whatever that means. It's a Dutch galliot leaving Kingston docks on the morning tide on the twenty-fifth.'

'Where's that?' Silas joined them.

'Look it up, James,' Archer directed as he fetched one of his almanacks. 'Must be a shallow harbour to suit a galliot, though it'll be a rough crossing. They're built for coastal waters.' He opened the almanack and brought it back to his desk, pecking Silas on the cheek as he passed. 'High tide on that morning will be... Five-sixteen.'

'And Kingston is a good six-hour ride from Inglestone,' James said. 'At least, that's what I'd reckon from the map.'

'Ha!' Archer dropped the book on the desk and lifted his glass. 'Your health gentlemen,' he said as if he just won a point.

'What on earth have you go to be cheery about?' Silas smirked, waving his whisky in return.

'The high tide.'

'What about it?'

'In order to make the distance, he must have his business with me done by midnight at the latest, earlier if possible. Keep looking for other ships, James, would you?'

'It's the only one on the east coast,' James said. 'I already checked. There's others, but they're leaving from Cornwall, couldn't get much further away, and some aren't until the next day.'

'Very well. We will assume that's his escape. We must make sure he is time-limited, Silas,' Archer explained. 'I shall keep him waiting to the point of distraction and when he is concerned about his getaway, shall attack with the advantage of confidence.'

'Yeah,' Silas considered. 'You could do that. Or you could just wait for him on the ship.'

'He would be suspicious,' Archer reasoned. 'And is probably expecting that. No, we must make him think he has me dangling from his puppet-master strings. This whole thing is just a game to him, but he's a man who can't bear to lose. He could have simply vanished by now, but no, he is taunting me, and he knows I won't stand for that and must react. I shall, but on my terms. Ah, Thomas.'

'All done,' Thomas said as he swept into the room. 'I spoke with Saunders. Her Ladyship has visitors. He will send his under-butler and a maid Lucy is friendly with to be her companion. Clearwater will be guarded and so will the maid.'

'And we now know how Quill means to escape.' Archer told him the details, noting Thomas chose to take his books to the couch rather than sit near James. 'We have the time,' he said as he crossed to the chalkboard to write. 'The eve of St Crispin's day is tomorrow and let's say midnight is when I will show myself. The accuracy would suit him, his envisaged battle taking place on both the eve when the speech was made and the day itself. He will appreciate the neatness of it, and I will enjoy delaying his departure.'

'You're assuming our destination is near Inglestone,' Thomas pointed out. 'It could be closer to the port.'

'True,' Archer admitted, frustrated despite marvelling at Thomas' quick mind. 'Without knowing the place where he intends to kill me...'

'Er, *hopes* to kill you,' Silas butted in. 'He ain't going to do it. We'll make sure of that.'

'Indeed we will,' Thomas seconded.

'Thank you, friends,' Archer said. 'I have yet to think on the best way to fight the madman, but until I know the lie of the land, I can't say if it is a job to be done alone. I am not prepared to put any of you in danger. You are to accompany me for your minds, not your muscles.'

'I'm pretty good in a scrap, Sir,' James said balling a fist. 'I'll give him a grim time the way I fought the bullies at...' He broke off, staring into the distance, his mouth open. 'No!' Picking up a pen, he began scribbling.

'I don't doubt your muscle power, James,' Archer said, wondering what he had thought of. 'But this man has been trained in all manner of combat, and you have read in the newspaper what he is capable of.'

'James knows?' Thomas was surprised.

'We must all be aware of the facts and Quill's history, Tom,' Archer said, placating him. 'What we are not aware of is the place and his reason. Have you found anywhere in your guide books that look remotely like the ruin in the postcard?'

'Not yet,' Thomas sighed and returned to his reading.

'Then we must work faster. The train leaves in five hours.'

'Is there a place in your book called Ebb Bay, Mr Payne?' James asked.

'Ebb…?' The name rang a bell with Archer, but it was one of his fluttering, caged birds; a memory that needed time to find its way out.

Thomas turned pages. 'Yes, why?'

James took the postcard and sat beside Thomas, holding it above the book so they could compare the pictures. Thomas made room for him, but although there was plenty of space, James chose to sit with their bodies touching. As he held the postcard aloft, he leant in and their heads connected. Encouragingly, Thomas didn't pull away.

'Well?' Archer prompted. 'Any similarity?'

'Ebb Bay Castle,' Thomas read. 'Ruined since the Cromwell era, only the church is in use. It's on the cliffs above Ebb Bay, popular in the summer…' He compared the card to the book. 'Completely different angle, but yes, that's your destination.'

'Our destination,' James emphasised, and in his enthusiasm, gave Thomas a nudge.

Thomas frowned and moved away, denting Archer's hopes.

'Is that a guess, James?' he asked.

'No, Sir.'

'So how d'you come up with it?'

James grinned with confidence cocky enough to put Silas to shame. He came to Archer offering the postcard. 'I don't know much about what's happened, My Lord,' he said. 'But if I'm not mistaken, being caught up with this Doctor Quill must have been a pretty ugly time. You might even call it "A grim era".'

Nineteen

Archer read the message he had read many times before, and it still meant nothing. 'I have no idea what you are alluding to,' he said looking at the words and trying to see how they might connect to the name of a tourist location in the north-east.

'You're an elegant man, Sir,' James replied.

'Thank you for the praise, but…?'

'What did you call it? An anagram? Elegant Man, same letters as *gentleman* but in a different order. Like marriage is *a grim era*, not that I'm likely to find out.' He turned the card to read the message. 'The way you twisted words to *a scabby tale B*… Except it's not "be" with an E, it just the letter B which makes no sense. Not unless you take the instruction hinted at there at the beginning and change the order of what follows. In that case, you can make Ebb Bay Castle.'

'Once more unto the breach, Ebb Bay Castle… Good Lord, James, you're a genius.'

'I bet you could make a hundred words out of that nonsense,' Thomas grumbled.

'Give me half an hour, Tom, and I'll prove you right.' James sat at the table and began writing furiously. Twenty minutes later, surrounded by pages of scribbled text, crossed-out letters and mistakes, he announced. 'I think I have something.'

The others gathered behind him, leaning over to look as he took them through his findings.

He pointed to the first line of the coded message. 'Here, we have the call to battle with the quote from the play. Lord Clearwater and Quill are going, once more, into battle. After that, the reference to the act and scene as you pointed out, Sir, a scene which takes place on the eve of St Crispin's Day. The next line, *The way you twisted words*, made me wonder if perhaps there was an incident in your past where he was angry at something you said, or misinterpreted.'

'There were plenty,' Archer said.

'Either way, I just thought, what if he means you to twist his words around? When you mentioned anagrams, I was reminded of some of the coded messages I've seen on telegrams, when, for example, a man doesn't want his wife to know he is contacting his mistress. Not that I read other people's messages.' He coughed. 'Very often. Apparently, it's quite a thing nowadays, the puzzle of unscrambling letters I mean, not reading private letters.' His blustering was amusing and endearing. 'I didn't see any truncations as we call them, and the odd letter B and the strange word, *ireded*, stood out as being so obviously wrong they could only be intentional. I tried all manner of combinations from the word "to" until the end, using everything that followed and twisting the words. There were too many letters, so I broke it down.'

Archer glanced at Thomas, standing over James and regarding him distrustfully through narrow eyes. Silas, on the other side, was more interested in what the footman had to say, and his face was a picture of admiration.

'Then,' James continued, 'I broke down phrases, so... Another example, *or your truth* which gave me all kinds of daft things like...' He referred to some papers. '"Hurry to tour", "Your truth or", and, "Try hour tour", none of which made sense. But, I was able to make sense of others. *Embed publica*, gives us *a bumbled epic*, which I like, but also makes no sense in this context, and *public bade me*, where I thought I might be getting closer. "Bade me" is an anagram of "be made".'

'You're losing me,' Thomas said. 'What's the message?'

'Alright, Tom,' Archer placated him for a second time. He would need to speak to Thomas; he couldn't have his men at odds with each other. 'James is doing his best.'

'If I'm right,' James said, seemingly unaffected by Thomas' curtness, 'the whole message reads as follows: "Once more unto the breach. (IV. III) The way you twisted words. To Ebb Bay Castle, be prepared to die or your truth be made public."'

All heads turned to Archer.

'So,' he said after consideration. 'He is baiting me and threatening blackmail. He threatens to make my true nature public if I fail to meet him.' He put an arm around Silas and drew the man's light frame close, kissing his hair. 'Good luck with that, Benji Quill.'

He let Silas go and resisted the temptation to congratulate James with a hug.

'Good work,' he said. 'We now fully know his intentions. What he doesn't know are ours.'

'Which are what?' Thomas asked.

'Now I have this information which, if nothing else, confirms my suspicion, I will redraw my battle plan.'

'Perhaps while you are doing that, James should see to your dinner,' Thomas suggested.

'For all of us, yes please.' Archer noticed the time. 'The hours are passing swiftly, men,' he said. 'We must prepare. Once again I feel we should be disguised. Silas and I will attend to that while you two assist Lucy and bring us all some supper. Fecker too. Tom, if there's anything lying around the pantry we can take for the journey, will you see to it?'

'Certainly. James?'

Thomas headed for the doors where he waited impatiently as James, the wind taken from his sails and crestfallen, joined him.

Dinner was served in the breakfast room and followed the usual conventions of the butler serving the viscount, and the footman his secretary. The unusual aspect was Fecker who was invited to join them, so he could be clued in about the journey and task ahead. The coachman was his usual self, unbothered about anything he was asked to do and unimpressed that the man who had tried to kill Archer previously was trying again. Albeit in a more convoluted, crazy way than before.

'I break his neck,' was all he added to the suggestions of the best ways to trap Quill.

'I would rather capture him alive,' Archer said. 'So that he can be brought to justice, even if it would mean scandal be brought upon me. Quill has gone far enough, and I am coming to the opinion that I should have told Inspector Adelaide everything.'

'Then your truth would already be known,' Thomas pointed out. 'And Quill would be in the Netherlands seeing to the release of your brother. You've done the right thing.'

It was the most positive thing Thomas said throughout the meal.

Archer became distracted with thoughts of Thomas and James

and what he could do to mend the rift. He concluded as he returned to the study, that the best thing was to watch, and at some point on the journey, see if he could intervene. James was infatuated with Thomas, possibly in the same way Archer had been up until Silas changed his life. It was an easy thing to do, to fall for the handsome redhead and his gentle manner, his alluring eyes and manly figure, but, with James, it was more than infatuation. Archer could tell by the way he accepted Thomas' cold shoulder, and, sad though he looked, was prepared to wait for Thomas to heal.

He was less worried about Quill and his ravings than he was about James. Even if Thomas didn't return to his previous state of admiration for the man, James was a good worker, clearly loyal, and as he had proved, intelligent. With his stocky build and strength, he would also be a useful man to have near in case of a skirmish.

While Fecker arranged transport and Silas and Thomas saw to the clothing and provisions, Archer took James to the study for another private discussion.

'I will repeat once more,' he said, with James sitting opposite him at the table. 'If you are unsure about coming with us, I will understand.'

'No need, Sir,' James said. 'It makes a change from tramping the streets with telegrams.'

'It is not a holiday, Jimmy. Although I intend to see to Quill on my own, perhaps with the bulk of Fecker behind me, you may face danger yourself.'

'I didn't mean to make light of your predicament, Your Lordship.'

'I know, but I am not the only one in a quandary.'

'How do you mean?'

'Thomas.'

'Ah.'

'I tried to hint earlier,' Archer said. 'Tried to suggest that you persevere with him. You know why he is upset?'

'I do, Sir.'

'Do you want to tell me how you arrived at this impasse?'

'If you want me to.' James shuffled in his chair, his hands wedged between his knees. 'Before he moved back to Clearwater,' he said, 'he spent some time at my house, and we had to share the bed. I can't tell you how hard that was for me, having him right there and not knowing if it was safe to say anything, let alone do anything.'

'But you did?'

'In a way. You see, Mr Tripp had made me this offer, but I wanted Thomas so badly I would have done what I did even without Tripp's bribe. It was, as my mum says, the icing on the cake — that one man should pay me to get closer to another I already wanted.'

'Did Tripp know you are... of our persuasion?'

'Don't think so, Sir. I reckon he assumed that because I was a messenger boy, I was fair game. It goes on a lot with some of the lads, but not me. I told you I've not done anything about it, these feelings, this... persuasion? I don't need no persuading. I was in like a shot with a legitimate excuse to be closer to Tom.'

He sought assurance that they were alone before admitting, 'I should have told him from the start, but I didn't know him. Still don't, obviously. I thought he'd be happy I'd come clean. One of the first things he told me was the first rule of Clearwater. I should have been honest from the start.'

James was secure enough to talk freely, something Archer admired in any man.

'What do you intend to do about it?' he asked. 'I need you both focused on what's ahead. We must be ready to react to any situation, and if Thomas is occupying your mind, you will be distracted.'

'I'll try not to be, Sir. I'll try and square things up with him on the train. We have seven hours between here and Barrenmoor. I'm sure I can put this to rest by the time we arrive.'

'Good man. I will leave it in your hands. You best go and change now. Are you prepared to wear your own clothes? I'm not sure we have anything to fit you, except some of my old cadet uniforms.'

'My old uniform was like military garb,' James frowned. 'But, yeah, happy to wear whatever I have if you don't mind me looking third-class.'

Archer laughed. 'You're a first-class code-breaker, Jimmy,' he said. 'We're travelling in a private carriage, but no-one's going to ask questions if they see you in your civvies. Actually, I might have a few other things from my past that would do for you.'

'Understood, Sir.'

James rose and turned to leave, but something on the wall map stopped him.

'Hang on a minute.'

'What is it?'

'Trains.'

He approached the map and traced a line down the east coast as Archer joined him.

'What have you seen?'

'Details,' James said. 'Another backup.'

'Can you explain?'

'I'll try.'

The map was large and well printed, detailed, and if one could interpret its symbols and lines, filled with information. Archer could read it easily because of his ordnance training, and presumably, James was used to reading street maps, but this was a collection of roads, rivers and railway lines.

'Excuse me, Sir,' James said. 'Do you have those notes the station master gave you? The ones giving the speed of trains on this line?'

'I do.' Archer found the papers and handed them over. 'What have you seen?'

James took them, concerned. 'Something that I don't think Thomas is going to like.'

Twenty

At eight-thirty that evening, James stood looking at himself in the mirrored wardrobe. The party were to travel as unobtrusively as possible, and there was no-one more unremarkable in the city than him. Few were more remarkable either. He was Mr Average, a typical working-class young man who had found a reasonable job, the same as thousands of other fortunate people.

The jump from being ordinary to special, as the viscount found him, was another reason why it was hard to make sense of the way his life had changed. He supposed that most men would be trying to understand what on earth they were doing, chasing after a madman who had already claimed several victims. Others would have left the house and perhaps even taken their story to the police. For James, however, the only way to accept the events of the past few days was to see the journey as an adventure. Perhaps he didn't appreciate the danger they were walking into, he certainly couldn't comprehend it, but everything was so new and topsy-turvy all he could do was enjoy the ride.

What occupied his mind more were thoughts of the man currently changing in the room across the passage. Also new to him and just as exciting were the possibilities Thomas offered.

Had offered.

He had withdrawn them, and James couldn't understand why. Thomas had told him to be honest, and he had been, that was all. He didn't strike James as the kind of man to react so churlishly to the truth. If anything, James expected him to be happy he'd admitted Tripp's business.

'Jimmy,' he said to his reflection. 'You've got to sort it out one way or the other.'

To set off on the viscount's adventure with a bad feeling between him and Thomas would not serve His Lordship well, but to go to him and try and make things right could make them worse, and that thought scared him more.

'You're about to travel half-way up the country to help one man kill another,' he said. 'A quick chat with Thomas is nothing.'

His confidence mustered, he left his room and knocked on the opposite door. It was thrown open immediately, and Thomas appeared, frown-face and flustered.

'What?' he asked, pushing past and locking the door after him.

'Can I have a word?'

'On the way down. There's much to do.'

'We have time. Just a couple of minutes.'

'There is no time. Come along.'

'No, hold on, Tom...'

Thomas rounded on him unexpectedly, forcing James against the wall.

'From now on, it's Mr Payne,' he spat. 'If His Lordship insists on bringing you, then we must behave like gentlemen, and that means I am Mr Payne and you say nothing unless spoken to.'

'Can't you give me a minute to explain myself?'

'We are late.' Thomas was off, clipping his way towards the backstairs. 'Follow or be left behind.'

'Tom, please...'

'Follow or stay!'

Hurt and frustrated, James followed.

They arrived at North Cross terminus at different times and in two hansom cabs to avoid suspicion. James rode with Thomas in stony silence, trying to make sense of the man's disinterest, while the viscount, Mr Hawkins and Fecker travelled later. Each man carried his own ticket, the plan being not to meet as one obvious group until they were in the carriage booked for the viscount's exclusive use and outside of the city.

Alighting from the cab an hour before departure, James hurried to the telegraph office to dispatch a message according to instructions his master had given and waited for the reply. That done, he returned to the concourse.

Wearing a long overcoat and carrying a travel bag, Thomas

examined the platform information and compared it to his ticket. He looked to all intents and purposes like any other middle-class traveller, fine and smart in a top hat, carrying a cane and occasionally glancing at his pocket watch. He hardly looked at James, also dressed for winter weather, but in clothes borrowed from the viscount's wardrobe. Nothing too fashionable, he was, after all, a bird-watcher, but the cut of the coat and the expensive felt of the bowler hat brought an unaccustomed feeling of wealth that boosted his confidence. No-one gave him a second glance as he studied a timetable a few feet from Thomas.

A little before ten, Thomas left, walking quickly to the platform where he was swallowed by the hubbub and steam. James followed a minute later, carrying a bag containing the notes, maps and other useful books. He walked as calmly as he could towards the first-class carriages. None of them knew what they were heading into apart from a confrontation with a murderer who must, at all costs, be prevented from leaving the country.

A murderer.

Suddenly, the sound of the station intensified the dull thumping in his ears. Coal smoke clogged the air, but the hiss of engines and the whistles pierced it and chilled him. He gripped his case tighter and breathed deeply, inhaling steam and the taste of oil that made his head spin. His vision was darkening as his pulse climbed, and he was on the edge of panic when he saw the viscount's party.

They appeared from the vapour, backlit by the concourse lamps. Individual silhouettes striding side by side intent on a common purpose. Lord Clearwater was in the centre, disguised in country clothes, a cloak and a travel cap. Beside him, Mr Hawkins walked confidently, the steam billowing about his boots and tight-fitting box jacket, a knapsack slung from his shoulder. He proudly wore a military-style peaked cap, like a revolutionary in a resistance movement. Fecker advanced on the other side, tall and imposing. His greatcoat hung open, whipping behind and swirling the steam. All were self-assured, their faces grave.

James hung back as the viscount opened the carriage door and allowed Silas to enter first as if the master and secretary had swapped roles. Fecker climbed in after them, giving James a genteel nod as he entered the carriage by a separate door.

James was the last to board. He slammed the door with a thud of finality and cut off the outside world before sitting apart from the others as he had been instructed to do. Only the viscount and Silas sat together, away from the windows where Fecker drew the blinds.

James had never seen inside a first-class carriage. On the rare occasions he had travelled on the railways it had been on hard benches among noisy louts in third where there was no heating and smoke infiltrated in tunnels. This was a different world. The floor was carpeted, the panels were oak, there was a toilet with a lock, and the walls were adorned with the crest of the railway line rather than notices banning the practice of spitting. Although they were only five, the carriage was big enough for ten with velvet-covered seats at one end and armchairs at the other. Tables were fixed to the walls beneath gas lamps, and a heater warmed the air to the point of stuffiness.

Their work would begin when the train pulled out which it did promptly at the sound of a whistle at ten o'clock. It wasn't until the tickets had been collected and the train was shuddering along at speed, that the viscount called them to the table.

'Gentlemen,' he said. 'We know Quill's plan, the location and the time we shall be there. What we don't know is what to expect. We have twenty-four hours to get ahead of him, and for that purpose, I have drawn a plan. You sent the messages, James?'

'Yes, Sir.'

The viscount laid out the map of the North York Moors where he had drawn a route for the party to follow.

'We get off here,' he said, indicating the Barrenmoor depot. 'From there, we hike the five miles to Inglestone where we rest up until dark.' He regarded James, his downturned face devoid of any good humour.

'The coaching inn knows we're coming, Sir,' he said. 'I messaged that we would be arriving in the morning. They have one room.'

'Good. And a carriage?'

James extracted a telegram from his pocket and read. '"Carriage unavailable. Horses?" I replied demanding five. It looks like the best they can do.'

'That's a bugger,' Silas muttered.

'You can ride with someone else, Silas,' the viscount said. 'And,

James, from now on there is to be no Sir or My Lord. You must call me Archer and even then only if you must. We are five tourists, friends on a jolly jaunt to spot a lesser crowned moorhen or some such.'

'Moorhens are water birds,' Thomas said. 'But there is a nest of rare hawks at Ebb Bay, apparently. I suggest, if asked, they are what we are looking for.'

'Do they have quill feathers?' Silas joked. 'Get it?'

'Thank you, Silas,' Archer said, dryly. 'But it will take more than one of your bad wordplays to quash my apprehension.'

Silas huffed. 'Sorry, but it's about the only weapon I got. I don't ride, I don't shoot, I'm not fast like you and Tommy, not strong like Fecks.' He smiled weakly at James. 'And not as clever with words as you are. I feel like a fecking mascot.'

Archer took his hand, and James instinctively glanced around to ensure they were alone.

'You are my reason to stay alive,' Archer said.

'Should have brought one of Mrs Flintwich's baking tins.' Silas, seeing the look of confusion on James' face, explained. 'The last time we tried to catch Quill, I had to wear steel around my neck to stop him slashing me. Obviously, it worked, apart from this.' He touched the wound on his chin, healing well and now, thanks to Markland, free of stitches.

'We don't need anything like that,' Archer said. 'This time, we have the advantage. We will ride to Ebb Bay Castle in time to recce the field. We will find some vantage point from where I can aim. I will shoot to injure, disarm the man and, with Fecker's help, we will deliver him to the authorities.'

'Are you mad?' Silas said. 'I thought we were going to kill the bastard.'

'That is the last resort.'

'But they'll ask questions, and your name will be dragged in. I thought that was what we wanted to avoid.'

'I have been thinking more on that.' Archer removed his cap and ran his fingers through his hair, adjusting it where it had been flattened. 'And I can see no other way around it.'

'Bullet, head, go home,' Fecker said.

'If only it was as simple as that, Andrej.'

'And then there's the possibility that he may see you first and get a shot off, or that he is already there lying in wait,' Thomas put in. 'There are so many possibilities that we have no idea what will happen.'

'Correct,' Archer agreed. 'We will have to improvise, which is why orders only come from me and if there is any fighting to be done, it's me that does it.'

'So what are we here for?' Thomas asked. 'Not that any of us don't want to assist you, Archer, but surely it would have been safer if you'd gone alone or with Fecker. I'm not scared, don't take me the wrong way, but five of us together is more noticeable than two.'

Archer nodded to James, and he knew the time had come to explain the strategy he had earlier devised with the viscount.

'There won't be five of us,' he said, and everyone looked at him in surprise. 'His... Archer and I discussed this before we left Clearwater and, with your permission, Archer, I'll explain.'

Using the man's Christian same came more easily than James expected. He had only been his footman for two days, and during that time they'd hardly had a master/servant relationship. If anything, after this business was done, he would have more trouble adjusting back to calling him My Lord.

He turned the map so that each man could see more clearly and took the timetable from his case.

'As Archer said, here is Barrenmoor.' He pointed with a pencil. 'Here is Inglestone and there, roughly six miles away on the coast, is the castle, nothing between it and the village but open moorland.'

'Easy riding,' Archer said, looking at Silas who was dubious.

'I had a look at the map,' James continued, 'and a few things struck me. Quill needs to get from the castle to the boat by five in the morning. Overland that could take several hours, we know this, right?' The others agreed. 'But...' he unfolded the timetable. 'What if he doesn't intend to do that? I mean, what if he's not got a horse? So...' Back to the map. 'If he rode, then that's the route, but it's up and down, around towns and through a couple of villages, all a bit long-winded and not quick. If he has a carriage, then this is his route.' He showed them the quickest way from the castle to Kingston docks by road. 'As you can see, it's lengthy, heads inland and circles around. It would take even longer.'

'Yes, I see that,' Thomas said, the first thing he had said directly to James since they left the house. 'But you're assuming he is at the castle and that he waits for us until midnight. He could leave earlier, or even be gone by the time we get there, or this whole thing could be misdirection.'

'You depressing,' Fecker said, pulling an apple from his coat and biting it in half.

'No, Andrej,' Archer admonished kindly. 'Tom is right to point out the negative. It would be too easy for us to become so enthusiastic with our schemes that we fail to see other options. We are dealing with a clever man but an insane one. Who knows what action he will take? He could, for all we know, have left the country directly after sending the postcard and already be on his way to my brother. However, we must assume not, and do what we can.'

'Basically, James said, 'we don't know what he's going to do. Only that, for want of a better word, he invited Archer to Ebb Bay Castle sometime tomorrow.'

'True,' Archer said. 'And I am willing to hear all voices. Go on, James.'

'Right, so...' He returned to the map. 'The meeting place is here, his getaway is here, and between them are serval hours hard riding either across country or by road. That's risky, I reckoned, so I looked for another escape route, and that is right there.'

He planted his pencil, and Thomas leant in to look.

'Highcliffe?' What has that to do with anything?' He looked at Archer for a reply, but James answered.

'Highcliffe Halt,' he said and turned to his timetable. 'It's on a branch line from Haverpool, and a freight train passes there at twelve-twenty every morning on its run south.'

'So?'

'Its next stop is Kingston docks where his boat will be waiting to sail.'

'Then we should put someone on alert at the docks,' Thomas reasoned. 'I've been saying it all along.'

'No,' James corrected him, bringing a scowl to the butler's face. 'Sorry, Tom, but as we know, this must be kept between ourselves.'

'Then you go and wait at the docks while we do the men's work.'

'Thomas,' Archer snapped. 'You being sceptical suits our purpose, but you being sarcastic doesn't.'

Thomas said nothing, but withdrew deeper into his sulk.

The more James tried to help the viscount, the more he alienated Thomas. He couldn't win and wondered if it was best to accept that Thomas was no longer interested in his affections. It was the last thing he wanted, and the thought left him cold.

He drew another paper from his bag.

'This is the speed information Archer acquired from the station master,' he explained. 'On its way to the docks, the freight train crosses the moors close to Ebb Bay. Quill could reach it easily and board it at Highcliffe Halt. It slows to...' He checked the specification. 'Five miles an hour, not much faster than walking speed. It's quite possible to climb on before it picks up again and reaches... Well, stupidly fast speeds as it travels downhill towards Kingston.'

'Yeah, I get that,' Silas said. 'He's got a way to escape, but what's your point and why are only three of us at the castle?'

'Because,' James continued. 'The train then passes through this junction.' He showed them the symbols on the map. 'Here, the up-line from Haverpool splits, the train either continuing to the docks some miles away or here to this siding. It's a dead end. Well, it's a depot where they turn the engine and shunt the cars backwards to the river.'

'And,' Archer picked up the explanation, 'if we change the points, the driver will see, stop the train and we'll have Quill trapped. That is if we haven't caught him before. It's a backup, and we have James to thank for it.'

Thomas was not impressed at the way Archer praised the footman and crossed his arms as he sat back. Fecker and Silas were more appreciative and declared it a good idea.

'Which,' Archer said. 'I think sets us up, and we now know what we are doing. Andrej, James and I will go on to the castle, while Thomas and Silas make their way to the signal junction. When you see the train approaching, switch the points. If Quill is on it, it will be up to you to fall on him. Thomas, thanks to his country upbringing, has experience with the shotgun.'

'My place is with you,' Thomas complained. 'Why can't James change the points? Silas, you want to be at Archer's side, don't you?'

'I do, Tommy,' Silas said. 'But I can see his logic.'

'Which is what?'

'Tom,' Archer said, placing a hand on the man's arm. 'It's not because I do not appreciate you. You played your part last time and with great valour, but it's a question of skills.'

'Are you saying I can't fight? Or I'm not willing to put my life before yours?'

'Not at all. It's simply a case of who is good at what. Fecker, James and I all ride…'

'So can I.'

'Yes, but Silas can't. If this turns into a cross-country chase on horseback, I need my strongest riders. Meanwhile, from the castle to the junction is only a couple of miles. Silas can ride there with you at a slower, safer pace in good time for the train should he seek escape that way. Also, sorry about this, Silas, but you are not quite as physical, and your strengths lie elsewhere.'

'Yeah, well that's 'cos of being homeless and starving for the past four years,' Silas agreed, appearing not to mind being called weak.

'But together, you and Tom will be strong enough to pull a signal lever. Also, Tom, you might need to break into the signal box, something Silas could probably do in his sleep.'

'Well,' Silas laughed. 'Never done a signal box before, but locks generally ain't no problem.'

'And finally, Tom, and again, no disrespect to Silas, you have a level head. You can keep an eye on him.'

'Like a nanny in the nursery?' Thomas was not impressed.

'No, as my trusted first officer,' Archer said, through gritted teeth. 'I am asking you to take care of the man I love, and if you are with him, I will not be worried. You do understand?'

'We're a team, Tommy,' Silas said. 'I don't mind being called weak, or having a nanny if it's right for Archer's plan. I'm happy to do anything to get rid of Quill, as is Fecks, yeah?'

'Da.'

'And as am I,' James said. 'And do you want to know why, Tom?'

'Not particularly.'

James' anger was rising at an equal rate to Thomas' belligerence. 'Well. I'll tell you anyway.' The words came from below as if spat from a bubbling cauldron. 'Because, I know how much you think of that man.' He pointed to Archer. 'I know how much you care about him and I get why. But, I'm here 'cos of you, Tom. I'll do whatever Archer says is best, so that no harm comes to him, 'cos I couldn't bear for you to lose him.'

'Very righteous.'

'Thomas, please.'

'No, Archer,' Thomas' face was ugly with anger. 'I should be with you. I know you, he doesn't. He can't read your thoughts like I can. He doesn't know what you're likely to do. How can you trust someone who lies to you?'

'I haven't lied.'

'You led me on.' Raging, he mocked James' voice. '*I have to think about this, Tommy*, you said. *Give me time.* Aye, time to wheedle your way into his house, so you could spy on us.'

'This ain't helping,' Silas barked.

'When what you were really doing was using me so you could make a little money.'

'It wasn't like that,' James pleaded. 'Honest.' His anger was crumbling into loss. 'I knew it from the second I first saw you.'

'Knew what? That I was an easy way into Archer's life?'

'No. Saw that I fucking loved you, Payne. And if you can't get that through your thick head, then shut your mouth and do what your boss tells you, right?'

James kicked himself away from the table and let free a growl of frustration. He stomped away and threw himself into a window seat.

'Hm,' Fecker grunted, unimpressed. 'Wake me when you've finished.' He rested his legs on the facing seat, pulled down his cap and closed his eyes.

Twenty-One

He had been dreaming about telegrams. He stood on a high bridge spanning a wide river with his house behind him and a castle ahead. The bridge, for all its strength, was swaying. There was no wind, just an uneven back and forth motion catching him on the wrong foot as he tried to approach the castle. The closer he came, the further it withdrew, and it vanished completely when he woke with a start.

Silas was standing over him, shaking his leg. 'We're nearly there,' he said. 'It's just on five.'

James' eyes stung, he was groggy, and his face was clammy with sweat. The carriage lights had been dimmed, but despite the gloom, the others were collecting their bags, talking in whispers. The bench he had been lying on had left him with a crick in his neck, and he rolled his shoulders to free it. He had been asleep for six hours and had not had time to talk to Thomas.

The man was at the far end of the carriage, leaning from the window. He clicked his fingers to attract attention and pointed ahead.

Understanding, James gathered his things along with his wits, making sure he had all the notes and maps as the train slowed with a grate of metal on metal and several loud screeches.

'It has been doing that at every stop,' Archer said in hushed tones. 'I'm surprised you were able to sleep.'

'Sorry,' James replied, aware that his mouth was dry, and his breath probably stank.

'It's alright,' Archer reassured him. 'We took turns staying awake, so we didn't sleep past the stop. I couldn't bring myself to disturb you.'

'You should have.'

'And I was going to, but Thomas volunteered to take your watch.'

The viscount leant closer. 'It's a start.'

'Only two men about,' Thomas said, closing the window. 'We'll need the lamps once the train has pulled away.'

The carriage jolted, and with a steamy hiss of relief, the train came to a halt.

The distance from the footplate to the ground was a fair one. Fecker jumped first and then helped the others, lifting James as if he weighed nothing. He was shocked at the change in temperature as an icy wind blasted the last of his drowsiness into the night. They hurried from the tracks, concealing themselves behind a brick building until the two workmen were too busy with a water pipe at the engine to notice.

Putting on gloves, and pulling their dark clothing tightly about them, they waited for Archer's signal, and on his silent order, followed him, keeping low. The moon, not quite full, afforded them a silvery light when passing clouds allowed, and once free from the depot and descending a hill, they were sheltered from the wind.

The engine built up steam behind them, its whistle sounded, and the heave-pull-clunk of its wheels gathered tempo, slowly fading to an eerie silence as it continued its journey. Archer stopped to light torch-lamps and examine the map. He looked to the sky, found his bearings and said, 'East is that way. If we take a direct line we should come to the back of Inglestone before dawn. Tread carefully.'

He led them into the night with Thomas at his side and Fecker bringing up the rear. James walked with Silas.

'You alright, mate?' Silas asked.

'Yes, thanks. Are you?'

'Doing my best,' Silas replied.

James hadn't had the opportunity to get to know the viscount's lover. With two hours walking ahead, now seemed like a good time. 'I heard you say something about being homeless?' he said.

'That's right. I was on the streets in the East End until a couple of weeks ago. Same as Fecks.'

'He's your mate, right?'

'The best. You had to have good mates around you.'

'And you were caught up in Quill's business?'

'His murdering of renters? Yeah, we put a stop to that. I hope.'

'You were lucky to escape. Because of what you used to do.'

213

'Had no other choice, Jimmy.' Silas was unbothered by the topic. 'Came easy to me, but Fecker only did it when he needed to. He prefers women, see?'

'I get it. It must have been hard on the streets.' James couldn't imagine a life without the comfort of a home.

'You get used it. It's fecking freezing out here.'

They walked a little way without speaking until Silas moved close enough for their clothing to rub at the shoulders.

'What's going on with you and Tommy?' he whispered.

'Nothing.'

'Ah, mate, we can all see the change in him. I can't work out if that's 'cos of you or Archie.'

'Eh?'

Silas lifted his lantern to his face where it threw shadows beneath his eyebrows, but caught in his eyes, turning their deep blue to flickers of yellow. Even with a letter-box view of his face between his scarf and his hat, James could see he was smiling.

'Tom's a bit of a man's man,' he said. 'In love with his master.'

James' heart hit his boots, and he stumbled on a tuft of grass. 'Is he?'

'You must have seen it.' Silas spoke directly into his ear, his words barely reaching it before they were taken away by a gust. 'I saw it straight off, but it ain't what you think.'

'What do I think?'

'That Tom's not interested in you, 'cos he thinks old Tripp put you up to it. Fancying him, I mean.'

'It's not like that.'

James had explained this to Archer and now to Silas, who appeared to know already, but he was unable to get the message through to the one who needed to hear it the most.

'Yeah, I can see that.' His companion's words were reassuring. 'Here's the thing, Jimmy, if you don't mind me saying. I've only known them a short time, but they're both easy to read. I got a skill at mimicking people, see, came in useful in my old job, and you learn to read men when you do work like that. Those two are in love with each other.'

If James' hopes were dashed any further, they would be nothing but pulp on the moorland.

'But…' This kind of thought was not easy to express. James wasn't used to being able to speak so freely. 'You and Archer are together, aren't you? Like a couple.'

'Oh, we are, mate,' Silas replied. 'I don't mean love like that. They're two best mates, only there's always been this sexual thing, so Archie says. I don't get jealous, so it's not a problem for me, but if you want to win Tommy back, you're going to have to accept it as well.'

'I can accept that they are friends despite their stations in life,' James said. 'I've never had anyone that close, so I can't comment on the other stuff.'

'The sex stuff?'

'Yeah. I don't have your… experience. Not with people so honest, nor with other men. Only person I've told I love is my mum. Oh, and me sister once, but that's only 'cos I thought she was dying.'

'Ah, sisters,' Silas sighed, but James didn't understand what he meant. There was no time to ask, Silas continued. 'You don't have to worry about that side of things with those two. Archer would never let it happen. You know what it's like. If you want something, but can't have it, it makes you want it more? Same with them.'

'But if Thomas feels that way, what hope is there for me?' The words were coming more easily due to Silas' openness.

'You've got more than hope on your side, Jimmy,' Silas said, and nudged him. 'Tommy fancies you rotten if you ask me. What he's having trouble with is accepting it. I bet he feels disloyal to Archie even though he's never going to have him.'

'He was fine until I admitted Tripp had paid me to seduce him.' That was the crux of the problem, surely? Thomas no longer trusted him.

'That's his excuse for his behaviour,' the Irishman said. His breath puffed before his face and was whipped away into the night. 'All Tommy needs is time and your understanding. You willing to give him time?'

'If it's the only way I can prove what I feel, yeah.'

'Good lad.' Silas' arm was suddenly around James' shoulder. It rested lightly, but the man's fingers held him tightly enough for the gesture to be a friendly hug. James didn't object. Although Silas was shorter and lighter, his presence gave James strength.

'Any idea how long I'll have to wait?' he asked.

'Oh, come off it, mate,' Silas laughed. 'I ain't got all the answers. Now, watch where you're walking, and don't you worry about Thomas. Okay?'

'Thank you, Mr Wright.'

'And you can feck off with that Mr Wright stuff and all,' Silas said. 'We're mates.'

That was the end of that discussion and little more was said as they trudged cautiously across the moor. Where the ground rose, so did the wind, blowing in off the North Sea. It cut through James' overcoat and threatened to rob him of his hat. Silas tightened the scarf around his face and James copied. It warmed his skin a little, but the chill troubled his eyes making them water and, perversely, he sweated beneath his clothes while his flesh stung as if he was being pinched by an icy demon.

The ground was springy beneath his feet one moment, and then rocky the next. The smell of heather scented the air when the gusts died, and the only sounds were footfall and the rustle of clothing.

After an hour's silent walking, they rested to eat what Thomas had provided, and Archer took another reading of their position from the stars. James was impressed. His father had tried to explain navigation to him, using the night sky over Riverside, but he had never been able to understand the method. He wondered what his dad would make of what he was doing now and his new position working for a viscount who thought nothing of chasing down a killer.

Their lamps refuelled, and with the eastern horizon showing a slice of grey through the black, they continued towards the village, reaching it with enough dawn light to extinguish their lanterns and let them cool before packing them away.

Archer stopped, overlooking the grey stone village below, and took a telescope from Silas' knapsack.

'We are bird-watchers after all,' he said. He wasn't looking for birds, he was figuring the best way to enter the village. 'Down and through that copse to the road,' he decided. 'If anyone asks how we arrived and why so early in the day, we tell them we are watching for owls, spending our nights on the moors and our days asleep. That should do it.'

No-one did ask, in fact, they saw no villagers only animals as they slipped and skidded down the hill and weaved through the thicket. At its edge, Archer checked them over and declared they looked like expert ornithologists.

'But.' He added a note of caution. 'If someone engages you in conversation, it's best to say little, unless you know the difference between a chaffinch and a sparrow hawk.'

'Well, a chaffinch is a finch, and a sparrow hawk is a hawk, Archie. Ain't no mystery there.'

'Yes, alright, Silas, you know what I mean.'

Their footsteps changed tone when they reached the road, a rough track of mud hardened in some places but claggy in others. They followed it to the main street, a collection of limestone cottages where lights appeared behind the netted windows as people started on their day.

They reached the inn, raised the owner and, as they gathered in the lobby, discussed the weather and how cold it had been on the moors all night.

'Which is why we are in need of a bath and beds,' Archer said.

The landlord was not impressed that he had been called from his rooms at seven in the morning, but adding up the income from five paying guests in October, he put on a brave face. It wasn't a pretty one, James thought, saggy and pale, with grey stubble showing through, but the man was the gatekeeper to hot water and sleep, and that was all that interested him.

'It were a bit short notice.' The landlord's northern accent was thick and his voice deep. 'Some of me rooms be empty this time a year, and it takes time to get 'em up to scratch. Still, I'll have the little woman set up the attic room for you. Two beds, bathroom on the landing, a fire you may light, five-pence extra a day, mind. I thought as you were all acquainted, you'd not mind sharing. Hope that be right?'

'That'll do fine,' Archer said. 'I shall pay for us all in advance. Include the fire and food if you will. I think we may be away by the early evening, so will you require payment for two nights?'

The landlord's sallow eyes came alive. 'If that's convenient, Sir,' he beamed. 'I can see you're a gentleman of breeding.'

Silas pushed through. 'Aye, mate,' he said. 'We all be that, but we're also all of us in 'urry, so take your money and give us key.'

James nearly laughed. He had copied the man's accent perfectly.

'Right away, lad,' the man replied, producing a ledger. 'If you'd put your names.'

'Allow me.' Archer took the book.

'You're from over past Barrenmoor if I'm not mistaken.' The landlord nodded at Silas before turning to unhook the key from a rack.

'Aye, you'd be right.'

'What place?'

Silas pulled a panicked face, and James pictured the map on Archer's wall. It seemed like days ago since he had seen it.

'Westington, isn't it?' he said and glanced at the register. 'Mr Dorrit?'

Surprised, but impressed, Silas did the same and said, 'That I am, Mr… Rudge.'

'Can't say it's a village I know well.' The landlord put the key on the counter. 'But welcome to our side a the moor.' Archer had completed the register, and the innkeeper turned it. 'And thank you very much, Mr Copperfield.'

As he paid the man, Archer caught James' eye with a mischievous twitch of his brows. 'Would you be so kind as to bring us some breakfast?' he asked, adding a yawn. 'After that, I think we will stay in the room until nightfall. We are planning to catch sight of a nocturnal Canadian goose.'

Thomas coughed loudly.

'Do I not mean that, Mr Drood?' Archer asked, suddenly out of his depth.

'You'd need a fair old scope to see a migratory bird at this time of year, Copperfield,' Thomas joked. 'You were thinking of a nocturnal Candida Gullerium.' He whipped the key from the landlord's hand. 'He's an amateur,' he confided, to which the landlord mouthed, 'Oh, I see,' with sympathy.

'What's a Candida Gullerium?' Archer asked as Thomas unlocked the room.

'I have no idea, but luckily, neither did the innkeeper.' Thomas rolled his eyes and shook his head. 'And, Archer, really? Copperfield?

Drood? What did you call Fecker? Martin Chuzzlewit?'

'Nicholas Nickleby,' he said. 'I thought it sounded the most Russian.'

The room was large. Under the eaves, it ran the full length of the building with two garret windows overlooking the moors. A double bed was pushed against the far wall, with another between the windows. It was well furnished with armchairs and a table, the fire was made up ready to be lit, and it was comfortable enough, being arranged, Archer supposed, for a family.

Maybe that's what they were, he thought as the others piled in and found themselves somewhere to sit. Not a related family of generations, but a band of brothers, with Thomas being the closest relative and James the newly adopted one. When he considered his relationship with Silas, he decided that brothers was not an appropriate analogy and gave up on the fanciful idea, resolved to consider them as friends. That was warming enough.

'There's not a lot of privacy,' he said, unfastening the chain of his cloak. Thomas was at his side in a second ready to take it. 'See to yourself, Tom,' he said. 'We are all the same here.'

The landlord brought them breakfast on trays, assisted by a short, wide woman who Archer took to be his wife. She said nothing but smiled pleasantly enough and ensured the fire was well alight.

'What news on our horses?' he enquired of the landlord.

'I can 'ave them ready when you like, Mr Copperfield,' the man said, helping himself to a view from the window. 'John Farley said he'll happily rent you three. I have two for the exchange when the coach comes through, so I'll need them returned come two days. You'll be back by then I take it?'

'We will,' Archer confirmed. 'We shall return in the morning. I'd like to inspect them, of course, so if you could have them saddled and fed by dusk, that's when we will leave.'

'Aye, Sir. I can do that, though decent saddles I can't promise.'

'Whatever you can manage.'

The rest of the morning was spent with each man taking his own time in the bathroom, where the water ran cold within minutes. Archer let his men have it, and Thomas and James benefited from what little there was. The temperature of the water made no difference to Silas and Fecker, they were used to it, as was Archer who commented that it reminded him of being aboard ship. They were not particularly happy memories, and he said no more, but he needed his men comfortable and rested, and so put their needs before his own.

At midday, the silent but smiling wife brought bread, cheese and beer for their lunch. After some remonstrations from Fecker, Archer ordered the same again and paid more for a hot stew and potatoes ordering extra portions for the Ukrainian and his bottomless stomach.

The wind died as they ate, and the roof tiles ceased their clatter bringing an eerie calm to the surrounding moors. Fortified and warm, James cleared the plates and put them out on the landing while Archer stood at the window contemplating the lie of the land.

The open country undulated lazily to the horizon, a grey and brown quilt with patches edged by ancient hedgerows and gale-weary trees. Stone walls and river channels scarred the landscape towards the east, and he was able to track the winding road from Inglestone towards Ebb Bay and the railway line. On any other day he would have found the view charming, but that afternoon it was marred by the knowledge that somewhere among the rocky outcrops and hidden valleys, Quill was lying in wait.

Shivering the thought from his mind, Archer called his men to order.

'Gents,' he said, turning to face the group gathered close to the fireplace. 'We know our roles, and we know our timing. I suggest we spend the remainder of the day resting.' He sat beside Silas on one of the beds. 'Someone will have to take a chair.' Indicating the second bed, he said, 'The other two can share that. Don't look so outraged, Tom.'

'I'd be happier on the floor,' Thomas volunteered with a sideways glance at James.

'Nyet.' Fecker wouldn't hear of it and grumbled his disapproval. 'I sleep on floor. I like it.'

'As you see fit, Andrej,' Archer said. He remembered walking into the stables on a recent morning and finding Fecker asleep on the straw beside Shanks, the larger of his two horses. Asking Fecker if there was something wrong, his coachman replied in the negative and explained that after years of sleeping on a rope-house bench, it was difficult for him to adjust to a mattress. It gave him backache to be too comfortable.

'If you can sleep, do so,' the viscount advised. 'We have a short enough ride to Ebb Bay, a little further for Silas and Tom to the junction. We three will find a place to stake out and watch for Quill. If, or when, we see him, we will watch until the time draws near for his necessary departure. Then, I will make my presence known and take the man down. Now then...'

James listened intently to the details which Archer repeated several more times ensuring that each man knew his role, answering questions and addressing concerns until they were fluent in the parts they were to play. As the viscount spoke, James kept his eyes on Tom, but when the sleeping arrangements were discussed, looked away, not wanting to appear too obvious. He was unsettled and harboured a need to put things straight with Thomas one way or the other. How else could he concentrate on what was expected of him? His most pressing matter was not how Archer would take Quill, but how he could make Thomas understand his intentions. When dusk came, they would ride out, and soon after, go separate ways. The only chance James had to be alone with the man was during the afternoon, and even then, other pairs of ears were close by.

He recalled Archer's advice to be patient, and Silas' words that Thomas was in love with the viscount. Whichever way he looked at it, he had little chance to make things right. It was a struggle, but he put the thoughts from his mind as he kicked off his boots and lay on the bed watching the room. Archer glanced at him before standing closer to Thomas, speaking inaudibly as he loaded his revolver. They were cleaning the pistols and shotguns and worked together in a practised way that made James envious. They knew each other so well they didn't need to speak. Archer lifted a gun and inspected the barrel, and Thomas had a cleaning cloth ready to hand to him before he asked. When the viscount loaded a revolver, Thomas passed him the bullets, and he took them without looking, each knowing exactly what the other needed.

It was the sight of the weapons that finally brought home the reality of what they were about to do, and the only way James could quell his nervousness was to look away and picture Thomas' face. It brought tears of frustration to his eyes. Tom was so near and yet so far away, and James had put him there. The last two days had been filled with excitement, erotic tension and nervousness. He had seen his ambition within his grasp. In fact, he had held it, fallen asleep with it, with Tom. He'd woken in the night knowing that he would be there the next day, and the one after that, and beyond to an endless future.

The future had been brief. Everything was now wrong, and he would do anything to put it right.

He lay on his side facing the wall where he could concentrate on how things might be, imagining fanciful scenarios where he saved Thomas' life and the man declared everlasting love. The vision only served to worry him more as he imagined Thomas shot or stabbed, dying in his arms.

The tears came more freely to his eyes, and he closed them and thought of home instead. The dimly lit parlour of his youth, his mother sewing by candlelight with her painful fingers, keeping the family together through hardship and the bite of winter. Perhaps he had been wrong to have ambition. He didn't know how to be a footman, nor how to be a lover. He was a messenger and a son, and that was about as far as his life was meant to go.

Unable to sleep, he fell further into self-doubt until the bed moved. Someone sat beside him, but he didn't turn. It was probably Fecker after all, he thought. Thomas would have insisted that the big man take the bed as he was the one Archer needed most. Clothes rustled, and he heard breathing, a sigh and a sniff before the mattress came to rest, and the only sound was the crackle of the fire.

The bed moved again, and the man behind shifted as though he was uncomfortable. He heard a growl of frustration. Whoever it was couldn't rest either, or was annoyed, but James remained motionless, feigning sleep. There was nothing he wanted to say to Fecker.

'Are you asleep?'

It was Thomas whispering in his ear, and James' heart leapt.

'No,' he said.

Thomas made no reply, but he put an arm tentatively over James and shifted his body to press against him, his head nuzzled into James' neck.

James had a choice, he could do nothing and let Thomas stew in his own juice, or he could show him he was able to forgive his churlishness — not that he needed excusing, it was all James' fault. Understanding his confusion, he took Thomas' hand and clutched his arm tightly to his chest relishing the intimacy. A gentle kiss on the back of his head brought hope.

Twenty-Two

Under any other circumstances, it might have been a pleasant ride if a bitterly cold one. Night had fallen and brought with it a clarity of air that seared Archer's lungs. The horses' hooves struck the road in a steady though unrhythmic mismatch as the five rode through the village in single file with Archer leading the way. The main street gave way to the country track, which the horses seemed to know well, and before long, cottages and hedgerows were replaced by dry stone walls and open moorland. The ground rolled gracefully, cresting hills and dipping into valleys. Above, the cloudless sky afforded them good light with the rising moon subduing only those stars nearest its glow, and the Milky Way severing the night sky in a scar of light and dark.

Archer was reminded of his own scar; the wound his brother inflicted in their battle when Crispin's madness boiled over into attempted fratricide. He was unable to make sense of why Quill would want to set Crispin free, or why he should want him restored to the title of viscount. The man he had known and served with, befriended and liked, had decided Archer was not fit to live on this earth. Both Quill and Archer's brother would see him dead and who knew what else Quill would mastermind should he succeed in freeing Crispin. Two devils would be let loose on the world and the only thing preventing it was Archer and the fellows who followed him on this unknown path.

He twisted in his saddle to talk to Silas riding behind.

'How are you doing?' he asked.

Silas, gripping too tightly with his knees, held the pommel firmly and swayed from side to side. 'Still upright,' he said.

Behind him, Thomas sat elegantly on his mount, tall and erect taking in the close scenery before it was lost to distant darkness, and behind him, James rode steadily. Fecker had taken the horse with no saddle, the innkeeper unable to provide more than four, but he was as assured on horseback as he was with everything. Archer didn't have to worry about the Ukrainian.

Night creatures rustled in the scrub to one side, and bats flitted from a farmhouse on the other. Without a breath of wind, the night was tranquil as they left Inglestone behind and progressed in silence.

The group came together a few miles further on when they arrived at a crossroads.

Archer pulled the map from beneath his cloak and lit his lantern to read as Thomas trotted up beside him.

'Highcliffe Halt is to the south,' the viscount said, peering into the silvery gloom. 'Two miles, Tom, and you should see the track. Cross and follow it. The signal box should be on your left.'

Thomas nodded. 'We'll be there in plenty of time,' he said. 'No need to panic Silas with a canter.'

'Don't be cheeky,' the Irishman replied. 'I'm getting used to the beast.'

Archer caught his arm as he began to slip from the saddle and righted him. 'Relax,' he said. 'She knows what she is doing.' The horse whinnied in agreement. 'See? She'll take care of you.'

'Yeah, maybe,' Silas frowned. 'But who's going to look after you?'

'Me, Banyak,' Fecker grunted.

'And I'll look after him,' James put in, making Fecker laugh.

'We must all look out for each other,' Archer said, his tone grave. 'We may be riding into a trap, it may be a pointless mission, or we may find ourselves face to face with a man bent on evil. I can't stress Quill's unpredictability enough. Just a few weeks ago, he was a gentle, trusted friend, but now? We have seen his work, we have witnessed his dementedness, and we don't know what he has planned, or why we he has brought us here. But what we do know is, he must be stopped no matter what. You each have your duties, and I know you will carry them out without cowardice, but I can pull rank, and you will not do anything to put yourselves in danger. That is an order. This battle is mine. You are here to support, but I want no heroics.'

'You will have whatever you need from me,' James said, and the other agreed.

It was heart-warming, but Archer could not throw off the insidious feeling that he was leading his friends into an indefinite future where the only thing they were sure of was that they were working blind. He intended to take the advantage from Quill, but the truth was plain. Quill would stop at nothing to see Archer dead, and that would include killing anyone who stood in his way.

'Your loyalty has lit my fire,' he said. 'Your trust and your bravery are more than any man could ask, and if any one of you feels he can go no further, I will not...'

'Aye, well you can stop right there,' Thomas said, among similar complaints from the men. 'Give us our orders, Archer. It is what we are here for.'

'James? You are the newest member of our band. Are you certain you want to be a part of this?'

'As I understand it,' James said, 'you have a message to deliver to Doctor Quill, and my job is to deliver messages. If that communication is his death, and you ask me to be the cause of it, then that's what I will do.'

'Even though it might mean your own?'

'Whatever it takes to keep you and Thomas safe, Sir.'

The sentiment nearly brought a tear to Archer's eye, but he remained focused. 'Then we must proceed,' he said. 'Silas? A word.'

He dismounted and helped Silas from his horse, drawing him to one side.

'I will not be harmed,' he said, taking his lover's hands. 'I have a reason to win this fight, and that reason is you. You are not to worry about me. I have been trained for such things, and I have fought foes more capable than Quill.'

'But you're still making a speech in case I don't see you again, right?'

'No, Silas.' Archer drew him close and embraced him. 'I love you, and I will see you in a few short hours.'

'I'm only not making a fuss because I trust you,' Silas complained. 'If I had my way, you'd wait here while me and Fecks go and fuck up the lunatic.'

'I'll have Fecker with me,' Archer reassured him. 'And James is a tough one too. You look after Thomas as I have told him to look after you. I'll be back before you know it.'

They kissed until Silas' horse snorted impatiently.

'I do love you, Archie,' Silas said, and turned the ring on his finger. 'I know I don't say it much, and I'll never be able to give you something as special as this, but you know I love you, yeah?'

'I do. Now, mount up and let Tom lead you downhill to the junction.'

Back at the group, Silas complained as Fecker lifted him into his saddle by his collar. The comedic sight brought brief cheer to the party.

'Whatever the outcome,' Archer said. 'We will rendezvous at the end of the branch line once the midnight train has passed the points. Wait for us there, Tom.'

They shook hands solemnly, and without another word, Archer took up his reins and turned his horse to the east. He swallowed hard. It was painful to leave Silas, but he could not let his fears for the man's safety cloud his judgement.

Fecker and James flanked him, facing the road ahead. A shared glance to ensure they were ready, and they flicked their reins.

They trotted onto open moorland where the heather muffled the horses' hooves. Half an hour later, they crossed the railway track, a single line which, James knew from his timetables, took freight to Kingston docks miles to the south. The distance to their destination was but one mile uphill. As they climbed, Ebb Bay Castle came into view, looming against the starry night like a shadowed blemish on a vast canvas. James had never seen such a sight and it, along with the lung-biting cold, took his breath away. He wished Thomas was there to share the moment, but then he wished many things about Thomas. Why had they lain so close together without words? Was his embrace one of apology or goodbye? Why hadn't James found the courage to dismount, hold the man he loved and give him words of encouragement? Why had Thomas not done the same?

He had no choice but to ignore his concerns, and his sadness left him when the viscount altered their course, and they crested the hill to arrive at an outcrop of rock.

'We should tether the horses here,' Archer said, once they had drawn to a halt. 'There is cover behind the boulders, and the battlefield is in plain sight.'

James saw the sense in his decision. They were opposite the castle looking down a short incline which, should they need to ride, would give them added speed. At the same time, there was an uninterrupted view of the ruins and, towards the cliff edge, the church.

He dismounted and tied his horse alongside the others.

'Keep behind me,' Archer whispered. 'From now on, stay low and stay quiet. We have some time to wait, but Quill may already be there.'

James and Fecker followed as the viscount skirted the rocks to find the best vantage point. A cleft between two massive boulders gave them just enough room to squeeze in side by side, lying flat on the damp ground. There, Fecker loaded and prepared a rifle while Archer produced his telescope and trained it on the ruins, scanning every inch in a slow, deliberate sweep.

'It's the right place, but I see no movement,' he said, and directed the scope inland. 'And I see no-one approaching. He's either not here, or already there and hiding.'

'I smell no other horse,' Fecker said. He wet a finger and turned it above his head. 'Small wind from the sea.' He tasted his finger and nodded. 'Da.'

'Good Lord, Andrej.' The viscount was impressed. 'Were you trained in the militia?'

Fecker grunted something that James didn't understand.

'Resistance movement?' Archer queried.

'Da. Before I escape.'

'Wish I could be of more use,' James muttered. 'The only training I've had is from the post office, and morning exercise ain't quite the same thing.'

'You're here for your logical mind.' Archer collapsed the telescope. 'Like Thomas. You and he have much in common.'

'Not as much as he wants,' Fecker said, reaching over Archer and ruffling James' hair.

'Meaning?' The viscount turned his head to James.

They were a few inches apart, and his skin was the colour of pewter in the moonlight, but even in monochrome, James could see the man's inquiring expression.

'The only thing we have in common,' he said. 'Is you.'

228

Archer's eyes narrowed in thought, and he breathed out a cloud of vapour. 'Then I am glad I've brought the two of you together.'

Maybe it was tension, or perhaps his chattering teeth, but James was unable to utter the words that fought for release.

He didn't need to.

'You keep them apart,' Fecker said, and pointed to the stars, sighing. 'Ah, Myslyvets, the Hunter. Same as my home.'

'What did he mean, I keep you apart?' Archer's face was clouded by more than moon shadow; concern was also evident.

'Best not go into it now,' James said, embarrassed. 'Sorry about that.'

'No,' Archer insisted. 'Tell me.'

James took a breath. Here he was, on the Yorkshire Moors, lying in wait for a killer and with two men he hardly knew, cold, scared and with his mind in disorder because of man he had met on a doorstep. He would have laughed if his situation had not been so perilous.

'You want it honest, Sir?'

'Of course. And remember it's Archer tonight.'

James gave a hopeless, short laugh. 'He has no time for me when all he can see is you,' he said. Strangely, it didn't feel wrong to tell the viscount.

'Well that's ridiculous,' Archer replied, amused. 'And it's not what he told me.'

'Eh? I mean, sorry, what?' Hope poured into James' chaotic mind and thickened his confusion.

'You'll have to ask Thomas,' the viscount said with a grin. 'But for now, I can tell you...'

'Zamovkny!' Fecker pressed Archer and James against the ground. 'No speak. I hear noise.'

James' heart thumped with a sudden stab of panic. Archer raised the scope and carefully extended it. He aimed in the direction of Fecker's pointing finger, and James squinted into the gloom to see.

Nothing moved in the gully below. The only sound was the dull and distant boom of the sea hitting the cliffs, and everything appeared as it had before, except now there was a light. Weak and flickering, a lantern glowed behind a tomb in the graveyard.

'You want I go?'

'No, Andrej,' Archer hissed. 'It's too early. James, watch the railway line. Andrej, towards the cliff. If our nonappearance unnerves him and he means to escape, we will be ready to give chase.' He focused on the graves. 'We need to delay him as much as possible so he will be off guard. The longer we can keep him worried, the better it will be.'

'What time is it?' James whispered.

'Just after eleven. Time a while before I take the battle to him.' Archer said. 'Stay vigilant. He doesn't know we are here. We have the advantage now.'

With those words, they settled in to wait.

Thomas and Silas found the train track and followed it towards the signal box. Thomas lead at a slow pace, referring to his pocket watch from time to time and keeping an eye on Silas even though he was more assured in the saddle than he had been when they set out. The track sloped gently from the moor through embankments cut into the hillside where shrubs and trees had been allowed to grow wild. Moonlight lit the way, glinting on the steel rails and offering a straight path marked out in sleepers and gravel to its vanishing point. He couldn't help feeling it represented his life as one dull, repetitive journey, except, his life of late had been anything but dull.

The steady rhythm of his days had been interrupted and changed irrevocably by Archer's elevation to viscount. Now able to be his own man, free from the intimidation of his father, he encouraged Thomas to follow suit by allowing him to be not just a footman, but a person in his own right. It was a difficult transition to make. Thomas had been the hall boy, the young viscount's playmate, the second footman, the first, and now the butler, all in twenty-seven years, but there was more to his current state of flux than a change in roles. There was also the freedom of expression that Archer insisted on and which, after some false starts, Thomas was now able to enjoy.

Their earlier conversation, spoken in hushed voices as they cleaned the guns, had set his mind to his future and his desires, but he was still unable to accept them.

'I can see you have strong feelings for James,' Archer had said, watching the man prepare to rest. 'And I know you have similar feelings towards me.'

Thomas had been uncomfortable, but only for a moment. 'I can't deny the truth,' he said.

'No more can I, Tom. I have told you, my feelings towards you must be platonic only, and they are. I cannot give you what you want, I can only give you my most ardent friendship, and I do. But you have a confusion which only you can pick apart.'

'I'm not confused,' Thomas said, inspecting the shotgun. He'd used his father's breech-loader to kill rats on the farm, but this was a Browning with a lever action repeater that self-loaded. A modern model and unfamiliar.

'Then why your reticence towards our new friend? Is it because of his involvement with Tripp?'

'It was,' Thomas admitted. 'When he said that Tripp had put him up to the job... I mean, he was keen, and then he said that. How am I supposed to know that he has any true affection for me?'

'You just have to open your eyes,' Archer advised. 'We have discussed this before, and I see no reason why we should go through it again.' He put down his Webley. 'I think I understand. You feel foolish and don't know how to get him back.'

'That's partly it,' Thomas admitted. Two months ago he would never have had a conversation such as this with anyone. 'The other part is having to apologise.'

'You don't need to. You've done nothing wrong. Neither has he.' Archer took the shotgun from him and loaded a magazine. 'All you need do is go over there, lie down and pretend nothing happened. He is genuine, Tom, and he will understand. I know it.'

'You're saying I made a fool of myself?'

'No. I'm saying you let yourself down.' Archer's honesty was often difficult to accept, but always on target. 'You behaved like a child, and flouncing about hurt and haughty doesn't suit you.' He attached the shoulder strap to the weapon. 'You trust me, don't you?'

'Of course.'

'Right. Then go and rest. With James. I'm here for you, Tom, but as a friend. He's waiting to offer you much more, and all you need to do is let him.'

Archer smiled, touched Thomas' cheek and, for a moment, Thomas thought they would kiss. The idea, once all he ever wanted, was now inappropriate. If anyone was going to kiss him, it had to be James.

'I can see you understand,' Archer said. 'Go and rest.'

He was reliving his inept attempt to apologise to James by hugging him when Silas whispered, shattering his thoughts.

'We're not alone.'

Fifty yards ahead, a lantern danced unevenly as two men climbed the steps to the signal box.

Thomas took Silas' reins and led the horses from the track. In the cutting, they were head height to the rails and deep in shadow.

'Keep still,' Thomas instructed, hoping their horses understood him as much as Silas.

Gruff voices wafted through the night, but the words were nothing more than deep grunts. A set of keys rattled, a door creaked, and the signal box came into light.

Thomas wished he had the telescope. He had no idea how to change signals, and that's what these men were doing. A loud clank was followed by a dull thud that vibrated through the track, and his horse shied away.

'Easy, girl.' His words were barely audible, but the animal understood.

For a minute, nothing else happened, and they watched in silence, their breath curling before their faces. Thomas began to worry that the men wouldn't leave. The train they needed to redirect was due in just under an hour.

'What's that?' Silas nudged him. 'Listen.'

A fragile rustle of trees, the distant screech of an owl, the horses' hooves impatient on the mulch and then a faint, metallic rattle Thomas couldn't place. Beside them, the vibration in the track increased and grew to a clatter.

'Under cover.' Understanding what the sound meant, Thomas dismounted.

He helped Silas down, and they led their horses away from the tracks and into the trees. The sound increased, and the vibration became so great it affected Thomas' breathing. The night grew lighter along the rails as an engine steamed closer, and the rattle

232

developed into a rhythm. The turning of wheels, the pushing of pistons, a thundering scream of iron and steel, smoke and steam; the engine roared by at full speed. The horse reared, but Thomas calmed it. Trucks rattled and shook their way past, throwing coal dust and debris into the air. The train was long, and by the time the last car passed, the engine's roar had faded. Stillness returned, but the train had damaged it irrevocably and Thomas' legs were trembling.

'Bloody hell,' Silas said. 'That was fecking fast.'

'Aye,' Thomas agreed. 'It was going straight on, the same as ours is expecting to do.'

They stepped from the cover of the trees to the cover of their shadows and saw the lights of the train fade to nothing.

'We need to check that siding,' Thomas said. 'If we change the points and an engine takes a corner at that speed it's going to come off the tracks, isn't it?'

'Makes sense to me,' Silas agreed. 'Unless the driver slows down.'

'How will he know to do that? No, we must go and look.'

Silas shushed him. The men were leaving the signal box. They extinguished its lamp and descended, their lanterns swaying. A 'Goodnight' floated through the air, and they separated. Thomas waited for the sound of their horses to fade and waited two minutes more for good measure.

'That was the last train before ours, right?' Silas asked.

'Aye. Then nothing else until morning.'

'Then we better make sure it's not going to crash.'

Twenty-Three

The glowing tomb became Archer's focal point. He was tempted to investigate, but he bided his time. If Quill could patiently plan his revenge over the years, Archer could wait another hour. Time passed painfully, the night air chilled him to his bones and his fingers hurt. James and Fecker pressed against him, and their body heat gave some relief as did their presence.

Every rustle of grass and unfamiliar night sound, the swoop of owls and each darting shadow from the ruins to the church tower caused his heart to pause and take notice, but the lamp at the tomb burned uninterrupted. No sound filtered up from below save for the wind among the heathland and the vibration of the sea through the ground as it pounded in relentless rhythm far out of sight. The damp gradually soaked through his clothes, and each time he examined his pocket watch, he found only a few minutes had passed.

What was this graveyard to Quill? Ebb Bay was not a place Archer had heard of, and yet it rang a muffled, distant bell. He could find no sense in it but refused to allow himself to think he was wrong. James' deciphering of the anagrams may have been incorrect. Quill might have sent the coded message as a diversion. He could be on the boat making his escape while Archer's party chased nothing but a distracting will-'o-the-wisp.

He comforted himself with reason. If Quill wanted to leave the country unnoticed, he would have done it already. Why send a sealed, obscure message if not to tempt Archer's curiosity?

It wasn't until midnight neared that James whispered, 'Maybe he's not coming.'

'He's here somewhere.' Archer was sure of it. There had been no movement, but someone had lit the lamp, and that was surely a sign. 'That's where he wants me,' he said. 'And it's time to give him what he expects. Have you ever fired a revolver?'

'Never even held one,' James admitted. 'But I'll give it a go.'

Archer drew his knapsack close and took out a gun. 'Hold it away from your ear,' he said. 'It's loaded and the safety catch is off. Be ready for a kickback. Aim at the moon and gently squeeze the trigger.'

'What good will that do?'

'I want you to lead your horse back to the halt,' Archer instructed. 'No lantern, but there's enough moon to light your way. If you see anyone trying to board the train, fire a shot as a signal. It fires six, but just let off one. If there's trouble ahead, fire two shots in quick succession as a warning.'

'Then what?'

'Stay where you are. We'll come to you.'

'Okay. Now?'

Archer nodded, and James took the revolver. 'Good luck, Archer,' he said and slipped away.

Fecker was gathering his bag.

'You stay here, Andrej,' Archer said. 'I'm going to investigate.'

'Nyet. I come with you.'

'No, my friend. I know what I am doing.'

He backed from the crevice on his belly, checked his revolver and spun the chamber. As he crouched and slid down the slope towards the graveyard, he didn't hear Fecker's words.

'Nyet,' the Ukrainian repeated. 'You don't.'

The ground was rough and wet against Archer's hands as he half-crawled, half-scurried, his cloak streaming behind like pitch. The moon cast its ghostly light on a crumbled wall beyond which uneven headstones stood in random disorder, some bearing crosses, some with weeping angels, all potential hiding places. Archer was alert, adrenaline pumping not with fear, but with the thrill, his pulse was steady and his breathing silent.

He reached the wall and crouched, but listening, heard no sound from beyond.

Cautiously raising his head above the wall, he scanned the graves picking out a route through to the mysterious light, yellow and warm against the wintry cast of the moon. No shifting shadows, no sense of another man, the scene might have been serene were it not for the uneasy feeling that Quill was somewhere close. If he had a gun, Archer would be dead before he heard its report, but Quill was no marksman. He preferred the soundless sword, the knife, the blade that sliced in silence and surprise.

Archer pictured the bodies in the Greychurch morgue. Youths lost to the world by Quill's demented revenge; his calling card a succession of pointless deaths strewn on the path he made Archer follow.

There would be no more.

Judging the time right, he followed the wall towards the cliff edge where there had once been a gate. Still crouched, he slipped through the gap and ran for the cover of the nearest headstone, pausing there to listen.

Looking towards the glow, he saw only the silhouette of the tomb. Quill could be behind it. He could be between the buttresses of the church, or even at one of the slitted windows in the tower. If he was at the tomb waiting to pounce, he had the advantage. All Archer had were his wits and time, which was fast running out. Enough of it had passed to allow James to reach Highcliffe Halt, Fecker was above, his rifle trained.

Whatever Quill had in store, now was the hour.

His revolver at the ready, Archer rose from behind the stone and crept towards the tomb. The glow increased and drawing near, he saw it came from a lantern placed on a mound of fresh earth.

A rustle behind made him spin, the firearm aimed.

There was no-one there, just the names of the dead weathered on worn stone. He took another step towards the light, rounding the corner of the tomb and there, he saw what Quill had prepared.

An open grave, deep, dark and newly dug. But it was not empty. The lantern cast light on only half, but it was enough to show him the coffin, its nameplate tarnished, its wood split. The headstone above read, 'Simon Harrington, 1859 to 1888. Beloved son and brother.'

He had been so much more to Archer. Friend, colleague, lover, he had been all things, but now he was a rotting corpse in a decaying box.

Archer didn't know where he had been buried. He was forced to deny his relationship for the sake of Simon's family and his own,

236

and only two people knew of it. His brother, and his once best friend, Benji Quill.

It hit him.

Jealous of what he and Simon had, Quill betrayed them, and when Crispin failed in his attempt to kill Archer, Quill, out of loyalty, spite or insanity took up the reins. He had driven their lives to Simon's resting place. Where more suitable to leave the viscount buried beneath the waiting pile of earth?

Another sound snapped him back to his predicament. He turned, his gun poised but saw nothing but endless stars and tombs.

It was a diversion after all, he thought, a false trail laid to tease and annoy, Quill was…

Suddenly, someone grabbed him by the ankles. He grunted in surprise, his feet vanished from under him, and a second later he was winded as his chest thudded into the ground. Bright flashes sparked before his eyes, and powerful hands dragged and wrenched him into the pit.

Stones scraped his flesh as he clawed at the earth to find purchase. The revolver was wrenched from his grip and he slid backwards and helpless to land in a heap on the coffin. He was yanked to his feet by his hair, and the next thing he knew, a blade was at his throat.

'Couldn't resist, could you, Riddington?' Quill breathed in his ear. He pressed hard against Archer's back, forcing him against the dank, earth walls. His breath smelt foul and his voice grated. 'You're so easy to trap, you'll be easy to kill.'

'Quill, don't be a…'

Archer was ignored. 'Know everything don't you?' Quill spat. 'What I want, where I'll be, but you never knew where he was put. Never cared to find out.' He laughed bitterly. 'Shows you what you thought of him, you depraved, disgusting sodomite. Well, here he is.'

With a strength he didn't know Quill possessed, Archer was spun and thrust forward. A savage kick in his back sent him crashing into the wall of earth, and Quill was on him again, kicking the back of his legs. Archer crumpled to his knees, the force splitting the coffin lid. Flailing with his cumbersome cloak, he tipped as the wood gave way.

'On your front.' Quill hissed, bunching Archer's cloak at the collar and pulling. The chain dug into his flesh, strangling him and the razor point of the knife stung the back of his neck. 'Face to face with your boy. Like you were those nights.' Each statement was accompanied by a tightening of the chain. 'The sea churning at the hull. The hammock empty while you took your sport on a dark deck.' A yank. 'With *my* desire. With *my* love.'

The knife pierced Archer's skin. He struggled to free himself, but Quill's weight had him pinned.

'It's going to kill you slowly.' The blade twisted, and a fireball of pain shot through Archer's spine. 'Penetrate inch by inch the way you defiled him in your abhorrent, filthy…'

'You're sick, Quill,' Archer croaked, his mind sprinting towards an escape it had yet to conceive. 'They'll hang you.'

'Then we'll all be together in hell, Riddington,' the doctor growled. 'It's where I've been since I learned your truth. It's where Crispin wants you, and it's where I promised to put you.'

Archer's tried to turn his head, but the knife cut deeper.

'Slowly,' Quill panted. 'Enjoy your last breaths.'

Archer's helplessness fuelled his anger. There had to be a way out of this, but, as the knife burned, he knew there was none.

He pictured Silas standing beside his grave, lost and alone, because Archer had allowed the madman to get the better of him. It was shameful. The image shocked and spurred him. He could not allow it to happen. He had to fight back.

He sucked in his stomach, raised his hips and forced his head against the wood as hard as he could. With one thrust and a flailing kick, he slammed himself into the coffin. The rotting lid gave beneath the weight of two men, and he dropped. It was only a couple of inches, but enough to draw the knife free of his flesh.

The collapse put Quill off balance. He grasped for the walls, giving Archer enough time to spin onto his back. Blood ran warm on his neck, and the wound raged, attacked by earth and splinters. He yelled in fury as he scrambled to stand.

Quill was a mass of darkness silhouetted against the spread of stars, but he had found his feet. As Archer backed against the pit wall, struggling to find purchase inside the coffin, Quill lifted the knife high in both hands and, before Archer could react, screamed like a demon and brought it down.

The end had come suddenly, but he didn't fear it. He was with Simon, Silas would understand and in time, join them. He would miss Silas' life, he wouldn't know if Thomas found happiness with James, he would never know how their lives ran, but this was how his was to end.

The stars were extinguished as the shadow fell. The coffin shuddered, and Archer was smothered. His head cracked against the wood, the stench of decay engulfed him, and a great weight pressed and writhed on his chest.

Helpless, he waited for the blade.

Thomas watched as Silas knelt at the signal box door. He held the lantern close so his friend could see the lock which he picked at first with a knife. When that didn't work, Silas rummaged in his knapsack and produced a length of thin steel. He inserted it, moving it as if trying to catch something in the barrel, but Thomas doubted it would be strong enough to act as a key.

'Ah, feck it.' Silas swore when the metal buckled. 'This ain't no good.'

'Can we break a window?'

'We could, mate,' the Irishman said, standing. 'But I have this. The thing is, see, you need to treat these old locks properly. Tease them to do what you want, you know? Go carefully and with respect.'

He raised a foot and slammed it into the door. The splintering of wood fractured the night in one sharp crack, and, after a second kick, the door flew open and crashed loudly against the wall behind.

'You might as well send up a flare,' Thomas mumbled, glancing behind and expecting to see the railwaymen come running.

'Yeah, well...' Silas entered the box. 'Now what?'

The lantern cast shafts of light across a row of levers set beneath the windows facing the tracks.

'How many do they need for one bloody set of points?'

'I'd have thought only one,' Thomas said. 'But which?' Each lever had a nameplate, but the words meant little. 'Shunting up main to four,' he read. 'Signal nil or goods yard two. Shunting goods yard to up main five. Any idea?'

'Only that our set of points is one of these, and if we pull the wrong one we could kill a few people.'

'You stay here. I'll ride up and see what's out there. Maybe our points are identified.'

'Be quick,' Silas encouraged.

'Scared?'

'Feck off, mate. No, it's late. If Jimmy's right, the train will be through in twenty minutes.'

Thomas descended the stairs and, mounting his horse, set off to investigate the siding. The mention of James' name lit an image in his mind. He pictured his round face and chubby cheeks, the neat cut of his short back and sides, the way his expression changed from thought to realisation in a second with a smile of excited surprise. He remembered the touch of his hand that night which now seemed so long ago, lying beside him in bed, pressed together, their breathing strained with anticipation.

'Concentrate,' he admonished himself, approaching the points.

He held the light to the sign there and read the number painted on it. If the upline ran south towards the capital, down was therefore north, and the lever they needed to pull was now apparent. Holding the lantern high, he followed the siding to check the angle of the bend. It curved away gradually, but he didn't know at what speed a train could take it without tipping and derailing.

As Thomas rode further, the night ahead darkened as the rails led him between trees raised from the ground on a bank of shale. The horse picked its way over the sleepers, slipping occasionally and jolting him. The darkness grew more intense but, after a few minutes, was pierced by a pinprick of red light. He saw the reason. An arched, brick tunnel spanned the track, the signal warning light to one side. The horse was unwilling to go further, and Thomas agreed. There was no end to the blackness, and only a map would tell him how long it was and what was on the other side.

He headed back, checking the time and wondering what was happening at the castle. The thud and grate of hooves accompanied him in their steady rhythm. His gloved hands chilled through the leather, and his lack of vision gave him no focus, leaving him disorientated and dizzy until Silas' lamp in the signal box appeared and guided him.

He found his companion trying to make sense of the controls.

'We need to change the up point number one,' Thomas said,

rubbing his hands together and breathing on them. 'Have you seen it?'

'Yeah, last one on the end,' Silas said. 'What do the others do?'

'I can't tell you. There's a tunnel about a quarter of a mile ahead.' Thomas found a map in his bag, and they studied it, but it was not as detailed as the one Archer carried. 'There's a river not far beyond, and it looks like the track ends at a jetty, to load coal into ships, like Jimmy said.'

Silas pressed his hand to the window and peered through. 'What d'you think?' he said. 'The driver sees a light so he knows he's been sent on another route and slows down?'

'I should think so. Railways are new to me, but I didn't see any lamps at the points, so it must change one further down the line.'

'The wonders of modern science, eh?' Silas joked as Thomas inspected the row of levers. 'They can build stuff like this but can't get the shit off the streets of the East End.'

'Aye, but not our concern at this moment. No. Nothing here about lights. The curve's not too severe. Here, help me.'

Silas joined him at the lever. 'We press the handle and pull it back?'

'Can't see how else it works.'

Thomas wrapped his fingers around the handle, pressing his palm against the wooden shaft. Squeezing the two together was easy but pulling the lever towards him took both men. Once it started to move, however, it slid into place and landed with a satisfying clunk.

'I'll go and check,' Thomas said. 'The train will be passing in a few minutes.'

The words made no sense.

'Dyyavol. Ublyudok. Ebat.'

Were these the words of the devil? Was that who was kicking him? Was Lucifer on him, thumping the breath from his body, yelling, screaming, smothering his face with foul smelling cloth and pressing him further into the pit of bones? Where was the sting of the knife?

Fecker's voice cut through Archer's confusion.

'Dyyavol!' He was growling, struggling to drag Quill away.

A punch, a gasp, the glint of steel, the taste of earth and then the stabbing cold of the night air. Archer's chest was free, but the shadows fought on his legs, trampling them and sending shards of savage pain from his shins to his groin. He kicked and elbowed his way from them until the pit wall pressed against his back.

A yell, words screamed in Russian and the sudden realisation that Fecker was scrambling from the pit.

'You alive?' he called down.

'Get after him!'

'Give me your hand, Geroy!'

Archer didn't understand the word but scrambled to his feet. He didn't want to picture what he was standing on as he reached. Fecker grabbed his wrist and with a jerk that nearly ripped the limb from its joint, dragged him up to the side of the grave.

'Are you hurt?'

'No, Geroy.' Fecker collected his shotgun. 'I don't shoot or I hit you. Look, he runs for horse.'

'We must get to ours.'

'You bleed,' the Ukrainian grunted, checking Archer's neck.

'No time for that, Fecks.' Archer pulled away. 'We must ride.'

Twenty-Four

James wrapped his coat tighter about his shivering body as he sat in his saddle listening for any sound of approaching horses or the train. The bitter, barren moor was a far cry from the busy streets of the capital. There, he had been just another runner in a maze of buildings, an inconsequential cog in a machine that relied on every other insignificant component. He kept the machine communicating, but his was only a small role. Unimportant, he had been replaceable.

Here, he was surrounded by space and open heathland, with a vast sky overhead, and he had never felt so small. More accustomed to spending his nights by the hearth helping his sister to read, the smell of grass and countryside was alien but thrilling. A week ago, he could never have imagined that he would be in the middle of nowhere working with devoted, noble men to catch the Ripper. He never knew that men like the viscount existed. Men who were willing to put their lives on the line for the benefit of others. He had never been so accepted and trusted. He had never been as valued, and he hoped he was man enough to rise to Archer's challenge.

He tried to read the time beneath the signal's red stop lamp, and the horse shifted beneath him. Also feeling the cold, it was impatient to be on the move, but his orders were to stay and watch. Beside him, the signal remained raised, but as he squinted into the gloom, watching the ridge between him and the castle, he heard it clunk, looked up and saw it had dropped and the lamp glowed green.

'Not long now,' he said, patting the horse's neck.

Steering his mount away from the tracks, he dismounted and tethered the horse to bushes where it could graze. There, he gathered his nerves, determined to do well by the viscount, and took strength from the cold steel in his pocket. He wasn't sure if he could shoot someone with it, but he was ready to try.

He sensed the train before he saw it. The track hummed and vibrated at his feet, and he looked as far as he could along its incoming path. He saw no locomotive, but a movement on the hill drew his eye. A shape crested the ridge, a horse galloping south, the rider's head down and his back bent. He was too far away to make out the face, but, instantly alert, James followed its trajectory to assess its intention. Whoever it was, they were racing and dropping below the ridge, angled for the tracks further up the line.

Closer, he could see it was not Archer or Fecker; it could only be Quill. He crouched.

The track began to clank and, as Quill neared the embankment, the scene brightened. James could now hear the throb of an engine, a quiet monotonal hum that intensified and, as it grew louder, broke into beats. Watching Quill dismount, he slipped from the bushes and drew out the revolver, raising it over his head, his finger on the trigger.

He hesitated. If he fired, Quill would know he was there and might bolt; if he remained silent, he was on his own.

The rhythm of the locomotive slowed, the light brightened, and he turned to look. Shielding his eyes from the headlamps, he made out the chimney ejecting puffs of dark smoke. They fumed upwards into one column before being dragged back along the carts, clouding the stars. It slowed as it approached the halt and, turning again, James saw Quill slap his horse's rump. It took off, following the tracks south. James lay low, the revolver in his hand and his heart in his mouth. If Quill climbed onto the moving train, he would do the same and fire the signal from there.

Gasping and wheezing as if it had just climbed a mountain, the stocky engine laboured past. The ground shuddered, and glancing up, James saw he had to act. Quill was scurrying, bent low and keeping up with the engine. He grabbed a rail on the coal-car and heaved. Mounting the steps deftly, he disappeared into the tender.

James ran back to the track and alongside the cars. They passed him as the locomotive, once past the halt, gathered speed, but there were no steps, no handrails and nothing to give him easy access. He stumbled as he searched for a handhold; he was quickly running out of cars and options.

A warning shot was the best he could do, but there was no sign of Archer or Fecker. Even if they heard the report, they wouldn't reach the train in time.

The last car was approaching. Thinking quickly, he grabbed the rear rail with both hands and clung on. The only way was to pull, jump and hope his feet found purchase on the buffer, but he missed his footing on the first attempt, and his shins slammed painfully into metal. His feet dragged, catching on sleepers, but he fought to regain his rhythm, found it and tried again. This time, he made the leap and hauled himself onto the backplate.

He pulled out the revolver and, looking away, let off a shot. The sound was barely audible above the rattle and clatter of the cars, but he hoped Archer had heard it. That done, his job was to watch for Quill. If he jumped, they would lose him. He had two miles before the points and another beyond them to the river.

With the train now running at full speed, he approached the side of the carriage and looked to the front. The slipstream immediately whipped his cap from his head, and the cold watered his eyes. It was hard to make out anything along the edge of the cars, but the engine lamps illuminated the track, and if Quill appeared he would see his silhouette. That was unless he jumped from the other side.

James couldn't watch both at once, and he had to move. He pocketed the revolver and leaning out, cautiously groped for something to hold. The side of the truck was smooth, and to traverse it meant pinching the lip of the roof with his fingertips and stretching his toes to a narrow ridge of metalwork just above the wheels, a few feet from the fast-moving embankment. The wind fought to whip him from his precarious position as he stepped out to inch his way towards the front.

"One step at a time." Thomas' words gave him hope and drove him on. He would be waiting at the points. James was not doing this alone.

As he squinted against the soot, his fingers explored the way, each grip more painful than the last, each less powerful as his hands numbed. A figure emerged from the tender. Huddled, it scurried along the footplate to the engine and slithered inside. James moved faster and reached for the corner of the car.

His boots slipped, and he was buffeted away from the ledge, his legs flailing. His fingers screamed in pain, and he was thumped back into the car, winded. He thrashed, but found no support, he'd lost his footing, his grip was weakening, and he couldn't hold on any longer. He had tried, but he was not up to the task. Knowing he was about to fall, he yelled in bitter frustration.

A hand slammed into his back without warning, pressing him against the truck, and held him there until his feet touched the ledge. Perhaps this was his mother's "unseen hand of God," he thought in a detached moment of clarity, and with the hand supporting him, he was able to stretch for the end of the car and find a handhold. As soon as he was safe, he was let go and shaking, looked to see who had saved him.

Fecker made a fist and thumped the air as he angled safely away from the wheels. With his hair and his coat streaming behind, he raced the train like the devil bearing down on the souls of the unrighteous.

Archer wasn't far behind, galloping from the ridge to the rear of the train and encouraging his mount with his crop. The horse knew its purpose and worked with him, delivering him up the embankment to the backplate. The viscount drew level with the last car, stood in the stirrups, and grabbed the rail. With one great leap, he left the saddle and swung his legs across to the car. He landed first time and clambered aboard as the horse veered off and slowed. Archer wasted no time climbing to the roof, and James turned his attention to the engine.

'Jimmy!' Archer was above him, fighting the wind for his balance. 'Warn the driver. Stop the train.'

Everything was shadows and speed, gusts and fumes as James fought his way to the next car. Wooden, it offered a narrow walkway, making it easier for him to pass, but there were no handholds apart from cracks in the planking where he dug his fingertips, pressing his body flat against the side. He didn't know how many more cars there were before the tender, but the headlamps were still a way off. The driver was expecting to continue straight on and was steaming the engine hard.

Knowing there would be a bend after the points, but not knowing if the engine would take it at that speed without derailing, James reached the next car to find it shuddering dangerously. A warning

246

of things to come. He ripped off his gloves with his teeth to gain a
better handhold and swung out once more into the howling wind.

'I can hear it,' Thomas whispered.

'Yeah, there's a light.'

Sure enough, a glow emanated from the distant trees and the
tracks hummed.

'Mount up,' Thomas instructed. 'We should follow it. I'll gallop,
you'll have to walk.'

'How do you gallop?' Silas stood on the steps where it was easier
to lift his foot to the stirrup.

'You can't even trot.'

'I can fecking try, mate.'

'You'll injure yourself.'

'Ah, away with you.'

Thomas shook his head. 'Do what you must. Just don't get in
front of the bloody thing.'

The locomotive was closer, puffing on each fourth-beat until it
broke through the trees with a glare of light. Thomas' heart pumped
as hard as its pistons. He'd never chased or hunted, but if Quill
was on that train and making his escape, he would do whatever
it took. No-one was taking down Archer's good name. If he had
been a religious man, he would have prayed Archer was safe, but
he didn't need prayers. He believed in the man, and thanks to him,
he believed in himself.

He tightened his reins and addressed Silas.

'Ready?'

'Fuck me!'

Silas was agape, and when Thomas turned to face the oncoming
locomotive, he saw why.

The engine bore down on him, and in a surreal flash of clarity,
he saw James clambering at the side of a coal-car edging towards
the cab. That was not the only worrying sight. Fecker was on the
coal heap, and Quill stood atop a boxcar in the middle, a knife
raised in one hand. From the back, Archer was battling towards
him resolved but struggling to aim his pistol. His cloak hampered
him, stretched out behind like a flapping sail, dragging him back
by his neck. As he sped past, he threw it away, and it took off into

the night. Releasing it allowed him to stand erect, and with Quill's advance empowered by the wind, he raised his weapon.

'It's turning,' Silas shouted.

The train took the points protesting the curve with a screech of metal and listing as it juddered onto the branch line. The men on the roof fought to keep their balance. Fecker was staggering to keep upright, Quill was on his knees, and Archer was battling the wind.

'Shit!' Thomas spurred his horse to action.

He had to reach the tunnel and warn them before their bodies splattered against the arch. He galloped head down and, reaching behind, swung his shotgun from his back. Tucking it beneath his arm, he found the trigger and looked ahead. The track was straightening, and he was gaining on the train. Driving his horse with shouts and jabs of his heels, he manoeuvred the shotgun to his shoulder.

He was too low, there was no way to aim up at Quill. He could only see his head as he crawled closer to Archer. If Thomas fired, he might miss, or worse, hit the viscount. Cursing, he let the gun hang from its strap. Pounding hooves now matched the rhythm of his heart as he drew level with James at the side of driver's cab.

'Tunnel!' Thomas yelled, but his words were snatched away and useless.

The tiny red dot appeared among the blackness. He grappled for the shotgun, aimed it skywards and fired twice. James heard, ducked and turned.

'Tunnel!' Thomas hollered again, pointing. He swiped his hand across his head, ducking.

James understood. He stooped into the cab, and a second later the whistle sounded. Two short bursts, a pause, two more. The rhythm continued as Thomas fell back and the engine steamed into the tunnel. He heeled his horse and yanked the reins, directing her up the slope and into the darkness.

The last he saw was Fecker throwing himself flat and Archer aiming his revolver.

Passing through the arch, James prayed his friends had seen the tunnel wall in time. Sounds were amplified, paining his ears, smoke burned the back of his throat, and the open furnace blasted his legs.

248

That was hellish enough, but nothing compared to the sight of two railwaymen slumped in a pool of blood, their throats sliced.

The cab suddenly brightened as they broke from its stinking darkness into the moonlight. He was faced with the regulator; dials and valves, handles and levers that meant nothing. The only obvious thing was the whistle chain, and he pulled it once, signalling they were free. In a mile, they would be at the depot, through it and, unless he could stop the train, straight into the river.

He kicked shut the furnace door. It might dampen the fire but only a little, there was still too much momentum, and even if he extinguished the flames somehow, the engine would take too long to slow on its own. There had to be a way of reducing speed by applying the brakes, but if he pulled the wrong lever, he could derail the train and kill them all.

He wished Thomas was with him.

Thomas was. Galloping beside him again, crouched over his saddle, shouting across the distance and beckoning with one arm. James couldn't hear his words, but he understood the gestures.

He hung from the open doorway, the ground a fast-moving blur. 'I can't!' he bellowed.

If he missed, he would break his neck. If he stayed, he would plunge into the river with the full weight of the locomotive on top.

Thomas was gesturing madly, one second looking forward and then next desperately at James. Buildings flashed past. They had reached the shunting yard.

'Jump!'

James tried to reach the outstretched hand, but Thomas was too far away.

'Trust me.' Thomas shouted, fixing James with his eyes; green, the colour of safety like a signal. 'I'll catch you.'

The sound beneath the wheels was suddenly hollow, and the vibrations worsened as the train thundered over a turntable. Sparks flew from the horse's hooves, its mane streamed wildly, and Thomas leant dangerously from his saddle, his fingers beckoning.

James reached for the whistle and gave two final blasts before pulling himself to the footplate.

The gap between him and safety was a chasm, but on the other side was Thomas.

All he had to do was jump.

'Now!'

James threw himself into the wind.

They had taken the points and careered onto the siding. The unexpected turn threw Quill to his knees, giving Archer the advantage, but even without his cloak, it was a struggle to remain upright. Taking accurate aim was impossible as the smoke blasted around him, watering his eyes and clouding his vision. He choked against it, gripped the revolver with both hands and, bracing himself, aimed.

The Ripper grinned, his twisted face visible in flashes of moonlight one moment and lost in smoke the next. He was crawling, his cloak flapping like the wings of an insect as he lurched to his knees. Behind, Fecker clambered from the tender, pushed unevenly towards Quill by the slipstream. He too was struggling to find his target, his arm buffeted and pulled.

Archer was aware that someone was riding below, and from the corner of his eye, saw two quick flashes of flame and heard Tom's shotgun. Quill recognised the warning, and when the whistle pierced the cacophony of pistons and coupling rods, he turned to see Fecker advancing. The Ukrainian threw himself flat on his stomach. Quill dropped, his hands covering his head, and between the billows of smoke, Archer saw the tunnel lit from inside as the engine plunged in.

He hit the deck with such force he lost his grip on his revolver, and it skidded over the edge. Suction pressed him flat against the boxcar, the tunnel roof an inch above his head. The acrid tang of smoke made him gag. His lungs burned from it, and his eyes streamed. The sound was deafening. The engine wasn't slowing, and they were running out of track. He dragged himself towards Quill. Unless Fecker could take the man down, Archer was on his own. It was just him, the Ripper and a knife.

They broke into open with a roar and a single, ear-splitting whistle. Clean air swept away the soot and stench, and he dragged his sleeve across his eyes. Quill rose to his feet, the night sky behind him a confusion of streaming stars and smoke.

Archer forced himself to his knees, his arms wavering as he

fought for balance. Quill was nearly on him, his blade swinging, his eyes flaming. The viscount had only his fists and his wits. Fecker, still on his front, wrestled to aim his rifle against the jerks and shudders. Between them, they had the man trapped.

'No way out, Quill,' Archer yelled. 'Give up. Jump. Turn yourself in.'

'You'll never be free of me, Riddington,' Quill laughed. 'I'm taking you to hell, and your pretty boys are coming with you.'

He spun to Fecker.

The crack of a gunshot and the hiss of pellets made Archer duck. He expected to see Quill fall, but he was still standing, although now he was raging at Fecker whose shot had hit his arm.

The train charged across a turntable. In the distance, the track ended on a jetty that reached out over a wide, slivery river. Sheds and carriages sped past and the engine thundered towards disaster, unstoppable.

Quill understood their fate, and his face contorted in elation. With an insane cackle, he directed his rage back to Archer.

'I have you!' He screamed. 'You see? Dying together!'

'Quill!'

'I don't care about me. But without you…'

'Benji!'

Quill attacked. Archer sidestepped, but his feet slithered on the curved roof. He grabbed Quill's arm, determined to yank him from the car, but his footing was unstable. He was slipping, and the Ripper's knife was jabbing ever closer.

'Without you, Crispin will be free to continue my work.'

Archer caught his wrist, the blade an inch from his face, and yanked it away, catching the man off balance. He forced Quill to his knees, using him as an anchor as he clambered over, determined to kick him from the train.

He bent his legs, and the engine ploughed through the buffers.

It left the tracks and arced over the river, weightless for a second before gravity sealed its fate. The boiler hit the water, the tender bucked, and the impact shot back through the cars. Each one reared as it slammed into the one before, each shunt rippling through to the next sending the shockwave towards Archer.

Fecker's car bucked, throwing him, and he was lost to the river.

There was nothing Archer could do but save himself. He ran towards the rear of the train, jumping the gaps and searching for safety. The jetty sped past beneath him, but he was running on the spot with the last car coming up fast.

The rest happened in individual flashes like a spinning zoetrope. The trucks rose and tipped, each one dragging the next into the water. They collided, piling up in an explosion of burning coal as the boiler blew apart.

Silhouetted by a ball of fire, Quill was tossed into the air and tumbled backwards into the chaos as the car disappeared from beneath his feet.

Archer was out of options. He dived.

He fell through the sound of screeching metal and the flare of flame and hit the water. It slammed against his head with a muffled thump, cold and hard, and the sounds distorted.

Around him, the murk flashed red and yellow. Coal and debris rained from above, and waves swamped his mouth as the final cars derailed. Shockwaves hampered his race for the surface, his arms working instinctively, his feet kicking. He broke water, sucked in filthy air and swam, not daring to look back. Spitting, gasping and thrashing, he heaved himself towards the riverbank.

His neck wound throbbed angrily, his legs were weak, and his lungs burned, but the waves created by the plunging train washed him shoreward. Clawing at the muddy bank, he dragged himself to safety in time to see the caboose pulled from the jetty and sink. The surface bubbled and calmed beneath a dissipating cloud of steam, and the noise faded to shocking silence. There was no sign of his men or Quill.

He struggled to his feet, coughing up a combination of river water and soot and heard his name.

Thomas rode towards him, a lantern swinging from his saddle and James clinging to him behind.

'Thank heavens,' Archer gasped, collapsing onto his back.

Thomas was at his side in a second, wrapping him in his arms and cradling his head. Calm and reassuring, he knew exactly what Archer wanted to hear.

'Silas is safe,' he said. 'You're hurt.'

'It's nothing. Where's Andrej?'

'Over here!'

James was at the river's edge throwing off his coat and wading in, and when Thomas released Archer, he saw Fecker thrashing helplessly in the river beneath the jetty. He was trying to make it to shore, foundering between the pylons. James reached him just as Fecker disappeared beneath the surface. He dived, his legs kicking the air and, a moment later, Fecker reappeared. Impervious to the Ukrainian's struggles, James flipped him onto his back, held up his chin and heaved him towards safety.

'Go, Tom,' Archer panted.

Thomas ran, and he and James dragged Fecker to dry land.

Archer crawled from the mud until he found grass where he fell shaking, cold and shocked. Fecker had lost his greatcoat but showed no signs of cold. All the same, James rubbed his arms and his back until the big man, realising what had happened, stopped him and did something Archer had never seen him do. He wrapped James in his arms, smothering him, and kissed the top of his head.

'I lost your gun,' Fecker said when James had struggled free. 'Man dead?'

'He followed the wreck into the river,' Thomas told him, crouching to inspect Archer's injury. 'I didn't see him surface.'

'Silas is coming, Archer,' Thomas reassured him. 'Stay still while I tie something around this cut.'

He had just bound it with his scarf when Silas rode up leading two of the horses. He slipped from the saddle, landing in an ungainly heap, righted himself and was at Archer's side in a second, kissing him and fighting Thomas to be the one to attend to his wound. Thomas allowed it and saw to the horses. He and James tethered and calmed them, and gradually, peace blanketed the scene.

'We must go,' Archer said when he had recovered sufficiently to stand, shivering and wrapping Silas in his arms for warmth.

'I see no Quill.' Fecker had been scanning the river. It sparkled beneath the moon, now low on the horizon.

'He couldn't have survived,' James reasoned.

'We did.' Archer winced at his own words. After tonight, who knew what Quill was capable of?

'We need to get you two warm and dry.' Ever practical, never ruffled, Thomas took Archer's hand and pulled him to his feet.

Twenty-Five

They paired up to ride the available horses, Archer cradling Silas on his mount, and James clinging to Thomas more tightly than was necessary on another. Fecker ambled behind, saddleless. The moon was fading, but with lamps lit, there was enough light to see their way. They found Archer's horse grazing not far from where he had left it, and James' still tethered to the bushes at the halt, but they remained in their pairs for warmth and led the spare animals with Fecker taking the front of the line.

'We go this way,' he announced as they set off. 'Follow.'

'The castle?' Archer queried. 'No, we must go back to the inn before we all catch cold.'

'Nyet, Geroy.' Fecker was insistent. 'First castle.'

Archer was too exhausted to argue. There would be a reason, and he owed the Ukrainian his obedience. He owed all of them, and when his head cleared and he was able to assess his position in the hopefully warmer light of day, he would think of some way to repay his team. He could lavish money on them, but that was too easy, and if he kept doing it, the gesture would mean nothing. He had given Thomas the chance to be with the man he desired, but the pair also worked for him, and both had proven their worth in more ways than one. They deserved more, but with his head thumping and his neck wound throbbing, he was unable to conceive what else he could do. It was too late at night and too cold to think about it now. He turned his attention to another question.

'What does Geroy mean?' he asked, resting his chin on Silas' shoulder and holding him tighter.

'No fecking idea.' Silas kissed his cheek. 'When we get back, I'm going to learn to ride properly, so I can do more next time.'

'Next time?' That was a hideous thought. 'You're here,' Archer said. 'That's enough.'

They followed Fecker uphill and across the top of the moor until the castle appeared, darker and more brooding than before. The troubled sea pounded and boomed on the cliffs away to the east, but the bats darted undisturbed from the ruins to the tower through peaceful starlight.

Archer shivered. He imagined the devastation back at the shunting yard and wondered what the authorities would make of it in the morning. They might find his cloak, or Quill's body, Fecker's coat, or any other pieces of evidence that could, with detailed research, lead them back to him, but that was the least of his concerns. If necessary, he would admit the truth to Inspector Adelaide and leave his fate in the man's hands. He was prepared to stand up and be counted, but would not let anything untoward to happen to his men.

His men? His staff? No, they were his friends and no harm would come to any of them.

'What are we doing here, Fecks?' Silas asked, when they reached the graveyard wall and dismounted.

Fecker swamped him beneath one arm, and whispered in his ear. Silas reacted in surprise, considered for a moment, and shrugged.

'Come,' Fecker said and led them to the open grave.

Archer followed, watching Thomas and James who walked ahead saying nothing to each other. They approached the pile of earth where the lantern still burned, and Silas looked into the open pit. He nodded to Fecker, but prevented Archer from coming closer.

'Don't look in there, Archie,' he said. 'Please? Don't say anything.'

Shivering, Archer agreed. He had no desire to see the remains of Simon Harrington, simply being at his resting place was difficult enough. Flanked by Thomas and James, he waited, confused when Fecker lowered Silas into the ground. He disappeared for a few seconds before being lifted out. Brushing dirt from his knees, he returned to Archer.

'Fecks says he saw this earlier,' he explained, holding out a fist. 'I don't know if this is the right thing to do, but he thinks you should have it, and so do I.'

He unrolled his fingers to reveal a signet ring, identical to his own, and engraved with the initials A.S.

Tears welled behind Archer's eyes brought by the memories of

Simon's death . 'I gave that to Simon in the weeks before he died,' he said.

'Yeah, I guessed as much.' Silas offered it. 'He took it to his grave. Shows how much he loved you. You should wear it.'

'I can't.'

'It'll remind you of how much you were loved.' Silas showed Archer his own. 'Like this one tells me how much I'm loved. Same initials, see? Archer and Silas. When I see you wearing it, it'll remind me of the scars you bear, both here…' He touched Archer's side. 'And here,' and put his hand over his heart. 'Carry him with you, Archie. Carry us both.'

Thomas stepped forward. 'Carry all of us.'

Silas slipped the ring on his finger, and Archer kissed his hand. 'I will,' he said. 'My heart was broken, but this will mend it.' He kissed Silas on the forehead and held him. 'You know, the initials don't just stand for Archer and Simon or Archer and Silas. There's another meaning.'

'Yeah, well nothing's simple with you, is it?' Silas grumbled blithely. 'What?'

'Amore Salvet,' Archer said, holding Silas' face in his hands and blinking in adoration. 'It's Latin for *Love Saves.*'

'Take.' Feck was at his side offering the spade.

The tears pressed harder as Archer lifted the first earth from the pile. Silently, he said his goodbye to Simon Harrington as he let it fall. His friends stood solemnly at the side of the grave with their heads bowed, each lost in private thoughts, until one by one, they took their turn. Using the spade and their hands, they worked in silence and without being asked until the grave was filled. Archer stood the lantern before the headstone and wiped the tears from his eyes. He placed his damp hand on Simon's name, leaving behind some of the sorrow he had suffered then along with some of the joy he had now found.

He turned to the others waiting patiently in a row.

'"This happy breed of men, this little world, this precious stone…"' He quoted as he regarded their lamp-shadowed faces and turned the ring on his finger. He pulled himself together. 'Men,' he said. 'We have been through much these past days, but we have been through it together. Whatever happens in our lives from this moment, remember this: You are my friends. You men have changed my life, and I will never be able to repay the debt of gratitude I owe. I shall try. Every moment of my life will be dedicated to you, your happiness and wellbeing. You have my esteem, my respect and my admiration, but above all, you have my love. Yes, even Jimmy whom I hardly know. Men like us face a far greater challenge than the madness of Quill.' His words flowed as he regarded each one in turn. 'We live in a world that chooses not to understand. It is not forgiving, and we must tread carefully the path our fates have mapped. Where Andrej faces discrimination and mistrust as an immigrant, the rest of us face the same hatred because of who we love. I thought my life would be lived alone and unloved as the world would have it be, but none of us need be alone now. I can say no more.' His voice was cracking. 'But, inadequate though it is, you have my thanks.'

'Ah, you old softie.' Silas took Archer's hand.

Fecker approached and threw his arms around the viscount, tugging him to his muscular chest for a second before kissing each cheek.

'You are Geroy,' he said.

Archer warmed at the unexpected embrace. 'I don't know what that means,' he said.

'Is old word from my homeland,' Fecker explained. 'It means honourable.'

The moon sank behind the hills as they rode, battered, bruised, but safe. The darkest hour waned, and before long, the first grey strip of dawn appeared on the horizon. Thomas had lost track of time, but it was of no concern.

The landlord was none too pleased at being woken early for a second morning in a row, but when Archer ordered hot water for five men and enough breakfast for ten, adding a substantial sum for the man's trouble, the inconvenience was forgotten. He did, however, look at their filthy clothes and soot-blackened faces with suspicion.

'We had a run-in with a rather common grouse,' Thomas explained with a wry smile. He handed the innkeeper a pound note. 'Would you have your wife bring me some gauze and, if you have it, antiseptic? As I am sure you know, the common grouse has quite a snap to its beak.'

The landlord took the money and set about heating the water under instruction from Thomas to ensure there was enough for every guest.

Back beneath the eaves, they took turns to bathe, and changed into whatever dry clothing they had. A substantial breakfast arrived, and the room soon warmed. Tiredness pricked at Thomas' eyes. They were exhausted, but they were not home and safe yet.

At nine o'clock, Archer gathered the party together.

'Fecker has gone to attend to the horses and return them,' he explained. 'I am told there is an omnibus to Haverpool at eleven. We should reach there by two and from there can take the night train home. I must dispatch a telegram to the sanitorium in case Quill has once again eluded us. I will instruct them that if he arrives, he is not allowed access to Crispin and they should immediately inform myself and the authorities.'

'I'll send it, Sir,' James offered.

'No, Jimmy, but thank you. Silas and I will go. You and Thomas stay here and pack our things. We will return in one hour.'

It was the first time James and Thomas had been alone since they had left Clearwater, and they stood facing each other saying nothing long after the door had closed.

'I think this is what you call a setup.' James broke the ice.

'I need to apologise,' Thomas said.

'No, you don't.'

Thomas took a step closer. 'I do. I have mistreated you.'

'No, you haven't.'

'James, please. Let me explain.'

'I lied to you.'

'You didn't.'

'Tom...' James took his hand. 'We ain't going to get anywhere if you stand on ceremony all the time. It's a simple argument to settle. Can you love me?'

'I don't know what that is,' Thomas said.

'It's this.'

James lifted his head and pressed his lips against Thomas' mouth, tentatively and once before stepping back.

A rush hit Thomas instantly. His body filled with warmth as if his heart had opened releasing a flush of joy which tingled every pore of his skin. It was not the same rush he enjoyed when Archer called him Tom or hugged him. It was deeper and more difficult to understand.

James led him to the bed. 'We have an hour,' he said. 'And I'd like to spend it lying next to you. We don't have to do anything. I just want to feel you beside me and know you want to be there.' He lay down. 'But it's up to you.'

Thomas sat beside him, admiring his smooth face. Washed and cleaned of soot, it glowed warmly in the cold morning light.

'I don't know what to do,' he whispered.

James opened his arms, and Thomas fell into them, turning to face him.

'Neither do I,' James replied. 'So that makes us even. We can find out together.' He ran his fingers through Thomas' thick hair. 'I love this colour.'

'You understand that things will have to be different when we get home,' Thomas warned.

'Yeah, I get all that.' James flashed a devilish smile.

'I may even have to tell you off.'

'Will you have to spank me, Mr Payne?'

'Don't be filthy.' Thomas' cheeks flushed as he kissed James' nose.

They looked at each other in silence. James pecked his lips cautiously, but even the light touch stirred passion. Thomas shifted closer.

'Have you ever worked for the Central Post Office?' James asked out of nowhere.

'What? No. Why?'

'Because it feels like you're sending me a message.' He pressed a leg between Thomas' so their hardening cocks touched. 'Can I help you deliver it?'

Thomas nodded. His heart was pounding, and his breathing was hard to control. It became more difficult when James fumbled at the front of his trousers.

'Here,' Thomas said, seeing to the buttons himself.

James fumbled inside for his cock. 'Fucking hell!' he exclaimed wrapping it in his fingers.

His own was hot and rigid. It offered Thomas an unfamiliar feel of soft skin covering an iron hardness.

Slowly, their hands began to stroke as their lips met.

Thomas was lost in pleasure as James' hand massaged and his tongue explored. Their teeth clashed, and their bodies rubbed. It was inexpert, but it felt so right. James clutched Thomas as if he couldn't hold him tight enough and wanted the two of them to meld together. He drew himself free of Thomas' lips, and they shared a look of amazement before James was on his neck, exploring it with kisses that caused Thomas to gasp with new pleasures. He returned every one of them, learning what gave James joy while all the time their hands maintained a steady rhythm.

'I wanted to do this from the moment I saw you,' James whispered.

'Me too.'

'I wasn't pretending, Tom. I didn't lead you on that night, I just wasn't sure back then.'

'Hush. I understand. Just don't stop doing what you're doing.'

'You neither.'

Pressure built quickly in Thomas' balls. He'd known it before, alone in his room with his imagination, but this was more intense. Where it had been a dream, it was now real. Where he had imagined Archer, he had James; a man who appeared from nowhere to turn Thomas' life on its head with the wonder in his eyes, his honesty and his acceptance. They kissed and stroked more urgently, driving each other closer to orgasm.

'I shall never get enough of you,' Thomas gasped. 'I was stupid to doubt you.'

'Hey, shush, it's okay.'

'I'm sorry, Jimmy.'

'I'm going to…' James gasped. 'Tom, fuck it. You're making me…' He panted hard. 'Don't stop.'

His back arched as Thomas quickened his stroke, and when James did the same, Thomas moaned loudly. His head thumped. He was unable to hold back. Every part of him glowed, but not just from the pleasure below. That was where it gathered, but it started from the touch of James' skin, the scent of his hair, the feel of his firm body.

They belonged to each other, they always had, and the joy

erupting through him told him this was always meant to happen. They were meant to be.

'It's coming,' he whimpered helplessly. 'Jimmy, I'm going to… I love you.'

Their mouths clashed, their moans of pleasure mingled in their throats, and they bucked and grappled until James' back arched and he spurted hot jets onto Thomas' flesh.

Thomas buried his head in James' shoulder to muffle his cries as he stuttered and gasped, unloading himself uncontrollably.

Gasping staccato exclamations of pleasure, they slowed their damp and sticky fingers, twitching and fighting for breath until their hands came to a natural halt. Neither let go, and for several glorious minutes, they lay joined as one in happiness.

Every muscle in Thomas' body, until then taut with anxious excitement, relaxed. He had never known such freedom, such understanding of himself, nothing had made this much sense in his life.

Still holding James' stiff shaft, he faced him, drinking in the sight of his hazel eyes, dewy and wide. He was biting his bottom lip as if he had done something wrong, but knew he was not to be punished. It was adorable. They held each other, kissing now and then, and explored each other's eyes, trying to read what lay behind. Nervous smiles spread into broad grins as they realised there was no need to ask.

'You know,' James finally said, 'there's other stuff we can do.'

'One step at a time.'

'Ha! The old Payne motto, eh?' He laughed briefly, before falling serious. 'There will be more times, won't there?'

'If you'll have me.'

'Was rather hoping you'd have me,' James replied with a leer. 'You know, back door delivery? Always wondered what that fuss was about.'

'Then,' Thomas said. 'If you will have me, we can explore together. Plenty of time.'

James pulled away drawing down his face in an expression of surprise. 'Are you asking me out, Mr Payne?' he smirked.

'Mr Wright.' Thomas returned the humour. 'I would be honoured to call you my man if you will acquiesce.'

'Gawd, you can sound pompous.' James snuggled closer. 'I love it. And yes, I would be honoured to acquiesce, as long as you know what you're letting yourself in for.'

'And what's that?'

'Oh, inexperience, fumbling, getting things wrong.'

'I don't see that,' Thomas said, 'I see bravery and heart, intelligence and loyalty. That's what you are, Jimmy, but whatever else you come with, I want it all.'

'You've got it.'

They kissed with sore lips.

Exhausted, Thomas felt the pull of sleep behind his eyes. 'We mustn't doze,' he said. 'The others will soon be back.'

'I reckon the viscount knows what's going on.'

'I don't have another clean shirt.'

'Don't fuss.'

'I shall smell of semen all day.'

'And I'll smell of you. Couldn't be happier,' James sighed. 'But you're right.'

Reluctantly and with a final lingering smooch, they rolled from the bed to wash and tidy themselves. Despite breaking off their tasks to grin at each other like adolescents and embrace at irregular intervals as the moment took them, they packed and were ready to leave, flushed and ecstatic when Archer and Silas returned.

They caught the omnibus from the village to Haverpool and made directly for the Station Hotel where the viscount procured them a suite while the concierge arranged tickets for the night train. Archer gave each man money to replace lost clothes, and they spent the afternoon in hat shops and tailors where Fecker bought a new greatcoat, smarter and better-fitting than the one before. James bought a canvas Duster coat with a wide collar and turned back cuffs in the new American style, and Thomas found himself an Inverness with a shoulder cape that James said made him look like a highwayman.

'Is there no end to Archer's generosity?' he asked as they left the shop.

'If there is, I've not found it yet,' Thomas replied.

'Should I pay him back? Or will he take it from my wages?'

'You could ask him, Jimmy,' Thomas smiled. 'But he'd only tell you not to be ridiculous.'

Dusk was approaching when they met in the hotel tearoom looking, to anyone who cared to notice, like any other party of travellers. What the public couldn't see were the bruises and scrapes beneath the clothing, nor could they detect the intensity of friendship that now bound the five together.

They spoke quietly of Quill, each man reliving what he saw in the final moments when the train hit the river. There was no conclusive evidence that Quill had died. Although Archer had seen him tumbling backwards into the flames, no-one had seen him since either alive or dead.

'The telegram has been dispatched to the sanitorium,' Archer said. 'I am watching the newspapers for reports of fatalities.'

'I don't reckon he'll come after you again, Archie,' Silas said, swigging tea.

'Hold it by the handle and sip,' Thomas tutted, slapping his knee. Silas grinned in reply and ignored him.

'We will have to wait and see,' Archer said. He was already reading the local evening news, and the crash dominated the front page. 'I did feel guilty that the signalmen might get the blame,' he said. 'But it says here that the driver and fireman were found with their throats cut and robbery is suspected, though who would want to rob a coal train isn't yet a question this journalist has thought to pose.'

'Poor sods.' Silas glanced at the paper. 'What does that make Quill's total? Eight, nine?'

'That we know of.' Archer turned a page. 'Ah, the men are exonerated due to the signal box door being smashed. "Clearly a case of robbery or vandalism by persons unknown", it says. If only they knew.' He looked at Silas accusingly, and his lover shrugged. Putting the newspaper aside, he turned to James. 'Everything good with you?' he asked.

'Good?' James smirked at Thomas. 'You could say that, Sir. I'd say better than.'

'Then I think I should be grateful to old Tripp for sending you to us,' the viscount said.

James' face clouded. 'Hm.' He put down his cake. 'Tripp.'

'Take no notice of him,' Archer said. 'If he seeks you out, it won't be at the house. At the pub maybe, but if he gives you any more trouble, just inform Thomas or me.'

'Very good, Sir.'

'I'm still Archer until we get home. Does that confuse you?'

'No.' James shook his head. 'I've got it sorted, no worries there. Archer…?' He was momentarily distracted by Fecker loading a scone with three layers of jam and cream. He waited until the Ukrainian had fitted the whole thing in his mouth before continuing. 'Sorry, Archer,' he continued. 'I wanted to be sure that you understand I only went along with Tripp's plot as a way of getting closer to Tom.'

'Were you prepared to see it through?' Archer asked. He had bought himself a pipe and was filling the bowl with tobacco.

James remembered the first rule of Clearwater. 'At first, yes. It was exciting, see? I mean, Tripp said he'd pay me, so that was a reason to prick up my ears. When he said that he suspected…' He lowered his voice. 'Unnatural acts took place in the house — his words, not mine — of course, my ears pricked up even more.'

'You want prick?' Fecker questioned through his mouthful causing Thomas to choke on his tea.

James blushed as he slapped Thomas on the back. 'Well, not this minute.'

'Well, when you do,' Silas said. 'Keep it down, yeah? Your room's right above mine.'

'He don't want cock?'

'No, Fecks, and definitely not yours, now shut up and stuff your face.' Silas pushed the cake rack to his friend, and Fecker set about it with nonchalant gusto.

'But I was telling the truth,' James insisted. 'I was prepared to give it a go, see if I got the job and then see what happened, but only for my benefit, not Tripp's. There was no way I was going to betray Thomas, and there's no way I would betray you, Archer. You have to believe me.'

'I do,' the viscount said. 'But I am left with the uneasy feeling that Tripp will find some other way to carry out his intentions. Whatever they may be, I am sure they will be nothing compared to Quill. However, we must all be careful, gentlemen.'

'Being in service is playing a role,' James said. 'Thomas told me that, and I get why. I'm just looking forward to being at home.'

'To your mam and sister?' Silas asked.

'No, to my new home. Clearwater.'

'The city is so dreary in winter,' Archer sighed. 'As soon as I have the East End charity up and running, and Her Ladyship has thrown her parties, I think I may spend some time at Larkspur.'

Thomas took a sharp intake of breath. 'That will be interesting,' he said.

'You'll do fine, Tom,' Archer reassured. 'Some of the staff will be loyal to Tripp, of course, they've grown up with him, but others will be happy to work under you. Besides, they won't have a choice, and they can leave if they don't like it. We live in changing times, as someone told me once. Our country has recently legislated against us. That's one thing, but in our smaller world, Larkspur needs dragging from my father's legacy, and part of that is the staff he left behind. Tripp for one, others at the estate are another, Tom. We will review the servants when we go to the country.'

'What's Larkspur like?' Silas asked. 'Will I have to be super-posh?'

'You shall have to be very discreet,' Thomas warned.

Archer agreed. 'Clearwater is relaxed, because there are not so many servants,' he explained. 'But I have several at the country house, all are my father's appointments, and there are none that I know or trust well enough to share a discussion such as this.'

'I see,' James said.

'But that is all for the future.' Puffing on his pipe, Archer looked at his pocket watch. 'Not long to wait now. I, for one, am looking forward to a decent night's sleep.'

Sleep didn't come easily or quickly. Archer lay in his berth as the train rattled and pumped its way south, his mind mulling over the events of the past few days. He could make sense of Quill, but not of Tripp. Did the man mean to shame him by engineering a scandal? Archer had never given him a reason to suspect his sexuality, apart, perhaps, from his occasionally foppish behaviour, but many men, married and single, behaved that way. He had never given him an excuse to seek retribution either. Tripp had been well paid, well looked after, and it was his own fault he was given his marching orders. He only had himself to blame, and Archer had sent him on his way with a fortune in silver. As soon as Tripp saw that James was no longer prepared to play his game, he would tire, count his blessings and vanish.

Archer lay with Silas pressed against his chest and listened to his breathing as he slept. The rhythm of the train numbed him as it steadied into monotonous motion, and drowsiness crept closer. His men were contented and safe. His life was settled, and the future he planned would see him and his friends living their lives their way, free from the machinations of Quill and the duplicity of Tripp. He had found Silas. Thomas, his dearest friend, had James, and together they could look forward to a life that was, finally, peaceful.

It was not to last.

Night after night Tripp had waited in the Crown and Anchor, the newspaper his cover, James Wright his intention.

The boy hadn't shown since the night Tripp prepped him for his interview. The sodomite, Payne, no doubt had him in his clutches, perverting him in his appointment to fall in behind Clearwater and indoctrinating him towards his abhorrent ways.

That the boy, the catamite, had betrayed his loyalty and chosen his path, was obvious. What Tripp could do about it was less apparent until he turned the pages of The Times and read the headline.

"The Clearwater Foundation announces its intention to host a night of opera."

He read more.

"Although no specific date has yet been set for the launch of Viscount Clearwater's new charity, an announcement is expected soon. A gala has been announced and it promises to be an occasion of glamour.

The philanthropic, the great and good, the titled and landed are expected to come forward to show their support at a gala performance at the City Opera House sometime in early December. Famed countertenor, Cadwell Roxton and international diva, Miss Cantanelli have been booked to appear at the star-studded gala which this publication will report with interest.

The Clearwater Foundation will also be in the spotlight, and the occasion could be 'make or break' for the viscount."

266

Tripp folded the paper neatly and placed it on the adjacent chair.

'Make or break,' he whispered to himself. 'If young Mr Wright refuses to return to me, I will simply engineer another way to ensure Clearwater's... breakage.'

He cast his calculating eyes to the group of messenger boys at the next table and tuned into their conversation.

It took only a minute before an idea slithered into his mind, and his lips twisted into a devious grin.

Look out for 'Unspeakable Acts'
The Clearwater Mysteries book three

If you have enjoyed this story, here is a list of my other novels to date. With them, I've put my own heat rating according to how sexually graphic they are. They are all romantic in some way apart from the short stories.

References to sex (*) A little sex (**) A couple of times (***) Quite a bit, actually (****) Cold shower required (*****)

Short erotic stories
In School & Out *****
13 erotic short stories, winner of the European Gay Porn Awards (best erotic fiction). Boarding schools and sex on a Greek island.

Older/younger MM romances
The Mentor of Wildhill Farm ****
Older writer mentors four young gay guys in more than just verbs and adjectives. Isolated setting. Teens coming out. Sex parties. And a twist.

The Mentor of Barrenmoor Ridge ***
It takes a brave man to climb a mountain, but it takes a braver lad to show him the way. Mountain rescue. Coming to terms with love, loss and sexuality.

The Mentor of Lonemarsh House ***
I love you enough to let you run, but too much to see you fall
Folk music. Hidden secrets. Family acceptance.

The Mentor of Lostwood Hall ***
A man with a future he can't accept and a lad with a past he can't escape. A castle. A road accident. Youth and desire.

MM romance thrillers
Other People's Dreams ***
Screenwriter seeks four gay youths to crew his yacht in the Greek islands. Certain strings attached.
Dreams come true. Coming of age. Youth friendships and love.

The Blake Inheritance **

Let us go then you and I to the place where the wild thyme grows
Family mystery. School crush. A treasure hunt romance.

The Stoker Connection ***

What if you could prove the greatest Gothic novel of all time was
a true story? Literary conspiracy. Teen boy romance. First love.
Mystery and adventure.

Curious Moonlight *

He's back. He's angry and I am fleeing for my life.
A haunted house. A mystery to solve. A slow-burn romance.
Straight to gay.

The Clearwater Mysteries
Deviant Desire ***

A mashup of mystery, romance and adventure, Deviant Desire
is set in an imaginary London of 1888. The first in an on-going
series, it takes the theme of loyalty and friendship in a world
where homosexuality is a crime. Secrets must be kept, lovers must
be protected, and for Archer and Silas, it marks the start of their
biggest adventure - love.
(Book one in the series)

Twisted Tracks **

An intercepted telegram, a coded invitation and the threat of
exposure. Viscount Clearwater must put his life on the line to
protect his reputation. His life is complicated by the arrival of
new servants, a butler and a footman both experiencing the
confusions of first love.

Twisted Tracks follows on directly from Deviant Desire. There are
now eight books in this series, and details can all be found on my
Amazon Author page.
Please leave a review if you can. Thanks again for reading. If you
keep reading, I'll keep writing.

Jackson

Printed in Great Britain
by Amazon

78723961R00155